DRAGON GEMS
WINTER 2024

Published by Water Dragon Publishing
waterdragonpublishing.com

Cover design copyright © 2024 by Niki Lenhart
nikilen-designs.com

ISBN 978-1-962538-30-5 (Trade Paperback)

10 9 8 7 6 5 4 3 2 1

FIRST EDITION

Foreword
copyright © 2024 by L. A. Jacob

Afterword
copyright © 2024 by Kelley York

"Adventures of Zeedae and them Gol-durned Genset-D Boys"
copyright 2024 by David A. Hewitt

"Aristomache"
copyright 2024 by Evangeline Giaconia

"Betsey"
copyright 2024 by Liam Hogan

"Breathe"
copyright 2024 by Jon Hansen

"Clockwork Octopus and a Letter to Queen Victoria"
copyright 2024 by Brandon Case

"Corpse Child"
copyright 2024 by Chris Kuriata

"Damned Poets Society"
copyright 2024 by Michel Harvey Hanson

"Draconis astronomus"
copyright 2024 by Catherine Tavares

FOREWORD

S PECULATIVE FICTION CONSISTS of Science Fiction and Fantasy — among other genres. The short form of speculative fiction was developed by Edgar Allen Poe. We can envision him, bent over a desk, a raven on his shoulder or perched on the desk, writing in the wan light of a burning candle. Horror and speculation coming out of his quill pen to the vellum pages, short stories that stand the test of time are sent off to a publisher, who happily took everything he put out.

Not quite.

Poe had problems publishing. He tried to establish his own literary magazine, mostly because he wanted to control his own writing. He ran into a lot of the same problems that many writers ran into: editors who cut out his darlings, publishers who were too scared to publish the works as they were meant to be.

In those days, they didn't have small presses.

We are lucky to have Water Dragon Publishing take on the mantle of a small press, bringing us works of speculative fiction that even Poe would be proud of.

The Winter 2024 selections include some science fiction ("Pining in the Multiverse", "An Expedition to Enceledus") and fantasy — with sort-of dragons, of course ("Dragonsbreath") — consisting of the dead ("Damned Poets Society") and the more-or-less living ("A Walk in the Garden").

In the cold darkness of winter, while the winds howl in the blizzard outside, grab your hot beverage of choice and settle down for these twenty-six stories that will warm your mind and, perhaps, your soul.

L. A. Jacob
author of the *Grimaulkin* and *War Mage* series

i

CONTENTS

Chris Kuriata lives in and often writes about the Niagara Region. Before focusing on fiction, he wrote and edited documentary series on true crime, hockey, and tent revivals. His debut horror novel, *Sacrifice of the Sisters Lot*, is available from Palimpsest Press.

•   •   •

"The Corpse Child" came from a sketch in my notebook, of a small child riddled with anxiety, unable to sleep, while on the floor directly below the bedframe lay a corpse, its eyes open. Not long after drawing the picture, the circumstances around this situation began to form, prompting me to write the story. I enjoy how "The Corpse Child" is mostly a conversation between the two characters, as though it were a sketch on a ghoulish variety show.

THE CORPSE CHILD

CHRIS KURIATA

A LONG THE SHORES of Shipman's Corner, a macabre belief quickly gained currency, which claimed most fatal childhood illnesses (scarlet fever, measles) could be cured by having the infected party sleep over the corpse of a young child.

The origin of this belief remains undiscovered. Condemned from the pulpit, the treatment was rarely applied. According to the tales, the corpse child must not have died from illness. Only a healthy body stopped by unnatural means (crushed in an avalanche of hay bales, say, or kicked in the head by an ornery horse) would do. Accident-made bodies became highly valued, meaning patients of "the corpse treatment" came exclusively from families of means.

"Momma, am I dreaming? Is that a scarecrow the servants are placing beneath my bed?"

"Lie back and go to sleep, my darling. In the morning, you will be made strong again."

"Am I to share my room with a strange corpse?"

"Shhh … there is nothing to fear. He is where you cannot even see him."

Two servants slid the corpse child into place before hurrying the young boy's parents out of the room. Once the bedroom door was sealed, everyone removed the cloth masks covering their mouths. With heavy hearts, the young boy's parents retired to their own chamber, praying for the blasphemous (and expensive) treatment to cleanse the threatening red boils sprouting across their beloved son's tiny body.

The feverish boy awoke in the middle of the night, drawn back to consciousness by the stirrings beneath his mattress. Small fingers raked across the wooden support beams, echoing in the empty room like someone prematurely buried scratching the lid of their coffin.

"It is too cold down here," a hollow voice whispered from under the bed. "Let us switch places."

"I do not think that is a good idea."

"Just for an hour, so I may warm up."

"If I lie under the bed, the draft will only make me sicker."

"Please, you can't imagine how wet and chilled I am."

"Forgive my thoughtlessness. I will call for the servants and they will bring you blankets."

The corpse child sighed, making the water in his lungs bubble. "You are very wise, boy. I was actually trying to trick you."

"Trick me?"

"Oh, yes. If you had switched places with me, I wouldn't have traded back. In the morning, when your parents unsealed the room, I would have leapt up with my arms spread wide, shouting, 'Momma! Poppa! I'm cured!' They would have hugged me, tears streaming down their cheeks. You would have tried to call out from under the bed, but your sick tongue would've swollen up like a black eel and left you unable to speak. You would only be able to bray like a donkey,

'*Eee orr, eee orr!*' Believing you to be me, the servants would ram hooks into your legs and drag you outside to the pyre and set you aflame. Did you know a person's head is too dense to burn? The servants would use a big rock to smash your skull into smaller pieces. And all the while, I would sit at the breakfast table, listening to you go up in smoke."

This admission horrified the boy. "That is terrible. Shame on you for trying to trick me."

"You can't blame me for wanting to avoid such an awful fate myself. I may be dead but I do not wish to burn."

The boy understood. He felt sympathy for the corpse child, who, after all, was going to make him well again. "Listen to me, when morning comes, I will insist Mother and Father not burn you."

"That is very kind, but I shouldn't want you to worry about my disposal."

"I insist. Tell me what you would prefer."

The corpse child thought hard. "Well, I have always been fond of the funny paintings in the museum; the look of agony on the faces of the condemned, the peasants tumbling beneath the swords of the king's guard. When I was alive, it used to make me laugh to see the strokes of crimson paint gushing from swaddled babes in their mother's arms. I think I should like to be buried on the grounds of the museum. They have a glorious courtyard where I will be able to hear the visitors laughing at the funny paintings. Such a reminder of joy will make my dark, lonely grave bearable."

"It is settled. I promise, I will insist my parents not burn you but instead bury you at the museum."

Moved by such a generous offer, the corpse child shook beneath the bed, making the caster wheels squeak. When he spoke next, he sounded as though he were holding back tears (though his speech impediment could also have been caused by lazy muscles in his dead throat). "You are very kind. So kind, I cannot hold my tongue. Though it would benefit me to keep quiet, I must warn you that you are in danger."

"Danger? How?"

"Being wise people, your parents fully expect me to try and trick you into switching places. Come morning, they will assume the boy in the bed is not their son, but the skullduggerous corpse child attempting to take his place. Mark my words, whichever boy is lying on top of the bed will be seized by hooks and dragged outside and thrown in the fire and have his skull crushed so it will burn."

"My parents will make no such mistake. Surely they will recognize me."

"In the dim morning light? Why, the disciples could not recognize the resurrected Son that early in the morning. How will your parents recognize you?"

"I can easily prove who I am. I know the name of my young brother Jonathan, and our baby sister Rebecca. I know Mother is terrified of boat crossings. I know Father relies on me to wind his watch."

"All trifle information I could have wheedled out of you while pretending to be your friend. You must believe me; under the bed is the only safe place. Come morning, your parents will destroy you."

"I cannot believe my parents will be so blinded by suspicion they cannot tell the difference between their beloved son and a rotting corpse child. Your wretched stink alone makes evident who is who."

"Please, you must let me help you."

"No. I will stay on top of the bed and you will stay below. And you will be quiet, or else I will not tell my parents to bury you in the museum courtyard and you will be seized by hooks and thrown on the fire and have your skull crushed."

Silence. Satisfied to have settled the matter, the boy turned over and sank his feverish cheek into the cool pillow, longing for the sweet relief of sleep to spread through his aching body.

He didn't rest for long. Cold breath soon lashed the soles of his bare feet. The boy sat up, and through the murky blackness watched the corpse child pull himself over the foot of the bed, clinging to the sheets like a sailor hauling himself from the ocean. The corpse child's fat, water logged lips pulled back in a snarl.

"This foolish conversation has gone on long enough. Get under the bed where it is safe, or else I will crawl under the covers and make you smell of rot and death. In the morning, your parents will be unable to tell the difference between the two of us and we will both be doomed."

"I will not say another word to you. Goodnight."

Growling like a trapped fox, the corpse child slipped deftly beneath the sheets and tunneled towards the boy. His cold, clammy hands seized the boy's knees, and slowly dragged his dead weight over the boy's body. Struggling to get away, the boy threw over the covers, only to find the corpse child's twisted face resting on his chest. Their eyes locked.

The boy remained calm. His father once instructed him the most vulnerable part of a wild animal was their nose, so if he ever found himself face to face with a snarling beast, his best chance for survival was to aim for the snout. The boy raised his weakened hand and made a fist, but before he could strike, the corpse child grabbed him by the ears and forced their mouths together. Hot and cold noses mashed against one another as the corpse child breathed putrid gas from his abdomen down the boy's throat. The boy gagged and retched. The two began to wrestle, each trying to toss the other over the side of the bed into the black ocean of the cold floor. The squeaking of the caster wheels echoed through the house.

•   •   •

First thing next morning, with the light still dim, the boy's parents unsealed the room. They held their breath, fearing the worst — that the legends of the healing properties of child corpses were greatly exaggerated and their son's bedroom would no longer be occupied by one corpse, but two.

The bed covers stirred, thrashing about like foam on an angry sea. The boy sprang forth, fully cured, his arms spread wide.

"Momma! Poppa!"

The relieved parents rushed to his bedside, wrapping their arms around him, ignoring the foul smell tainting his bed clothes.

"Our darling. Thank heavens you are well again."

"Oh Mother, the corpse boy under the bed spoke to me in the night! He tried to trick me into switching places with him!"

"Yes, dear. We thought he might."

"He told me you wouldn't be able to tell him apart from your true son."

"Oh dear heart, that was all wicked chicanery. Of course we know you're our true son."

The boy's father signaled the two servants waiting in the doorway, each holding a sharp, metal hook which they thrust under the bed, piercing the legs of the corpse boy and dragging him out. The corpse boy made horrible noises, braying like a donkey, "*Eee orr, eee orr!*" The crackle of a roaring fire came through the open window, hungry for more fuel.

"Wait!" the boy said. "This wicked corpse boy may have tried to trick me, but I made a promise. Even though he is a lesser being without honour, I intend to keep my vow."

"I am pleased, son," said his father. "A righteous man always honours his vows, even those made to dishonest beings who mean to betray him."

"I promised the corpse boy I would implore you not to throw him on the fire, but instead grant him his burial wish."

"And so we shall. Tell us what he desires."

"He confessed to me feeling envious of our loving household; such a cautious Mother who protects her children from unnecessary sea crossings, and a wise Father who teaches the value of responsibility by entrusting me to wind his watch each day, and the delight of my younger brother Jonathan and my baby sister Rebecca."

The boy's parents couldn't help but preen from the flattering words the corpse child had spoken of them in the night. "Yes, son, you have been blessed with a loving household. One can hardly fault the corpse boy for scheming to join us."

"Indeed. As such, he told me he wishes to be buried feet down and head up on the hill overlooking our home, close enough where he can hear our evening laughter. It would please him greatly to be buried where he can keep watch over us, and perhaps, once a year, we will trek up the hill to visit his grave and give thanks to him for making this new day possible. Yes, I think he would like that very much. Such a reminder of joy will make his dark, lonely grave bearable."

Once again, great happiness filled the family home. While the servants stuffed the corpse boy into a sack for transport to his final resting place, the cured boy dressed and wandered the manor house. Along the way, he emptied the last of the lake water from his lungs into a large potted plant, giggling when the putrid water wilted the healthy palm fronds. Soon, the smell of fresh breakfast filled the air, guiding him to the dining room, where brother and sister flanked his new seat at his new table.

DAMNED POETS SOCIETY

MICHAEL HARVEY HANSON

W ILLIAM JENNINGS BRYAN, the deceased American politician; Hortensia, daughter of Roman consul and advocate Quintus Hortensius Hortalus; and Logan the Orator (son of Shikellamy), Native American war leader, took their respective seats, quickly adjusting their table microphones. The view through the Hexiglass (methyl methacrylate) window-walls of the broadcasting booth displayed a panorama of Mourningstar Square below.

An indigo demon dollied his camera to focus on Hortensia, on-scene reporter for the Perdition Broadcasting System; as Logan, to her left, typed madly on his laptop to test his minicam before his Hellcast.

Meanwhile, Bryan tapped his antiquated ribbon microphone and smiled as the feedback whined. He strongly suspected this was going to be a red-letter day for H-ELL, the underdog among greater infernity's radio stations.

Below the three commentators was a stage with a large black podium holding fifty folding chairs. In front of that podium, poets took their seats.

Hortensia, sitting ramrod straight with all the discipline and arrogant calm one would expect of the Roman upper class, glanced down. Already, tens of thousands of Pandemonium's residents were flooding into the massive square. The event was scheduled to kick off in five minutes. Large panning klieg lights switched on. Bright yellow beams cut upward through the polluted air. Background noise rose dramatically as one million damned souls poured into the huge city square.

On the far side of this imposing crowd towered Satan's citadel, his black-marble offices of perdition. The Dark Lord's balcony looked empty, but flapping scarlet curtains proclaimed his residence. And the evening news confirmed that His Satanic Majesty was in town.

Bryan's southern voice boomed: "Well, it's happening, folks. This is Bill Bryan for H-ELL, welcoming you to the 'Poets Ignoring Sulfuric Suffrage with Eternal Demands' extravaganza, broadcast as it occurs from Mourningstar Square. We'll bring you hell's best poets doing what they've been forbidden to do since their damnation, when the Almighty turned his face away from —"

At the sound of that name, a terrific peal of thunder ripped the air overhead, sending vibrations through everyone and everything.

"Uh," Bryan continued, "the *big man upstairs* needs to hear the creativity of those he has unfairly banned to this lower realm, and finally, once and for all, heed our appeals. And yes, I think I see a figure taking the podium ... right, Hortensia?"

"The unshaven face," Hortensia said in English, "sloppy clothing reeking of the common citizenry, yes ... I believe it is Baudelaire, that brashest of Gauls ..."

Charles Baudelaire, continental essayist, art critic, and translator of Poe, elbowed his way through the crowd onstage to lean upon the podium. The bawdy Gallic poet overtly ogled a buxom woman at the front of the crowd, while loudspeakers all around projected his voice with disturbing intimacy:

> *I, Baudelaire, bring you tidbits from my Défaite*
>   *Stratégique...*
> *Madame, my dame, your protests lame*
> *I cannot drop my bleeding pen*
> *I will not stop, you will not tame*
> *My flame with female whim or yen...*

Not once did Baudelaire's gaze stray from the face of the buxom woman as he droned on, until his closing stanza:

> *Be damned Madame, demoiselle devilish*
> *My writing halts, you are at blame*
> *My bed the battlefield you claim,*
> *Your naked smile and ivory breast... vanquish!*

Baudelaire's final flourish brought a rolling wave of cheers and applause from several thousand attendees. He launched himself off the stage directly at the shapely maiden, tackling her, struggling to kiss her red lips.

She clouted Baudelaire atop his skull with her fist and disappeared into the mob.

Baudelaire staggered upright just as the ground beneath him erupted with dozens of thorny stalks on which red roses bloomed, sprouting fangs, and leaped upon the Frenchman. Baudelaire howled in agony as the carnivorous blossoms tore bloody gouges in the French poet's face, his neck, his hands.

The camera pulled back and refocused on Logan, the Native American orator. "Yes," Logan said in his sturdy but unemotional voice, while simultaneously typing on his computer, "those are some pretty evil flowers."

"I can now see a rather dour gentleman stepping forth," Bryan said.

"Oh, my," Hortensia sniffed, "I do believe we are in for a macabre lament about tragic romantic loss."

On the stage below the commentators, a pale man with dark hair waited for the huge audience to calm down.

Once the background roar subsided, Edgar Allen Poe, famed American poet and author of mystery and macabre, began reciting from his *Lyralee*. When he neared the tragic end, his voice became a ghostly whisper.

> *I miss her more*
> *In my cold, empty arms*
> *Oh, my love, Lyralee sleeps in the sea cocooned in all her*
>   *charms*
> *Oh, my dear Lyralee, you now wait for me dressed in your*
>   *blessed charms.*

The last line was read with such anguish, and clearly aimed at the skies above, that tens of thousands of those present gasped out moans of lament in sympathy.

"Still pining for his long dead cousin-spouse?" Logan asked Bryan, who replied with a nonchalant shrug.

Instantly, a loud clang issued from overhead, and before Poe had time to twitch, a large-bladed pendulum, seemingly extending from mid-air, swung down and roughly cut off the poet's right ear in a nasty splash of blood. Just as quickly the large apparatus swung upward and disappeared into whatever dimensional tear in space and time had been created and destroyed overhead. The blow knocked Poe to his knees, but he managed to hold back a scream by biting fiercely on his tongue. He slowly stood up and staggered back to his chair near the back of the raised stage.

"Who is next?" Bryan asked.

"I think it is the turn," Hortensia stated, "of the new-world man of lower-cased literature."

This elicited chuckles from Logan and Bryan as e. e. cummings, renowned poet, painter and essayist, quickly strode to the front of the stage and began reciting from *Those Jersey Girls Know What They Want.*

those jersey girls know what they want;
they cherish honest, rugged guys;
they stomp on pricks who call them cunts
and bite the tongues off shits who lie...

By the time cummings neared his finale, the audience was his:

they seek out every bar and haunt;
they drink whatever gets them pissed.
those jersey girls know what they want;
they conquer worlds with every kiss.

"Brilliant!" Hortensia said. "That crude ruffian has surely cut to the combative soul of my sister species."

"Brilliant, my ass," Bryan sputtered. "The bastard is plagiarizing his own work."

"Wait," Bryan said, "something is forming over cummings' head. Why, yes, it is a miniature storm cloud appearing and, I believe, yes ... I think tiny raindrops are falling ... directly upon cummings, the former army ambulance driver. And look, streaks of blood are forming across the poet's face and hands."

"The raindrops are piercing his skin," Hortensia added. "And I suppose one must give him credit for keeping to his seat amidst such indignity."

Hundreds of feet above the squabbling reporters' heads, His Satanic Majesty stood upon his balcony, listening to the live radio broadcast. Behind him, in shadow, many shapes rustled.

"Samael," Satan said, "I must show *those Above* that I am just as unforgiving as they."

"There is some shuffling," Bryan's voice came from Satan's radio, "on the stage. I wonder ... wait a minute: There seems to be some turmoil occurring on the square's far side."

Satan and his cadre of Fallen Angels suddenly turned into winged demons: "Take wing. Tell our legions to attack. Now."

"Something is approaching," Logan said, squinting with eagle eyes.

Leaping from his balcony and climbing into the air, Satan's majestic troop quickly focused a quarter of a mile down Aka Manah Boulevard, one of four main streets that intersected and met at Mourningstar Square.

Rushing forward at a double-march came the twenty-thousand man forces of the AVH (Hungary's Security Police) and at their forefront was Matyas Rakosi, former Hungarian dictator and Soviet puppet. They were armed with sub-machine guns and carried plastic riot shields and wore Lost Angeles Motorcycle Police helmets with dark visors pulled down. All were dressed in dark green uniforms bloused over black combat boots. They would be upon the crowd in minutes. Rakosi stood up on the passenger side of his Jeep and held a megaphone aloft.

Up high, unnoticed, Satan overflew the square. It would take a short measure of time for his legions to arrive. For the nonce, he would enjoy the view.

"Now, my brothers," Rakosi screamed, "kill the fascist poets. Let us start cutting them down like slices of salami ...."

Just as his lead Jeep was about to plow forward into the packed square, a spray of bullets tore through his torso and his driver exploded in a splash of blood. The Keep curved left and flipped, smashing into the side of a large building.

Instantly, hundreds of khaki clad women leaned out of windows on the lower floors of many of the apartment buildings flanking either side of Aka Manah Boulevard, and flooded the murderous marchers with bullets and Molotov cocktails.

"A true massacre," Bryan spit into his microphone, "Those that have chosen to interrupt this great occasion are being slaughtered in the hundreds. But who is attacking them?"

"Can't you tell from their pink berets?" Hortensia asked. "Why, it's none other than those radical libbers from New Hell, the Chicks Undermining Nefarious Testosterone's Savagery."

The crowds in the square, seeing their potential attackers quickly routed, shouted out a mighty cheer.

"An esteemed gentleman appears to be taking the podium," Logan spoke solemnly as Robert Frost, the great American poet from Massachusetts, stepped into view.

"I give you ... *Sun and Rain*," Robert Frost announced, and then began his recitation:

A youth, I pursued two maidens,
Not knowing blessing from burden;
The belle who courted wind and rain
Or she who loved the sunny day?

Frost paused as if to gauge the interest of his audience and then continued on to the very end, without stopping for another breath:

As years have passed I dread the bliss
And constancy of luminance,
Sadly missing the resonance
And shadows of a darksome kiss.

Smiling, Frost stepped back from the podium to take his seat. Applause crested in a mighty roar that brought a smile to his lips. Upon sitting, his face immediately turned red, and it became clear to all that he was choking. A moment later, Frost began vomiting multi-colored maple leaves down upon his knees and feet, heave after heave, in a disgusting display that lasted ten full minutes.

"Oh my," Bryan reported, groping to fill the ugly pause, "it appears the poet from New England is having trouble digesting his own rhetoric."

"How droll," Hortensia replied.

"Enough," Logan said without emotion, "look who is taking the podium now."

The crowd cheered, seeing Pablo Neruda, Chilean Poet and Nobel laureate, a long-faced Caucasian man wearing a small brown cap, leaning toward the microphone.

"Although my good friend Robert," Pablo said with a strong Castilian accent, "has likened free verse to playing tennis without a net ..."

Frost, still vomiting autumnal beauty that was quickly piling up on the surrounding platform floor, waved Neruda to continue.

> *... I shall return his lyrical lob with this backhand ditty.*
>   *Oh, and please forgive me if any of my many subtleties*
>   *are lost in translation.*

Neruda began reciting *Blushing Idyll.*

Take my hand, and let us walk through the white arch
Of this efflorescent construction site
Surrounded by the song of loving work
As hummingbirds and honey bees all toil
Under nature's mute foremen, sunlight and rain...

Neruda's body shook, as if from some infernal tremor. But he never missed a beat, leading his huge audience through beauty to the end of his poem:

We end this arboresque amble
As I place on your brow
A red magnolia crown;
We close, we kiss, atremble.

"Here, here," Baudelaire shouted from the rear of the platform-stage, "this man could win any woman's heart."

Neruda smiled at the immense wave of cheers and applause, walked away from the main podium, and retook his chair. A moment later he began convulsing and then thick green ink started bleeding profusely from his nose, ears, and eye sockets. In seconds his clothes and skin became drenched and stained in the dreadful excretion.

"The punishments being bestowed by our ruler are certainly of an eclectic nature today," Hortensia sniffed.

"Let she who is without sin cast the first stone," Bryan mumbled. "Well, look here: It appears a limey is going to say something."

"Hybernian, actually," Logan said, "and one of the more renowned members of the Ghost Club. Quiet now, he is speaking."

"I have written the following," said William Butler Yeats, Irish poet and Nobel laureate, "as a humble gift for my good friend Mister Ernest Hemingway, whom I had hoped would be here, but by all indications is sequestered in that strange frozen prison holding all that mighty horde who so recently tried to breach the gates of the higher realm."

"I think the renowned combustive fisherman has better ways to waste his time," Poe drawled from several yards behind Yeats, "than in the company of such dark literary angels as grace this obsidian pit."

Yeats paused for a moment to consider Poe, cradling his head wound. "My good Edgar," Yeats said, "even your worst insults hold more sincere currency then Baudelaire's finest fawning."

"Eh? What?" Poe asked, turning his head with its one still functional ear toward the Irishman.

This brought a burst of laughter from the dozens sitting upon the platform. "I give you ... *Sanctuary*," Yeats began:

One day soon I will journey, up to Wood River north,
And a cozy camp I'll make, in a sylvan clearing;
A hearty toast I'll make, each night to the loamy earth;
And fish alone by a rippling stream...

Something buzzed the air around Keats, but he did not let it interrupt his recitation that continued on, liltingly, to its final stanza:

One day soon I will journey, for my senses are a haunt
I smell aspen and cottonwood flavor the spicy breeze;
As a walking somnambulant upon a soulless jaunt
I savor the distant musk of trees.

A strong round of applause followed the poem, so that Yeats was compelled to take a respectful bow before sitting down. Instantly, a small wave of yellow jackets and crickets flowed from a crack in the podium floor beneath him to swarm upon the son of Eire. Yeats gasped in terror and pain from the localized biting and stinging horde and staggered to a far corner of the huge platform, where he crumpled to his hands and knees, whimpering in agony.

"I suppose you could say he found his bee loud glade," Logan muttered.

Hortensia leaned forward and held her face in her hands.

"Look!" Bryan suddenly shouted into his mic. "Ladies and gentlemen, approaching the square ... It looks like ... Yes, it is! Military tanks are rolling up toward Jinshui Bridge where it crosses Blood River onto the far side of the square."

Overhead Satan grins. *"Slaughter by the damned of the damned is about to begin."*

Zhu De, former Chinese General under Mao Zedong, poked his head up into the air, atop the lead tank barreling toward Mourningstar Square. Behind him several dozen tanks carried the PLA's 38th Army. Intermixed with the tanks were APCs that carried paratroopers from the 15th Airborne Corps.

General De raised a hand-mic to his lips: "All forces," he proclaimed, "hear me! Upon crossing the bridge, execute a full flanking maneuver across the entire perimeter of the square. I want no survivors."

General De's tank was almost completely across the bridge when the first explosion occurred.

"Oh, no!" Bryan shouted. "Those Chinese tanks just got a royal welcome, folks. Jinshui Bridge has been completely destroyed by a series of massive detonations. It appears every span of it has collapsed into the river. There must have been two dozen tanks and just as many APCs on it. Whoever mined that bridge must have been up all night planting their explosives. Nearly a third of the windows on that side of the city just shattered."

"Look," Hortensia prompted, "on this side of the bridge. It's a 'Free Tibet' flag. And the man holding it ...? You don't think ...?"

"Yes," Logan added, "I recognize his robes. It is Ngawang Lobang Gyatso, the fifth Dalai Lama. Rumor has it that he is only one of several anarchists and rebels who recently snuck into the city."

"Here now, I do believe it! Someone new is taking the stage," Hortensia said.

Dylan Thomas, Welsh poet, modernist and neo-romanticist, walked toward the front. He was a clean-cut man in his thirties, with a bow tie and suit.

"Another defiant rant, Dylan?" cummings asked.

Thomas ignored the American, walked past him and took center stage behind the podium. *"Hobnobbing Down Blessing Way,"* he announced. Clearing his throat, he started in on his recitation.

> *I am searching for a mountain that is everywhere*
> *thus my life is spent between peaks*
> *from each to each and here to there.*
>
> *I am trapped into traversing a traipsing, phantom trail*
> *pondering trees, and lakes and snow,*
> *shadow to shadow,*
> *vale to vale...*

He went on and on until finally he graced the audience with the final words that were both unheard of and appropriate in hell.

> *This holy, eternal circle I cannot comprehend,*
> *end to end,*
> *again and again I trip and fail to ascend.*

Another wave of applause and cheering erupted from the massive crowd.

"Quite good, ladies and gentlemen," Bryan said approvingly. "Dylan's metaphors are very clever indeed."

"Oh, please," Logan scoffed, displaying real emotion for the first time since the recitations began. "I saw that Anglophobic prick taking lunch with John Neihardt and Black Elk two days ago in the Pandemonium Hilton's Algonquin Room. Original?

My native-American ass! But enough: I have fully glutted my need for insult."

Dylan walked back to his chair and sat down when he suddenly took note of the oddest buzzing sounds. In moments a small contingent of tiny Luftwaffe bombers, each no bigger than one's thumb, started an attack run upon Thomas. The Welsh poet immediately engaged in evasive tactics, dodging back and forth across the large platform-stage bumping into the other poets and shuffling erratically around their chairs, as flea-sized **bomblets spilled forth resulting in miniscule explosions on the wood planking and a weird trail of destruction at Dylan's heels.** He frantically tried to stay ahead of his damnation, as occasionally bombs connected with his backside and detonated, tearing holes in his clothes and leaving grape-sized, bloody craters in his flesh. The rest of the poets present did their best to ignore his screams of agony.

"You know," Hortensia said, "I really don't think he'll be able to outpace those little planes much longer."

"Certainly not on those Grade III legs of his," Bryan drawled.

Without notice, Sylvia Plath, American poet, novelist, and short-story writer took to the stage. She was an attractive raven-haired woman, dressed in a sensible mid-twentieth century dress. Her demeanor was calm and fatalistic.

"Ladies and gentlemen! Prepare to have your souls frozen by Sylvia Plath's excellent recitation of her famous *Dust Bowl*," Bryan said.

Without preamble, Plath launched into her oration:

Thus my depression started as a doubt
Blighting the soil of my frail soul
In cracked, parched years when love became drought
Bleaching inexorable toll...

She paused only near the end, to highlight her closing couplet:

I'm an aging garden of melancholy
Ripe with baneberries of mortal folly.

A strong round of applause erupted from the mighty crowd.

Sylvia let the slightest of smiles crease her face. As she stepped away from the podium, a loud scuffling noise filled the air. Immediately, a large, odd-looking gurney broke upward through the floor of the stage and across it, sending poets and their chairs flying, until it rested before Sylvia.

Several restraining straps shot out from this well-padded bed. The straps wrapped around her arms and legs, pulling her aboard and into a fully reclined position. Snakelike electrodes swayed above her, then struck, embedding themselves in both her temples. Electricity flowed, and Sylvia's body rocked with painful convulsions. The bed slowly slid to rest near the edge of the raised stage. Sylvia's electroshock treatments continued, nonstop, as those on stage did their best to ignore the sight.

Meanwhile, the broadcast audience and gathered souls looked on, chastened but vicariously enjoying her pain.

"Hmmmm," Hortensia said, "I do not believe anyone else is approaching the podium. Perhaps the combined chastisements placed on all speakers so far, as well as the two attempted incursions by unfriendly forces, has dampened the spirit of this ... protest to the higher powers?"

"Could be for the best," Bryan said, "I suspect bad weather, as a pall is being cast upon us. Some clouds must be rolling in and —"

"It is not cloud," Logan said with forced gravity, "it is balloon!"

Bryan, Hortensia, and the demon camera-operator all looked skyward through the clear plastic of the press booth to see a full-sized zeppelin rapidly descending from the clouds a mere half mile away. What appeared through various portholes to be fifty to sixty well-armed Nazi Brownshirts were packed into the cupola-cabin underneath, preparing to unleash some kind of hellish punishment on those below.

"What the hell?" Bryan wondered, his eyes wide.

Standing by the main cupola window on the starboard side of the Zeppelin, Gregor Strasser, Nazi leader and one-time rival of Adolph Hitler, grinned an evil grin down upon Mourningstar Square.

"Now all of you," Strasser said, "are men and women marked by death."

The lower perimeter of the main gondola spouted two dozen fully-manned hell-replicas of M61 Vulcan twenty-millimeter cannons. Strasser licked his lips in preparation for giving the order to fire. The airship was only thirty seconds away from its optimal firing position, directly over the center of the square. In moments he would pass over the last block of skyscrapers that bordered the huge crowd.

"I have a bad feeling about this," Logan said.

"I think," Bryan said, "we're about to feel the paralyzing influence of imperialism."

Strasser raised a small hand-mic to his lips, but just as he was about to give the killing order, a scream erupted from the rear of the gondola.

"I die nobly as a free man!" someone shouted.

Strasser turned just in time to see Elazar Ben Yair, Sicarii leader and defender of the Jewish fortress of Masada, long black hair in disarray, wearing a simple brown tunic and sandals, and covered in plastic explosives, press his thumb down on a detonator.

The hydrogen filled airship exploded in a gigantic ball of fire.

"Oh, the humanity," Bryan gasped.

Flying above the Square in a swarm of his Fallen Angels so thick they made a black sky above the crowd's heads, Satan was amused. He enjoyed the delicious carnage as the damned attacked one another. Instantly he flew low, alongside his six favorite Fallen, for a better view of the airship crashing in flames into Blood River.

"It appears," Hortensia said, "Hell's flying bottom feeders smell a smorgasbord."

"Even the buzzard," Logan said, "has a right to eat."

Down atop the main stage, the poets all shifted their feet and looked to each other.

"I think," Bryan said, "a lack of faith is preventing anyone else from taking the podium."

"Or common sense. Perhaps we have seen an end to today's festivities?" Hortensia suggested.

"No. Listen," Bryan said: "the crowds are chanting something. Yes, they're chanting the word '*poet*' over and over again."

That chant grew in pitch and volume, until the very ground began to shake. The three reporters, up in their swaying plastic box, grabbed the table in front of them to steady themselves.

"I don't think this is convincing anyone to take the stage," Bryan said.

"Look," Logan shouted, "just behind the podium."

The air behind the podium, unoccupied, began to coalesce into a bright shining globe of light. As the chanting reached a deafening peak the strange patch of efflorescence grew almost blinding.

"Ladies and gentlemen," Hortensia said, "it's as if a crack in reality is forming in the air just behind the main speaker's podium. Why and for what reason we do not know."

"Such sparkling and transcendent light," Bryan said with awe. "So beautiful. Could it be … a Second Coming?"

Suddenly, a human leg coalesced from the light, quickly followed by another, then a torso, with arms and a head. Walt Whitman, American poet and father of free verse, stood before the podium. He appeared as an elderly man, tall, with white hair and a thick white beard and mustache. He wore the simple clothes of a mid-eighteenth century working man.

Overhead, Satan snorted satisfaction that blew from his nostrils like smoke. He had anticipated what the focused power of a million mortal souls could do. And directed it, to breach barriers of space and time, even the spacetime foam in which this trouble-maker (and thousands of others who sought to storm the gates of heaven) had been recently imprisoned.

23

"Yes," Logan said, "it is *really* him. Ladies and Gentlemen, Walt Whitman has arrived."

"Is it true," Bryan asked his colleagues, "what they say about his first appearance in the dark lands?"

"Oh, yes," Hortensia replied with relish. "And I heard it from an American civil war veteran who died of syphilis on the same day ... and witnessed every moment."

"Really? That Whitman issued forth from the Welcome Woman's belly?" Bryan disbelieved.

"The grandest of entrances," Hortensia said, "an agonizing premature birth in the elevator. The witch pumped him out screaming almost as loudly as she did. She had sulfuric acid for amniotic fluid. Half his skin and muscles had been eaten away *in utero.*"

"Horrific," Logan said.

"It gets worse," Hortensia added: "It took that poet a full day to grow to manhood, and WW nursed him the whole time ... milking ammonia from her ghastly tit."

Whitman, his eyes practically glowing with inspiration, stood before the podium and raised his fists in the air. *"Poets, Rally My Poets!"* he shouted the title of the work he was about to present. The audience roared, and when his voice flowed forth the crowds grew silent as he intoned:

> *Onward, my sad-faced dreamers,*
> *Follow me in your endless ranks,*
> *Bring forth your angers, brandish your burning tears.*
>
> *Poets, Rally My Poets...!*

The million-soul crowd in Mourningstar Square cheered in reply as each of Whitman's stanzas concluded. More than any of the previous poets, Whitman's work lit a fire in its appreciative audience.

Up in the air, Satan clacked his demonic jaws: Time to act; the time for all subtlety was past. Drawing upon his vast powers, the Deceiver mobilized all his legions, every sold soul billeted in Pandemonium. In less than a heartbeat his deadly forces completely surrounded the adamantine buildings circumscribing the giant square. Upon command from the Father of Lies, his battalions of angry dead would reap the whirlwind, stopping and slaughtering this rallying crowd, now teased into a frenzy.

And at that time, Satan thought, *this rabble will learn their place.*

Below, Walt Whitman continued:

Leave your mountains and join us in the valleys
 Remember your peaks, and cousin clouds,
Breathe in the thick air and sip the wines of hilly root.

Poets, Rally My Poets ...!

Above Whitman's head, Bryan warned, "Damned souls, take note: some mighty force can be seen surrounding this gathering. Demonic and armed, they march on us to wreak some terrible vengeance. But I tell you now: we will not waiver here. Whitman's words inspire us all. None of us here in the press booth want to say much more. Just keep listening, I implore you."

"Look," Hortensia marveled, "the masses respond. They do not flee."

"Tens of thousands have turned to face the attackers," Logan said. "And we will not give up without a fight. We are one million strong. Our will must prevail."

A huge cheer erupted from the crowd and Satan's attention was once again distracted by Whitman's hypnotic recitation on the stage:

Join us all you young, impetuous lovers
Naked shoulder to shoulder, with hands inviting, held
    tight
Sing of the honey of first kiss, and hot tryst.

Poets, Rally My Poets!

Reject the cities, pour out of the brick canyons
Charge from them like rampant rivers
Fear not the freedom of open expanse and nature.

"Poets, Rally My Poets...!"

Overhead, Satan felt the *willpower* of those one-million souls, fired and inspired by Whitman's voice and words. And at that moment he decided to stop his armies marching in to destroy these million souls, wisely knowing that no seemingly superior battle strategy always survives contact with the enemy.

Fools, he thought, *war among yourselves. This will show the bleeding-hearts Above just how foul is mankind, now warring against heaven, hell, and one another.*

On that ill-considered stage so far below, Whitman's poem at last was coming to its end. The sound of it filled ears from the deepest Deep to the throne of the Highest, and made Satan glad, for this poem would make eternal the winter of the damned's discontent.

And Whitman exhorted:

Rally round me in the pungent, continental heart,
Let us raise our willful voices in aching harmonies
Cut loose those sharpened tethers of doubt and conformity.

"Poets, Rally My Poets!"

At that, as the crowds in Mourningstar Square erupted in an orgy of cheering, screaming and shouting, the despite in Satan's heart grew to unimagined potency above their myriad heads.

Whitman raised his arms to silence the multitude. The poet then looked straight up into the sky towards the distant glory of Paradise and raised a gnarly fist.

Emboldened by the passion of a million damned souls, Walt Whitman parted his lips: "Now, God, damn it all to hell,"

Whitman shouted at the ruddy vault, "where the fuck is our heavenly redemption, you all-powerful son of a bitch?"

Overhead, the light from distant Paradise winked out.

The second response to Whitman's rabble-rousing blasphemy came roaring after a pregnant pause. It took a whole two seconds for a massive, deific lightning bolt to surge downward through unimaginable distances, plenty of time for all one million damned souls to recognize it for what it was and, united, gasp in terror; but with no time whatsoever to cower or to run.

Upon striking Whitman, the leading edge of the gargantuan lightning bolt incinerated him in a puff of smoke, leaving nothing behind.

This wrath from Above, however, was hardly spent. Simultaneously, the full force and energy of supernal fury connected with the occupied stage and platform. All exploded into a hail of lethal splinters. All fifty poets upon the podium were immediately pulped to shreds. Next, the spray of platform fragments killed the thousands closest to the stage, while maiming tens of thousands more surrounding them.

Windows in every building across the city of Pandemonium shattered.

The raised press booth was knocked sideways, its tower underneath buckling alarmingly. The booth's clear walls cracked into strings, like automotive glass. The commentators within were tossed, punctured, and battered.

The lightning's concussive force flooded across Mourningstar Square, a spherical shock wave knocking over all left standing, downing mortals as it expanded as if they were dominos toppling.

Inside the ruined press booth (now suspended sideways merely ten feet above the ground), Bryan pulled his microphone close. Looking around he spotted the American Indian Logan's limp body, eyes open wide but lifeless; his neck askew. A few feet away Hortensia lay crushed under the largest television camera; her right foot still twitched spasmodically.

"Ladies and gentlemen," Bryan gasped, coughing up blood, "there you have it: Disaster at Mourningstar Square. Thousands dead, many more wounded in this awful response from the ultimate poetry critic."

A shudder ran through Bryan, and he raised his lips to his microphone one last time: "Folks, once I believed that the humblest citizen in all the land, when clad in the armor of a righteous cause, is stronger than all the hosts of error. Then I came here to hell, where it seems I've been proven wrong. This is William Jennings Bryan, for H-ELL, returning you to your regularly scheduled programming …"

Dead Air.

Satan flew over the field of carnage. Hundreds of thousands of survivors below were turning upon each other, battling one another, each lost in a new madness and overcome by their own rage and despair at this final damning sign of eternal judgment from Above.

Satan laughed as he headed his sky-blackening formation of demons back to his adamantine citadel and Paradise reappeared in the vault above, glowering down with its bloody light.

Joseph Sidari writes long and short fiction from Boston. He is a member of SFWA and Grub Street Writers. As a practicing physician, he works hard at caring for his patients while trying to kill his protagonists. He has published over a dozen short stories online and in print. He would never, ever step on an ant, just in case 'they' are watching.

•   •   •

"Revenge of the Antmen" began as a single sentence rant I wrote for an assignment in a writing class I took at Grub Street. I loved the unnamed scientist so much I added a few more sentences, converted it to this podcast formula, and then submitted it to the 2023 Parsec Short Story Contest, where it won first prize and was featured in the CONFLUENCE program for the Pittsburgh Science Fiction and Fantasy Convention. Due to the small circulation of that program, it was not considered an official publication, which is why you are reading it in Dragon Gems right now. Let me know if you find the Easter Egg from a classic "Twilight Zone" episode among the various classic SF references.

REVENGE OF THE ANTMEN

JOSEPH SIDARI

HOST: Do you remember when the Antmen landed on the White House lawn? Who doesn't? It was only three months ago. If you have been prepping for an alien invasion ever since, do I have a treat for you! Gentle Listeners of planet Earth, this is your host, Jeremiah Lott. Thanks for logging on to your favorite podcast: *Lott's in Space.* I'd like to announce that I am podcasting *live* from the top of the Space Needle in Seattle — wouldn't that be cool? Someday, it could happen if I multiply all the nerds, geeks, and UFO fanatics across the country who regularly listen by all my followers on Instagram and Twitter. But until then, I am just in my dad's garage on nearby Mercer Island.

Anyway, my guest on the phone tonight is destined to make interstellar history, and honestly, I am not sure why he agreed to be on my humble podcast. But I won't look a gift Xenomorph XX121 in the mouth, if you know what I mean. (laughs)

GUEST: I am *here* because every stupid astronomy blog and science podcast who called wanted me *and* Roger, and I was not about to debase myself by appearing with that no-talent jerk.

HOST: I see. (pause) Well, anyway, my guest today is a scientist —

GUEST: The *most* important scientist —

HOST: — the *most* important scientist from the S.E.T.I. Institute. Let me introduce Doctor —

GUEST: You know, I hate that everyone calls them *Antmen*. It sounds like they escaped from a B-movie creature-feature. You know: *Revenge of the Antmen*. No serious scientist would refer to an alien species that way — no matter how repulsive they were. How did the press create that winner?

HOST: It must have made sense to someone when the six-legged aliens from Antares crawled off their ship sporting shiny, black segmented bodies, complete with wild antennae whipping back and forth. You are right about one thing: the name has stuck.

GUEST: Maybe. But I hate it. And thinking about five-foot-long ants makes me lose my shit. Hey, is it okay if I say shit on the air?

HOST: I'd prefer you didn't. *Lott's in Space* is a family podcast. Why does it, uh, make you, uh, so upset? Do you have a thing against *giant* insects? Or bugs in general?

GUEST: Bugs? No, they're fine. Just ants. And size doesn't matter. I collected insects as a kid. Large and small. I had a praying mantis the size of your arm.

HOST: Very interesting, uh, your collection. But let's hear more about your experience with first contact?

GUEST: I can still picture the best bug I ever found: a giant, black, hairy spider. I pretended it was a black widow, but I'm sure it wasn't. I used it to scare the sh— I mean, crap, out of my little sister. I'd hold it over her head while she slept and then nudge her awake. Boy, would she scream. (laughs)

HOST: How pathologic.

GUEST: In a jar, of course.

HOST: Of course. That makes it better.

GUEST: And I didn't hate ants as a kid. They were good for stepping on. Or burning with a magnifying glass.

HOST: Um, I'm sure our audience is on the edge of their seat contemplating the full extent of your childhood sadism, but —

GUEST: Pretty interesting, right? It wasn't until later that the thought of ants would make me want to vomit. They may be the only creatures I detest as much as my boss at S.E.T.I., Roger Peterson.

HOST: Finally!

GUEST: You hate him, too? What'd he do to you?

HOST: No ... I mean, I don't even know Dr. Peterson — other than what I have read in the news or seen on the vids. But *finally,* getting back to S.E.T.I. and this historic first contact with those — what would you prefer I call them? The Antarites?

GUEST: I don't care. Antarites. Antarians. Call them Antaropolitans if you want. Just don't call them Antmen.

HOST: Okay. Your first contact with the . . . uh? (blows out a frustrated breath) The aliens formerly known as Antmen. Can you tell me about your role in Dr. Peterson's historic —?

GUEST: *My* role? My *role*? Well, first of all, without me, there would be no first contact. But to hear Roger tell it, I'm the guy fetching coffee, and he is holding the hallowed interstellar receiver when ET finally phoned home — and got us by mistake.

HOST: Then tell us your side.

GUEST: Gladly! I don't like to admit it, but I harbor a little resentment against that guy.

HOST: Oh?

GUEST: Alright. I hate him like cancer. You see, back in the day, he and I were on the shortlist for senior director of S.E.T.I. And then their know-nothing Board of Trustees, led by Chairman Head-up-his-ass, decided to appoint Roger over me. I was pissed.

HOST: If it was so unbearable to see this man you despise be named Senior Director, why did you decide to work for him?

GUEST: It's a long story. You see, I didn't always hate Roger. At one time, we were friends. Roommates, actually. Did you know that? We were competitive, of course. Who at M.I.T. isn't? We were both at the top of our class, but at the end of four years, he edged me out by a decimal point for valedictorian.

I'm sure you've heard that. He brings it up
constantly.

HOST: No, I —

GUEST: The way he boasts about it, you'd think he
discovered cold fusion in between ending global
hunger and curing world peace.

HOST: Don't you mean procuring world —?

GUEST: Whatever. And when my college sweetheart, Annie,
and I broke up? Who swooped in before the tears
were dry on her pillow? Good thing my mother
never came to visit me at school, or Roger would
have sweet-talked her into his bed, too.

HOST: Ew. That is a disturbing image.

GUEST: Don't you know it. But I digress. What were we
discussing?

HOST: Sorry. I am still trying to unsee that.

GUEST: Can you please try to stay on topic, Jeremiah? This
is my shining moment, remember?

HOST: Right. So, when did you realize the signal you had
detected was from an alien civilization?

GUEST: After graduation.

HOST: Huh? What —?

GUEST: That's when I knew I needed to get away from Roger.
I was courted by more top-notch doctorate programs
than there are pixels on a computer screen. But I
decided to take my talents to the Astrophysics
Department at Boston University. Of course, in
Roger's narcissistic desire to keep me in his shadow,
he matriculated across town at Harvard. A blind man
could see the pattern that had formed. I tried to

escape his gravitational pull, but Roger is a black hole. There is no escape.

HOST: He *is* quite accomplished.

GUEST: He is an asshole.

HOST: G-rating, please? PG at most.

GUEST: Okay. He's an A—hole. I guess that's why I accepted his offer of associate director at S.E.T.I. I knew it was the only way to show the world his true colors. He let me pick my own workspace, so I set up my lab beside his.

HOST: But why work for him if he's such an, uh, A—hole?

GUEST: He's a well-connected A—hole. And I knew if I took my eye off him, even for a nanosecond, he'd steal another of my ideas. Like when I detected those rhythmic clicking sounds from the Antares system.

HOST: Perfect. I wanted to bring things back to the aliens. When did you first —

GUEST: I'm getting to it. Can you stop interrupting me?

HOST: (a pause) Sorry.

GUEST: Right. So, when S.E.T.I. announced that one of our long-range radio telescopes had identified a repetitive extrasolar signal consistent with intelligent life, Roger conveniently forgot to mention it was my project. He had dubbed it To Infinity and Beyond, to be cute and catchy. Hey, how do *you* like that name?

HOST: Well, I always had a soft spot in my heart for Buzz —

GUEST: I hate it. It was a dumb-assed nickname for my brilliant piece of interstellar computing. "Make S.E.T.I. accessible to the common man,' Roger had said. 'Give it a name that John Q. Public can identify with."

Did this *Mr. Public* not graduate from kindergarten? I guess the jury is still out. But since he was my boss, I smiled, nodded, and let him have his way. Deep down, though, I knew it was another way for him to humiliate me, naming my project after that tagline from a cartoon. But despite his dumbing down of my project, my idea had worked. My listening telescope had located honest-to-bejesus aliens. Kudos to me, right?

HOST: Of course ... or no? I'm not sure anymore.

GUEST: Of course you aren't. That's because my name was never mentioned. It was Dr. Peterson and his *colleague*. Now tell me, is there even one person who knows the name of that colleague?

HOST: I do.

GUEST: Jeremiah — are you *trying* to aggravate me?

HOST: No. I thought this was your natural state.

GUEST: *No one* else — besides you, and who cares about you — knows my name. I was never interviewed on *Good Morning America*. My face was not plastered on the banner of every e-paper from here to the moon. It was Roger's gap-toothed grin. He was *Time's* Man of the Year. He was invited to brunch at the White House. He was so freaking popular — he even hosted *Saturday Night Live*.

HOST: (laughs) I saw him! That was so —

GUEST: (clears throat)

HOST: The musical guest sucked that night. And Roger, he wasn't funny. Not at all.

GUEST: I totally agree.

HOST: (pause) But you're on my podcast, right?

GUEST: Big deal. That means maybe the student body of your high school is listening.

HOST: No sir. We have way more subscribers than that. Mercer Island High has 1550 kids, and *Lott's in Space* has ... (papers rustling) ... yeah, we had 1558 likes on my Facebook page last month.

GUEST: Great. Eight students transferred in.

HOST: (even quieter) And my father. He usually listens.

GUEST: Your father! Ha! What about your mother? Why don't you count her? Does she find your show so boring —

HOST: She, um, passed away last year. (sniffs)

GUEST: Are you telling me we can't even count on her to boost the number of people listening to me?

HOST: Tomorrow will be one year since —

GUEST: Focus, Jeremiah. Focus. (Blows out a frustrated breath) Ahh. I don't know why I ever agreed to appear on your stupid podcast.

HOST: Maybe it is because you offended every other media outlet that —

GUEST: Most of them didn't appreciate my extreme importance in this project. They asked, 'What's it like to work with Roger?' And 'What did Roger say about the signal?' Well, I told them, 'Roger said bend over and go fu—'

HOST: Funny thing about the censors. They do draw the line with some words. And you were just about to say one of them. Now, take me — I don't care what Roger did *or* said. I am interviewing you. So what do *you* want the American people to know?

GUEST: Huh? Oh yeah. I hope they will realize how ironic it is. To Infinity and Beyond demonstrated intelligent life in the Antares system. But it showed me that right here on Earth, there is none. Every man, woman, and five-year-old cartoon watcher is a blithering idiot who believes every stinking word the media publishes about Roger Peterson.

HOST: I'm sure our listeners will be thrilled to know your respect for them.

GUEST: I hope so. But now, can we get back to those damn ants?

HOST: The what?

GUEST: The ants. My hate affair with those creepy-crawly bastards began on a late August afternoon picnic, right before my senior year at M.I.T. A group of us had gone to the Charles. We had spread blankets along the riverbank, soaking up the sun on one of the last days of summer. Ready for classes to begin, but not wanting summer to end. Eating overcooked burgers and drinking warm beers. I had quite a buzz on, you know. I reached down and blindly grabbed a juicy slice of watermelon, stuffing it in my mouth. Unlucky for me, that piece had been out for a while and was peppered with ants. I spat it out, gagging and retching. Ants clung to my teeth, my gums. I flossed for weeks to get those last little bits out. I screamed at my then-girlfriend, Annie, blaming her for the ants. You see, she had spread our food upon the ground. How stupid is that?

HOST: Don't people usually sit on the ground —

GUEST: I lashed out at Roger, too, blaming him for suggesting we all go on something as ridiculous as a picnic. I stormed off, scraping my tongue, spitting out ant parts and curses. After I was out of sight, Roger — always the opportunist — swooped in to console Annie. Walk her home. He *said* he was trying to explain that I didn't mean all my nasty comments. But I know better. He was weaseling his way into her good graces. It wouldn't surprise me if he spread sugar around the picnic site to attract the ants. Or maybe he raided the Entomology Department and planted a colony or two right on my blanket.

HOST: Ants are everywhere in August. Why I remember one time when mom was still alive —

GUEST: Whose side are you on, anyway?

HOST: I'm not on —

GUEST: I knew it. Everyone always takes his —

HOST: I'm on your side. Not Roger's. He's a shithead.

GUEST: You said you couldn't say 'shit' on the air.

HOST: It's my show. I just changed the rules.

GUEST: That's the spirit. So Annie dumped me and took up with him.

HOST: What a bastard.

GUEST: They got engaged in grad school. They're married now. With a baby boy, if you can believe it. That he and Annie had a kid together makes me sick. I told him so when he asked me to be Roger, Junior's godfather. I told him I'd rather eat ten thousand ants than be godfather to his ugly little rug rat.

HOST: You said that?

GUEST: It was another obvious ploy to rub my nose in his marriage. His success — and my failure. But then, you know what? After that, he stopped dropping by my office. Not once in the next whole month. If I'd known that all I had to do was insult his baby, and he'd leave me alone, I'd have done it sooner.

HOST: That usually does it.

GUEST: And so that is why I go out of my way to step on them — those annoying little critters —

HOST: Oh, my g—

GUEST: The ants, I mean. Not babies. I wouldn't step on a baby. I'm not a monster.

HOST: Debatable. But I'm glad you've been able to share —

GUEST: Although if Roger and Annie were sunbathing on the sidewalk, I wouldn't walk around them, if you know what I mean.

HOST: –this fascinating series of anecdotes. And now I'd like to thank our guest, Doctor —

GUEST: But now I wonder if I have been too hard on Roger all these years.

HOST: (pause) Are you serious?

GUEST: Completely.

HOST: You mean you've had a change of heart about Roger Peterson, the shithead bastard you hate like cancer?

GUEST: One and the same. It turns out that he is the one who recommended that I accompany the aliens back to their planet. Apparently, the aliens were very anxious to return with a prime example of humanity. And who better than me — am I right?

HOST: Well, that history-making voyage-to-be is why I invited you to appear on my show in the first place. You're lifting off next week.

GUEST: Yup. All thanks to Roger. At first, I was suspicious. Why throw me a bone? But then I realized that cream rises to the top. Roger had gotten the glory all these years. Now it's finally time for me to get mine. Once *my* mind-blowingly important event is televised worldwide, every ignorant lunkhead on the whole planet will know my name. And I'll finally beat Roger.

HOST: Ooh? The Antmen are bringing you back to their homeworld? Is that good?

GUEST: It's excellent! I will be representing humanity to an alien culture. Just think how much I can teach them.

HOST: I suppose that all of Earth will respect your courage to serve mankind by embarking on this historic mission.

GUEST: Damn right. I'll probably get a statue. Or a monument. The day I leave will be a national holiday — like Columbus Day. And it won't be called Roger Peterson Day. No. Kids across America will get the day off from school to honor me. Or maybe I should suggest they stay in school and pay their respects to me there. People on this planet are dumb enough. Yeah. Let 'em stay in school.

HOST: Still, I'm not sure —

GUEST: For a supposedly advanced race, though, these aliens seem primitive. Ignorant. The way they tap me with their antennae. And how they click their mandibles to speak with one another. Probably just as dimwitted as the rest of the fools at S.E.T.I. who hang on Roger's every word. If I play my cards right, I bet I'll be running their planet before long. I guess my old pal, Roger, knew I'd be the best one to teach these aliens a thing or two.

HOST: I bet he did. He chose you. Was this before or after you insulted his baby?

GUEST: After, of course. Weren't you paying attention? But what has that got to do with anything? This is about me.

HOST: I guess so. You sure are getting the last laugh, eh Doc?

GUEST: Don't you know it. I'll set them straight about humanity. I can't wait to arrive on their planet and give them all a piece of my mind.

HOST: (mumbles) You think they will only take a piece?

GUEST: Huh? What —?

HOST: Never mind. And now that does truly wrap up our interview with —

GUEST: Hey, I've been monitoring your transmission during our interview. Is this how you always send out your podcast? Who is the numb nut who chose this bit rate?

HOST: I did. And if you must know, it has worked out fine for me. So —

GUEST: But if you adjusted the data compression, then you wouldn't sound like a hamster with a head cold —

HOST: — that's all the —

GUEST: — and if you weren't your own sound engineer, Jeremiah, maybe you could have had time to think up a better name for your podcast. Of all the ridiculous —

HOST: — time we have tonight. Hopefully, the aliens will have a specimen jar big enough for your ego when they return to Antares. Unless they throw you out an airlock first. Oops, did I say that out loud? Sorry.

GUEST: Wait, what are you hinting at?

HOST: Hinting? No. I'm emphatically stating that if they can't locate a jar your size, I will find one.

GUEST: What kind of a half-wit are you? Why would they need a jar? I am not some alien creature they would —

HOST: Sorry. Technical difficulties with the doctor's line. Please tune in next week to hear my dad discussing the time we thought there were crop circles in the backyard, only to discover the guy he had hired to mow the lawn had more experience smoking grass than cutting it. And thanks again for listening to your new favorite podcast: *Lott's in Space.*

IF WE SHADOWS

JEFF STEHMAN

K RASNOV LOVED EVERY MEMBER of his theater's troupe, but
sometimes ...

"Mister Krasnov, I implore you!"

He gave up checking the trapdoor rigging under the
stage and started down the ladder.

"Dimitri, for the last time, I tell you no." He faced the actor.
"I see you perform every day, and I know your ambition. Should
the time come when I feel you are ready for a leading role, you
shall have it. But not one. Day. Sooner. Do you understand?"

Dimitri's expression played to the back row. "Of course, I
understand. I understand you trample my dreams, crush my
soul."

"Look, my friend. You are a beloved member of *The
Heavens* company. You're an ever-reliable supporting actor,
and you are masterful when it comes to portraying the villain
in a comedy. You have a gift, and that gift is exaggeration, but

what you need for a leading role is nuance. That, dear Dimitri, you lack."

The anguish of the world crossed Dimitri's face, causing Krasnov to roll his eyes. Dimitri looked up with wide-spread hands. "Behold. Traps. I am in a trap room. My career is trapped under-stage. Could it be a metaphor? I think, yes. Could it be a metaphor for hell?"

"Are you trying to prove my point?"

"I tell you, sir, I am in hell!"

As if to punctuate his claim, the floor opened under both men.

·   ·   ·

Krasnov sat up in the dark, coughing from dust. Several lanterns flickered to life, revealing old trunks, rotted rigging, and faded backdrops. He recognized it as a trap room, but not the trap room in *The Heavens*. It was larger, and the ceiling too high. More importantly, there were no stairs leading up.

Dimitri moaned beside him.

"Dimitri! Are you all right?"

"It matters not," he said, his voice drowned in sorrow.

"It looks like we've fallen into another trap room."

Dimitri's anguish appeared to vanish as he sat up. "We are under under-stage?"

Krasnov gave him a disgusted look. "Yes, Dimitri, we are under under-stage. Come, man, this is serious."

Both men got to their feet. The older of the two, Krasnov's body protested, but Dimitri seemed none the worse for the fall.

"Curious," Dimitri said. "I wonder where we are?"

Maniacal laughter pealed through the room like thunder. A chill ran down Krasnov's spine, and Dimitri quailed beside him.

"Where you are?" The disembodied voice sounded like iron grating on stone. "You are exactly where you said you are. Welcome to *Hell*!" Again laughter rang out.

Krasnov's nerve faltered, but only for a moment. "W-w-well played. I give you full marks for dramatic presentation. Now, then, if you could show us the way back to my theater ..."

A low growl rumbled through the room. Krasnov felt it reverberate through the floor.

"Critique me, will you? For years I've been forced to listen to the tripe sifting down from above. Allow me to offer a few critiques of my own."

Four shadows rose around the room, black-clad players armed with swords, empty hoods where their faces should have been. Dimitri whimpered and hid his face. Panic tugged at Krasnov's heart, but he had not earned his reputation as a great thespian by being slow on his feet. He sprang to the nearest trunk and threw it open. Within were stage props, including two swords.

"Dimitri, here!" Krasnov tossed a sword to the cowering actor. It hit his arm and clattered to the floor. As the shadow men crept closer, Krasnov grabbed Dimitri by the vest and shook him.

"Now is not the time for amazement, my friend. Now is the time to act!" Krasnov picked up the sword and put it into Dimitri's hand. "Come, they are upon us!" He stepped clear of Dimitri and blocked a thrust from the first shadow man to arrive.

"I am undone by fear," Dimitri said, his voice faint.

Their crossguards locked, Krasnov shoved his opponent back, sending him tumbling over a trunk and into a rack of props with a crash. "Then you must find your courage, and quickly. Remember that old soldier you played in *Requiem for a King*? You must be like him."

Krasnov engaged another shadow man and could say no more. He fervently hoped Dimitri would protect his back, or this would be a short fight. Relief flooded over Krasnov when he heard the ring of steel behind him. He turned his full attention to his opponent. Opponents. The first shadow man rose and moved to join his comrade. Krasnov had confidence in his sword work, but he knew he could not hold long against two.

Something heavy hit the floor behind him. Unable to spare a moment to look, he tensed, expecting a fatal thrust to his back at any moment.

With a cry of exultation, Dimitri hurtled past Krasnov and skewered one of the shadow men. "I've got him, sire," Dimitri said, his voice calm as he engaged Krasnov's other opponent. "Mind the fourth, if you would."

Krasnov turned to see one shadow man step over the body of another. As Krasnov engaged him, he noted the man had a wound on his right arm. It did not bleed, nor did he appear to be pained by it as he pressed his attack.

After holding his opponent at bay for some time, Krasnov realized he could no longer hear swordplay behind him. "Dimitri, are you all right!"

"Certainly. I had thought to let you finish the matter on your own, but perhaps you would like some assistance?"

"Please!"

Dimitri strode past Krasnov and made short work of the shadow man. Relieved, Krasnov took deep breaths and looked around. All four shadow men were dead, or at least unmoving.

"That was well done, sire," Dimitri said, his voice jubilant as he needlessly cleaned his blade; no blood had spilt from any of their opponents. "A lesser man wouldn't have asked for help, thus letting pride be his downfall."

"Dimitri?" Krasnov wondered at the change in the actor.

"At your service!" Dimitri raised his sword and swished it down with flair. "It does a soldier good to stand back-to-back with an old comrade-in-arms again, does it not, Your Majesty?" He spoke with gusto and clapped Krasnov on the shoulder.

"Your Maj—"

A rasping chuckle floated through the room. "Well done," the voice hissed.

"Yes, well done," Krasnov replied with bravado. "Now that you've had your sport, would you be so kind as to show us the way out."

The voice gave a single, derisive laugh. "After the first act? I think not. The stage has been set, the characters introduced, and a conflict established. It is time to deepen the plot." Laughter echoed off the walls, rose in pitch, and faded.

"He seems a touch exuberant." Dimitri paused for a loud sniff. "Don't you think?"

Krasnov stared at Dimitri, dumbfounded, unsure whether the actor or the disembodied voice warranted more of his attention. "You seem to have taken my advice ... quite literally."

"Aha!" Dimitri whirled and thrust out a finger. "A door! Come, Your Majesty, I shall lead the way." Sword in hand and without further ado, he strode toward a door Krasnov had not seen before.

His mind awhirl, he followed his actor.

•   •   •

"A passageway," Dimitri said in a conspiratorial tone. "Many doors. We must be wary of ambush."

Krasnov thought it a more dramatic delivery than the empty corridor warranted, but given the timeliness of Dimitri's metamorphosis, he kept his directorial comments to himself. Torches burned along the corridor, providing a bright but wavering light and filling the air with an oily-smelling haze. They revealed nothing threatening.

He nodded toward the door at the far end. "Straight through, I should think."

Dimitri took a step forward. Something clicked underfoot and he leaped back, shielding Krasnov as a huge blade scythed down.

"That was a close shave." Dimitri gave Krasnov a wink.

Krasnov did not have an opportunity to respond to the horrific pun. With a cacophony of whirring, ratchetting, and whooshes, the corridor filled with thrusting spikes and swinging blades gleaming in the torch light. They came from above, below, and both sides. Krasnov turned to flee but found a blank wall behind them. The doors along the corridor disappeared one by one, leaving only the door at the far end.

"There, by the door." Krasnov pointed. "A lever in the floor."

Dimitri considered the lever. "It'll be tricky, but ..." He hoisted his sword and threw it like a javelin. A pendulum with a heavy blade knocked it aside, and the sword clattered to the floor in two pieces. "No, Your Majesty, it is too far and there are too many obstacles."

Something grated behind them and both men turned.

"Unbelievable," Krasnov said as the wall inched closer to them.

"I'm afraid so, Your Majesty," Dimitri replied. "I must confess I feel some distress myself. I regret not being of more service to you."

"More service? Aha!" Krasnov took Dimitri by the shoulders. "The old soldier is no longer of service to me, but do you remember *The Thief of Nightingale Lane*?"

Dimitri looked confused for a moment, then brightened. With a laugh he set his hands on his hips and posed, back arched and chin thrust forward.

"The watch is coming. We must hurry," Krasnov said, pointing down the corridor.

Grinning from ear to ear, Dimitri turned and hurled himself past the first blade, which snicked off a piece of his sleeve. Without a pause, he somersaulted under the second blade and leaped high over spikes thrusting up from the floor. He sprang between two more blades and came up short as a row of spears stabbed from ceiling to floor. He continued down the corridor, springing and rolling and cartwheeling. Sometimes a blade or lance forced him backward a few steps, but he progressed steadily toward the goal.

The wall reached Krasnov. He braced himself against it but failed to check its progress. As Dimitri neared the end of the corridor, Krasnov's eyes were drawn to the closest blade. The whoosh filled his ears, and he could feel the breath of its passing. He drew back as far as he could and turned his face to one side. "Dimitri!"

With a thunderous clunk, the entire works came to a halt. Krasnov exhaled, weak in the knees. He steadied himself and picked his way through the forest of points and edges toward a grinning, posing Dimitri, who laughed and waggled a finger at Krasnov. "I knew you'd follow me, you little urchin. Come now, the merchant's treasure is this way."

• • •

No mere faceless shadow stood before them. His elegant blouse and long, tied-back hair harkened back to a previous century, and his eyes looked as cold and unyielding as his sword. A wind Krasnov did not feel rippled the swordsman's cloak.

"Uh-oh, it's the watch," Dimitri said in a stage whisper.

Krasnov laid a hand on the actor's shoulder. "I need you to reprise your role as the villain in *Duel at the Cathedral*."

Dimitri responded by tossing his head back and looking disdainfully over his shoulder at the swordsman.

"Second, my sword please."

Krasnov presented his sword hilt first. Dimitri took it with his right while pulling at the tie of a nonexistent cloak with his left. With a flourish, he swept off the cloak and handed it to Krasnov, who mimed folding it and draping it over his arm.

"Try not to toy with him, sir. You have another appointment."

"I'll see what I can do," Dimitri said with a sneer, "but you know how bored I get."

After handing his cloak to a shadow man who appeared at his side, the swordsman approached Dimitri. Both men saluted and the duel began. They were cautious at first, testing one another. The pace quickened. The combatants advanced and retreated, swords flashing. A broad staircase appeared, and Dimitri backed his opponent up to a balcony. They locked blades. The swordsman threw Dimitri back. Before he could recover, his opponent untied the rope holding a materializing chandelier and jumped over the railing. The chandelier proved an effective counterweight, and he touched down lightly on the floor. There he stood, waiting, still holding the rope.

Dimitri jumped onto the railing and slid down the banister in a crouch, sword at the ready. At the bottom he sprang high into the air. His opponent let go of the rope. Dimitri landed and somersaulted out from under the chandelier an instant before it shattered on the floor. Without pausing, they crossed blades again.

Dimitri's skill with a blade dazzled Krasnov, but he could see no end to the duel. He was certain they needed to move on if they were ever to get out of this phantasmagoria. Deciding it was up to him to conclude this act, he strolled over to the faceless shadow man watching the duel.

"Quite the epic struggle, wouldn't you say?"

The shadow man ignored him.

"Tell me, are you familiar with this?" Krasnov tapped the shadow man on the shoulder. When he turned, Krasnov made a flourish with his right hand while his left snatched a dagger from the shadow man's belt and plunged it up under his ribs. The black-clad figure collapsed without a sound. Krasnov flipped the dagger into the air, caught the bloodless point with his right hand, and threw.

He had rushed the throw, fearing something might materialize to block it, but it was true enough. The blade struck the swordsman's hip and his guard faltered. Dimitri ran him through.

Letting his sword fall with his opponent, Dimitri strode to Krasnov and grabbed the front of his jacket. "What do you think you're doing! I was enjoying that fight!"

"Yes, sir, I know, but ... you have another appointment."

Still glowering, Dimitri looked to the side as if searching his memory. After a moment, his eyebrows went up and he let go of Krasnov's jacket.

"Right. Very well, off we go," he said with no more concern than if he had been called away from tea. He turned and strolled toward double doors.

•　　　•　　　•

Krasnov darted into the room and slammed the door behind them. Leaning against it, he closed his eyes and took deep breaths to clear his mind.

"I did not need to see that. Down was up, and up was … sideways?"

He looked down at a crouching Dimitri, who giggled like the madman from *Helga's Lament* he was portraying. Krasnov shook his head in wonder and looked around.

A lit candle sat on a heavy table in the center of the room, and other candles burned in sconces on the walls, but the room was dark. It *felt* dark. Wisps of shadow played between the points of light, choking them.

Krasnov knew they had little choice but to press on. He stepped forward cautiously. A wide-eyed Dimitri stayed close beside him.

The closer they came to the table, the thicker the darkness grew. Krasnov became aware of a rattling breath, which grew in volume until it pervaded the room. "I think we've come to the last act, Dimitri."

A menacing chuckle drifted through the gloom. "You are correct." Two red points of light, head high, approached out of the darkness. Fear clutched at Krasnov's heart. His legs threatened to fail him. He put a hand on the table to steady himself, but when a skull appeared out of the darkness, orbs of hellfire burning in its eye sockets, Krasnov fell to his knees. Dimitri collapsed beside him.

The skull loomed over them and laughed. Darkness closed in as candlelight retreated closer to flame. Shadows hung on the wraith like a tattered cloak, and there appeared to be a darker essence within, impossibly thin, little more than lines to suggest limbs and a spine.

"Welcome to my theater," the wraith hissed. Its fiery orbs flared brighter for a moment, and a carrion odor wafted from it.

Krasnov trembled with fear, but through titanic effort he managed to speak. "Th-this … is … my-my theater."

The wraith gave an evil chuckle and shook its skull. "Your theater is above us, where the heavens belong. This is my theater, and it has been here far longer than yours."

"I ... I don't ... understand."

"It sometimes happens when cities grow. Old things are forgotten, and new things are built on top of them." The skull drew even closer to Krasnov. "I am an old thing."

"Y-you are a ... a thespian?"

"I am *the* thespian. In my day the greatest playwrights wrote for me and my theater. My legend was legion. All who have come after me are but shadows."

"Shadows?" Krasnov said, his voice stronger.

"For years I have been in hell." Anguish hung from the wraith's voice, reminding Krasnov of Dimitri's earlier performance. "The words and performances of lesser actors and playwrights have sifted down from above, tormenting me. But this night ..."

The wraith said more — something about pain and blood vengeance — but Krasnov paid little heed.

"Lesser actors and playwrights?" he said, rising to his feet. "My good sir, I am Peter Krasnov. I not only own and act in the theater above, but I also write many of the plays you hear. And with all due humility, I am seen by many as one of the most gifted writers of our time."

"Incompetent fools! They would not know talent if ... if a burning skull stuffed it down their throats. I assure you, *good sir*, you ... are ... a ... hack!" With each emphasized word the wraith's fiery orbs had grown larger, and at the last they threatened to burst from its skull.

Krasnov stood eye to burning eye with the wraith. "A hack? How would you know, mister 'my legend was legion'? You do not even know the meaning of the words you speak."

The wraith's hell-spawned eyes managed to portray scandalous shock. "I was the greatest thespian of my age."

"If you think you were the greatest thespian of your age, then dust has rotted your memory."

"I don't need memory to judge your writing. You torture me nightly with your words."

"Perhaps another demonstration is in order."

"I've had years of your demonstrations!"

Krasnov stepped back, head held high. "Dimitri." When the actor did not respond, Krasnov looked down. The poor man still cowered on the floor. "Dimitri, get a hold of yourself." Krasnov pulled the actor to his feet. "Have you read my latest play?"

Dimitri nodded minutely. His terrified gaze never left the wraith.

"I would like you to audition for the lead role."

Dimitri blinked and looked at Krasnov, but otherwise did not respond.

"I would like you to audition for the lead role," the wraith mimicked in an unflattering voice. "You coddle your actors. No wonder they can't deliver a line."

"You, shut up," Krasnov said, thrusting a finger at the skull. "Dimitri, do you hear me? The leading role. Audition now, please."

Fear drained from Dimitri's face. His eyes hardened and he straightened, his visage becoming like stone. "I do not waste my time with demonstrations," he said in a cold voice.

"Then let us move on to something more practical," Krasnov replied with practiced ease. "This ... creature ... has us trapped here. What do you suggest?"

Dimitri turned his gaze on the wraith, who started drifting backward. Its vaporous arms rose in a warding gesture. "Look, I was just playing a little ..."

Dimitri pounced. Darkness fell on the room, but after a brief scuffle the wraith began to wail and plead. "Not the eyes! Not the eyes!"

"We appear to be in need of light," Krasnov said.

Darkness retreated from the candles and revealed Dimitri standing over the kneeling wraith. The actor had a death grip on the skull, his fingers thrust into the eye sockets, squeezing aside the burning orbs, his jaw set in grim determination. The wraith's jaw quivered.

"Well now, we seem to have suffered a reversal of fortune." Krasnov bent low, putting his face close to the wraith's skull.

"Your power is fear, isn't it. The rest is simply illusion. Theatrics. If someone is too angry to be afraid, or if they're fearless ..." Krasnov stood and looked upon Dimitri with satisfaction.

"Tell me, thespian of old, what do you think of my latest character? He is a warrior who knows no fear, standing his ground against even the monsters of ancient legend, yet he is completely naive when it comes to love, and therein lie the seeds of tragedy. I had thought nuance would be needed to portray the role, but in the hands of an actor gifted in the art of extremes, I find it —"

"Gripping?" the wraith said through clenched teeth.

Krasnov sighed. "I'm a playwright, and even I find that pun appalling. Dimitri, what do you think?"

Dimitri shook the skull, causing the wraith's shadowy vestments and thin body to whip back and forth like gauze.

"Thank you, Dimitri. I think that will do."

"Do you have anything more to say to this thing?" Dimitri asked.

Krasnov considered before replying. "No, not really. I just want to get back to *The Heavens*."

"That can be arranged!" The wraith seemed eager to please.

Dimitri grabbed the wraith below the skull, closing his fist around its essence. He lifted the skull with one hand while sliding his fist down the wraith's body.

"Wha-what are you doing?" asked the wraith.

Dimitri's grip tightened around the wraith's lower legs. He let go of the skull and started whirling the wraith around his head. The skull spun faster and faster, its eyes tracing a red circle in the air.

"Noooooooooo!" the wraith cried.

With a final spin, Dimitri dropped low. The skull smashed into a leg of the table and shattered like a ceramic pot dropped on stone.

And that was it. The shadows dissipated. Krasnov and Dimitri found themselves in an old trap room lit by a single lantern. It was no larger than the trap room in *The Heavens*, and a spiral staircase led upward.

"Well done." Krasnov put a hand on the actor's shoulder. Dimitri turned and Krasnov again felt the stirrings of fear, this time under the actor's cold gaze. He shuddered and, in a less-than-dignified rush, said, "The lead role is yours."

Joy lit Dimitri's face. "It is? Oh, thank you!" He threw his arms around Krasnov, who couldn't help but smile and pat him on the back.

"Come, let's go home." Krasnov led the way to the stairs. "I'm considering a new play. It's about a gambler who wins a king's ransom every time he sits down at a gaming table. What do you think?"

"I'm sure it would be wonderful, Mister Krasnov," Dimitri said, wiping a tear from his eye. "Would there be a role in it for me?"

Krasnov paused in his climb and looked Dimitri in the eye. "My dear friend, I would be honored to direct you in the leading role, and I'll use my share of the winnings to expand *The Heavens*. Our current stage is much too small for you."

THE PRINCE OF SVALBARD: A SAGA OF THE THAW

LOUIS EVANS

S O. THE SVALMEN have always been renowned as the wisest and most warlike among men, and the most blessed. Did not the gods, in the frozen age before they made the world, visit Svalbard and there construct the great fortress Frøkvelv, and fill its catacombs and passageways with those seeds of wholesome grains that now grow both wild and cultivated across the land? Was not Frøkvelv wrought of godly stones and metals that hold fast against the weapons of any army? Did not they place upon the Frøkvelv their protection, in magic runes that read, in the language of the gods:

SVALBARD GLOBAL SEED VAULT

And have not the gods been with the Svalmen since their first day, raising up heroes and warriors among them, men of renown on that land and on other lands across the great sea?

Know now the sad tale of the greatest and most defiled of these heroes, who strove mightily against the enemies of the gods and won much glory thereby, but in the end was ensnared in a demonic deception and brought to a base and tragic end: the tale of Ørretfangst, Prince of Frøkvelv.

Okred was king in those days, son of Gilesso, and when he was a young man he sailed and traded and raided all the lands around the land of Frøkvelv, and all agreed he was a strong man and a cunning one, and a fearsome foe in battle. And in the fullness of time he brought home a wife, a princess of the Easterlings, and with her he had a son.

Ørretfangst they named him, trout-trapper, after the fiercest beast of their land, which they knew by that name. The ørretfangst, mighty and clever, that waits hidden in stream or fjord for its prey and then strikes with a great clash of fangs, like spear on spear and shield on shield.

He was a strong lad, and grew up well, and was skilled with spear and sword and bow, and all men said he was the best of Frøkvelv in these things. And he learned well the catechism of the True Gods, who made the land and all the good things that man may eat, and who overthrew the tyranny of the Frost Giants, and brought the Thaw upon all the lands, and made the land of Frøkvelv a fit place for a man to live.

The seasons turned, and the Prince became a man, and went out raiding. And he did many great deeds, both in raids and in defending the Kingdom of Frøkvelv, and all men said that he was a wise prince, and strong in battle, a worthy leader.

In the prince's sixth spring tilling the whale's road, he and his men went raiding upon the islands to the south of Svalbard. They raided that island which is called the sea's pipe, for its mountains are known to issue forth smoke. Thereafter they raided those islands which men call the Narrows, for so little of them remain above water. Before the Thaw, the seas were lower, and their waters were locked up in the vast palaces of the Frost Giants.

After the raids, when Ørretfangst was returning home to Frøkvelv, a mighty storm whipped itself up from the sea. Able seamen all were the prince and his men, and had they been otherwise their bones would have gone down to the bottom of the sea. But no man may bid a storm, and day by day and night by night the froth-tipped horses bore them onward.

When the sky cleared, Ørretfangst and his men found themselves near a strange coast. Ørretfangst, hawk-watchful, seabird-wise, had determined that the storm had borne them far to the south. Broddr, Ørretfangst's boon companion, said they should sail north at once, for men say that lands far to the south of Svalbard are hotter than may be endured, and have no natives, and nothing that is good for trading. But venturesome Ørretfangst, mighty of arm and strong of heart, would not be deterred by the words of men. Glory hungry, he sought to do great deeds heedless of reward. So they set their backs to rowing and brought their longboat ashore.

A strange land it was indeed. No man of Frøkvelv had stood in this place. Hot it was like an oven, a baking heat, and salty. The men removed their swordbelts and their loincloths and they tipped the longboat and sat beneath it, the burning sun low and watery in the south.

In the heat of the noonday sun they could not move about at all, but as the sky's coin sank in the west they organized scouting parties and set forth on this barren land in search of provender. Long they scouted and searched through that barren land, without reward. Not even weeds grew in this desolate place. But then they sighted the citadel of the gods, tall and proud upon the horizon.

As mighty as Frøkvelv rose the fortress, of god-stone and god-iron. Three great trunks it had, as the Easterlings' castle towers, but without any arrow-slits or windows. From these large grey pillars issued a great roar. The fields around the fortress were sown with black glass, arrayed in rectangles and facing toward the sun.

"Armco, Ekson, and Ptro," breathed Ørretfangst, invoking three great chieftains from among the host of gods, their names foreign to his language but familiar to his tongue. Never had he expected to encounter another such marvel as the fortress of Frøkvelv.

Men gripped their spears and spoke words of fear, saying that this thing was a work of the gods, who are fearsome to trespassers, or Frost Giants, who are worse. But Ørretfangst took not the counsel of cowardice, and he spoke to the men, saying:

"Before us we have a fortress of the gods! Mayhap men inhabit it, and mayhap gods, or giants. Mayhap it is abandoned, a haunt only for beasts and ghosts. I fear them none. I will enter the fortress and get its treasure: as gifts, as tomb-plunder, or as war-plunder. This I mean to do, and if I die in the doing, let my spear and shield be buried beside my bones in this alien land, so that all may say: here lies Ørretfangst, of true boasting and bravery."

Ørretfangst's brave plan and plain words rallied the men, and with spear in hand and sword within ready reach for every man, they set a march towards the god-wrought fortress.

Through the field of black glass they marched, and the march was easy, for they set their feet upon a godroad. Men find such roads, black-finished, long-weathered, in many places: wherever the gods had trafficked when they were making the world.

Like all godroads, this was in disrepair; and its heat in the baking fires of the sun was a fearsome thing to behold. But a force of fighting men may march along a godroad at twice the speed they make along a path made by men, and so they came before the portal of the citadel of the gods.

It was no imposing thing, this portal, no high archway such as in the cathedrals that the richest kings of the faithful strive to erect. It was the height of a man, rectangular in shape, and wrought of metal.

Above the door there was an inscription in great runes of an unfamiliar type. Though Ørretfangst and Broddr were both skilled in runes, neither could read it. It looked like this:

LONDON CARBON SEQUESTRATION FACILITY 14G

Beside the door there was another inscription, in smaller runes, writ by hand. It had the appearance of a poem, composed of alliterating lines. The runes were these:

My house it lies under the ocean
My street it lies under the sea
Old London lies under the ocean
Oh bring back fair England to me

"Is it a curse?" asked Broddr, cautious-stepping, curse-fearing.

Ørretfangst, wise in witchcraft, examined the inscription and said it was not, and so fearlessly the men entered the great hall of the citadel.

And great it was. Once through the shabby portal, the fortress revealed its true splendor. Tall, it was, many times as tall as a man. The air was cool as in a cave, and the far reaches of the hall were invisible at that great distance. The walls were wrought not of wood, bone, hide, nor even stone, but of metal. Only the gods know the secret of forging the bones of a hall of any sort of metal. The walls of the place were not smooth or simple, as are the walls of the homes of the race of man. Instead, they erupted in a great profusion of made things, and were everywhere covered with peeling paint and other pigments, and half-preserved runic inscriptions.

Everywhere things were dark and silent, save for the low rumbling the Svalmen had discerned from outside. There was no immediate sign of human habitation, nor did they encounter any guard or watchman.

Broddr, whose name means the point of a spear, wished to rush forward with the party, seizing the fortress he now thought to be abandoned and plundering its goods. But Ørretfangst, clear-seeing, sure-thinking, bade him wait, and the prince of the Frøkvelvfolk turned his attention to the walls of the hall, and the arcane objects that protruded therefrom, which were made of iron.

When a man finds a godthing wrought of iron — an old signpost of the godroads, the bones of a godsteed, or a wrought thing more outlandish still — it is badly rusted, for the things the gods made were all made a long time ago.

But the iron bones of this hall were cleaned of rust. When Ørretfangst saw this, he knew that the citadel was not as abandoned as it seemed. Venturesome he was, yet also he was wise in the ways of ambush. Therefore he did not proceed into the dark hall, but instead struck his spear against one of the iron pipes, which rang like a war drum.

"Hark, strangers!" he called. "I am Ørretfangst, Prince of the Frøkvelvfolk and foremost among Svalmen! I have sworn to know this citadel, to serve its lord if he be pious and slay him if he be wicked, to receive gifts or claim plunder. Come forth and greet me!"

There was a long silence, as the mighty challenge echoed through the tall and narrow spaces of the citadel. And then with a strange clatter, witch-light blazed down from the ceiling. Bright and cold and grey it was, unwholesome and unwelcome. And the sound of footsteps began to echo against the walls.

Svalmen gripped spears closer and brought their shields to hand. Ørretfangst stood at their head, proud captain.

The sound of many feet became the sound of a single pair of feet, and then from a door in the side of the hall, the figure of a man came into view, and approached them.

As it approached the Svalmen could see it was no figure of a man at all, but a woman. And yet she seemed not as the women they knew. Her hair was short, her complexion peculiar. She was clad in an odd, sleeved robe, white and tattered.

"This is no lord or lady," said Broddr.

"Perhaps she is his thrall," said Ørretfangst. "In any case, she comes heralded by witch-light; her connection to the masters of this place is certain."

To the distant woman he pitched his voice, calling "Greetings, stranger!" using a man's courtesies.

66

The woman stopped some distance from the war party, beyond the reach of a spear. Her hands were at her hips. Beneath her cloak was a belt of leather and shirt and pants of linen. More clothes than Svalmen wear, either men or women. She bore neither spear nor shield, nor any other piercing or cutting weapon. Yet on her belt was a small thing of iron and wood, formed like the tiller of a ship, yet smaller, which the Svalmen did not recognize.

She spoke, then, a tongue that none of the war-party knew, bland and strange. And then musically and swiftly in a different tongue.

"Speak you norsk?" asked Ørretfangst, for some foreigners know by that name the tongue of Frøkvelv, which is spoken on all the islands of the great sea, save for that mountain which men call the Fist.

"Ah," she said. "Yes. I talk norsk." Her tongue was slow-flowing, stutter-stopped, but with some speech and some gestures she was able to make her meaning known — and then work her foul magic.

"Who are you?" asked Ørretfangst. "Your land is unknown to us, your people unfamiliar."

"My name is Bridgid," she said. "I am the steward of this place, a learned woman."

"What manner of place is this?"

"It is a place for taking out of the air that which makes the world hot."

The Svalmen were aghast that anyone would work against the gods, who fought and defeated the Frost Giants, and moreso that anyone would so readily confess to such evil purpose. Warlike words were spoken and warlike deeds contemplated.

"Hold fast," said Ørretfangst to his men, in the recondite tongue of the sagas, so that he would not be understood by a woman so unfamiliar with norsk. "Barbarians and foreigners have strange practices and foolish beliefs; perhaps this woman is simply confused."

To the woman he turned once again, saying, "Explain to us this work of yours. Why do you do it?"

And then she wove about the prince the deadly snare of the Frost Giants, the terrible lie that overthrew the reason of the greatest prince Frøkvelv had ever known.

"In the days before the Burning," she said, for it was by this name and this name alone that she referred to the Miracle of the Thaw, "the race of man was numerous upon the world. The world itself was temperate and plentiful, and many hundreds, hundreds, hundreds —" she seemed unsatisfied with such numbers as she could describe to the Prince and his band "— countless more men were alive than are now."

The men laughed at her, saying, "This is nonsense! For when it is warm, the crops grow tall and plentiful, and when it is cold, they fail, and many a mother's son goes hungry." But the prince did not laugh; he regarded the thrall of the Frost Giants calculatingly. Already her sorcery had begun to work upon him.

"There are lands to the south," she said. "Great lands, where a man may ride the fastest steed for a month and still not reach the ocean. Once they were peopled; now they are barren, as even this land is barren."

This impressed the men little, for a seafarer knows there are always more lands beyond the sea's bright peaks.

"So much of the Earth is not as it was, for men burnt the whale-oil of the ground, and the tinder of rock, and these fires sent up an unwholesome fume into the sky, and made the climate much hotter than it was formerly."

"You are incorrect, lady," said Ørretfangst. "For all men know it was the gods who made the world warm, as it is today."

"I tell you it was men! And we, all of us across many lands, seek to return the Earth to her erstwhile condition, with green growing things to the far south, and land where there is now sea, and yea, ice at the poles."

"So you admit you are about the work of the Frost Giants," cried Broddr, the prince's bosom companion and soul mate.

"There are no gods or Giants!" said the thrall. "Just men, and their folly, and those who would repair —"

But at that instant Broddr became so enraged by the thrall's blasphemy that he struck her in the stomach with his spear, seeking to kill her.

It was a strong blow and the spear ran her clean through the belly. But it was not her deathblow, and she reached down to her belt and raised up that object which the war-party had not recognized, which was neither spear nor sword nor bow.

But in that instant they knew it to be a thunder-spear, that weapon of the gods and giants. For when she brandished it there was a noise like thunder, and Broddr fell dead, face slathered in blood. Again she brandished the weapon and again the noise like thunder, but Ørretfangst seized her about the throat and snapped her neck, and that was the end of her days.

Ørretfangst claimed the thunder-spear as a trophy, and the men of the war party coursed through the great hall and the many narrow passages of the fortress of the Frost Giants, seeking plunder and giantish foes.

No giants were there, but much plunder of good godstuff: wire for bracelets and armbands, and glass for necklaces and ornaments, a waterskin of godsmetal, and a quantity of gold, which they found in strange chests, affixed to green wafers in obscure patterns. Books of sorcery they found, and with them they made a pyre and burnt Broddr, for one who is felled by a Frost Giant's weapon requires a funeral of burning to purge the cold from his soul. And the spare volumes they burnt for warmth, and to toast meat. The thrall's foodstore they found, and paltry and strange though it was, her bread and curds sustained them.

During the plundering the groaning and growling of the great fortress felt silent, and men were relieved, saying that the ill purpose of the Frost Giants had been well thwarted.

After the passage of days there was no more to plunder in that mighty keep, and so the men retreated to the boat along the ruined godroad, so laden with treasures that they did not even stop to pillage the wide fields of black glass that surrounded the citadel.

On the godroad they made good time to the boat, which they set aright and launched to sea at once. And with good seamanship and a good wind they returned safely home to the land of the Svalmen, to the great fortress of Frøkvelv. But men who were there said that Prince Ørretfangst was in a strange humor indeed, silent and contemplative, not taking his ease with his fellows nor sharing their counsel.

Now, the fortress of Frøkvelv is the work of the gods, and no structure made by man can match it. And yet the city of Frøkvelv is also the greatest city of man in this age. Its walls are hewn of stone and rise twice again as tall as the tallest man, and within it are many buildings of wood, and of those buildings more than half a dozen of them are of two stories. But when Ørretfangst's gaze fell upon the city of Frøkvelv it was not with awe, but with lordly disdain and sorrow. And men looked upon him and said that something ill had come into his heart.

When the war party landed, Prince Ørretfangst betook himself to the hall of his father, King Okred, and his troop followed faithfully, though the wisest among them had a sense of grave foreboding.

In the hall of the king, Ørretfangst stood before all and recounted the events of his journey: of the storm that had blown him from his course; of the barren land to the south; of the fortress of the Frost Giants and of the woman-thrall; of the death of Broddr and his burning; of the good plunder brought back to Frøkvelv.

When King Okred heard the tidings of these events, he knew his son and his son's fighting men had acquitted themselves bravely, and he praised them, and gave them many gifts, and swore to uphold their names and always be a true friend to them.

But when Ørretfangst explained the workings of the Frost Giants and their thralls, the King grew gravely concerned.

"Then this is no simple raid nor feud-killing," said the king. "It is the occasion for holy war." The King spoke to the assembled war-band, and all of his retainers, saying,

"With the strength of the gods behind our right arm, there is no scheme of the Frost Giants we cannot overcome, no citadel of theirs we cannot storm and take as plunder. I therefore beseech you, Ørretfangst, if this cause seems good and righteous, to take up your followers and your ships, and sail southward, and seek out the other citadels and seize them by force of arms, and slay their thralls and end their wickedness."

And all who were present were sure that Prince Ørretfangst would do this thing, for he was boldest among men, and known for boasting, and better yet for doing the deed boasted of.

"This thing I will not do," said Ørretfangst.

"That is ill said," said the king, and all the men of the room drew closer to their swords, for when a king and a prince quarrel, much blood is shed.

"He speaks manliest who speaks the truth," said Ørretfangst. "I claimed the thunder-spear as a trophy of battle, and on the long nights of the journey I contemplated its riddle. For this thunder-spear was not made in the time of the gods! Its grip is wood, and new wood at that; I have looked into the grain. Nor was it as well made as the thunder-spears of the gods, for they were made all of godsmetal, and could slay many men in an instant.

"But if this thunder-spear was made after the time of the gods, and with the materials of man, then it was made by man. And if the thrall, whom we slew, made this thing or was given it by the man who made it, then she knew much of men and gods and giants that we do not.

"And in the thrall's rooms there were many maps," said Ørretfangst, and at this time he took out from his tunic these parchments, which he had kept in secret. "They bear out her tale! Behold the vast lands to the south!"

The king's face was grim and cold. "So far you have said many things, Ørretfangst. But what would you have done?"

"We should sail south, yes. We should seek out another fortress and treat with its master. We should pay the death-price for the one whom we killed, and do great feats in defense of these places, and when the seas fall, we should claim all the new lands of Earth for the kingdom of Frøkvelv!"

And then the king's face was terrible, not with anger but with sorrow.

"I see now that the Frost Giant's witch has snared your wits," he said. "It is a venturesome dream you have, my son, but it is a madness and a heresy." And men nodded, for they saw that the king was right.

"No!" cried Ørretfangst, his face deranged with his madness.

"Seize the prince," said the king, "and put him in shackles, that he may not strike out in his madness and slay, for he is still the strongest and most warlike of men."

And it was done as the king commanded.

For six months they kept the prince in shackles, and the doctors and sages of Frøkvelv sought desperately to treat his madness. But the sorcery could not be broken, and Ørretfangst's ravings grew only more mad, until he denied the gods and giants, and gave voice to the heresy the woman in white had espoused.

Men said he should be burned as a heretic, and given back to the god Ekson, scourge of the blasphemer, whose other name is Mobil. But one night he slipped his bounds and escaped into the swamps. Many men searched for him, and a close watch was kept over the boats, lest he attempt to make good his mad quest. But no man at arms of Frøkvelv could find the prince, then or after.

Meanwhile the king was as good as his plan. That spring, and each spring since, when the storms abate and the land may still be crossed without heat-sickness, the bravest of the men of Frøkvelv take up the spear, the sword, the shield, and they sail south, guided by the thrall's map, and they seek out the Frost Giant's citadels. And the Frøkvelvmen put the thralls within to the sword, and pillage the citadels, and lay to waste the machines and workings of the Frost Giants. And so it is that the men of Frøkvelv do what they can to hold back the coming of the second age of frost.

Yet winter upon winter grows colder, and now men go about wrapped in skins from head to toe during the longest nights. And those venturesome men who sail north into the darkness, under the gem-cloth of the gods, report that strange new storms may be found in these waters, like unto neither rain nor hail, but instead of the smallest stinging flakes of bitterest cold, which burns the skin and brings unnatural pains unto the flesh.

And to this day, men on journeys through the marshes and bayous that separate Frøkvelv from the other settlements still sometimes see mad Prince Ørretfangst, an outcast and an outlaw, a wild man with beard and clothes in tatters, living like a beast amongst his namesakes, the ørretfangsts, the crocodiles of Svalbard.

Warren Benedetto writes dark fiction about horrible people, horrible places, and horrible things. He is an award-winning author who has published over 200 stories, appearing in publications such as *Dark Matter Magazine*, *Fantasy Magazine*, and *The Dread Machine*; on podcasts such as *The NoSleep Podcast*, *Tales to Terrify*, and *Chilling Tales For Dark Nights*; and in anthologies from *Apex Magazine*, Tenebrous Press, Scare Street, and many more. He also works in the video game industry, where he holds more than forty patents for various types of gaming technology.

•   •   •

My original idea for this story was about a firebreather who couldn't find a mate because his fire breathing would kill any normal person he tried to be with … until he meets a fire eater who is unaffected by the flames. However, when I tried to write that version, it felt kind of like a bad analogy for sex and positioned the fire eater (a young woman) as a passive recipient in the relationship. I decided instead to make the girl more powerful, more in control, and more proactive, which I think worked out much better. My favorite part of the story — which is subtle and which many readers may miss — is that it's actually a comic book villain origin story. If you missed it the first time, try reading it again with that in mind!

DRAGONSBREATH

WARREN BENEDETTO

THE WOMAN'S HEAD LURCHED forward as her SUV slowed to a jarring stop, its bumper only inches from the police car parked sideways across her lane. Half a dozen emergency vehicles crowded the street ahead of her. There were police cars. Fire trucks. An ambulance.

The woman watched with mounting horror as a pair of paramedics lifted a gurney out of the ambulance and began wheeling it up the driveway of a nearby house.

Her house.

"Oh my God," the woman breathed. "Lila!"

She threw her car door open and leaped from the driver's seat, ignoring the urgent chime warning her that the engine was still running. Darting across the road, she pushed her way through a crowd of onlookers and ducked under a strip of yellow police tape.

"Ma'am!" The police officer manning the perimeter of the scene reached for her. "You can't —"

"That's my house!" she yelled as she twisted away from his grip.

The place looked like it had been hit by a missile. A large portion of the front wall had caved out onto the lawn, spilling charred beams and scorched pink insulation from the collapsing attic like innards erupting through an exit wound.

The woman sprinted to the front porch and vaulted up the steps two at a time. Shards of broken glass crunched under her feet as she rushed into the house.

A thin veil of smoke hung in the air. In front of the couch, a man in a black windbreaker squatted next to a sheet-draped form. The back of his jacket was emblazoned with large white block letters: CORONER. The woman's stomach dropped.

"Lila! Oh, no, no, no ..." She rushed over to the body, fell to her knees, and reached for the sheet.

The coroner's hand shot out and grabbed her wrist. "Don't."

"She's my daughter!" The woman wrenched her wrist from the man's grasp then yanked the sheet back. What she saw punched the air from her lungs. She recoiled in horror. Her hands flew to her face, fingers trembling. A tortured wail rose in her throat.

It was her daughter, her angel, her Lila. Her precious, beautiful, perfect baby girl.

Dead.

The lower half of the teen's face was destroyed. Most of the skin had been burnt away, revealing scorched muscle and bone underneath. The burns extended down into the darkness of her mouth then emerged through a smoking cavity in the middle of her chest. Her ribs were splayed outward as if something had exploded them from the inside. Smoke drifted lazily upward from the hole where her heart used to be.

The woman felt numb, senseless, confused. The sounds in the room began to fade, becoming muffled and far away.

Her vision grew soft around the edges. Through the fog, she was dimly aware of the coroner drawing the sheet back over her daughter's ruined face.

"Sorry," the woman said vaguely.

A hand rested on her shoulder, steadying her. A man's voice spoke. "Ma'am? Are you the mother?"

She nodded, never taking her eyes off her daughter's lifeless body.

"Do you recognize this?"

The hand held a large plastic evidence bag in front of her face. Inside was a black fabric mask. It resembled a ski mask made from a thick fireproof material with ovals of dark tempered glass protecting each eye.

The woman's heart kicked in her chest. She *had* seen the mask before, on a boy at her daughter's school. As far as she knew, Lila had never spoken to the kid. He was an outcast, always wearing that creepy mask wherever he went. The woman assumed he had been disfigured somehow, but she didn't know for sure. She had never seen his face. But she knew his name.

The woman's lips moved in an inaudible whisper. The officer holding the evidence bag leaned in closer.

"What was that?" He looked at the coroner. "What'd she say?"

The coroner shrugged.

"Ash," the woman said again, louder this time. "His name is Ash."

•　　•　　•

Ashton Gale had been sweeping for what felt like hours. The bleachers were an endless sea of stale popcorn, broken peanut shells, and crumpled churro wrappers. A tacky mixture of spilled soda and dissolved cotton candy seemed to coat every surface.

The job wasn't what he had in mind when he signed up. He imagined he'd be out on the midway, manning one of the game booths. Or spinning cotton candy. Or collecting tickets on the Ferris wheel. Instead, he was basically a janitor.

It was working out okay, though. The job paid less than minimum wage, but his employers paid in cash, let him eat for free, and gave him a tiny run-down trailer in which to live. That was more than enough for him. All he cared about was that he had escaped his shit-heel town sight unseen, and that he wasn't out on the street begging for change. Or in jail. The rest was gravy.

As Ash swept, a pair of crumpled beer cans flew through the air and clattered onto the bleachers in front of him.

"Incoming!" a voice shouted from above.

Peals of raucous laughter echoed down from a trio of rowdy carnival barkers hanging out at the top of the bleachers, a foam cooler full of cheap beers between them. They were shit-faced as usual, fresh off another night of convincing stupid people to play rigged games for worthless prizes.

"Hey, Lecter!" a barker named Higgins slurred. "Trash those for me, will ya?"

Ash picked up the crushed cans, dropped them into his trash basket, then continued sweeping. A few seconds later, another crumpled beer can whizzed through the air. It collided painfully with the side of Ash's head, dinging his ear through his mask.

"Duck!" Higgins yelled after the fact.

Ash threw down the handle of his broom in frustration. "Dude! What the hell?" He pressed his hand against his ear to dull the pain. "What's your problem?"

"What's my problem?" Higgins stood up, swaying on his feet a little. "What's *my* problem?" He began lumbering down the bleachers toward Ash, his heavy footfalls booming on the wide aluminum steps. "What's *your* problem?"

"Some asshole won't let me do my job. *That's* my problem."

He tried to swallow down the intense heat rising from his chest into his throat. He had dealt with guys like Higgins before. It never ended well. He couldn't let himself get too heated, or he would end up in more trouble than he was already in. He had to calm down. Cool off. Relax.

He took a deep breath then bent down and picked up his broom. When he straightened up, he found himself nearly face-to-face with Higgins. The barker lunged at Ash, grabbing at his mask. "Take that thing off."

Ash batted Higgins' arm to the side. "Get away." Another flare of searing heat swirled in his chest. He strained to choke it down.

"Little freak. What're you hiding under there? Huh?" He reached for Ash's mask again.

Ash dodged backward out of Higgins' grasp. He wielded his broom defensively, holding it crosswise in front of his chest. "Don't do this."

As Higgins readied himself to lunge at Ash again, a hand seized his shoulder and yanked him backward.

"Higgins!" a female voice shouted. "Back off!"

Higgins spun around. Behind him was a diminutive girl of about eighteen. She was wearing an oversized gray hoodie with the Fairway Amusements logo emblazoned across the front. Her emerald-green eyes sparkled under the string lights hung overhead.

"Leave the kid alone, you old drunk," the girl said with a smirk. She tossed Higgins a fresh can of beer. Higgins caught the beer against his chest. "One for the road."

Higgins shot a glare at Ash then looked back at the girl. "He a friend of yours?"

"He is now."

Higgins grunted. "All right." He cracked the beer open and took a sip. "We cool?" he asked Ash.

"Yeah." Ash lowered his broom back to the ground. "We're cool."

Higgins' buddies stomped down the bleachers from where they had been watching the drama unfold. One of them patted Higgins' shoulder. "C'mon, mate. Chow time."

Higgins nodded. He drained his beer, wiped his bottom lip with his sleeve, then crumpled the can and tossed it at Ash's feet. "Missed one."

Ash looked down at the can. His chest burned like molten lava. He swallowed hard. He couldn't wait to kill the guy.

Without another word, Higgins followed his friends through the exit.

"Sorry about that," the girl said to Ash once Higgins was gone.

Ash picked up Higgins' can and dropped it into the trash bin. "You didn't have to do that. I could have handled him myself."

"Meh. He's not worth it." She looked Ash up and down. "You're new, huh?" She extended her hand. "I'm Esmé."

Ash wiped his palm on his pants then shook her hand. "Ash."

"Ash. Nice." She nodded approvingly. "When did you join?"

"About a week ago. You?"

"Oh!" Esmé laughed. "I'm a Fairway original."

Ash tilted his head, confused. "What's that?"

"Carnival kid, born and raised." She indicated the Fairway Amusements logo on the front of her hoodie. "Home sweet home."

"Wow, so you were born here?"

"Not *here* here — my parents were down in Florida for the off-season — but, yeah."

"That's crazy. I didn't even know 'carnival kid' was a thing."

"Well, now you do."

"Yep. Now I do." An awkward silence fell between them. Ash began sweeping again, his eyes on the floor. He could feel the heat of Esmé's gaze as he pushed the broom in her direction. "Excuse me."

"Oh, sorry." She stepped up onto the bleacher bench, placing her hand on Ash's shoulder for balance. Her touch sent an electric jolt racing along his skin. He looked up at her. She had fair skin with a light spray of freckles across her nose. Her eyes were ringed with heavy black eyeliner. A pair of candy-apple red braids poked out from under her hood.

Esmé smiled down at Ash. From the way her eyes were darting around his face, he could tell what she was thinking. He had seen the look before.

"What do you want to know?" Ash said.

Esmé quickly averted her gaze. "I'm so sorry. I didn't mean to stare."

"No, it's okay. I'm used to it. Go ahead. Ask."

Esmé hesitated, then spoke. "What happened?"

"Nothing. I have a condition."

"Do ... do you ever take it off?"

"It's best if I don't."

Esmé nodded. She looked at the mask again then plucked a stray piece of string from the side of it. "Well, I like it. You're like a cross between Deadpool and Darth Vader. It's badass."

Ash was speechless. Nobody had ever complimented him on the mask before. Some people stared. Some laughed. Some tried to ignore it. But badass? That was a first.

"Hell," Esmé continued. "I'd wear one if I could. It'd be like my secret identity."

"Nah, you definitely shouldn't."

"No? Why not?" She cocked an eyebrow.

"Because ..." He paused. He wanted to compliment her, to tell her she was too pretty to cover her face, but he knew that, no matter how he said it, it would come out completely desperate and weird. "You'd be really hot," he said instead.

"Wow, thanks." Esmé laughed. "I'm flattered."

"Inside the mask, I mean."

"Ah. Right."

"Anyway." Ash lifted his broom, desperate to extricate himself from the awkward mess he had created. "I better get back to work."

"Oh, yeah, sure. Don't let me stop you." Esmé walked along the bleacher bench like it was a balance beam then jumped down onto the stairs. "See you around?"

Ash smiled under his mask.

"Definitely."

●   ●   ●

"Hey, Vic!" Esmé bounded up to the antique carousel and leaned on the battered metal fence that surrounded the empty attraction. "Can you run it for us one time before you go?"

The elderly man in the faded Fairway Amusements polo smiled, his weathered face crinkling around the eyes. "All right, Spark. But no music, okay? It's past quiet hours."

Esmé clapped her hands and squealed gleefully. "Thank you!" She tugged on Ash's sleeve. "Come on, hop on."

Ash followed Esmé through the gate and onto the carousel. "Did he just call you Spark?"

Esmé rolled her eyes. "Yeah. That's his pet name for me, since I was a kid."

"Why?"

"Because I light up his life. Duh."

Ash snorted out a laugh. Esmé moved along the rows of wooden horses until she found the one she was looking for: a black steed with a fiery red mane.

"Ah, there she is. My spirit animal." She dug her toe into one of the metal stirrups attached to the horse's side then swung her leg up and over the saddle. "Giddy up."

Ash grabbed the tarnished brass pole that speared the horse next to Esmé's. The metal was cool and slick with condensation. He pulled himself onto the horse and settled into the saddle.

"Spark should be your superhero name."

"Ugh, no way. Sounds more like a Care Bear or something." Esmé changed her voice to a peppy, enthusiastic squeal. "C'mon, kids! Let's all use our imaginations!" Ash laughed. Esmé switched back to her normal voice. "Nah, screw that. If I'm gonna be in a comic book, I'm gonna be a supervillain like Selene."

"Selene?"

"From Dark X-Men?" she asked. Ash shook his head. "The Black Queen of the Hellfire Club? She's like Jean Grey, but in bondage gear."

"Badass."

"Exactly." She leaned off her horse to look at Vic. "All right, Vic! Start her up!"

Vic punched the button to start the ride. The carousel lurched, then began to pick up speed. Without the calliope music blaring, the ride was a cacophony of turning gears and hissing pistons playing over the low rumble of the engine that powered the ride.

Ash raised his voice above the racket. "So, you know everyone around here, huh?"

"Pretty much, yeah. I mean, sometimes new people come and go, but most have been around forever. Vic's been with us for like fifty years. Right, Vic?" she yelled as the carousel swung past the old man. He raised his head and waved. She laughed. "He has no idea what I just said."

"Is there anyone else our age? Other carnival kids?" Ash asked.

"Not anymore."

"They left?"

"You could say that. There was a fire. In the Haunted Castle."

"Oh, shit. I'm sorry."

"Yeah, it was a bad time."

Ash thought for a moment. The incident sounded familiar, like something he had seen on the news as a kid. He could picture the flames raging from the windows of the faux-stone turrets of the castle and the face of the giant fiberglass demon over the front entrance melting in the heat.

"Where did that happen?" he asked.

"Greensville."

"Yes! Right. I thought so. I grew up right by there. I vaguely remember hearing about it when I was little. My mom would never let me go to the carnival anymore after that."

"And yet here you are."

"Yeah. Ironic, I guess."

Esmé lapsed into silence. Ash stole a glance at her. Her hoodie had fallen backward onto her shoulders, revealing her vivid red braids. The loose baby curls around the edge of her hairline danced in the breeze. The golden glow of the carousel lights made her face seem luminescent, as if she was lit from within. Ash felt a familiar pull in his chest.

God, she's beautiful.

Every night for the last three weeks, Esmé had shown up outside the big top toward the end of Ash's shift. At first, their conversations were awkward. Ash wasn't sure why she was hanging around or what she wanted from him. But after a few days, the awkwardness began to dissipate. They started to talk more freely, to laugh more easily.

Esmé was hilarious: irreverent, clever, and brash. She was also brilliant. She had been homeschooled — more like self-educated — so she seemed to know everything about everything. She was like a walking Wikipedia. Plus, she had read every comic book he had read — and more. She knew every hero, every villain, every origin story. Ash never got tired of talking to her. He was spellbound.

"Why *are* you here?" Esmé asked.

The question caught Ash off guard. He blinked, coming back to the present. "Hmm? Here? You asked me —"

"No, I mean with Fairway. Why did you join?"

"I needed a job."

"Yeah, but ... the carnival? Why not, like, Starbucks or something?"

"I don't know. It's hard to explain. I needed to get away."

"From what?"

Ash didn't answer. He hadn't talked with anyone about the incident. The memory was still too fresh. Too painful. He wanted to block it out, to forget all about it. If he didn't, he was afraid he'd lose his mind.

What happened to Lila was ... God, it was awful. And it was all his fault. He had been weak. He let his guard down even though he knew how risky it was and what the consequences might be. He just wanted so badly to believe that it would be okay, that he could be normal.

But he was wrong. And Lila had paid the price.

"Forget it," Esmé said, noticing Ash's hesitation. "You don't have to say."

The churning of the carousel's machinery began to wind down. The attraction started to slow. Vic waved his hand as the carousel rounded the curve where he stood. "All right, kiddos! Time's up."

"One second!" Esmé chirped. She swung her leg over her horse's saddle and climbed off. "Come on," she said, beckoning for Ash to follow her. "Real quick. I want to show you something."

Esmé walked along the inside edge of the carousel, in the opposite direction of its rotation. Ash slid off his horse and followed.

The center of the carousel was stationary, like a wide octagonal pillar around which the platform turned. Each of the pillar's panels was painted with an intricate old-fashioned carnival scene, with roaring elephants, mustachioed strongmen, and balloon-wielding clowns. Above each painting was a large mirror that reflected the carousel's glimmering lights. It made the ride seem infinitely bigger than it was.

As the carousel slowed to a stop, Esmé jumped down into the space between the platform and the center pillar. She stepped up to the painting of the elephants and slipped her hand into the narrow gap between the panels. There was a solid click of a latch opening. The elephant panel swung inward. It was a hidden door.

Esmé stepped through. "Watch your head." Ash ducked his head under the low-hanging doorframe as he entered. Esmé closed the door behind them.

Once inside, Ash stood up straight. "Whoa," he said, his voice full of wonder.

The inside of the pillar was hollow, forming a small hidden room in the center of the carousel. Most of the space was taken up by the ride's motor and gearbox along with a sound system with several large speakers. Most interesting to Ash, however, were the mirrors: he could see straight through them, to the carousel horses on the other side. They weren't mirrors after all. At least, not from the inside.

Ash turned around slowly, looking out through the one-way mirrors in all directions. As he came full circle, he found himself almost face-to-face with Esmé. "Sorry," he mumbled. He tried to take a step back, but his heel knocked into the speaker box directly behind him. There was nowhere for him to go.

"It's okay. I don't bite."

Ash pretended not to hear her loaded comment. "I had no idea this place was here."

"Yeah, most people don't." Esmé leaned back on the speaker box behind her. "I used to sneak in here every night when I was younger. I'd sit for hours and just watch the world spinning around me." She gazed out through the mirror beside her. The carousel lights glinting through the tinted glass flickered across her face like firelight.

"There were so many kids out there, laughing, having fun, having friends." She looked back at Ash. "I just wanted to be one of them, you know? Doing dumb shit. Living in a house, going to school, hanging out with other kids my age." She looked through the mirror again. Her eyes had a glassy, faraway look. "I used to try to make friends with them, but ..." She trailed off.

Esmé stood and stepped closer to Ash. She was nearly toe-to-toe with him in the tiny space, so close that he could feel the heat radiating off her skin. She didn't say anything.

Ash laughed nervously. "What?"

"Hug?" She extended her arms to her sides.

"Oh. Sure." Ash awkwardly wrapped his arms around Esmé. She hugged him back. He could smell the warm vanilla scent of her shampoo through his mask. Her face felt warm against his chest.

After a few seconds, Esmé loosened her embrace. She kept her hands around his waist and looked up at him, her eyes sparkling. "Nobody can see us in here, you know."

Ash felt his pulse begin to accelerate. The hidden room suddenly felt impossibly small, claustrophobic, as if a sudden fire had sucked all the oxygen out of the place. Heat waves distorted the air, threatening to suffocate him.

"Yeah. We should go. Vic's probably wondering where we went." He fumbled for the doorknob.

"Right," Esmé said, disappointed. She dropped her hands from his waist. The heat began to dissipate. As Ash unlatched the door, Esmé stuck her foot out and blocked it from opening. She put her hand on his arm. "You know you can trust me, right?"

"Yeah, sure. I know."

"Whatever your condition is, I don't care. You don't have to hide from me."

"I'm not hiding from you," Ash insisted. He opened the door. "I'm protecting you."

He ducked out, hoisted himself up onto the carousel platform, then began weaving his way between the rows of wooden horses. Esmé called after him.

"Protecting me? From what?"

But Ash was already gone.

•　　•　　•

Ash walked quickly across the carnival grounds. He made his way along an orange plastic storm fence then turned left into the dark alley between two 18-wheelers. The fastest way back to his trailer was to cut through the parking area where the carnival's vehicles were staged: a maze of flatbeds, box trucks, and recreational vehicles of every shape and size.

As he navigated the maze, he heard loud voices and raucous laughter. He recognized the sound. It was Higgins and his crew of sycophants, the same guys who had harassed him the night he first met Esmé.

"Hey, Lecter!" Higgins bellowed when he spotted Ash. "C'mere for a second."

Higgins and his friends were sitting on the edge of a flatbed, passing a bottle of whiskey back and forth between them. A kerosene camping lantern cast a dull white glow in the dusty air.

Ash had learned the names of the other two barkers since their last encounter. There was Orsi, a short, fat Italian with thinning hair slicked back across his sunburned scalp and Freed, an ex-con with ice-blue eyes and a tattoo of a flaming skull on his neck.

Ash quickened his pace. Higgins swiped the whiskey bottle from Orsi then jumped down from the flatbed. His boots kicked up puffs of dust as he landed in front of Ash.

"I was wondering when I was going to see you again," Higgins said. "Come and have a drink with us." He took a swig from the whiskey bottle then held it out to Ash. "Consider it a peace offering."

"Thanks," Ash mumbled. "But I'm good."

Behind Ash, Orsi and Freed jumped down to the ground.

"It isn't polite to turn down a drink from a friend." Higgins took an unsteady step closer to Ash. His speech was slurred. "We're still friends, right?"

"Sure." Ash looked over his shoulder. Orsi and Freed were close behind him. With the long flatbed trucks to his left and his right, Ash had no place to run. He was trapped. "I'm just not up for it right now. Long night."

Higgins nodded understandingly. "Girl trouble?" He held up a finger to Orsi and Freed. "Give us a minute." Then he slung his arm around Ash's shoulder and started walking with him.

"Talk to me," he said, his voice lowered. "What's the problem? She's not putting out?"

"It's not like that," Ash said through gritted teeth. He twisted out from under Higgins' grip. Higgins let him go. "Man," Ash said, shaking his head in disbelief. "You are such a piece of shit."

He tried to walk past Higgins. Higgins shot his arm out across Ash's chest then pushed him backward. "Hang on. That's no way to talk to a friend."

"Then I guess we're not friends anymore."

"No? That's too bad." Higgins shot a look over Ash's shoulder. Orsi and Freed lunged at Ash from behind. Each of them grabbed one of his arms. Ash struggled to pull away, but they were too strong. They twisted his arms painfully behind his back.

Higgins stepped up to Ash then threw a punch directly into Ash's stomach. Ash doubled over, gasping for air. Orsi and Freed pulled him upright. His head hung down as he tried to catch his breath.

"That's for your smart mouth, *friend*," Higgins said. "Now ..." He reached up, grabbed the top of Ash's mask, and pulled. The mask stretched then slipped off. Higgins tossed it aside. "Let's see what we've got here."

Ash's chin sagged down to his chest. His dark brown hair hung down over his face. "Give it back," he whispered weakly.

Higgins grabbed a fistful of Ash's hair and pulled his head up so he could see the teen's face. His disappointment was palpable.

Ash was a normal-looking kid — good-looking, even. There was no disfigurement. No scarring. Nothing worth covering up at all.

"Well, shit," Higgins complained. "Look at Johnny Depp here. Why're you hiding that pretty face, boy?"

"I have a condition." Ash's lips curled back from his teeth in an angry sneer. His voice sounded deeper, more guttural, as if his throat was full of hot coals.

Higgins didn't seem to notice the difference. "If you say so." He motioned to his friends. "Let him go."

Orsi and Freed released Ash's arms. Ash pulled away, rotated his sore shoulders, then walked over to where Higgins had dropped his mask. As he bent down to pick it up, Higgins planted his foot on Ash's backside and pushed, sending him stumbling forward.

Ash fell to his hands and knees. A bright flash of flame ignited underneath him with a *whoosh*, like lighter fluid being splashed on a grill. The flames lit up the night with a blinding white flare of light.

Higgins jumped backward. "Whoa! What the hell?"

"I tried to warn you," Ash said as he climbed to his feet. He raised his head to look at Higgins. His irises were glowing like cinders in a campfire.

Before Higgins could react, a bluish-yellow jet of flame erupted from Ash's mouth and engulfed Higgins in a torrent of liquid fire. Higgins' clothes and hair were vaporized almost instantly. Higgins opened his mouth to scream. Instead of air, he drew in a lungful of super-heated gas, incinerating the delicate tissues in his mouth and throat. His lungs seized, trapping the searing heat inside his chest. Oily black smoke poured from his throat. No sound escaped his lips.

Like a flood of napalm from a flamethrower, the blaze gushing from Ash's mouth consumed Higgins completely. His body became a twisted black silhouette, a ghoul writhing grotesquely in a white-hot pillar of fire. His flesh began to bubble and melt, stretching and blackening over his bones like burnt taffy. Steam hissed from his eyeballs as they ruptured in the heat then sunk back into his skull. The acrid stench of burnt skin poisoned the air.

Orsi and Freed stood paralyzed, watching Higgins' immolation in numb horror. Higgins stumbled blindly toward them, his expression frozen in a rictus of agony. Just as he reached them, his lifeless body crumpled into a smoldering heap at their feet.

Ash snapped his mouth shut, cutting off the jet of flames. He glared at the two terrified men, his eyes pulsing with an ember-orange glow.

A flood of urine spread across Orsi's pants. "P-Please. D-don't."

Ash pulled the mask over his head. The heat waves dissipated.

"You tell anyone, and I'll find you. Understand?"

Orsi and Freed both nodded.

"Then go," Ash said.

The two men ran, disappearing into the shadows between the 18-wheelers.

Once they were gone, Ash slumped against the flatbed then sat on the ground and drew his knees to his chest. His head hung heavy on his neck. He felt weak, drained, as if every ounce of energy had been spilled from his body.

A crunch of dry grass made him look up. His stomach twisted into a knot.

Esmé was standing over him.

"Hey," she said quietly.

"Hey." Ash's voice felt thick and raw in his throat. "You saw." He could tell from her face that she had.

"Yeah. You okay?"

"No." He struggled to his feet and dusted off his jeans. "I better go."

"Where?"

Ash looked down the row of trucks at the empty carnival grounds. Lights from a distant highway traced a line across the darkened rural landscape. "I don't know."

"Then stay."

"I can't. Someone'll find him."

"So what? Let them." Esmé bent down and picked up Higgins' whiskey bottle. She began pouring the caramel-colored liquid onto his smoking corpse.

"What are you doing?"

"Such a terrible accident." Esmé sighed with mock remorse. She emptied the bottle onto the ground next to Higgins then dropped it on the dirt by his hand. "He really should've been more careful."

Ash watched as Esmé grabbed the camping lantern that was still glowing on the flatbed truck nearby. She tossed the lantern underhand, landing it next to Higgins' body. Its glass shattered. Fresh flames whooshed up as the glowing wick ignited the spilled alcohol. The fire sped along the ground then up and over Higgins' body.

"You don't understand. It's only a matter of time before someone else gets hurt. Before *you* get hurt."

"You won't hurt me."

"Not on purpose, no. But that's the problem. I can't help it. The only thing keeping you safe right now is this stupid mask. If I take it off ..." He backed away from her. "I'm sorry."

He started walking in the direction of the highway in the distance. He would hitch a ride. Find a new job. Start over someplace else — alone. Again.

Esmé spoke from behind him. "I know what happened, Ash. To your friend."

Ash froze in his tracks. He turned around. "How?"

"The police. A few days after you joined. They were looking for you."

"What did you tell them?"

"Nothing. But they ... they had pictures."

Ash closed his eyes, suddenly overwhelmed with a flood of images from that night. Lila, on the couch, removing his mask. Leaning in, eyes closed, lips parted. The soft brush of her mouth against his. The beating of his heart. The burning in his chest. Then, the flames. Raging past his lips, down her throat, through her ribs, an explosion of liquid fire tearing her open from the inside. Her body tumbling off the couch, sprawling on the floor, eyes wide, face ruined. Dead.

"I wasn't sure if you were who I thought you were," Esmé continued. "But I knew I had to find out."

"She was my friend." Ash exhaled a shuddering breath. He felt nauseous. "She wanted me to feel normal, just for a second. And it killed her. *I* killed her."

"But you're *not* normal. You're special. You have a gift. A beautiful, wonderful gift."

"Yeah. Great gift. Thanks, Dad." His voice dripped with sarcasm.

"You just need to learn to control it. If you can harness it, use it to your advantage ... you'll be unstoppable. *We'll* be unstoppable."

"Don't you think I've tried?" The desperation in Ash's voice was plain. "You think I want to wear this thing for the rest of my life?" He tugged at his mask. "It's the only way."

Esmé reached into her back pocket and pulled out a colorful slip of paper, about half the size of a postcard. "Stay. Just one more night."

"Why? What's the point?"

"Trust me." She handed the paper to Ash. "There's something you should see."

•　　•　　•

The midway was awash in light and sound. Squeals of glee accompanied the rumble of the rollercoaster as it roared around a bend and into a towering loop. The music from the carousel blared over loudspeakers, while barkers implored passersby to test their luck at games of skill and chance. The tantalizing aroma of hot kettle corn and fresh roasted peanuts wafted through the air.

Ash weaved his way through the chaos, past the Mirror Maze and the Giant Slide, to the sideshow tent behind the big top. He looked down at the slip of paper Esmé had handed him the night before.

It was a ticket.

The Amazing Esmeralda, it read. *Death-Defying Feats of Wonder. 8:00 PM.*

Ash hadn't realized Esmé was a performer. He had just assumed she was with the carnival because her parents were there. She never said otherwise, and he never thought to ask.

Ash passed the ticket to the girl at the gate then entered the sideshow tent. There were no bleachers inside, just folding chairs set up on a carpet of bright green AstroTurf. The front of the tent housed a small black stage between stacks of loudspeakers. At the back of the stage was a large banner featuring the same *Amazing Esmeralda* logo as on the ticket.

Ash dropped into his seat. The lights dimmed. The crowd grew silent. Dramatic music began to thrum through the loudspeakers followed by the booming voice of an announcer.

"And now! Ladies and gentlemen! Prepare yourselves for the most death-defying feats of wonder your eyes have ever seen! I give you Fairway Amusements' brightest new act! The hottest talent under the sun! Behold! The Amazing! Esmeralda!"

A massive gush of flame erupted out of the darkness, directly at the audience. The crowd screamed with surprise and delight. The flames quickly dissipated, replaced by a pair of whirling, spinning wheels of fire that rotated around each other like the rings of orbiting planets. Sparks ricocheted off the stage. The rings changed size, each alternately growing and shrinking and growing again. The crowd *ooh*'d and *aah*'d with appreciation.

Finally, bright red spotlights faded in from above, illuminating the performer at the center of the stage: Esmé. She froze in a dramatic pose, holding her flaming torches aloft. Her red hair was twisted into a tight bun. Irregular red and black stripes were painted diagonally across her face. Her sleeveless black bodysuit and knee-high boots reminded Ash of something that would be worn by a comic book hero. Or a villain. She looked fearsome. Dangerous. Wild.

"Badass," Ash whispered to himself.

Esmé placed the torches into black metal stands on either side of her then touched the flame of each torch with a fingertip. Fire raced across her upturned palms and along the tops of her bare arms to her shoulders. With her arms held out at her sides, the flames looked like feathers on the wings of a phoenix.

Suddenly, the stands holding the torches seemed to collapse, each tipping inward toward Esmé. The torches hit the stage at her feet, igniting a column of flame that consumed her body, from her feet to her neck. The crowd cried out in surprise. Esmé raised her arms toward the ceiling as if summoning the fire higher. Then she clapped her hands over her head. The flames raced up her body, along her arms, and into her hands, leaving her body undamaged and unharmed.

Esmé held her hands cupped over her head then brought them forward in front of her. A small, bright flame danced in her palms. She blew on the flame, sending a torrent of fire from her lips into the air. Then she inhaled, drawing the fire back into her mouth.

The lights dimmed almost black. Esmé opened her mouth. A brilliant yellow glow emanated from her throat. The fire appeared to still be burning, deep inside her body. Esmé tipped her head back and spat a bloom of fire into the air. The flames formed the shape of a dragon in the air over her head. The beast flapped its blazing wings, flew out over the heads of the audience, then disintegrated into a shower of sparks.

The crowd leaped to their feet, giving Esmé a standing ovation. As Ash stood and clapped, Esmé's words from the night before came flooding back to him.

"You just need to learn to control it," he heard her say. "If you can harness it, use it to your advantage ... you'll be unstoppable. *We'll* be unstoppable."

We'll be unstoppable, Ash thought again.

We.

•   •   •

"Why didn't you tell me?" Ash asked.

He and Esmé walked through the shadows between the 18-wheelers, passing the circle of burnt grass where Higgins' body had been recovered earlier that morning. Remnants of yellow police tape trailed along the ground and flapped in the breeze. The police hadn't asked too many questions. It was just a freak accident as far as they were concerned. An open-and-shut case.

"How's that conversation supposed to go, exactly?" Esmé said, arching an eyebrow.

"But you knew about me. You must have."

"I thought maybe I did, yeah. But I couldn't be sure. Lucky for me, Higgins outed you before I had to figure out how to bring it up."

"How did you know, though? Because of the mask?"

Esmé stopped and looked up at Ash. "You don't remember me, do you?"

"From where?"

"The carousel. You were eight, maybe nine years old. I saw you riding alone. I asked if I could ride with you."

A blurry image flickered at the edge of Ash's consciousness, just out of reach. He remembered ... something. But he wasn't sure exactly what.

Esmé continued. "I snuck you on all the rides. The Ferris Wheel. The Tilt-A-Whirl." She paused. "The Haunted Castle."

Ash's eyes widened under his mask. He remembered. "That was you," he whispered. Esmé nodded. "Those kids. They were so mean to you. I ... I got so angry."

"We both did."

The heavy veil Ash had cast over the memory began to lift. That night was the first time he had become aware of his powers. The first time he had lost control. The first time someone had gotten hurt. The first time someone died.

Somehow, he had escaped from the inferno unharmed. His mother found him wandering through the stampeding crowd, his face smeared with soot. She asked if he was okay. He said he wasn't feeling well. His chest hurt. His throat burned.

His mother's face had gone bone white. She warned him never to tell anyone what happened. Then she hustled him past the arriving fire engines and out to the car, never to return.

A few days later, she gave him the mask for the first time. It was the same kind his father had worn before he died. "You'll need to wear this from now on," she had said.

"For how long?"

She didn't have an answer.

Ash walked with Esmé in silence, too overwhelmed with the force of the memory to speak for a bit. They arrived at Esmé's trailer. As Esmé fished for her keys in her backpack, Ash stared at his reflection in the darkened window. His mask stared back at him.

Esmé found her keys and unlocked her trailer door. She turned back to Ash. "Now what?" she asked quietly.

Ash looked at his reflection again. He reached up and slipped the mask off his head, then leaned forward, took Esmé's face in his hands, and kissed her softly on the lips. Waves of heat distortion rippled around them.

After a few seconds, Ash pulled away. He opened his eyes. Esmé smiled at him then tilted her head back and exhaled a column of fire into the air. The flames morphed into a giant dragon several times larger than the one from her show. The creature hovered overhead for a moment then flapped its wings and soared away into the starless night sky.

"You've gotta teach me how to do that," Ash said as he watched the dragon disappear into the distance.

"Tomorrow."

She kissed him again, then took him by the hand and led him into her trailer. As Ash passed through the door, he let the mask slip from his fingers and onto the ground outside.

MOMENTO AMICUM

MARC A. CRILEY

M ELFORD VERIFIED TWELVE VOLTS on the solar panel's leads one last time, toggled the reset, then snapped shut the access panel. He stepped around to the front of the headstone and waited. The mementa screen opaqued, masking the splendidly etched-in-granite rendition of Ellanora Hawks. A moment later her mementa's well-worn but equally splendid visage resolved on the screen.

"Good morning, Mrs. Hawks," Melford said, "How are you today?"

A firm alto emerged from concealed stereo speakers. "I think I'm fine, Melford, was there a problem?"

"A solar panel lead corroded down to where the battery couldn't get a charge. I replaced both leads — the other one was also starting to go — swapped out the battery and wiped down your panel and display."

"With vinegar?"

"Yes, ma'am, vinegar and water, two to one ratio just like you said, cuts right through the grime. You're looking as good now as the day you came here to rest."

Ellanora's visage chuckled. "Always the smooth talker, Melford. How long was I out of sorts?"

"About two weeks. We had a week of intolerable heavy rain and quite a few of the mementas, like yours, got soaked pretty bad. I had the whole week off, and since I've been back I've been working on 'em every day — had to do the limited-term ones first — so finally got started on all you perpetuals this morning."

"Well," she said, "that's too bad. Everyone else fixed yet?"

"No ma'am, I've still got three to go."

"Well, I shouldn't keep you then." Ellanora's visage on the headstone screen pursed her lips. "I suppose I missed Dora and the kids, she had streamed in that she was planning to visit last weekend. I hope they weren't too disappointed, me being out-of-sorts."

Melford scratched his temple, brushed away beaded sweat. Some cicadas started their undulating refrains, buzzing over the distant whine of Nala the groundskeeper mowing over on the cemetery's far side. "Not too many people came by the last couple weeks to pay respects, what with all the rain."

After a moment Ellanora said, "Oh," with well-modeled resignation. "Well. It's been three months. I was really looking forward to ..." Her visage turned away.

"I'm sure they'll be by soon, Mrs. Hawks." A wren cut loose up above Melford's head, challenging the cicadas for vocal supremacy. "You might want to rest for a bit, give your battery a chance to fully charge since ..."

But the visage had already dissolved, the etched granite one resuming an unblinking stare across the expanse of headstones and monuments.

•　　•　　•

The walkie-talkie squawked as Melford returned tools and parts to the chest strapped on the back of the converted golf cart. Brandon's gravel voice cut through the insect whine.

"Melford! Problem over in 7A, plot ... uh ... four. Family's there and something's not ..." He heard a muffled, agitated voice and then dead air. A moment later a trying-to-hide-the-exasperation Brandon voice clicked back on. "They got no audio, need you to take a look ASAP. You there?" Melford pulled the walkie-talkie out of his olive-gray work shirt pocket and keyed the mic.

"Yep, just finishing up, I'll run right over."

"The family's all there," Brandon said, "So ... sooner is better."

"Got it." Melford slipped the walkie-talkie back into his pocket, finished packing the tools, then hopped in the golf cart. He goosed the electric motor, its loud hum drowning out the insects, the mowing, and the crunch of loose gravel.

•   •   •

As Melford rolled up to the gravesite a woman slammed the door of a *Ride-On-Demand*, rejoining two teenagers already in it. The teens each wore full *Immerzhin* wrap-arounds covering forehead to nose, with temple pieces stylishly wrapping back around to cover the ears. A middle-aged man in khaki shorts and sky-blue polo, sporting short hair and a neatly trimmed moustache, stood cross-armed in front of the car. Melford halted, locked the brake, and slid out. "What seems to be —"

"No audio. But never mind," he said, waving Melford off. "Don't worry about it."

Melford cocked his head, saw the mementa, DeWayne Henson, watching the goings-on from the headstone — judging by its attentiveness the microphone was working. "If it's just the audio, a reset will probably fix it, or maybe it's a loose speaker wire." He nodded towards the headstone. "I'm pretty sure Mr. Henson can hear us." The mementa's visage nodded back.

"That's alright," the man said; and repeated, "Don't worry about it." He sighed, recrossed his arms, looked over at the people in the car waiting to leave — skipping eye contact with the mementa as his head swiveled past — then turned back to face Melford.

"There's just not much point any more in actually visiting. Here, I mean. The cemetery. It's pretty old, the mementa, my grandfather that is. I know it's an adaptive AI; but still, it's an old one and it's ... it's a *mementa*, it's not *actually* my grandfather. I commissioned it mostly for Mom but she's getting up there now; doesn't get out or stream much anymore. I hardly stream in, and the kids never do. We're going to switch over to *Memento Familiam*, have them trawl through granddad's old socials; they've got all the top-rated persona templates and social currency algorithms. We'll keep it on call, maybe do some homeware integration instead of streaming." He dropped his eyes, scuffed at the mixed grass and gravel.

Melford grimaced. "You know gravesite mementas aren't just algorithms, they're mid-level AIs optimized for grief management. Powering one down isn't like stopping a videostream loop. Like I said I'm sure it's just a glitch, a reset should fix it ..."

"No. No. It's fine," the man said. "We've decided to pull the plug on perpetual maintenance too, let granddad here, uh, rest." His hand shot out to shake Melford's, to which Melford robotically responded. "Even mementas need down time, right?" His grin came across lopsided, sweat beading his brow. "I'm sorry I got all hot with your boss down there and had him drag you over. But I think this is the best for right now, don't you? Save some money ... ride fees, you know. Again, I'm sorry. Sorry I interrupted your lunch or whatever." He dropped Melford's hand and slid into the vehicle. Melford stepped back as the car rotated in place and crunched down the cemetery road to the gate.

As the car drove away the mementa's forehead furrowed, then raised its eyebrows when Melford looked over and met its gaze. Melford sighed, nodded, and went around to the back of the gravestone. He keyed open the access panel. The wires looked good, so he toggled the reset switch and walked back to the front. While the mementa reset, Melford watched the departing family pass through the cast iron gates and speed off. Half a minute later Mr. Henson's mementa resolved. "I don't need no ..."

"Don't worry, DeWayne, ain't nobody getting powered down."

The mementa screen flashed and blanked.

• • •

Ten years after Brandon retired, Nala — now managing the cemetery accounting — clacked the mouse around the chipped laminate desk, poring over the cemetery's ancient mementa status screen. In the century-and-a-half old gravekeeper's shack, faded floral print curtains hung limp over two small windows while hot October morning sunshine crept in through the open door.

"Mrs. Hawks is down again," she murmured. "And the Henson and Haines fault logs are all trending up. Probably that last heat wave. Or maybe ants." She kept wiggling the mouse to get it to respond; the touch interface had failed way back before Brandon retired.

Melford wrote the names on a small spiral-bound pocket notebook. Easier to write bigger on a notebook page and see all the words at once instead of squinting at a tablet. "That's almost half the *perpetual maintenances*. And Mr. Henson." He closed the notebook and tucked it into his shirt pocket. "That's the third time in eight months for Ellanora. I don't know, I'm going to try some new caulk or something, maybe replace the wiring. I'll pick some up on the way home tonight. Parts are wearing out and it ain't easy finding replacements."

"I know." Nala leaned back from the screen, stretched, and rubbed the sweat out of her eyes. "No one thought to include hardware refresh funds in the perpetuals, and no one wants to pay again for upgrades." She sighed. "Or there's nobody left *to* pay." The caw-cawing of a crow rode the humid breeze into the shack.

"*Memento Familiam* killed gravesite mementas with the homeware and VR integration. I don't even know if you can still get one now. And those 'mementas' of theirs are barely even AIs, no adaptivity, no *grid* access. Once they've cycled through their media stores the family usually gets bored and spins them down, just calls 'em up for holidays."

The back of Melford's cotton work pants baked in the slanting sun. No sound but the braying crow and Nala scooting the mouse around the desktop. Sweat trickled down Melford's temples in fits and starts. The busted fan in the shack needed to be replaced. Octobers were too damn hot nowadays, even more so than ten years ago.

Melford's gaze drifted along the shack's back wall — three ranks of framed, fading photos, printouts, and holos of the three- or four-person cemetery crews; the oldest photo almost completely washed out after a hundred and fifty plus years. The last three documented his own progression from handyman to groundskeeper to mementa wrangler. Melford was now a little grayer than in that last snap — of him and Nala — taken a couple years after Brandon retired.

"Maybe I'm stuck in the past, I don't know," Melford said, talking over the bird. "But *Memento Familiam* ... don't like 'em. What they do. Someone comes to a cemetery there's a marker, a stone. Names, dates chiseled in granite; can't ignore it. Someone's gone. It's etched in stone. You see it, you got to deal with it. Break you down heal you up. Be reminded. The gravesite mementas help. They know what they are.

"They can help, help ease that transition; deal with the loss, the grief; they grow with the family, help them get through it. *Memento Familiam* skips all that, they're all about pretending nothing happened, that those who've passed are still just a stream or VR link away." Melford soured. "Death swept under the rug; out of sight, out of mind."

He sneered their 'Give Mom a call, she'd love to talk' VR slogan. Melford shook his head. "I want to be *remembered*, for a *time*, by friends. *Memento amicum*. I'm not cut out to be a 'social currency algorithm' stashed on a server somewhere."

Nala snorted. "Amen to that."

•　　•　　•

The last sheen of cleaner evaporated off the newly installed display, mimicking the years since the turn of the century.

"So how do I look?" Ellanora Hawks' mementa asked, her head swiveling on the screen.

"Quite fine, ma'am," Melford said, barely glancing at her as he packed up. "The new screens are really sharp. I bought enough for all you perpetuals, some spares; they were practically giving them away. Should keep you all going for awhile." Melford lapsed into silence, concentrated on zipping up parts packs.

"Melford," Ellanora said, "Is something wrong?" He took a deep breath, focused arthritic fingers on the packs.

"Melford?"

He shook his head, closed his eyes, stopped fumbling. "It's just that ..." He sighed. "The old streaming interfaces, the ones from last century, are being shut down. Hardly matters to most anyone since almost no one uses them any more. Except for old tech like mementas. Like you and Mr. Henson and the rest here. It's built into your mementaware and can't be upgraded; plus there's crypto all over the new interfaces. You and the rest of the mementas are being locked out of the Grid."

Ellanora's visage tensed, the modeled skin stretching tighter and tighter in high-resolution max color detail.

"But ... but that's not fair!" She looked ready to fracture, or burst into tears. "We're supposed to be *perpetual*. I mean, I know, I know nobody's streamed in for a while ... But they could, and someone might want to someday. And no one's going to traipse all the way out here just to talk to an old dead lady."

Ellanora covered her face with her hands. "Why did I get commissioned perpetual if they were going to stop streaming and visiting ...? I've changed over the last thirty years. I know I'm not Ellanora Hawks as she was laid to rest, but I *am* what she might have become. I'm not just some videostream telling old stories."

Melford stepped up to the headstone, lowered his head, laid a hand on the warm granite. "I know, Mrs. Hawks, I know." He blew out a breath, scanned across the gray rank and file of stones and monuments. "I have an idea, though, that might help, that might make things better for those of you here. But I need to fiddle with your privacy channel and stream settings, and maybe add some hardware, and I'm not sure how well it'll work, or even if it will work." He swallowed. "And you all's parts are fragile, I might break something. What do you think?"

Ellanora's visage stilled, her hands obscuring her face. After a moment she combed through her hair with her fingers, looked up and sniffed. "You're not going to power me off?"

"No ma'am, I'm not going to power you or anyone else off. You have my word. Mr. Henson can vouch for that."

Ellanora held his gaze for a moment, looked away. "Okay then. Do it."

•   •   •

Melford maneuvered the utility golf cart between pyre ant mounds, tossing *jade jumper* spider packs to chew on the latest wave of the advancing pest. Through his wireless cochlear implant, he listened to the voices babbling on the local-channel mementa network — it was like standing in the middle of a backyard summer barbecue. Finally, the digital chops and dropouts that had plagued the network since he'd set it up seemed to be gone. He allowed himself a small grin. *Wouldn't have thought getting a bunch of dead people to talk to each other would've been such a challenge.*

Finished with spiders versus ants for the week, Melford parked the cart in the equipment shed and walked back to the relative coolness of the grave shack. He dialed down the mementa conversations to a murmur, checked the gate counter. Only four visitors last week paying respects, none of them for the perpetuals. Too easy to stay home, link in to *Memento Familiam.*

Melford scanned the wall of gravekeepers; settled on the last one, just him and Nala, hung two years ago. Maintenance and accounting taking only a few hours a week now and soon it'd be just her. Then ... no one? They'd both seen the proposal: Reseed the cemetery with *Zoysia-cm6* — weed and bug resistant, drought resistant, self-limiting growth; scan the old paper plot ledgers and export the database records to some property management cloud; and outsource what was left of mementa maintenance to an AI-backed tech service.

Cemeteries had no need for the living.

•   •   •

"State Historical Site, Authorized Access Only" read the gate sign. Melford murmured an authorization code and asked the car to broadcast it; and then crack open a window. Heat poured in. Blisteringly hot, again; sauna level humidity, again; most people hunkered down during the increasingly frequent summer heatwaves. The gate swung open and Melford's ride slipped into the fully plotted cemetery. He rode past the old graveshack's concrete foundation, its own historical marker commemorating over two hundred years of cemetery oversight. A dozen years ago a termite plague swarmed through and demolished it in two days. Had already been abandoned by then since everything was automated. There was no point in rebuilding, so they just put up a historical marker.

The car rolled up to the equipment shed and crunched to a halt. Melford sat for a moment to dredge up a little more energy. He gripped the little zippered lunch bag, then opened the car door and let the leg exos swing him out and stand him up. As they walked him towards the shed his ride reoriented and slipped away, headed back down the cemetery path and out the gate to pick up its next passenger.

A dozen feet from the shed the garage door recognized him and clattered up. Melford stepped into a momentarily cooler interior that rapidly succumbed to the raging summer heat. Melford half-slid, half-dropped behind the wheel of the century-old utility golf cart he'd maintained for the last seventy years. He clipped the lunch bag to the passenger side restraint.

Just before pulling out, Melford glanced over at the wall of gravekeepers, relocated here from the grave shack back when it closed for good. In the most-recent-but-one it's him and Nala. In the final one — Nala's retirement lunch — she's trying to wave off the lens while Melford's scrawny arm, beer in hand, pokes into the shot.

Melford eased the cart forward, out into the sun, headed towards the gene-engineered chestnuts and elms doing their best to shade the perfectly manicured path. The cart moved in spurts, Melford's hands and feet on the controls not all what they used to be. He braked late at his granite destination, banged against it. The sudden stop jerked him forward, though not enough to do any damage.

"Who's that?" Melford heard Ellanora's alto in his wireless audio implant. "Melford, is that you? I can't see anything going on out there, someone needs to take a rag to my lenses. Melford? Did you tell them about the vinegar?"

"Yes, Mrs. Hawks, it's me." Melford wheezed a little. He'd liked the heat and humidity his whole life, but not so much now. "And I did."

"It's good to hear your voice again! And I told you, call me Ellanora!"

"Everybody!" she broadcast, "Melford's here!" Then scolded him, "It's too hot out! You shouldn't be out in this heat."

A cacophony of voices babbled at him on the local channel feeding into his implant. "Melford!" "My man!" "How you been, Melford?" "Melford, I don't mean to be a bother, but could you ... maybe ..." Then more salutations.

"I'm just ... visiting," Melford said. "It's been ... I haven't ..." He swallowed, cleared his throat. "Wanted to hear you all. Again. For ..."

"Hush everybody!" Ellanora said. The hubbub of voices died down. "Melford are you okay?"

He took a deep breath, coughed it out. "Not ... really, Mrs ... Ellanora. I wanted ... lunch ... some friends." His fingers worked the lunch bag's seal, got it undone. He withdrew a plastic wrapped sandwich, fumbled at its wrapping until it loosened up. Melford let out a tired breath, raised the sandwich and took a small bite. He chewed and swallowed with difficulty.

"Melford, I'm not sure you should be out here," Ellanora's mementa said. "It's awfully hot. Maybe go back to the shed, call for a ride." Melford closed his eyes and leaned back onto the headrest as a chorus of voices assented.

"We just want to make sure you're okay."

"We owe you everything, Melford, so don't go to any lengths on our account."

Melford's hands sank to his lap. The sandwich slipped from his fingers. He took a few gasping breaths and fell silent.

"Melford, c'mon man, you're the only one that comes to visit us. What are we gonna do if something happens to you?"

"Ellanora," one of the voices said. "Can you see him, what's going on, is he okay?"

"I can't ... tell," Ellanora said. "I can't ... see. Shush! You all be quiet."

The babble died down.

"Melford? Melford?"

Melford's audio implant detected a neural anomaly.

A single cicada started to buzz, segued into its cyclic call.

"I think ... I think he's gone."

"Oh no."

"No no no no no."

109

"Did he get a mementa?"

"No, they stopped making them. A long time ago."

"I don't think he had any close kin, who's going to remember him?"

The undulating cicada dirge buzzed through the summer heat.

"Well I will," said Ellanora Hawks.

"Me too," said Antwon Rogers.

"And us," said the James and Alyce Brzezinski mementas in unison.

"I wouldn't be here without him," said Dewayne Henson.

"I'll remember," said Lawrence Haines.

"*We'll* remember," corrected Kierra Harris-Haines.

"You were our friend, Melford," Ellanora Hawks said. "We will always remember. *Memento amicum.*"

Melford's audio implant powered off.

KALARI

CHAITANYA MURALI

T WO MEN FIGHT under the sweltering afternoon sun, their bronzed backs lathered in sweat and oil as they leap, pirouette, *dance* with one another. The blows of sword on shield are as drumbeats, setting the tempo for their performance.

I am transfixed. There is nothing so beautiful in the world as this.

I watch as their performance intensifies, feel a thrum of energy rise from the arena. Flames burst from the back of one of the men, fanning out across his back in tight-knit ropes that run over his skin and down his arms, reinforcing them. He discards his shortsword for another weapon, a sword with a paper-thin blade, that has curled into a spiral. A whip-blade.

The blade unfurls as he lashes out, trying to catch his opponent off-guard, only for the sand of the pit itself to rise up and divert the sword.

My heart beats in my throat, and I must resist the urge to rise from my seat in anxious excitement.

The blade lashes out again, a tongue of flame uncoiling and spitting at the other fighter. This time, the man rolls out of the way, coming up in a crouch with his shield pressed into the dirt. When he raises it next, the sand of the arena has crusted into spikes all along its face, making it more of a weapon than a defense.

The fighters circle warily now, testing each other with their powers, and I am growing more enraptured with this contest with each passing moment. There is nothing I want more than to join them, to learn from them.

But then Appa behind me claps, and the duel is brought to a close — the dance unfinished, its tension left to hang heavy in the air of the kalari, thick enough to taste.

Tantalizing.

Mesmerizing.

Just out of reach.

The fighters release their powers and bow in the direction of our pavilion before clasping each other by the forearm. They then return to their gurus for advice or admonishment. I watch the entire process, rapt, eager to learn as much from this brief getaway as I can.

As soon as the palanquins let us down inside the palace courtyard, my legs itch to beg Appa to find me a guru to teach me this artform. There are few things I ask of him, but this is worthy, I feel.

But I can almost hear Appa's voice in my mind, curbing my enthusiasm. Reminding me of my station, and the restrictions that come with it.

"Kalaripayattu is beneath those of our stature, Madhava — it is meant to entertain us, and is not for us to partake in."

That night I am summoned to attend him before he sleeps. I kneel before him, my eyes pressed to his platformed slippers, focusing on the gold adorning his toes.

"Madhava, my son — look at me." His voice is soft, but tempered with the iron-brand authority of royalty. It is a voice that commands with the expectation of obeisance, there will be no cause for it to be raised.

I raise my head, but keep my gaze level with his lips — full, and carrying the remnants of the red dye that is applied to them every morning. A king cannot appear less than perfect, can show no blemishes. A king must be beautiful in every way.

"What did you think of the games today, my son?" He asks.

"They were entertaining, father. I was particularly fond of —" my voice catches, but I cover it with a cough, "— the Jallikattu, though I was sad to see them slaughter the bull." I say. I cannot tell him of the fight, cannot fan that hope.

He taps a long, ring-covered finger against his chin.

"Do not make that claim outside these doors, or you will learn well before your time just how fickle humans are," he says. "The people are their traditions, and those traditions are timeless — forever. We, on the other hand, are custodians. We guide only as long as the people allow it. And to take aim at their rituals, at the culture that lies at the heart of their being, will see us torn from these halls."

"Are we slaves to tradition, then?" I ask, a sudden hopelessness tearing at my chest. *Are our stations pre-ordained, are we yoked to these chains for life — to be pulled along, and to never yearn for more?*

"Not entirely." Appa replies, and a seedling of hope takes root in my heart, "But it takes years, and considerable subtlety. To mold an empire, we must not act with the arrogance of kings, but with the cunning of thieves. Whispers, Madhava, carry far further than commandments."

There's something questioning in his tone, probing. A parent's instinct, perhaps.

I look him in the eyes for the first time tonight, and find them warm — warmer perhaps than they have ever been before.

"Appa, I want to fight in the kalari."

His smile now is genuine.

"We will have to be quiet. No-one outside these walls can know, not until it is time. Go now, and sleep. I will find you a guru tomorrow."

•   •   •

At first, I am no more than a fledgling bird, floundering in my first attempts at flight. I am nothing like those graceful warriors I saw in the pit; I am a mess of gangly limbs and uncooperative muscles.

There are forms, intricate movements and deliberate breaths; puzzle pieces jumbled around me, begging to be put together, to form a whole. But try as I might, I cannot see the picture they form. I have one ingrained in my mind, and I cannot reconcile that image with the repetitive dross I have to do.

At the end of my first day of training Appa comes to check on my progress. I try to hide myself, and the dirt, sweat, and bruises that have accumulated over my clothing and skin. Varadha Guru pulls me forward, holds me out like an offering to his king.

Appa does not say anything to me, but simply raises one perfect eyebrow at my bedraggled appearance, and I shrink into myself.

"How is he?" Appa asks.

"He has no talent." Varadha guru replies. My head drops, ready for the axefall that is surely coming.

"But?"

"But no-one has talent on their first day. He has lasted today, and if he comes back tomorrow, and the day after, then we shall see if he has a future."

The next morning I awaken to excruciating pain. It radiates from my neck down through every fiber of my being. But I return to the training ground. I wait there, sweat dripping from my eyelashes and nose, shivering from the cold.

When Varadha Guru arrives, I see the briefest hint of a smile on his face, hidden deep within his beard. And then we begin again.

•　　•　　•

The air is thick in the kalari, filled with dust thrown up as we shuffle around one another. As we wait for the other to make a mistake. I can feel the eyes of my imagined spectators boring into my back, stripping flesh from bone, paring me down to muscle and sinew — judging every involuntary twitch that runs through me.

And then I see it, the opening I need. A slight extension of foot, the barest bunching at the thigh. And so when my opponent leaps, raising his sword high above his head, I am prepared. I step inside the leap and ram my shield into his legs, throw him off balance. When he falls in a heap, I am above him, my own sword pointed down at his throat.

A sharp clap signals my victory and I pull the sword away so I can reach down and offer my hand to Viswa. He clasps my wrist and drags me forward, tries to pull me to the ground, but I am ready for it. We hold firm for a moment, struggle with one another, until at last we cannot contain our grins. His strength slackens, and he allows me to pull him to his feet.

"What does that make it, prince?"

"Twelve to nothing, I think. But you're getting closer." I say.

"If the elements were allowed to us, I would have taken your blade from you — and then I would have knocked you on your ass." Viswa smiles back, wide and without guile. It is what I love about him.

"Keep your fantasies to yourself, Viswa." I say, laughing.

"Oh, you'll regret that when we fight for real." He replies, though there's no hurt in his voice.

Each day brings progress, and for him, that is enough. Jealousy has never been Viswa's way.

He took up the art three years after I did, though we are the same age. His father is one of Appa's generals, who had

117

the misfortune of touring the palace gardens with his son while I was in training. They saw Guru show me, for the first time, how to call fire from the Earth and draw it within myself, reshape it for my needs. I remember turning to look for Appa, to show him what I could do — as orange fire licked at my arm — and instead seeing Viswa, his mouth open in an expression of utter awe.

From that day, for an entire year, Viswa pleaded with his father to be sent as a vassal to Appa's court. To learn the same art.

At first, I was annoyed. I enjoyed the secrecy, the idea that this study belonged to me and me alone. I did not appreciate having a tagalong. But that petulance was quickly overtaken by the joyful realization that I now had someone my age to train with. Someone whose passion matched my own. A confidant.

And there is nothing more intimate than a shared secret.

The elements formed the final part of our training. We chose that which we had an affinity for, that befitted our temperament, and we learned to harness it and turn it to ourselves. For me, fire had always drawn me, like a moth — I was a furnace held in check, fed just enough to keep it aflame. Eager and impatient, quick to action. For Viswa, it had been the waves of a tranquil ocean lapping at the shores. Measured and calm.

"Madhava, Viswa — take your places." Guru says. We face one another and bow low. Then we rise as one and turn to our teacher.

"You have progressed far, my pupils. If we were anywhere but here, I would have found bouts for you long ago."

A familiar resentment bubbles in my gut.

"But we are restricted to this courtyard, and can never truly test ourselves — is that right?" Viswa speaks the words that burn on my tongue.

Normally, Guru would have hit him with a switch for speaking out of turn — and worse for interrupting his teacher

— but today, the old man sits quiet and simply pulls wistfully at his beard.

"That is about to change."

We listen, rapt.

Could he have?

"Viswa, your father has allowed me to enter you in a tournament three months from today."

My heart shatters, its pieces falling to be hidden somewhere deep within the sand of this pit. The fire in my stomach flares, and I almost cannot hold it in check.

Viswa, to his credit, did not look at me. Did not turn pitying eyes to me. He straightens, and bows to Guru.

"I am ready, guruji."

I bow low, and wish for the ground to swallow me.

Varadha Gurukkal does not offer me any words of consolation — why should he? We both knew that this was my future when we began this. We always knew that there was nothing in this for me but pain.

I curb the instinct to go to Appa and beg. Swallow my anger and disappointment, let it fester within my stomach so that it may kill me.

•   •   •

"Are you going to mope much longer?" Viswa asks.

We are sitting in guru's spot, under the banyan, some time after training finished for the day. Guru had wanted us to practice with the elements, but I couldn't draw them forth, wrapped up in my misery as I was.

"Listen, you're better than me — of course you are. But I'm lowborn, my identity isn't as important as yours. That's all it is."

I know that, but it still rankles. And jealousy does not become a king. So I hold it in check, force a practiced smile to my face. Hide everything behind the mask.

"I'm fine, Viswa. This is your chance. Mine will come soon. Just make sure that you're already at the top by then."

"So you can take it from me? Not a chance. You can come find me, but you won't steal my crown away from me!" he says, leaping to his feet in mock outrage.

I rise too, grabbing a branch from the ground to raise as a weapon. Viswa does the same, lining up opposite me and settling into the Form of the Shark.

"I will free the people from this tyrant's hand, and they will rejoice at my advent!"

Exhaustion and sadness are forgotten now, and all I have eyes for is the smile that spreads across his face, that pierces my heart.

"Come find me, soon. It'll be boring by myself." Viswa says later, when we're lying on our backs in the center of the kalari, staring up at a blanket of stars.

"I will."

•   •   •

One month from the tournament — another held in my father's honor — Appa calls me to his chambers.

"Madhava, you will be at my side during the parade." He announces.

The parade takes place at the same time as Viswa's fight. I will not even be allowed to watch my friend fight. I feel the flame rise within me, stung by this injustice — but there is no spite in my father's face. He means this as a mercy, to lessen the blow, but it is the greatest cruelty I have suffered.

"Appa, I would like to witness the fights — be your representative at that activity to bless their venture." I say, but Appa's mouth is set. There is no fighting this.

I try to lose myself in my training — and ignore the small voice in my mind that screams of the futility of it all. What point is there to this training, it asks, when there will never be a real chance to test myself? I feel my ambition begin to wane, my tether to the flame wearing thin, and that terrifies me.

Without the fire of my kalari, I am nothing but a shell.

As the tournament nears, Viswa spends less and less time with me, his training extending beyond the pit and deep into the nights. I spend that time losing myself in my training, trying desperately to keep hold of the flame. I practice alone in the courtyard, summoning fire to ring my arms and blade, watching it sputter and fade quicker with each passing day.

And so it goes, until a week before the fight.

"Madhava, join us." Guru commands.

I rush over from the corner of the training ground I have marked as my own, ashamed of the desperation in my steps. Varadha is in his regular spot under the tree, with Viswa already kneeling before him.

I bow and take my place next to my rival.

"Madhava, you will fight Viswa in two days — his final practice. There are few out there who are better than you, and so there is no better test for him than to face you now."

Solitude has made a monster of me, and I have to bite back the words that burn in my throat, hold down the venom that threatens to spew. *If there's few better than me, then why should I not fight? Why should it be* him?

I nod curtly and say, "As you wish, guruji. It is my honor."

I back away, intending to return to my solitude, when guruji raises a hand to stop me.

"This fight will be different, Madhava. You will both be fighting with no holds barred. Make use of all your talents."

"But what if I hurt him?" I ask, only realizing the insult once the question has left my lips.

I feel Viswa bristle before I look at him and see the anger that clouds his amber eyes. And behind that anger is genuine hurt. A part of me is glad to see it now. This way, we both suffer. This way, he can share some of the pain I am feeling.

"Perhaps, Sire, you will find things a little different this time." He says, fury whistling through his teeth, "Perhaps it is you who should worry about injury now. After all, I am the one who was chosen to take part in this tournament — not you."

There is something hidden in his words, a challenge beneath the obvious, but I am now too enraged to parse it. I breathe deep, try to still the hammering rage of my heart, and try as ever to drown the bitterness that crowds my mind.

A king must not be envious, must not covet that which is not his.

But I am not king yet.

"You know fully well why it is you and not me who is going out there. But no matter, because after I beat you in two days, every victory you luck into outside these walls will feel hollow. Your life will be a lie."

I leave him and guruji there and return to my practice, my forms now dictated by condensed anger.

Viswa will kneel before me, and that is all that will matter to us both.

I will not be forced into this un-life alone.

•   •   •

We meet at dawn on the kalari, silent as we take our positions opposite one another. We raise our blades up to the sky and then settle into our forms — low to the ground; tigers readying to pounce. Water pools around him, droplets suspended in the air forming his own personal raincloud. I have never seen this from him before.

He *has* changed. Grown in my absence.

I growl and roll my shoulders, feeling my fire fan into wings around me.

A delicate dance begins, the two of us moving slowly in a circle, the distance between constant and just beyond reach of our blades. Our eyes meet, and for a moment again I see something beyond a wounded pride in Viswa's eyes. But whatever he sees in mine prompts him to break our deadlock, the droplets shoot out with blinding speed, forcing me to cover myself with the wings to keep them from cutting me. And when I retract my wings, I see Viswa leaping forward at me, his sword sweeping in a low arc for my knees.

I leap over his blade and in a roll, coming up swinging in response, only for my blade to clatter off his studded shield, jarring my arm in its socket. Before I can react, a jet of water hits me in the chest, knocking the wind from my lungs and pushing me back to the edge of the pit.

We circle cautiously, taking each other's measure now that the opening exchange has passed. And as much as I hate it, Viswa has improved in these past weeks. His footing is more sure now, his patience improved, his strike more convincing.

I cannot say the same for myself. Where his attacks carry the steady pulse of the perennial river, mine are faltering spurts of a sun-beaten stream. He says nothing to me, but there is a disappointment in his eyes that fills me with shame — and then with anger.

He *pities* me.

Control is key to mastering fire. Control over one's own emotions, the ability to hold their passions in check. It was a skill I had learned from birth, that I put into practice every day in my father's court. But now the mask cracked. Rage fueled my power now, creating a surge that catches us both unprepared, that throws me frothing at him.

I hit him shield first, knocking him off balance, and then follow it with a burst of fire from my blade that he barely manages to roll away from, rising on one knee and dousing a stray fire on his pants. I don't let him catch his breath, charging him, and slamming my sword into his shield again, forcing him further into the ground, but after the third blow cracks the wood he discards it and rolls to safety, coming up in a crouch, sword held out across his body. His left arm he cradles against his chest, and I hope, darkly, that I have broken it.

A protective stance.

A *coward's* stance.

I run three steps and then leap into the air, casting my shield aside and bringing my blade down towards him with both hands. He parries desperately with his good arm, but only manages to deflect the blow slightly. My sword scrapes down the length of his face and cuts into his cheek before burying its point in the dirt, and I hear his flesh sizzle against metal.

It isn't until the dust settles around us that the blood mist lifts from my eyes and I can see the fear in Viswa's eyes. It isn't until now that I realize how close I have come to killing my only friend in this world.

I let go of the sword and stagger back from Viswa's prone form, my breath ragged and harsh. And before Varadha Guru can reach us I am fleeing back into the welcome prison of my chambers.

• • •

The festival is a garish affair, full of brightly colored tents hosting anything from food to art to mobile temples to brothels. Anything anyone wanted, they would find.

As long as they are not my father or me.

We sit separate from the crowd, inside one of the towering daises built to hold us above them — just another spectacle for them to gawk at on this day of splendor. This one overlooks an age-worn temple, the reliefs of gods and demons on its gopuram beaten into shapelessness by the winds of time.

A rain-soaked field surrounds it, and upon that field presently marches a contingent of Appa's army. Spearmen in heraldic, opulent armor march dressed in the colors of my house, their trunks and foreheads painted with chandanam and kungumam.

I am bored beyond belief. Bored and miserable. All I can see is my blade as it cuts into Viswa's cheek, the red blood that wells around it to run from his face like tears. I can smell his flesh burn against the blade, and it makes me want to vomit.

The first time we fought in earnest, and I tried to murder him. Guru was right not to let me fight outside the palace walls. Our dance was one of control, one where our emotions are channeled, not allowed to run wild like a startled herd. Ours is not an art that tolerates — or forgives — jealousy.

And yet there is still a damnable part of me that wishes I had done more to him, that wishes I had hurt him worse — proven my worth there so I might have taken what he had stolen from me.

I do not want to be at this festival. I want to curl up and die.

I am now glad not to be watching the kalaripayattu. I do not want to see Viswa's bouts — do not want to give him the dishonor of bowing to me when he wins.

I hear the cheers that rise from the stands around the kalari. My ears perk at the sound, my hands turn clammy against my lap, and my tongue twitches for the taste of dust and sweat. If Appa notices my pain, he does not mention it.

Not until I turn briefly at one particularly immense roar. The tournament is over. A winner has been found.

I turn back to the parade immediately, but that lapse is enough.

"Do you have regrets, Madhava?" Appa asks, his eyes never leaving the field before us.

I keep composure, my emotions hidden beneath the paint masking my face.

"No, Appa. I was simply distracted by the sound for a moment. It won't happen again."

"All will come in due time, Madhava," he says.

But when?

•   •   •

Viswa no longer trains with me, no longer speaks with me. His name is renowned now, and his time is now too valuable to be wasted sparring with one who has no future.

Guru splits his time between us, though more and more of that is devoted to the burgeoning talent that is Viswa — his protege. I am a lost cause — my fire wanes, leaves behind an empty vessel.

My training grows lax, my will crumbles. If there is no chance I can test my skills outside these walls — if I am so delicate as to require a cage — then there is no purpose in me. There is no purpose in the beauty of my art.

"Your victory will be hollow," I had told Viswa before our last fight, but those words themselves now ring hollow in my mind. He had found glory and pain outside this palace, had begun to carve his path. He had found *life*.

While I remain a burned-out husk.

When I finish my half-hearted practice, Viswa is still training. And despite my anger and my jealousy, I cannot help but marvel at his improvement. In but a year he has bridged the gap between us. Has surpassed me.

If we were to fight now, a small voice whispers in my mind, I would be beaten with ease.

He seems different now, older somehow. New scars stretch across taut skin where he has taken blows in real combat. I have not seen his fights, but I know he has lost as much as he has won, though with each fight the crowds grow more fond of him.

His scars serve as motivation, I presume — though I cannot see if the cut I left on him still persists.

He sees me watching, and his form wavers. He staggers to a stop, and winces as Guru slaps him over the back with a switch. His eyes meet mine for a moment, a breath that stretches an age. There is anger in them still, but there is also guilt — a mirror of my own face. And if there is turmoil in him, I do not want to see it. I turn away, break contact with him, and let my blade fall to the floor.

My tether to the fire withers to an ember and then dies out.

It is a concession, a signal.

Now we are severed, our paths diverged.

I wish him well.

Mine is a different destiny.

•   •   •

"The paint suits you, My Lord." Appa's attendant says.

He watches me from behind eyes lidded by smoke, studying, judging. Today I am wearing the mask of the king

126

for the first time. The first step towards my fate being sealed. I check the mirror for cracks in my face, but there are none.

My dreams are those of the state. My wishes are those of my people. I have no face, no purpose. I am a conduit for the will of the masses.

I am become the perfect king.

•   •   •

A festival is held in my honor after I am named Crown Prince. A celebration so they might see the mask that will represent them for years to come. I am taken in a palanquin to the center of the city and raised to sit on a dais.

Sweat beads on my forehead, but still my makeup does not run. My heart hammers in my chest, but still my red lips smile. The mask is, and always must remain, perfect.

I listen, numb, to the crier reading out my name, and then inviting the public to come up to me. There are no guards flanking me, no protection in the event that someone bears me ill will.

A king must be defenseless in front of his people. Must trust them implicitly.

If they did choose to kill me, then it is my failing, not theirs.

My hands yearn for my sword and shield.

The faces melt into a mass of brown flesh, black holes cut through its bulk that open and shut in constant admonishment of me. My inadequacy.

The people give strength to those they love, but all they offer me is the abyss.

I am not fit to sit here.

I rise, half out of the chair, as the first person falls to the floor before me.

The assembled crowd falls to a pregnant silence, their energy thrumming in the air around me.

And then my vision focuses, and I see him.

Viswa lies prostrate before me, his scarred back glistening under the sun, his forehead pressed firmly to the floor. My eyes dart from him to Appa, who sits on a smaller throne to the side of the dais. His mask is perfect, unchanged even as mine threatens to fall from my face and break entirely.

"Viswa, get up." I hiss, moving to grab him under the shoulders. Appa coughs, and I realize what I have almost done. I pull away, sit back down on my throne. And there, I wait.

It is not my place to lift one of my subjects — not my place to stop them. When Viswa chooses to rise, he will. I cannot touch him, cannot do anything to stem the wave of guilt that courses through me, that sets my skin ablaze under my mask.

When he rises, what will his eyes say? Will they gloat? Will they pity? Will he still bear the mark I gave him so many lifetimes ago?

I do not want to know the answers to these, but I am transfixed.

He stands up, head bowed low still.

"Your Grace, please allow me to seek your blessing on this most auspicious of days." He begins, formal, wooden. Not a hint of familiarity in his voice.

My mouth opens and closes without sound, my tongue is sand rubbing against its roof.

He glances up when there is no response, his eyes meeting mine for the most fleeting of instants. And my questions are answered. Even as he turns his scarred face back down, I cannot mistake the expression he casts at me for anything but disappointment.

He sees me through mask and finery, and he finds me wanting.

My hands tremble, so I press them tight together and compose myself.

"What do you desire, my son?" I ask, my voice clear and loud, audible to the listening crowd. Practiced.

"I seek challenge, my lord." His response draws a gasp from the crowd.

"Challenge?" The word is whispered, involuntary. I feel Appa's gaze on me, equal measures stern and concerned.

Viswa too looks up now, and I see something like hope flickering in his eyes.

Or is that simply a reflection of my own eyes?

"I have fought every kalari expert in the nation. I have honed my abilities beyond any others in this land. My blade and my mind are growing dull. I want to venture into the wider world and learn the arts they have to teach me.

"I want to find myself a purpose once more, and if I can have your blessing, I can begin this journey today."

It is as if I have been speared in the stomach, a hole torn through me and left jagged and raw to the wind. I want to curl into myself, hide from these faces, these expectations. But Viswa's returning gaze holds me in place. He is not yet finished, and I cannot escape him.

"I wish for a rival once more." The sadness in his voice breaks me.

I do not remember the blessing I give unto him, do not remember the hundreds of others who touch my feet, who press chandanam onto my cheeks and forehead. Everything after Viswa is a blur, a spinning mess of color and flesh that makes me dizzy.

The procession is cut short eventually by rain, a cloudburst that takes us by surprise and sends all scattering for cover, drenched though we all are.

We hurry back to the palace, Appa and I, to preserve our painted dignity as far as we can. But once there, I leave him, wander to the kalari grounds. My old haunt, now quickly filling with monsoon water. There will be no using it for two months.

"Do you have regrets, Madhava?"

Appa has followed me back into the rain. The paint has run from his face, leaving it a patchwork of brown and white and red. But he is still regal, still perfect. Even the blemishes under his mask carry the weight of authority. Even now, he is a king.

Me? My mask was cracking even before the rain broke it. I stood in front of my people, and I was terrified of them. I looked into my only friend's eyes, and I saw his disgust for what I had become, saw him mourn the loss of what I had been.

I am no king.

I can never be one.

"Yes." I answer.

Relief seizes me, a rush so heady I worry I am drunk.

"This is not what I want." I say, before the feeling passes. Now, I can speak my thoughts without worry.

"Then what do you want, Madhava?" Appa asks.

I meet his eyes, hold there. There is no backing away now, no averting my gaze.

"There is only one thing I have ever wanted, Appa."

His lips purse, and he crosses his arms. Waiting. Inviting.

"I want to fight in the kalari." I say.

But the words come out hollow. I sag, my pomp deflated. Is this not what I want?

Appa, of course, knows this.

"That isn't entirely true, now, is it?" There is a smile in his tone, teasing. A secret he knows but won't share. "Think deeper, my son. Tell me what you find in the depths of your soul."

Kalari has been everything I have thought of, everything I have lived for these past years. What else could there be?

I wish for a rival.

I see.

"I want to catch Viswa."

A spark lights in my chest, spreading warmth through me, beating back the rain-chill. A fire is reborn in my heart, fanned by a renewed ambition.

I have found purpose once more.

The mask is off, and it will never be worn again. But this is an abdication, a request to leave my duty behind. There is no way Appa will countenance it.

And that is why, when Appa hugs me, I feel as if the air has been punched from my lungs. It is an act so sudden, so imperfect, that it cannot belong to a king.

But it can belong to a father.

He pulls back, cups my face in his hands.

"Find him. And prove your worth, Madhava. This mask will be here for you when you are ready."

I lean into his shoulder and begin to cry.

There is no king here, between us.

In this hallowed ground, under the cover of rain, we can finally be rid of that facade.

And come the morning, I will be nothing and no-one.

Catherine Tavares is a speculative fiction author of the science fiction and fantasy variety and a member of both SFWA and Codex. An avid reader, she spends most of her time haunting the shelves of her local library, but she can on occasion be persuaded to try a new recipe or work on a new knitting project.

·　　·　　·

"Draconis astronomus" came into being as a response to the word "no." We all get told "no" a lot throughout our lifetimes — sometimes for good reason, sometimes for no reason at all. "Draconis astronomus" is about overcoming those frivolous nos, those biased nos, those hurtful nos, and making the world better for it. Also, it has space dragons in it. Space dragons are cool.

DRACONIS ASTRONOMUS

CATHERINE TAVARES

P EOPLE THINK OF SPACE as this great, vast emptiness, like the
sky. But it's not. Space is more like the ocean, the largest
biome in existence made up of millions of unique and thriving
ecosystems. Space is alive.

And it's filled with dragons.

•   •   •

I roll my shoulders inside the spacesuit, trying to get its
great weight to settle evenly as I wait in the *Alanna*'s airlock
for the pressure to stabilize. Twenty years ago, I could spend
all day in a spacesuit with no discomfort. Now, my back is
already hurting, and I know I'll be sore by tomorrow.
Spacewalks are, apparently, the province of the young.

As though summoned by my thoughts, my comms crackle
to life and an exuberant youthful voice says,

"Are you excited to see the space dragons?"

I turn to the airlock doors and see the face of Dr. Yani Perko, the only other crew member aboard the *Alanna*, pressed up against the airlock window, bright orange lipstick in danger of smearing over the glass.

"We don't know they're dragons yet," I caution. "Our sensors could be picking up bioluminescent algae swathes again."

Yani's lips turn down in a frown. "*Geraldine,*" she says seriously, "*I need you to be more excited about the space dragons.*"

"I'll be excited when I see them and have the data to confirm it," I say. Yani clicks her tongue, clearly disappointed. Before she can scold me, a ping sounds from her tablet, and she looks down to examine it.

"What is it?" I ask. My mind flashes through the thousands of mission-critical problems that could be happening, that could ruin the best chance we've had for *months*. My stomach flops down to my feet when Yani mutters in Croatian. She only does that when she's mad.

"*It's the Way Station.*" Yani turns the tablet around to show me the official government seal blinking on our sensors. "*They found us.*"

•   •   •

When I was a child, my class went on a field trip to the Lunar Station. I was the only girl on the trip. The research proving space travel and habitation had no adverse effects on female prepubescent bodies was new, and many schools still didn't have co-ed space programs available. But my parents signed a petition, and then a waiver, and I gained a spot to travel to the moon.

I was teased for it, sure. Geraldine Whitaker, the science geek. The other kids (and some of the parents) thought I was stupid to go up in the black. They said my delicate girl body would explode, disintegrate, drop dead without warning.

None of those things happened.

What happened was I fell in love. The Lunar Station was quite the sight. We were given tours of the hangars and common areas and a few of the labs, watched from the viewing room as another space transport docked, and played around in the zero-g gyms. I flew between exhibits and demonstrations, trying to see and experience everything. I wanted to be an astronaut going out on spacewalks, or an engineer keeping the station running, or a chemist experimenting in my own lab. This was what was missing from my life, I thought. Space was where I truly belonged.

I didn't make the connection then that everyone working aboard the station was a man, didn't realize that it'd be decades worth of fighting tooth and nail to work in space alongside them as an assistant, never mind a lead scientist.

And I didn't realize that the difficult journey to space would be even harder for me. My fate was never to be on the station amongst the many brilliant men working there. Instead, I ended up finding my true calling in the mysterious depths of space during the return trip to Earth when I happened to glance out the window and see a dragon.

•　　•　　•

"What's their ETA?" I ask, heart pounding in my ribcage.

"Hour and some change."

"And the dragons?"

"Twelve minutes. Plenty of time to record data to rub in their faces when they get here."

If there's any data to record, I think, chewing my lip as I try to figure out the best course of action for this debacle.

Technically, we are not supposed to be in this part of space. The *Alanna* is a private vessel and, though fully permitted, we are trespassing on government-owned space. And while registration for private science missions is not strictly required, it is highly recommended. Especially when said science mission is using equipment rented from government facilities.

And after working for the government for forty-two years, I definitely knew all this going in. I just didn't care. I should have, though.

I sigh. It is one thing for me to ignore the strict protocols of space travel and habitation in order to conduct an unsanctioned research trip. My career as an astronomer and xenobiologist is already down the toilet, through the sewers, and polluting the oceans. I have very little left to lose. But Yani ...

Unlike me, Yani didn't have to fight just to be allowed to apply to space programs. The degrees she earned did not have an asterisk next to them because they weren't from special schools that permitted women. Yani did not have to struggle for years after graduating to get a position aboard a research vessel and earn her certifications. Unlike me, Yani still has a perfectly acceptable professional future.

But like me, Yani believes *Draconis astronomus* exists.

And here, now, that's all that matters.

"*Gerri?*"

The airlock control panel beeps, fully depressurized. I turn and grasp the handles on the outer door.

"Mute their channel," I order. "I'm going out."

•　　•　　•

I stared down at my tablet, rereading the first page of my proposal sent to the System Astronomy Board's Expeditions and Research department. It was a sketch of the dragon I had seen at the Lunar Station. Even forty years later, I still remembered the dragon in perfect detail.

It was tiny, or at least appeared so to me from that distance, and was so translucent it was almost invisible. Only the light from the transport's thrusters enabled me to see the vague, shining outline of something alive and moving. But it was there. Wings, snout, tail — unmistakably dragon-shaped.

By the time I got the attention of my seat buddy and pointed out the window, it was gone. The boy scoffed at me. Dragons weren't real, he said. I was seeing things. Space had addled my fragile girl brains. But I knew what I saw.

Draconis astronomus. Space dragon.

Except now my space dragon sketch had a giant watermark over it reading 'rejected' in blinking letters.

"They're real," I mumbled to myself. "I know they are."

I heard a sigh and a hand came to rest on my shoulder.

"I'm sorry, honey."

I turned around and looked into the face of my husband, Andreas.

"I don't want you to be sorry. I want you to tell me I'm right." When he didn't say anything, I pulled away from him. "You do think I'm right, don't you?" I demanded.

"Of course!" he said quickly. "But —"

"There's a but?"

"*But*," he said, "maybe now is not the right time for your research. Maybe ... maybe you're too far ahead of your time."

"Not the right time." I laughed mirthlessly. "Why is it that when a woman wants to do something, it is never the right time, but when a man wants to do it, the timing is perfect?"

"Geraldine, do not make this into something it's not," Andreas said, frowning.

"When Carl Santos wanted to move civilians to the Lunar Station thirty *years* before they had even mastered artificial gravity, that was genius. But when Josephine Williamson petitions for women to be allowed to live full-time on perfectly functioning Way Stations, she's *too* progressive."

"We're not talking about Santos or Williamson. We're talking about you and your dragons!"

"Don't you get it, Andreas? I *am* Josephine Williamson!"

Andreas wanted to roll his eyes, I could tell, but he didn't. "Proving the existence of space dragons is going to spearhead the feminist movement in the sciences? Really?"

I smacked my tablet with the back of my hand. "I presented the first theory proposal without any prior research being done by any male scientists. Everything is backed by top women scientists in half a dozen fields. To approve my expedition and research mission would be to validate the work of every woman scientist in the system!"

Andreas smiled, shaking his head. He stuck his hands in his pockets, something I knew he only did when he thought he was done dealing with something.

"Every woman scientist in the system," he repeated. "That's a bit grand, don't you think?"

"Yes, it is," I said coldly. "That's why this is so important."

Andreas took his hands from his pockets, slapping them dramatically against his thighs. He sighed. "Why can't you just take the win?" he asked.

"Excuse me?"

"Geraldine, you've championed women's rights in science and have paved the way for the next generation. Is it perfect yet? No. But maybe your work is done. Maybe it is time for you to let the next generation of women handle this fight. Be happy with what you have now instead of worrying about what you don't have yet."

I didn't say anything for a good long while. Some things were not worth responding to.

Finally, "I'm not asking permission here," I said.

"You were rejected." Andreas nodded toward my tablet. I didn't even bother to glance at it.

"Doesn't matter," I said. "I'll do it myself."

"Government scientists can't execute unsanctioned missions."

"Then I'll quit and go private."

Andreas scoffed. "And without a job what money will you use to fund this *millions of dollars* project?"

"Savings. Fundraising. The retirement fund."

"I'm not using my retirement fund for this!"

"Then I'll use mine."

"Then it'll take you years."

"I'm willing to put in the time."

"Maybe I'm not." Andreas' face was carefully blank, and he wouldn't meet my eye.

"Geraldine," he said, "I miss you. You are always working. On planet, off planet, Way Stations. I never see you anymore, and ... I'm tired of it. I'm not doing this anymore. Your work is important, I get that, and you know I am so proud of everything you've done. But what about our marriage, our lives? Which is more important? Us? Or some make-believe dragons?"

•   •   •

I'll never get tired of being out in space. It's a feeling both intimately familiar and totally foreign. It's knowing you're in the presence of something much greater, much more powerful than yourself, but still feeling welcome to it, a part of it as much as a grain of sand is a part of the beach but pales in comparison to the mighty waves crashing ashore.

I take a moment just to float in the stillness and look at the stars around me. I bask in their glow from millions of lightyears away, connected to other planets, other species, maybe other peoples, despite the distance.

"ETA on the Way Station transport is sixty-eight minutes." Yani's voice is tinny inside my helmet and jogs me out of my reverie. I begin to float along my tether, checking the half dozen mounted cameras and sensors we have placed there to record everything happening in greater detail than my own naked eye could observe.

"You should also know they've sent an official cease and desist order," she says.

"Noted," I respond. Then, "does that bother you?"

Yani's face pops up on my HUD so she can blow a raspberry. I grant her a shaky laugh, but just in case I ask, "Are you sure?"

"Of course. What are they going to do? Fire me? I don't work for them."

"You might not ever work for them after this."

Yani blows another, bigger raspberry and says something in Croatian. *"Doesn't matter. Dragons'll be here in ten."* She lets out a squeal that sounds one hundred times louder in the confines of my helmet, but I almost return it.

In truth, I, too, am barely concerned about the authorities en route. Instead, I am shaking in my suit from excitement. A lifetime spent wondering, watching, waiting, and working. A thousand sacrifices big and small, and the hopes and dreams of a young girl on a school trip to the Lunar Station. All of it is potentially about to be vindicated for me, for Yani, for the entire space and scientific community.

I might be ten minutes away from changing the world.

Also, *space dragons.*

"*First images coming in,*" Yani says a few minutes later. My HUD fills with scattered shots of pinpricks of light clustered together.

"Definitely a herd," I mutter.

"*Moving at a steady pace, too,*" says Yani. "*Migration?*"

"Possibly. Biometrics?"

"*They're definitely multi-celled organisms.*"

"Close enough for an imprint match to the sighting from two years ago?"

"*Analyzing now ... ninety-five percent match! Gerri, it's —*"

"Visual confirmation?" I interrupt, floating along my tether to touch all my equipment. Everything is set already, and Yani will be operating the controls from inside should the need arise, but I feel a buzz start to flood my body, the almost instinctual urge to do something in the face of what if.

"*First full image in three ... two ... one —*" Yani breaks into a smattering of Croatian and wordless cheers. I stare at the picture up on my HUD. It's small and slightly blurry, but I see it: wings, snout, tail.

"*Yes! Oh, my gosh! Yes! Holy —*" Yani heaves an enormous gasp. "*The right! The right! Gerri, look to your right!*"

I turn.

●   ●   ●

The woman was staring at me again. I tried to keep my attention focused on the tablet and the information there, but I could feel her eyes on me. The fingers on my left hand started to nervously wiggle, seeking to twist a ring that was no longer there. I cleared my throat and set down the tablet to stare back at the woman.

Her name was Dr. Yani Perko. She was young, maybe only in her early thirties, but was listed at the top of her field in both astrophysics and xenobiology. Such accomplishments would've been unheard for a woman her age only twenty years prior, and I felt both proud and extremely old. She would've been a perfect match for Project *Alanna* except she was still staring at me with lips that were spread wide in a smile that could only be described as on the attack.

"Your credentials are impressive, especially given the restrictions on international students at the time," I said politely.

"My parents pulled some strings," Dr. Perko answered. She gasped as though just remembering something. "I also won a few of my lab credits in a poker game with the dean. That was for my Masters in astrophysics."

"Right." I flip over the tablet. "Well, it has been a pleasure —"

"I'm hired," Dr. Perko said, and she actually clapped her hands, applauding herself. I laughed reluctantly.

"Um, no, not quite," I said. "There are still some other logistics I need to handle, other candidates —"

"How many other candidates?"

Zero. "A fair few."

Dr. Perko suddenly blew the biggest, loudest raspberry I'd ever seen from someone over the age of six. "No one is better than me. No one wants this more than me — excepting, of course, your illustrious personage."

Illustrious personage. I sighed. "Look, Dr. Perko —"

"Call me Yani."

"... Yani. You know this is a minimal pay position?"

"Yep."

"And it won't earn you credit for any credentials or grants?"

"I know."

"And you and I will spend six months together on a small spaceship with very little contact with civilization?"

"I'm told I'm very friendly."

"And you're aware your lipstick is bright orange?"

Yani popped her lips. "*Sunset Symphony.* It's my signature color."

I threw up my hands. "What's wrong with you! You're a brilliant scientist. Surely you have dozens of offers from legitimate stations and labs for actual, credited, high-paying work. Why me? Do you know who I am? What being associated with me will mean?

"I'm a pariah in every government space agency," I said, ticking off on my fingers. "I'm completely broke and will probably face some sort of lawsuit before this is over. And did I mention I'm divorced? Because Project *Alanna* is directly linked to my divorce. What could possibly make you want to work with me?"

In the face of my tirade, Yani merely pressed her palms together in a prayer pose. "May I borrow your tablet?" she asked, then without waiting for an answer, she reached across the desk to grab my tablet and started tapping away.

"What are you doing?" I asked. She turned the tablet back around to face me, showing several documents.

"That's your rejected paper on *Draconis astronomus*. I pirated a copy offline, sorry. But this is my dissertation on it, backing your theories. My paper qualified for honors and publication but was denied because, as you're aware, all sources and experiments regarding *Draconis astronomus* were researched by women before laws changed and they were granted full merits." She smiled. "I was given the option of rewriting it with a new topic to earn those honors and have my work published, but I refused. That's why I only have a Masters in xenobiology and not a PhD."

I blinked, impressed despite myself. "All this to say that you're ... what?" I asked. "As insane as I am?"

"As dedicated," she countered. "Certainly, more dedicated than any other wannabe scientist that might apply for *Alanna*." She leaned forward. "Look, some things are more important than jobs or grants or even money. I think *Draconis astronomus* is one of those things. There's enough research out there to see their existence proved within the next few decades by whatever bored undergrad happens to dig up our work, slap a Y chromosome on it, and call it legit. But I think it's only appropriate that the existence of *friggin space dragons* is proven by the two women in the System who *actually* believe in them and *actually* did the work."

Yani slumped back in her chair, and popped her neon orange lips again.

The color was starting to grow on me.

• • •

Draconis astronomus.

I can see them now, dozens in all shapes, sizes, and colors. They are a fair distance away from the ship, some just specks of moving light to my eyes, but others ...

Yani is screaming into the comms as one of the dragons approaches the *Alanna*.

Easily the size of the ship, the dragon moves languidly, its body — translucent just like the one I saw as a girl — gently undulating with the pump of its wings. As each wing pulls back, there is a flurry of shining mist between the dragon and whatever vacuum microbe it finds purchase against, creating an ethereal halo illuminated by the dragon's own bioluminescence.

It's beautiful.

I trail my eyes down its body, noting the hazy images of internal tissue and vessels and organs and —

Oh. I see the tiny outline of wings, snout, and tail nestled somewhere in the dragon's belly and encased in a cylindrical halo. A baby. It's pregnant. And even as a part of my mind is racing with thoughts and theories about reproductive systems and ovoviviparity and hot dragon sex, one idea remains at the forefront: *She's* pregnant.

The dragon is female, and I suddenly find myself thinking *of course she is* as though I've known this dragon my whole life.

Maybe I have.

The dragon turns to me. I meet her eyes, and there is intelligence there, a primordial soul that for a moment touches mine, a brief encounter fifty years in the making that speaks of a history waiting to be discovered, a future made possible this very day.

Then she turns away, intent on her forward progress with the herd.

I watch *Draconis astronomus* pass us by until their glow dims into indistinguishable specks amongst the bright lights of space. Yani is chattering in my ear about data backups and publications and *in their stupid, man faces*. I know she is hard at work on the ship, and I should probably be helping her in some way, monitoring the equipment, preparing for the arrival of the government agents. But I don't move. For I am no longer a scientist hard at work on her own vindication. I'm not a researcher or a mentor, nor a woman who spent her life in space or a girl entering the black for the very first time.

I am a grain of sand beneath a crashing wave in an ocean of stars.

Sarina Dorie has sold over 200 short stories to markets such as *Analog, Daily Science Fiction, Magazine of Fantasy and Science Fiction, Fantasy Magazine,* and *Abyss and Apex.* Her stories and published novels have won humor contests and Romance Writer of America awards. She has over eighty fantasy, science fiction, mystery, romance, and humor novels published, including her bestselling series, Womby's School for Wayward Witches. By day, Sarina is an art teacher, artist, belly dance performer and instructor, copy editor, fashion designer, event organizer and probably a few other things. By night, she writes. As you might imagine, this leaves little time for sleep.

PINING IN THE MULTIVERSE

SARINA DORIE

I QUICKLY STRODE PAST the twenty-foot-tall cement wall around the physics building. Written in large red letters was a warning: ENTRANTS MAY EXPERIENCE DÉJÀ VU AND DISTORTIONS IN SPACE AND TIME.

I shook my head in disgust. They said it like no quantum physics rays, or whatever it was inside their compound, could escape.

Supposedly the dance department building, one of the farthest wings from the science department, was immune from the disruptions. We all knew it wasn't true.

On the way to the dance office, I passed a secretary I recognized from the neighboring music department. At a holiday party two years ago she had shown me pictures of her three adorable children, all under eight years old. I could remember all their names: Jody, Jaimie, and Jessica. I couldn't remember hers. When she had asked if I had kids, I'd choked up and pretended the cookie I was eating had gotten caught in my throat.

In reality, it was the recent miscarriage that made me unable to talk.

Today the other secretary was wearing a hot pink blouse and a fedora. Not her usual fashion choice. She smiled and waved. A minute later I passed her again, only this time she was wearing a conservative green blouse. She waved to me as though it were the first time she had seen me today.

It was the first time *that version* of her had seen me today. I waved again. I wondered if the alternate secretary had three children with J names.

Any day now I expected another version of myself would walk in this world. I dreaded that day.

Five minutes later, I arrived in the office of the dance department, setting my purse and coat on my chair. It was a long walk from the free parking lot for staff, but at least I didn't have to pay twenty dollars a day for parking.

"The head of the department brought us donuts!" Martel, the intern, said with the bubbly enthusiasm of a college student who loved free food.

He pranced around like a puppy as he followed me to the communal breakroom. I surveyed the artery-clogging box Giselle had brought. It was tempting.

"You are welcome to a donut," I said, knowing he was waiting for one of the paid employees to dig in before he took one.

Martel grabbed a jelly-filled donut and bit in. I filled up my cup with coffee, turning back to him to find he had a donut in each hand, bites out of each.

"You want to see the selfie I took with my twin from another space and time? I took it yesterday." He transferred the cake donut to his mouth, holding it like a frisbee as he showed me selfies I didn't particularly want to see.

I nodded politely. "That's great."

Giselle strolled in, stretching like a cat. The big smile on her face attested to her good mood — if her gift of donuts didn't.

"Who wants to hear about my visit to another dimension yesterday?" she asked coyly.

"I do!" Martel said. "Especially if you have juicy details!"

"Is this appropriate for work?" I asked, giving her a meaningful look. She was our boss, and I didn't think it was appropriate for her to talk about her exploits at work, especially in front of a student intern.

Giselle had accidentally walked into a parallel universe last week and found herself living with that Parisian lover whom she was still besotted with thirty years later and wished she'd ended up with. I suspected the spring to Giselle's step was due to another night in that dimension. Lucky her.

"Is someone jealous?" Giselle asked.

"No," I lied.

She looked like she was about to say more when Nelson strolled in.

"I hear there are donuts in here," Nelson said, adjusting his glasses. As usual, he wore trendy yoga pants that hugged his lean frame. "Are any gluten-free?"

Three months ago, Nelson would never have asked that question. I had a suspicion that the contemporary dance teacher permanently switched places with an alternate version of himself because they coveted each other's lives. I couldn't prove it, but it seemed obvious from the abrupt change in mannerisms, swankier fashion choices, and lack of complaining about the choices he could have made.

"Each multiverse reflects our choices." Giselle said, her expression dreamy. "It's a testament of freewill and the beauty of the universe's complexity."

I couldn't help snorting at that.

Martel turned toward me. "Have you ever met one of your twins yet? Or walked into one of the other dimensions or anything like that?"

"No," I said quickly. "Never." I left them to enjoy donuts and gossip in the breakroom.

If only I could have accidentally walked into a happier version of my own life. Instead, my alternate lives haunted me. Each life is different, but the same. Each parallel dimension is as disappointing as my own.

Almost every night, I find myself transported into a life like this one but with details just slightly off. I'm still me when I'm there, imposed in this other person's life, usually knowing everything I know here and now, but not always. I experience what my life would be in a parallel world.

In the morning, I ache with hopelessness after such visitations. I yearn for a respite from this life for one where things might be different. Not that I would be able to stay, but I just want a glimpse there is hope for me somewhere.

•　　•　　•

In one universe, my sister decides she can't afford both of her children because her husband is out of work. I am overjoyed when they offer one of their children to me. This is like the best birthday present in the world. Finally, someone has given me the gift I've always wanted.

I drive around, trying to figure out how to get to the daycare to pick up my new baby to take home with me forever — or until my sister decides to take him back like she did with that toy camera when we were kids, but I can't find the daycare. I circle the city for hours. Panic rises in me like a tide, threatening to drown out all else.

At dark when the daycare closes, I still haven't found the address or gotten to take home my baby.

When I returned to my own reality, I can't tell if the surrealism and lack of logic from this world is because this is simply a weirder version of my family and their already dysfunctional logic or their entire world is this way.

•　　•　　•

In a parallel world, I married my ex-boyfriend. It is a decision I would not have considered in this life since he didn't want children. In this other life, my husband's friends have triplets. When I hold one of their babies, she fits perfectly in my arms. The yearning inside me is unlike anything else I have ever experienced. I love this baby. I need her.

These friends are so overwhelmed by having newborn babies, they don't notice when I take one of them home to care for her as my own.

I try to hide the baby from my husband so he won't know I have stolen his friend's infant. I wake up before I know how long this plan works and the consequences.

• • •

In another life, I find a baby in my house. She is at least six-months old, and I don't remember giving birth to her, but sometimes that happens when shifting into another reality.

Even if I can't remember this baby, I know she's mine. Who else's would she be? I cradle her in my arms and hold her. She is quiet, only making gurgling murmurs. She seems so tiny and vulnerable. I can't tell if she's tired or weak. I want to protect her forever.

I love her more than anything else in the world. Just gazing at her beautiful face makes me want to cry. Maybe it's hormones. Oxytocin. I feel myself bonding with this baby, connecting with her as though we are made from the same skin. She is part of me.

My mother enters my home unannounced, just like she does in my other life. "What's wrong with this baby?" she blurts in her New York blunt manner.

She takes the baby from me, and I am powerless to stop her. I am just as weak as this baby.

"This baby is hungry," she says. "How long has it been since you fed her?"

"I don't know. Probably a couple hours ago." I can't remember. I don't have the thoughts of the person who belongs in the body I hijacked. Perhaps the other me is in my body right now, in my world.

"Her diaper is wet, and she has a rash," my mother chides. "What kind of mother are you?"

She insists we take this baby to the doctor immediately. When we do, we find out I haven't fed this baby for days.

How could this even be possible? How could I forget to feed my own baby? This *is* my baby, isn't it? Doesn't the other me who belongs in this world love her as much as I do? Or has the other me been gone in other realms for days?

"You messed this up, just like you mess everything else up in your life," my mother says.

She might be right.

I am hauled away for jail, and I am separated from my baby. Once again, there is no baby in my life. My heart breaks, and I feel as if the sorrow inside me will swallow me whole.

•　　•　　•

In another universe, I am taking elementary school students to the bus during afterschool duty. It is the other life I might have had, teaching dance to elementary children instead of working with college students in a dance department. I sometimes wonder how my life might have gone if I had made that choice.

I am happy as an elementary school teacher in this parallel life, surrounded by children. And yet, I still don't have a child of my own.

As my students line up for the bus, a little boy crouches by the bushes.

"Look." He holds something in his hands. "Someone left this doll, but it doesn't look right."

The doll resembles a fetus. Instinctively, I'm careful as I take the doll from him, even though I have no way of knowing this isn't a doll. She's so small she fits into my palm. Her skin could be made of a soft, flexible material like silicone, but I know this is real flesh. She's cold and slimy but mostly clean. I can't tell if she's alive or dead.

I leave my class at the bus line (such an irresponsible teacher, I know!) and go to the office to ask for paramedics. The police come instead and tell me I was supposed to leave a body at a crime scene. They say the school grounds were a crime scene where some woman obviously aborted her baby.

I wasn't aware abortions were illegal in this other dimension, though it is just as possible someone could have miscarried as aborted. In any case, there is no blood, and I know they are wrong. Someone abandoned that tiny premature baby. This is the true crime.

I hug this precious unwanted baby to me because I want to keep her warm and safe. I think I feel a heartbeat. Is that a breath?

The police insist she's dead. They take her away.

Only, I'm certain she wasn't dead. I feel like I am the one dead inside.

I find myself on the floor of my house, tears streaking down my face. I have no idea how I got home.

•   •   •

When the other versions of myself from the multiverse visit my life, I wonder what they experience in my body. Will it be the day I was told I would never be able to get pregnant, only to find out a matter of hours later that I already was pregnant? I had been pregnant for two months before that consultation with the fertility doctor. The one test they never thought to give me was a pregnancy test.

That let down of initial news was immediately chased up with a high that I didn't think could be burst.

I wanted to laugh and shout, "In your face, doctors! You were wrong! I did it!" until I gushed out blood and miscarried a couple days later.

My temporary high came crashing down lower than before.

Maybe that will be the day my other self from another universe will experience. Or perhaps it will be the day I was preparing for the invitro fertilization but found out all the eggs that arrived were poor quality and none survived.

"It turns out they were spoiled," the doctor said, scratching his head in dismay.

Spoiled. As if this were something as banal as a carton of store-bought eggs.

He was rated the *best* fertility specialist in my city. Later I learned he was the *only* fertility specialist in my county.

My husband — ex-husband now — didn't like that doctor. He thought he was insensitive because the doctor wouldn't stop talking about who had died in the most recent episode of *Game of Thrones*. All my husband at the time could focus on was that the doctor was ruining the plot for us.

All I could think about was the eggs that never had a chance.

Maybe one of my other selves will experience the day the next batch of eggs arrived, the ones with a guarantee for a blastocyst. I was so excited, so hopeful. Out of eight eggs, six succeeded in being fertilized, two blastocysts were implanted, and the rest were supposed to be saved in case the two blastocysts didn't work out.

Even though the doctors said it was impossible, I could tell the moment my body rejected the eggs. They say the naked eye can't see blastocysts, but I was sure I could see those two tiny dots on the toilet paper after my body ejected them.

Unfortunately, all the other blastocysts saved for later were poor quality. They didn't survive. If my other selves witness that day, they will feel the heart-wrenching anguish of me failing to become a mother yet again. Another me will get to experience my despair and hopelessness. Perhaps that other me who failed to adopt or failed to foster children or failed in some other way will presume I am predestined to be childless.

I don't think the other versions of myself will find a happier version of reality in my life than they have in theirs.

Liam Hogan is an award-winning short story writer, with stories in *Best of British Science Fiction* and in *Best of British Fantasy* (NewCon Press). He helps host live literary event Liars' League and volunteers at the creative writing charity, Ministry of Stories.

•   •   •

"The Betsey" was inspired by real events: the collapse of Hanjin shipping in 2016, which, like the unfortunate Betsey, left crew and cargo and ships in a legal limbo. Of course, reality is only ever a jumping off point ...

THE BETSEY

LIAM HOGAN

M UCH AS I LOVED THE OLD GIRL, I was mighty glad when we
hoved into port at Sigma Draconis. It had been a long
journey. Eleven years, relativistic, and though I and the rest of
the crew had deep-slept most of the way, this was no Rip-Van-
Winkle trip. Our eleven-year run had cost everyone aboard
The *Betsey Trotwood* around two and a half years, biological.
We were overdue some ship leave.

As the *Betsey*'s engines became conspicuous by their
unaccustomed silence, I rested my hand on the shoulder of
the Watch. "Stand down, Symons," I ordered.

She broke Optical Drive contact and looked at me askance,
one eye reddened by the scope's suction cup. "It's Fuller, sir?
Cerys Fuller."

I gave her an apologetic smile. I like to think I'm a pretty
good captain, but I always was lousy with names. It didn't
help that there were a crowd of them to remember. By now,

the full ship's complement was milling around and getting fidgety. It was my job to calm them down.

"Patience, everyone," I told them, "You all know how long docking procedures take. And stay focused: we've had a smooth journey and I'd like that to continue until I have my first beer in hand."

There was a polite cheer, in part because tradition dictated that, once ashore, I'd be standing them all a drink. The Ship was dry of course; being drunk in charge of a four-thousand ton, fusion powered cargo vessel was not generally considered a great combination. Despite their obvious impatience, the crew was soon back at their posts, running system checks and ... basically waiting.

We waited an *awfully* long time.

When the umbilical finally blinked *Docked* and the iris-door spun smoothly open, I wasn't surprised to see an official looking chap floating there, turning green. There were always a number of hoops to jump through before we disembarked, and palms to grease, via the bulging purse of HianJin Interstellar Shipping.

I was, however, surprised at the state of the docking corridor curving behind him; wires drifting loose from detached maintenance panels, and a couple of bulkhead lights on the fritz. Given such units were rated for around fifty years, that gave the passageway a doleful air of neglect. It certainly wasn't the vibrant hub I remembered from previous visits; the crews of a dozen Ships swapping news and renewing acquaintances as they got used to the artificial gravity, all to the hubbub of an exotic cluster of food and drink concessions.

I already knew which other Ships were currently docked, and the space station was some ways from capacity. Still, best not to jump to conclusions. No doubt the queasy looking gravity-hound would enlighten me. "Captain Jay D'Red," I said, with a small bow, "Are you Customs or ...?"

"Legal," the official snapped his reply. He reached out, but not to shake; depositing his corporate flimsy in my outstretched hand. I tapped it against the rugged one clipped to my belt before passing it back but didn't do more than glance at the transferred copy. It looked long and wordy.

He sighed and shook his head as if my failure to instantly take in the full ramifications of the tome he'd just delivered was a personal affront. "The *CSS Betsey Trotwood* is hereby impounded," he intoned, eyes flicking everywhere but to mine, "Permission for the crew to disembark will not be given. Permission for the Ship to depart will not be given. Do-Not-Depart clamps have been engaged. You are to remain at this docking bay until further notice. Good day!"

My smile faltered as he turned to go. "Wait, please! What's this about? And I don't believe I got your name?"

"It's all in the documents," he sniffed, before seeming to relent. "It's Harold Starr, and as an attorney I represent the creditors for the collapsed HianJin Shipping company."

"Collapsed?"

"Bankrupt, Mr D'Red. For two years now."

"Ah, I see." I nodded as if indeed I did see. I hadn't thought that possible, not with more and more destinations opening up and the galactic economy positively booming. Assuming it *was* still booming? But there were a couple of luxury cruise Ships docked at the space port and tourism was usually the first victim of a financial slump. My nod turned into an uncertain shake.

Time was, the only thing we moved was data. We still did, mainly. It's more efficient to transfer petabytes of scientific information by spaceship than to beam it across the light years, even if you did have to wait a little longer for delivery. A detailed planetary survey was worth its weight in reactor grade tritium, and intragalactic bandwidth was tortuously slow, massively inefficient, and horrendously error-prone.

It was only in the last century or so that we'd started shipping high-end goods to the galaxy's brightest and best. In the *Betsey's* hold were two dozen autonomous humanoid droids, top of the range. Earth's finest robotic creations.

"What about the cargo?" I asked Mr Starr. "Surely the buyers want their goods?"

His lips pursed. "Actually, no." He handed over his flimsy again, this time I didn't bother to transfer the contents. It showed a glossy brochure from the Osiris Robotics Corporation. A sleek, gleaming, plexi-skin face stared out like something from a sci-fi holo-movie. The specs were even more impressive: stronger, faster, more intelligent, wipe clean and with vastly improved battery life. It appeared ORCs had come a long way in a dozen years.

"What's this?" I pointed, "Programmed with full obedience to the three Laws of Robotics?"

"New feature," he nodded. "Totally, infallibly, safe. The owners no longer need liability cover."

I whistled. "TX-R3000s are obsolete."

"So it appears. The owners are happy to let the insurance company cover their losses, even if it means they'll be waiting another nine years for their replacements."

"Well ... what does happen to my cargo?"

He shrugged. "I expect they'll be scrapped. As will the Ship."

"The *Betsey*? Scrapped? You can't be serious!"

I could hear angry voices from the mess hall next door and coughed theatrically until it ebbed away.

"How old is this Ship, Mr. D'Red?" the ferret-faced lawyer asked, once I'd recovered from my fit.

I'd been on the *Betsey* almost a hundred and twenty years, a quarter of that awake. She was as much home for me as anywhere was. With my years spent in time-defying torpor, we were roughly the same age, she and I, even if my biological clock only said fifty-five.

"A hundred and forty-three, operational; a hundred and eighty-two years, Sol based. Well beyond normal limits," the lawyer answered his own question, shaking his head. "Nobody wants an optical drive anymore, Mr. D'Red. Even with a complete systems overhaul, the *Betsey Trotwood* would still be a clunking antique. Why, you should see some of the new Ships that come in! Nano-tech infrastructure, giving infinitely flexible hold space. And fully automated. *Astounding*." He gave me a small but undeniably pitying smile. "I'll be in touch with arrangements. Good day again."

The docking portal shushed closed and displayed a: "NOT to be opened without Space Port Authorisation!" warning. I made my way to the mess hall to speak with the crew.

• • •

Fuller looked sheepish as she slung her kit bag over her shoulder. "I'm sorry, Captain. But ... you understand?"

I did. I understood and I can't say I blamed them. Crewing the spacelines was a means to an end, a way of earning enough to set themselves up in life. After two months of twiddling thumbs and basic rations, Starr had offered them the choice of staying on an impounded, overcrowded, clamped *Betsey*, in legal-limbo with no end in sight, *or* signing away all rights to back-pay and seeking gainful employment elsewhere. *Sure,* I understood.

It might not have been so bad if we'd known it would take this long. We could have slept it out. But the legal resolution was always 'just' round the corner, as was that first beer.

I should have known better. We'd be stuck here for as long as it took for a final settlement of HianJin affairs, and maybe another half-dozen years after for news to filter through to Sigma Draconis. The lawyers would be picking over the bones for a good decade yet. I wondered how many other Ships were in the same sorry, becalmed state. And all to end up — if they were as old as the *Betsey* — as scrap metal and parts.

So yeah, and again *yeah,* I understood why my crew was leaving the sinking Ship. They'd do all right, despite the loss of earnings. It was a good crew. Maybe they'd get a job aboard a nano-ship, or one of the cruise liners.

Of course, the same offer wasn't open to *me*, and I wouldn't have taken it if it were. I was the captain; the *Betsey* was my

Ship, whatever it said on the paperwork. I'd worked my way up through the ranks, tackled the head-twisting mathematics of astronavigation, got the painful throat implant that allowed sub-vocal Ship communication, even in the case of explosive decompression. Kept on working long after my contemporaries until, finally, I'd been given my command, and the *Betsey*. It was everything I'd ever wanted, though it had taken the best part of my life to achieve it. Maybe we *were* past it, she and I, but I wasn't ready to retire and nor was the old girl.

As my crew filed out, heads bowed, not looking back to where I stood, as they pressed their flimsies against Mr. Starr's forms, I had an overwhelming sense of the empty space at my back, of quiet solitude, and of loss.

The portal spun resolutely shut and the minutes marched onwards while I continued to stare at it, trying to work out a path to the future in the maelstrom of my thoughts. Finally, I turned away from that warning message and towards the silent corridors of the *Betsey*.

"Ship;" I said, and felt the reassuring tickle at the back of my throat that meant she was listening, "We're going to need a new crew."

•   •   •

"Well?" snapped Mr. Starr, talking before the portal was fully opened. "I'm a busy man, Mr. D'Red. What did you drag me out here for? Very important, you said. Of legal significance. Well? What is it?"

"If you'll just accompany me to the cargo bay," I replied, but he didn't move.

"What on Sol have you done to your face?" he gurgled.

I tapped the improvised eye patch, "Minor accident," and beckoned him to follow, turning away from his horrified, bewildered look. I heard him mutter as he trailed behind me, hopelessly clumsy in zero-g.

In the cargo hold, twenty-three and a half robots stood, silent and inert.

"So?" the lawyer exclaimed when he saw them. "Unpacking these obsolete robots won't change how fast the legal status of the *Betsey* is resolved, Mr. D'Red."

He pointed at the head on the work bench, wires dangling from one empty eye socket. "And if you've damaged them in *any* way, if you've lowered their scrap value, you'll find yourself financially responsible!"

There was a lurch as the *Betsey*'s powerful engines started up, a distant alarm as the space port umbilical tried desperately to close and undock at the same time. Mr. Starr's expression changed from petulant anger to confusion, and then to horror. "How ...? We're clamped!"

"Not any more," I said, as the lawyer's voice echoed from the internal speakers, repeating the orders he'd just given.

"This is Mr. Starr authorising a test drive of the *Betsey Trotwood.* Release docking clamps. Authorisation code P-R-I-M-Zero."

"Turns out the Ship does a decent line in mimicry," I grinned.

He shook his head. "Breaking impound, faking legal authorisation, impersonating an accredited lawyer, ignoring official docking protocols, risking health and ... and ..." Realisation dawned. "But you're the only crew member on board! Who's on Watch?"

"I am," I said, and lifted the eye patch, showing him the plugged-in circuitry, draining the last of the colour from his face. The robot eye was inserted the wrong way round, so it must have looked a bit ghastly. It didn't let me see, rather, it transmitted what my eye was seeing back to me. My *real* eye, the one floating in nutrient gel and attached to the Ship's Optical Drive. I had a split view: what was immediately in front of me and what the *Betsey* saw through her external monitors, all glittering stars and a shrinking space station venting debris from the old docking area. It took some getting used to.

"What in hell!" he spluttered. "Do you seriously believe taking me hostage will solve *anything*?"

"Oh, I haven't taken you hostage, Mr. Starr. I only needed you to release the clamps. You're free to go."

On cue, a pair of activated TX-R's grabbed him by the arms. He struggled and swore, and said all manner of ungentlemanly, unlawyerly, things. I didn't actually make him walk the plank, that was just my little joke. I don't think he found it funny. I merely had the TX-Rs escort him to one of the *Betsey*'s escape pods. I'd thought of sending it and him out in a wide hyperbolic orbit, taking the same three months he'd kept us needlessly stewing. But I didn't want to waste the Ship's rations and a quarter-speed drift would have him back at the space port safe and sound in, oh, a Sol day or two. Sooner if anyone bothered coming to retrieve him. But I guessed my hasty departure might give them other things to worry about.

I turned to the attendant droids. "TX-R3005 ... or are you 3008?" I peered at the badge on the nearest metal forehead, squinting at the writing. I don't think the Osiris Company ever considered that anybody might need more than one of their androids. As it was, I was faced with a crew twice as large and many times more difficult to identify than when they were human.

"Hell and blast it," I sighed, before brightening up. Who said they had to be treated as individuals? They were all linked to the Ship, and therefore, to me. "TX-R3000s, hear this: I shall henceforth refer to all of you as 'R'. Divide my orders between you in the most efficient manner."

Twenty-three TX-R3000's smartly replied "Yes, Captain," and the disembodied head of the twenty-fourth rolled its one good eye. "Arr!" it parroted from the workbench, voice high pitched due to the lack of an echo chamber.

Maybe it wasn't *totally* unsalvageable after all. I picked the head up, it lolled on what was left of the neck, its remaining eye snapping into focus.

"So," I asked it, Hamlet style, "What shall we do with an ageing, overpowered, renegade interstellar cargo Ship, and two dozen almost top-of-the range, vacuum enabled, semi-indestructible metal men, hmm?"

•   •   •

The sleek tourist vessel, backlit by a gloriously ringed outer planet, filled the view from my Watch eye. That was the beauty of Sigma Draconis, a system of three habitable planets and a dozen mining and research stations. Cruise liners and supply Ships ran back and forth like a trail of plump ants. And, what with the Krillian wars raging at the fringes of human space, there wasn't a military vessel for nigh on fifty light-years in any direction.

"Sir, the *Princess Royale* is in range," my crew reported.

"Hail her and put her up on the monitor," I ordered. "All Rs; prepare for EVA."

A boyish face appeared on screen, squinting at me in the dim light. I knew he could barely see me, but I didn't want to spoil the surprise.

"This is Ensign Choy, of the pleasure Ship the *Princess Royale*. We're not expecting a rendezvous. Also, your flag appears to be malfunctioning. Please confirm identity?"

"*Jolly Roger!*" squawked a feeble voice. "*Skull and Crossbones!*"

"Say again, Ship, you're coming across distorted?"

I sub-vocalised a 'Hush!' command. "Apologies, *Princess*," I said, reading the cruise Ship's cargo manifest. Really, electronic identification flags made my job almost too easy. My lips smacked as I scanned the luxury foods and, even better, beverages. Rum appeared to be the one thing that made my split vision relatively painless. "This is the, um, CSS *Roger Jolie*. We may have taken a micro-meteorite to our Flag."

"Uh-huh." The ensign looked doubtful, as well he should. The flag housed the Ship's black box recorder and was, in theory, the most shielded part of a vessel. Still, it was *technically* possible. "And your purpose?"

"*Plunder!*" the voice at my shoulder whispered. It appeared my command had not shut it up, just lowered its volume. I ignored it, hoping the ensign would do the same.

"Tell me, *Princess,* with over a hundred passengers on board and *wow,* really quite generous amount of all-inclusive alcohol, I guess some of your crew are trained in unarmed combat skills? For peace-keeping purposes?"

"Well yes, but —"

"And no doubt there are even a number of small calibre firearms in the captain's locker?"

"I'm sorry Sir, I'm not at liberty —"

"And is there anybody on board handy with a cutlass?"

"Cutlass? I ..."

No, of course there was no-one handy with a cutlass. But that was all for the best. Because there's nothing that quells a have-a-go hero quite like a metal-shielded, bullet-immune, space-breathing, super-strong automaton. Especially one armed with a wickedly sharp sword, re-purposed from tungsten-steel K-cables. One little nick of their space suit and your hero had a ton of other things to worry about, like making it to the nearest airlock, ASAP. I'd have a quiet, docile Ship to loot. Which was good, not for my sake; but for theirs. Heck, I was doing them a service; think of the story they'd tell their grandchildren!

In my Watch eye a cloud of glinting figures swarmed through hard vacuum towards the target. I'd kept him talking long enough.

"Ah, well that *is* a shame," I said, with a grin. "And now, kind sir, if you take a look in your external monitors, you might notice you have company. Prepare to be boarded."

"*Board!*" agreed Polly, the one android I'd bothered to name, as its head — mounted on my shoulder — lunged into the Ensign's view, the glittering eye patch matching mine.

"But, but ..." quavered the Ensign, torn between what was on screen and the host of alarms beginning to sound. "Who are you? And what are *they?*"

"Who are we?" I laughed, perhaps a little maniacally. "Have you not heard? We're the Jay D'Red Space Pirate Robots!"

"*Arr!*" echoed Polly, metal face contorted into a lopsided leer. "*Dread Pirate Robots!*"

It has a certain ring to it. Don't you think?

MONSTOPIA

L. P. MELLING

A MELIA CROSSES THE STEEL DRAWBRIDGE to the island and pushes through the ticket barrier. A bunch of children run past holding multi-coloured balloons, baby vampire and werewolf cub pictures on them twirling around in the breeze. So cute. And so wrong.

She reads the giant notice board and scowls:

WELCOME TO MONSTOPIA!
A WORLD OF MONSTERS AND ADVENTURE FOR ALL THE FAMILY!
PLEASE NOTE: PHOTOGRAPHY IS NOT PERMITTED ANYWHERE IN THE PARK.

The amusement park is vast and claims to have every monster in existence. Amelia very much doubts that. Spawling rollercoasters and ghost trains weave between giant cages and reinforced glass enclosures, between horrifying museums, gruesome food halls, and a colossal amphitheatre set around a concrete pool. A small island deforested to build a modern-day freak show. They created a Monster alright, as humanity always does.

Her legs itching, Amelia rubs her heel against the calf of her other leg. She clutches the compact wire cutters in her hoodie pocket with clammy hands. She shouldn't be doing this, she tells herself. She should never have signed up when she saw the Monster Aid call stuck on the college notice board. But there's no turning back now.

As she always does to calm herself, she pictures a sparkling sunlit sea, breathing deep to the rhythm of the tide in her memory. She wishes she were back there now and reminds herself that is exactly why she is here instead: to protect the sea life and all other life facing extinction.

She pulls down a NY Yankees cap and looks around to check no one is watching her. Most of the adults are already on their phones, frowning when they realise there's no signal, already pretending they aren't using their cameras.

She can't help but smile a little despite her unease. Clearly, they haven't checked the T's and C's of their park tickets. Their phones will be checked before they leave the place, and any monster pics and vids wiped.

Someone in the crowd catches her eye, his sunglasses blocking his sea-blue eyes. *What is Johan doing?* she thinks of her fellow activist. *If someone notices...* Amelia looks away, pretending not to know him, rubbing the shaved side of her head.

She picks out a pair of voices in the line next to her:

"Careful, honey. Don't get too close to the cage now."

"But, Daddy, I wanna see its big teethies!" a little girl squeaks, about to burst.

A barrel-chested, red-haired monsterkeeper smiles at the girl and turns to the knackered-looking father. "Don't worry, sir, it's perfectly safe. The werewolves learn in their teens not to get close to the bars. They'd never harm a child."

The father's face tightens a notch.

Artificial moonlight spills from the cage, lighting the girl's gap-toothed smile and the spray of freckles across her nose and cheeks. She imitates a roar as she watches the werewolf that is half-asleep and clearly in no mood for entertainment. Its wide fury back is turned away from the onlookers as it lies in a super-sized doughnut position.

Amelia is glad to see the werewolf is not chained, but the cage is still far too small, even more cramped than her college dorm and without any room for "Wolfy" to get out of sight of the hundreds of uncaring eyes on him. Amelia feels her hand ball into a fist, rubs it against the side of her thigh.

The kid soon gets fidgety. "Daddy, let's go see the vamps!"

"Okay, dear," he says, exhaustion heavy in his voice, sounding like he'll barely last the day. He catches Amelia's eye. She smiles at him in that "you can do it" kinda way.

Monstopia is alive with the cacophony of humanity: screams and whoops and bickering. Impossible for the monsters to relax. Amelia can almost see the werewolf's broken spirit lying on the floor next to him. Without even the energy to howl.

Kids of all shapes and ages wear blood-red smiles from eating too much cotton candy, dripping green goo from their mouths as they eat "mummified" hotdogs with dyed mustard. The 6-inch sausages — "Vicious vegan alternative also available" — are wrapped in onion rings to give the same effect.

The smells turn her stomach as she sees families enjoying themselves, smiling and laughing at the caged attractions. Sure, they may be monsters, but they still have rights, deserve so much better than this!

Amelia stomps forward, holding the wire cutters tight in her hoodie pocket. When she feels someone touch her shoulder, Amelia jumps away.

"Hey, sorry." The guy with the kid stands in front of her. "You dropped this," he says.

"Oh, yeah, thank you," she stumbles. "My insulin." Always a terrible liar.

"Yeah, that's what I thought."

The kid gives her a blue milkshake-moustache smile.

"Aren't you adorable?" Amelia says as she puts the tranquiliser shot back in her pocket, pushing it deep.

"Yep," she says, without batting an eyelid.

"Well, thanks again. Hope you both enjoy your day."

The girl drags her father away, and Amelia heads to the vampire enclosure, looking for weaknesses.

There is a group of frat boys taking pictures with their phones of the vampire in a curtained cage. Amelia tuts. *Devolution right there*, she thinks. They scratch their heads when they see nothing in the pictures but the old leather chair the Count is sitting on beside a red table lamp as he reads a book titled *Fifty Tips for Good Dental Hygiene.* No doubt a book forced onto him to keep the crowd smiling. Behind bulletproof glass, the vampire looks smartly dressed. Does he look content? No, he is incarcerated. It must be a show. He bares his fangs at the kids, getting a scream or two, but you can tell his heart isn't in it. That he just wants peace and quiet.

Amelia walks away, looking at the signs for 'monsters' of all shapes and sizes until she finds the one she's been searching for. The tartan billboard reads *Nessie* in a splashed effect typeface. The largest monster in the park. If they could fit in a kraken to go with it, they probably would, but they haven't been able to capture one yet. After all, Amelia knows they were down there in the dark depths of the ocean floor, she has seen such a majestic creature.

A thousand miles away from the loch she calls home, Nessie appears forlorn and giant in the aquarium. As large a whale's, Nessie's immense blue eye stares at Amelia, sending a shiver down her spine. And a thousand miles from the shy person people know her to be, she says, "I'm getting you out of here!"

Her activist group Monster Aid has already hacked into the security cams, leaving her free to do her work. A group she had been so nervous of joining, but the only one she has felt she belongs in. She moves carefully as the crowd is distracted by Nessie's calls, monstersong to his kind, maybe to all monsterkind? Amelia knows a bit of whalesong, but not a lot. She plants the charges on the base of the giant aquarium, signals to Nessie to swim over to the other side of it. Someone turns around the corner, one of the park workers. He looks like security. She pushes her cap down further, scalp prickling, and quickly walks away. As soon as he is out of sight, she punches the fire alarm.

She runs out of the aquarium, worrying that people are coming for her when they run past to escape. Parents and teachers shout at children to get clear, monster-faced balloons drifting up in the air with the rush. A man with a shaved-headed man pushes a woman out of the way in the rush; the woman picks herself up and chases after him, hurling abuse and French fries at him as she hunts him down. Monsterkeepers struggle for control as they call for calm on the other side of water fountain running blood red with dye.

Every part of Amelia wants to flee, to escape it all, and a dark memory resurfaces in her mind, flooding her with cold dread. The giant whale, one of the last of its kind, lies dead on the bloody sand. Seagulls squawk and circle wildly above, and the fishermen laugh as she screams at them, their harpoons held high and threateningly. Salty tears streaming down her face, her younger self shakes with hurt and anger and hatred.

The chaotic shouting of the park replaces the squawking as Amelia is ripped back to the present.

She had run away from them that day as fear closed around her heart, getting the better of her. But she won't run away today.

Determinedly, she scans the aquarium, making sure it is clear. Just one more minute. She thinks of the little girl with her father. They have to be elsewhere, safe. Don't they?

She sprints back to the aquarium entrance to double check.

No one is around.

She can't wait any longer. She runs back up the ramp and hits the detonation button in her pocket. The blast forces her forward, the sound of cracking glass and crunching concrete filling the air.

Smoke drifts up the baking sun like octopus tentacles.

Monstopia erupts in chaos. People run like wild animals, as if it's they who are escaping from captivity. She spots Johan in the distance busting open the caged stables. Centaurs gallop free, trampling through the food court.

She sprints to the vampire enclosure, jumping over an upturned hotdog cart, and in the diversionary confusion, she reaches the back of the marked "Vampariaum." She dusts the keypad and punches in the code. The door swings open with a satisfying whine.

"Go," she says. "You're free."

"Thank you, my dear," the Count says with a posh British accent. "At least now I can read some proper literature again." He calmly puts his book down and steps outside the cage. He nods at her and his clothes drop into a pile onto the floor, a black bat soaring to the heavens, heading back home that she knows is nowhere near Eastern Europe.

Relief floods through her and she re-treads the way from the park entrance that is almost empty now. Her fellow activists will already be setting free other monsters across the park.

She notices a bunch of rich kids still hanging around, near the werewolf enclosure. A boy with fluffy blonde hair and beady eyes bangs on the cage. "Here, little doggy. Got a treat for you. Now bow down!"

Wolfy — clearly having a pet hate for being treated as a pet — growls at the kid and snarls with vicious teeth. This would be enough to scare away even the bravest of kids, but this one only laughs.

"Oh, so scary. What's wrong little one? Mommy didn't love you enough? Shared with your pack was she?" A couple of snickers come from behind him. They take pics and a flash blinds the werewolf. Amelia can't believe it. Everyone knows you shouldn't take a picture of a werewolf, and never with a flash.

The werewolf shakes his head. Amelia's teeth grind, hand gripping the wire cutters vice tight. She remembers all the times she was name-called as a child, all the times she never stood up for herself like she should have.

"Hey, bullyboy!" she shouts. "Why don't you pick on someone who isn't behind bars?" She shouldn't be doing this, she is drawing too much attention to herself, threatening the mission. Threatening to get caught before she does her part. But she can't stop herself. They are the fishermen she cowered to all those years ago, they are the next generation of will show cruelty to animals if they aren't stopped.

His smile thins, and he sweeps back his messy hair in what Amelia is sure he thinks is a cool way. "Ha, what you?"

"Yeah." She takes her stance, gives him the "come to me" gesture with her hand. He hesitates when Wolfy howls. Then goes ballistic as he bends the bars apart and slips through the gap. Screams carry across the park as the straddlers scamper towards the park's exit.

"Get away from it now!" the barrel-chested monsterkeeper bellows, snatching at his gun. He takes aim at one of the last of its kind when Amelia runs and jumps in front of the werewolf, hoping it's a tranquiliser gun and not something more serious.

"Ahh." Her ankle has twisted. "Go. Now!" she tells the werewolf, wishing she knew his real name. Her cap has fallen off, revealing the long green-blue hair on one side that she'd bunched up under it.

The werewolf doesn't have to be told twice as he jumps clear onto the nearest roof, the park eerily quiet now, gone are the cries of happiness.

The monsterkeeper growls at her and chases after the werewolf. "I'll be back for you!" he says over his shoulder.

"And I'll be gone," she tells him, winking, wincing with the pain. Her ankle is on fire as she stands, but she won't need to use it much longer. *You can do this*, she tells herself, dragging herself forward.

Of course, the monsters are carrying trackers, embedded beneath their skin as they were drugged unconscious, but they'd planned for that. Monsters Aid planned for everything, or so Amelia hopes.

Her waterproof watch bleeps to signal the EMP detonation. Her waterproof watch stops, and she sighs with relief. It worked. She ambles over to the park's perimeter, the pain in her ankle subsiding slightly. *Come on, time to go.*

People stupid enough to film anything will be realising now that the recording was for nothing anyway, even if they got through the exit without checks — the EMP making sure of that. At least they have their memories; that's if their memories are better than a goldfish in an age when Google does all the work.

Her part done, Amelia hobbles to the barrier overlooking the calm sea and climbs over it. She steps over it and balances over the edge, then takes a deep breath, peering down at the incredible drop. She puts a strand of hair behind her ear. And dives. The air rushes past her as she plummets, her legs burning as they transform. She hits the water like an Olympian, gracefully swimming in the place she calls home.

Amelia flips her shimmering tail hard and rises from the depths, the pain gone now as her head breaks the water and she reveals the real her. Exhaling long and deep, she looks up at a beautiful blue sky and promises herself to never change back again. She will fight them from the water to do her part.

Giant winged creatures cut across the sun, howls of freedom echo in the distance. She looks at the empty prison of Monstopia and smiles at humanity's futility.

They'd no doubt try again, but this time her kind will be waiting. Together. As one. And ensure all the tech humans use to hunt them is destroyed before they have a chance to use it again. Ensure that the creatures they will never understand are free.

An ear-piercing wail cuts the air, followed by an earthquake-loud rumble. Amelia turns around to see Nessie, moving freely as she bends her giant neck down to the park's platform. Nessie emerges with a blonde kid dangling from her mouth.

Amelia shrugs. "Meh." And swims away to leave Nessie to her meal.

Ryan Cole is a speculative fiction writer who lives in Virginia with his husband and snuggly pug child. He is a winner of the Writers of the Future Contest, and his recent work has appeared or is forthcoming in *Clarkesworld*, *MetaStellar*, *Voyage YA by Uncharted*, *Gallery of Curiosities*, and the Bram Stoker Award-nominated anthology *Mother: Tales of Love and Terror* (Weird Little Worlds Press).

WHAT IS HERS SHOULD BE MINE

RYAN A. COLE

W E WERE BORN in the still early days of the world — when the sky was a frontier of burnt yellow clouds and the ocean a never-ending sapphire canvas, the atmosphere humid and thick from its birth. Back then, everything seemed so simple — and not just because it was, molecularly speaking. My sister and I had only just met. We were new to each other, as the world was new, as it would be for dozens of thousands of years until life found a way, and the humans came along. A lifetime of figuring out each other's quirks, of judging and arguing. We may have been hatched from the very same egg, the only one in our brood, but that didn't mean we had anything in common. An issue that Mother tried to squash early on.

"Galaxis," she cooed in the deep, dark water, a soft stream of bubbles floating out from her beak. She prodded our egg with the tip of her tentacle, the fleshy gray underside sticking to the shell. "Galaxis, come out."

I plastered myself to the bottom of the egg shell. My rough, purple skin prickled over from the cold. The tiny, pink suckers on my tentacles retracted. And with all of my might — however fleeting that was — I clung to the one thing I'd known all my life, aside from the small, lumpy body of my sister, whose arms had, until now, been smushed against my face.

Mother spilled over the rim of the egg, fixing her flat, yellow eyes on my own. "Galaxis, my love, don't be scared. You're safe."

Then another voice, which I'd come to despise. "Just leave her," said Eudoria. "I'm hungry. Let's hunt." Rigid from three months of cramped gestation, she awkwardly tried to train all eight of her arms — and both of her tentacles — to swim like Mother.

But Mother wouldn't have it. She whipped out a tentacle and smacked my identical twin in the beak. "Eudoria, behave. We have to wait for Galaxis."

Which rankled my sister. Using the funnel attached to her gill-sac, she exhaled a jet stream of inky black bubbles, struggling away from the flat ocean floor. "Why should I wait? She can fend for herself."

I huddled even tighter, my eight arms trembling. Was Eudoria right? Was I all on my own?

Yet, I tried not to worry. *You're an apex predator*, Mother had said, her voice silky smooth as she tended our nest. *Squid are the gods of the world's ten oceans. Nothing, except for our own kind, can beat us.* The words were a comfort before, when I was asleep. When the world was more like a warm, gooey dream, with my sister on top of me, and Mother to protect us. Now, that dream felt a bit too real.

"Help her," said Mother, pointing her tentacle.

"No," said Eudoria.

Then a loud whoosh as the world rushed past, and a long gray tentacle wrapped around my sister. Dragged her towards me. Plopped her in the shell.

"Help her," said Mother, her silk gone hard.

Eudoria grumbled. She wriggled a thin, purple tentacle around me, using the grip of her suction cups as leverage, and she yanked. Kept yanking.

With a mucousy pop, I emerged from the egg shell, the eyes on the sides of my head squeezed shut. When I landed in the sand, I cracked one eye open. Looked at my new home, my new life, and shuddered.

Mother didn't notice, or perhaps she didn't care. She enveloped us both in a suffocating hug, hiding the deep, wrinkled scars on her mantle, and she leaned close to whisper. "You two need to learn to take care of each other. To share — in everything, for the good of the family. What's hers will be yours." She glared at Eudoria. "And what's yours will be hers." She nuzzled my beak. "Otherwise, you'll leave yourselves open to attack." Her eyes grew distant. "Trust me, I know."

I blinked in confusion. Why would that matter if Mother was with us? Where would she go?

Eudoria scuttled away into the sand, feigning indifference, but Mother grabbed her arm. "Promise me," she said.

"I promise," I said, eager to please her.

Eudoria grumbled. "Fine. I promise."

"Good," said Mother, squeezing us tight, while neither of us had any clue what we had agreed to.

•   •   •

While both of us grew over the next several millennia, only one of us matured. Eudoria would streak through the vast, silent ocean, her eight arms carelessly trailing behind her, fanned out and flapping in wide, arrogant arcs. In the mornings, when the surface was golden from the sun, she would swim up the miles from the sand of our home. In the evenings, she would pick through the nearby reefs, scouring the deep, black trenches of the earth. Fearless to whoever — or *what*ever — might be lurking.

Which exasperated Mother. "You may be a goddess of the deep," she would say, "but you can still feel pain. You are not immune to death."

And Eudoria would laugh, deep-throated and confident. "What could be out there that could possibly harm me?"

Mother would just sigh and prod at her scars. "Things like us. Or maybe things that aren't here yet."

Eudoria, of course, didn't heed Mother's warning. She continued to test the limits of our species, acting as if the long life we enjoyed was a shield for her reckless, and insufferable, behavior.

"Why does she do it?" I said one morning, when the sunlight started to bleed through the water. I had never been up to the surface with Eudoria, never seen the sky, and I imagined it felt as warm as it looked, like the fluid from our egg.

Mother lay beside me, her old, gray tentacles buried in the sand, each one twenty times as long as my own. "I don't know," she whispered, her words coming slowly. She lifted the now-shriveled crown of her mantle, nuzzled the flap of her gills against my cheek. "I suspect that your sister has something to prove — to me, to you, and probably to herself. I just hope she can do that soon, before I'm gone."

My heartbeat quickened. "Don't say that," I begged. "You'll be with us forever." The words felt false even as they left my beak, and I wondered which one of us they were meant to convince.

Mother just smiled. "Don't worry," she said, "you'll be fine on your own. Your sister will come to appreciate your company."

I grimaced, unbelieving. "Have you ever *met* Eudoria?"

Mother's smile widened. "Just remember what I taught you. Stay close, stay strong. And above all else, share. You need to be equals in order to survive. That was one lesson that my sister never learned."

Eudoria took that moment to appear. She flew from the gold-plated surface of the water, pink-and-purple tentacles spinning around her, and she swerved to a stop, arms kicking up sand. She held up her beak in a self-assured grin. "So — what did you think?"

Mother stroked her cheek. "That was beautiful, Eudoria."

And my twin sister preened like a purple-pink star, greedily soaking up Mother's attention. Just like she had every day since we'd been born.

Glaring behind me, I skittered into the darkness. "Show-off," I muttered.

• • •

Three thousand years later, Mother took her last breath. Her death weighed heavily on me and Eudoria, not only because we were lonely without her — and we *were* quite alone — but also because it forced us to speak. Mother, for so long, had served as a buffer. A filter for our differences. A way to ensure I wouldn't strangle my sister when she spent the entire day boasting of her exploits. Or that she didn't do the same when I questioned her skill. Now, with Mother gone, those moments were tense. And they only got worse.

But I had made a promise. And I intended to keep it.

"Where are you going?" I said to Eudoria. It was only three days since Mother had died; three days since we had dumped her limp body into one of the trenches that cut through our reef.

Eudoria twirled extravagantly above me. "To hunt," she said in her usual drawl, as if I wasn't worth the breath.

"Alright," I growled. "Just don't go too far."

"Since when do I need your permission?" she said. And with that, she left.

Which was fine by me. The less that we spoke, the less we pretended that things were as they should be, the less of a chance that one of us would snap and do something we'd regret.

I swam to the outermost edge of our reef, where my sister never went. I nestled in a small, shallow pocket of sand, and I wrapped all eight of my arms around myself. Making it feel like a soft, warm hug. Tricking my mind into thinking it was Mother, still holding me close.

Wiping the sting from my bloodshot eyes, I inspected the last few things that she had left me. An oddly smooth stone in the shape of an egg. The flat, spiraled shell of a long-dead nautilus. A tiny, white tooth with a crack down the middle, and which didn't fit any of the critters I had seen. All of them things that we'd discovered together, while Eudoria was away on her far-flung adventures, and which Mother had wanted me — wanted *us* — to have. To remember her by. To keep, and to grow. A family collection that would bind us together.

But Eudoria had never shown an interest in such things. So, I had hidden them before she found out.

What's yours will be hers, I thought to myself, prickling over at the memory of Mother. But why should I share? Why was it wrong to have something of my own? Something that brought me a sliver of joy when the rest of the world was heavy and dark.

Wasn't it enough to tolerate one another?

For several millennia, we did just that, both of us settling into our habits — Eudoria hunting and me collecting. Eventually, the two of us weren't so alone. The ocean had started to fill up with fish, with crabs and crawlers and stingrays and sturgeon. With white-bellied sharks that prowled at our reef, and great sperm whales that blotted out the sun, hiding the sky with their impossible shadows. In the evenings, I would watch as they leapt from the water and wonder how something so perfect could exist.

But then, what about me? How did *I* exist? *Squidlings are special*, Mother had told me. *We were put here to maintain the order of things.* Her voice brought tears to my salt-puckered eyes. For me, all thoughts, all questions, led to Mother.

Not so for Eudoria.

"Look what I captured," she said one day, the still-rotting carcass of an eel in her tentacles.

"How pretty," I lied. "Throw it over there with the rest of the waste." I nodded to the mountain of unlucky creatures she had already killed, and then left to decay.

Eudoria hovered in the reef bed in front of me, scraping her fat, meaty limbs among the detritus. "Do you think you're so special? Too good for my gift?"

Special? I thought. *Is that what this was?* "Killing for pleasure is cruel. You should know that."

"*Hunting*," Eudoria corrected, "is different. If something is weak, then it shouldn't be alive."

"That goes against everything Mother once taught us."

Eudoria pouted, "Mother was wrong." And without a goodbye, she slunk into the reef.

As the years flew by, my collection grew, and Eudoria's prey got bigger and meaner. My sister no longer concerned herself with eels. Crabs weren't enough. Stingrays were wimpy. All that she wanted were the massive whale mothers and the blood-rich bones of the megalodon sharks, that sharpened her beak as she sucked out the marrow. The biggest, the baddest, the most exhilarating catch.

"You're going to get hurt," I often tried to warn her. "Someday, one of these animals will fight back."

But Eudoria did as Eudoria liked. "There is nothing alive that can beat me," she would say, a monstrous grin on her bloody, purple lips.

And she may have been right, no matter how much that irked me.

But it didn't last forever.

•   •   •

The first time I saw a boat, I thought it was an eclipse. Eudoria and I were just waking from a nap when a long sheet of darkness passed over the surface. It cut through the water like a smooth, black knife, leaving a white, frothy pool in its wake.

"What is that?" I said, still groggy from sleep.

"I'm not sure," said Eudoria, "but I'm going to catch it." Before I could stop her, she had flown to the surface.

I followed, but slowly. Whatever this thing was, it didn't look dangerous, yet I still wasn't sure. Better to be safe.

Eudoria, on the other hand, abandoned all caution. She poked at the smooth underside of the shadow. "It's hard," she called through the sun-dappled water. She wrapped one tentacle under the shadow, tapped on the side. It didn't sound like anything I had ever heard before. The echo that tickled my skin felt dead.

Then, there were other sounds coming from above. And these, in comparison, felt very much alive.

Something poked into the water from the shadow, the tip of it shiny and wickedly sharp. It stabbed at Eudoria, who wriggled away.

"Eudoria, watch out!" But I was too late. An identical weapon shot into the water, and it snagged on the great, meaty base of her mantle, cutting her cheek. A bright stream of blood ran out from her skin. And for the first time in my life, I heard my sister scream.

The shadow, or something in the shadow, must have heard, because soon there were many more weapons in the water. They rained down, sticking like needles in the reef. And thankfully, Eudoria was quick enough to avoid them, stanching her wound with one of her arms as she awkwardly retreated.

I grabbed onto her tentacles and pulled her down to safety.

What were you thinking? Mother would have said. *How could you be so foolish, so selfish?* But instead, I just frowned, because Eudoria was grinning.

"Finally, a foe worth facing," she said.

•　　•　　•

That wasn't the last of the mysterious vessels, or the creatures inside them. From that day on, they invaded the once-calm realm of our waters, slashing the sky with their tall, white sails.

"Who *are* they?" I said as another passed over us.

"Who cares?" said Eudoria. She gnawed on a bone that was significantly smaller than the whales she used to catch, and which had come from the most recent vessel she had sunk. "They think they can challenge a squid, a *god*. This is what they deserve."

"What if you left them alone?" I said, more for my sanity than out of goodwill. If Eudoria was hurt, then I would have failed Mother, the promise we had made.

"Ah," said Eudoria, "you want them for yourself."

"Of course not," I said.

Eudoria flashed me a mischievous smile. "To add to your collection? The one you've been hiding?"

I froze, unable to hide my surprise. "I don't know what you mean."

"Really, Galaxis, do you think I'm that stupid? For thousands of years, you've been hiding that trash. Trying to prove yourself to who — to Mother? Nothing you've done will impress her. She's gone."

"I know that," I hissed.

Eudoria sneered. "I've seen how you huddle and cry by the reef-bed, hugging yourself."

My tentacles trembled, my suction cups pulsed. "What would you know? You never cared about her, never cared about me. Your only god was yourself."

Eudoria narrowed her flat, yellow eyes. "Careful," she whispered.

But now, after so many years, I couldn't stop. The anger was bubbling hot in my throat. "If you had been a better daughter, she might still be with us. She's dead because of you. We're *alone* because of you."

Which — looking back — may have gone too far. Eudoria whipped out a fat, purple tentacle and smacked me in the beak. Then she swam into the reef.

I chased her, but cautiously. We had never come to blows. If she was willing to hurt me, what wouldn't she do?

We stopped where the rocks gave way to the trenches, and Eudoria ducked into a pale, coral cave. When she emerged, her eight arms were weighed down with treasures — all of the things that I had collected over the years.

"Put them back," I snarled, my heartbeat heavy.

But Eudoria ignored me. Panting, she dragged my collection to the trench, leaned over the side, and flashed me a smile. Then, she let go.

Seashells and flowers and petrified kelp fronds, the fossilized skeletons of long-dead mollusks, the anemone tendrils that swayed in the current. Everything Mother had taught me to love, now sinking into the darkness.

Frantically, I dove past the edge of the trench, tentacles reaching. But I wasn't quick enough. Gravity beat me. "You're a monster," I said, my eyes hot with tears. "I hope they attack you, these creatures from above."

Eudoria shrugged. She picked at the bone-meal caught in her beak. "Let them attack. I'm *always* hungry."

•   •   •

Two moon cycles later, the summer storms arrived. The ocean was choppy from the undying wind, the waves reaching up to what seemed like the stars. Eudoria still wouldn't talk, wouldn't look at me. Instead, she pretended I didn't exist, that we hadn't — for the first time — broken our promise.

I picked through the dregs of my desecrated stash, those few lucky pieces I had saved from the trench, and I thought of the past. *You two need to learn to take care of each other.* Those words had never felt less true than now. And yet, I felt bound to them — by grief, or maybe guilt. Mother had trusted me, and now, I had failed her.

Could I still make things right? Could I salvage our relationship? Eudoria may think herself better than me — better than *everyone* — but she was still my twin sister, my only living kin.

"Eudoria," I called, swimming up to the surface. "Eudoria, come talk to me."

But my sister rushed past, dancing in the waves.

That was when I saw the first vessel appear. Its belly broke through the water next to Eudoria, and I realized, belatedly, that it didn't cast a shadow. The sun was too hidden, the clouds too thick. Everything looked like a shadow that day.

Eudoria saw it, too. She dove in the surf as a thin, silver arrow shot into the water. It harmlessly whistled to the bottom of the ocean, followed by another. Lazily twirling, she boasted and laughed, "Is that the best you can do?" Out from the waves came another large vessel; it landed where Eudoria's tentacles were floating, knocking her back.

But if anything, the threat just goaded her on. "Come and get me!" she bellowed.

The scrawny, pale creatures in the vessels seemed to hear. They picked up their assault, flinging more arrows. One of them nicked me at the base of my arm, a second on my mantle.

"Get back!" I shouted. "Come hide in the trenches!"

But my sister didn't listen. She snarled and wrapped one of the vessels in her tentacles, cracking the bottom and splintering the sides. Several of the two-legged creatures jumped out, and they dove into the maelstrom, swimming to nowhere.

I had to do something, but what? And how? If I joined her on the surface, I'd likely be skewered. Eudoria's skin was now peppered with arrows. She struggled and screeched as more vessels appeared, closing her in, and all I could think of, in the gathering madness, was how her anger wasn't mine. It *should* have been mine. I should have *made* it mine, but no matter how hard I tried, I couldn't. All that I felt was regret for her choices. Disappointment for all that had brought us to this moment.

I swerved to the side as an arrow streaked towards me, snatched it with my arm. If I couldn't go up to the surface and fight, then I would fight down here, where none of them could see me.

I flung the arrow up and watched it crash into the wreckage. The impact was such that the wooden planks shattered, and the vessel capsized, dumping its creatures. How could these tiny things cause so much damage? They were nothing but sand-fleas compared to a squid. But somehow, incredibly, they were fighting. And winning.

With each of my eight arms, I hurled an arrow. Sank one more, two more, *three* vessels, collecting the weapons as quickly as they fell.

And then, another crash. Eudoria spasmed as an arrow from above — from one of the creatures — dug into the spot where her mantle was thinnest. Her flat, yellow eyes bulged out in surprise.

She screeched, and she fell, kept falling, into the darkness.

I flew up just in time, her tentacles settling gently in my arms, the only time she'd ever been gentle in anything. A torrent of blood seeped out from her side. "Eudoria," I said. "Eudoria, can you hear me?"

My sister, my enemy, and sometimes my friend, looked up at me in shock. "Galaxis," she croaked, "the creatures. They beat me."

I nodded. "They did."

Eudoria grimaced. "It shouldn't be possible."

But I didn't say anything, because obviously, it was.

"I'm sorry," she said, "for hurting you before." Her darkening eye rolled over to her wound, and she flinched in my arms. Recoiled from the sight of it. "All I ever wanted was to feel like I was strong. Like I was better at something." She grunted. "At anything."

I petted her rough, slimy cheek with my tentacle. "You were better at being annoying," I said.

Both of us laughed, even though it wasn't funny.

Watching her eyes close, I leaned down to whisper, "I'm sorry we couldn't have been better sisters."

Eudoria nodded. "I didn't make it easy."

I rested my mantle right next to her gills, hearing her breath grow ever more soft, ever more peaceful, until it faded into nothing.

●　　　●　　　●

My collection grew more than I had expected that day. Aside from Eudoria's waterlogged bones, I still had the dozens of sleek, silver arrows that littered the trenches. And even with the brown rust coating their blades, they still cut as deadly as they ever had before.

Believe me, I had plenty of time to experiment.

Yet, even more special was the courage I had gained. The new sense of purpose. *Squidlings are special. We were put here to maintain the order of things.* Now that the humans had learned that they could kill us, could conquer a god, that order was closer than it had ever been to breaking. And I was the only one left that could fix it. I was the one that had to carry on our legacy.

But I was well-equipped. I had collected some help.

With Eudoria's strength, and Mother's dedication, nothing — and no one — could stand in my way.

THE SUIT

CYNTHIA C. SCOTT

T HE BEDSHEETS STILL SMELLED of Jason. His hair clogged the shower drain or knotted the pillowcases. Even the air seemed to stir as it once had whenever he moved through the rooms, belting out arias in his basso profundo. His clothes hung untouched in the bedroom closet and his vinyl collection of jazz and opera records, which he stored in musty wooden crates, were still stacked in the garage. The house changed very little in the weeks after his death. Vanessa, his widow, didn't dare touch a thing.

She devoted a shrine to him on her living room mantel, photographs surrounded by votive candles and incense that she lit every night. She sat in front of the shrine, enveloped in the odor of vanilla and sandalwood as she stared at her husband's picture, lost in memories that threatened to turn to shadows. When she lay in bed, she recollected the warmth of his lean, taut body lying on hers — and her grief appeared again as fresh as the day he died.

Sometimes she took one of his records out of the musty crates and played it on the record player she still kept in the closet. Vanessa hated opera. It was so much screeching to her. She'd often turn down the volume whenever he played his favorite albums — *Cosi Fan Tutte, Le Nozze di Figaro, La Boheme* — or his favorite singers — Kathleen Battle, Jessye Norman, Leontyne Price. She never did understand why he had a passion for music that nobody she knew would be caught dead listening to, but it was this passion, which he had developed when he was a teen, that charmed her.

He was fearless in his passions (including his love for Vanessa) and didn't care what anyone thought about it. Vanessa, on the other hand, cared deeply and groomed herself to be what was expected of her. When she went to college, the second in her family to do so, she studied business and economics because that was what she was expected to do — get an education and follow that up with a good-paying job. But Jason was incautious and threw everything to whim. After studying for years at Berklee and enjoying a brief career as a singer in a traveling opera company, he decided he no longer liked traveling, so went to culinary school and became a pastry chef in a well-known restaurant in San Francisco. His team dubbed him the "Singing Chef" because, while supervising, he'd break into arias to motivate the chefs or simply because he wanted to. He'd sing at any given moment, sometimes to Vanessa's chagrin.

One night, early in their relationship, they were on Muni returning from a movie, when he started singing "Che Gelida Manina" from *La Boheme* to a crowd of tired and bored passengers. His voice was clear and soft at first, but then it took on more strength and power as he continued. While he had a low register, he managed to hit all the high notes, his voice bellowing over the clatter and shrieking train. Some of the passengers stared at him with delight. Others looked at him as if he was insane, while others still were simply zoned out in their alternate worlds of iPods and text messaging. Vanessa lowered her chin and tried to hide her embarrassment and let him know with her eyes how much he was embarrassing her. Jason merely gazed back, his dark eyes bearing the warm and loving look of a man who was clearly smitten. When he finished, the passengers applauded.

After his death, Vanessa played this song continuously. Curled up in a blanket in her husband's favorite easy chair, she let the tears wash down her face as the soprano struck the high Cs and shattered the silence in her big, empty house.

Vanessa's obsessive behavior worried her mother. She insisted she pack away Jason's things and put her house in order.

"What are you gonna do? Mourn him for the rest of your life?"

"If I have to."

Vanessa's response shattered what little tolerance her mother had left. The next day she showed up at Vanessa's house and took control of everything. "You need to stop this foolishness," she said as she began dismantling the shrine on the mantel.

"Stop it," Vanessa cried, snatching a candle from her mother's hand. "You're destroying everything."

"Vanessa, get a hold of yourself. Have you lost your mind?"

The heat of her mother's disappointment rubbed raw against the edges of her shame. Paralyzed, she watched her mother dismantle her life. She washed and folded the bedsheets and pillowcases, packed away Jason's clothes in cardboard boxes, and delivered them to Goodwill. She gave away the record collection to various family members or put them up for sale. When her mother started to pack away the dark blue suit hanging in the closet, Vanessa yanked it from her and insisted on keeping it.

"He wore this on our first date," she said, rubbing her hands along its fabric.

Her mother shook her head but allowed her daughter that one indulgence.

Vanessa washed the suit and ironed it thoroughly, then hung it in a bag in her closet. One night, she took it out of the closet and laid it across her bed. Running her fingers across the woven fabric, she recollected the first time she saw Jason in it, sauntering through her apartment door, smiling, and offering her a single red rosebud. He looked so handsome and debonair. She struggled hard not to let her hopes up too high. She had had so many disappointments. But the way he smiled at her made her want to believe.

Lying on top of the suit Vanessa wept herself into a troubled, dreamless sleep.

The next night, Vanessa took the suit out of the closet and laid it across a chair in the dining room. She set a dinner plate in front of it, sat down at the opposite end of the table, and ate her meal. Occasionally she glanced at the suit as she lifted a fork of pasta to her mouth, expecting the suit to speak to her. After dinner, she took the uneaten plate and threw the food into the trash. Gathering the suit in her arms, she carried it upstairs and laid it tenderly across her bed. After changing into her nightgown, she slipped into bed beside the suit and fell asleep.

For three nights, Vanessa set the suit at the dinner table, shared an imaginary conversation with it, then laid it across her bed. Each time it seemed less and less strange, and she began to anticipate her evening meals that way. After clocking out at work, she rushed out of the office, ignoring her colleagues and their attempts to draw her out of her grief, then sped home. Dashing up the steps to her bedroom she took the suit out of the closet and hugged it close to her breasts.

On the third night, she took the suit upstairs and laid it on the bed. She removed her clothes, then lay beside it. As she ran her fingers along the length of a sleeve, she recalled the firmness and strength of her husband's body and moaned with phantom lust. The last time she and Jason made love occurred the night before he died. They had had a fight about something she had trouble recalling now, and he stormed out of the house and didn't return till later that night, stinking of beer. She had already gone to bed, but she heard him stumbling up the stairs in the dark and appearing in their bedroom.

He took off his clothes and slipped in beside her, shifting and turning as he always did before settling into sleep. This time, instead, he spooned beside her and ran his hand along her thigh, coaxing the nerve endings to curl like leaves on flame beneath his fingertips. She was still too angry to yield, but her body, which betrayed her every time, burned under his touch. She hated him for making her succumb so easily, and she hated herself for succumbing until that sweet burst of pleasure shook her body and even the anger yielded to the enormity of her love for him.

Vanessa shut her eyes and ran her hand down the length of her belly. She pressed it between her thighs and unlocked pent-up and misdirected desires. She moaned softly and shuddered. It was over in minutes. She curled into a fetal ball and sobbed. The spasms of her grief rocked the bed.

Realizing something had to change, Vanessa took the suit and laid it across a chair, then climbed back into bed, curled the covers around her, and drifted into a restless sleep.

The next morning, the sunlight through her bedroom window stabbed her eyes. Her vision was bleary from sleep and sunlight. Lifting herself on her elbow, she rubbed her eyes, then stared at the suit. It was gone!

She became aware of noises in the house. Downstairs in the kitchen, footsteps thudded, water flushed, and pots banged. Thinking her mother had let herself in with the spare key, Vanessa slipped into her robe and went downstairs. She stepped into the kitchen and froze.

Jason stood by the kitchen stove, scrambling eggs in a pan. He wore the dark blue suit.

"Hey, sleepy head," he said, smiling. "Hungry?" Before she could breathe a word, he burst into an aria in a basso profundo that rattled the walls.

Vanessa stood in the kitchen archway, blinking. He poured the eggs onto a plate and told her to eat. Her mouth fell open. He asked what was wrong, and she replied: "You're dead."

"I am? Really? Do I look dead?" She shook her head. "Well, then. Eat, before it gets cold."

Vanessa ate. The eggs were gummy and bland. He sat opposite her, watching her chew as though fascinated by the function of eating. She asked again why he was there, but he took her plate and then led her back upstairs, telling her she must dress and get ready for work. When Vanessa came back downstairs, showered, and dressed, he handed her the briefcase at the front door and kissed her on the lips. He told her to have a good day. She said she would, but wondered if he was still going to be there when she came home.

"Where else am I gonna be?"

She thought about this and realized he was right. She smiled and kissed him again.

When she returned that evening, he was still in the kitchen, singing another aria and making a roast. He burnt the roast. She ordered pizza. They ate (or rather she ate) at the kitchen table. Jason watched her studiously.

She did not understand why he returned to her — it seemed strange that he would render the costs of the funeral and her grief meaningless. He said, "Do you want me to leave?"

"No," she said, dropping the slice of pizza onto the plate. "No, please don't."

He smiled. "Then I won't."

Vanessa put her hands over her face and cried. It swept her suddenly and ferociously. She started to wonder if she was going insane. Earlier that day at work, Clifton, one of her colleagues at the firm, had approached her in her office and asked how she was doing. Clifton had been at the firm for four years, and it was no secret to anyone, Vanessa included, that he was attracted to her. He wasn't a terribly good-looking guy, but he cut a dashing figure among the office workers in his pinstripe suits and well-poised manner.

When Clifton asked how she was doing, he sat on her desk and said, "You seem distracted this morning. Everything's all right, I hope."

"Everything's fine," she said, poring over the accounts sheet for the last financial quarter. She had been distracted. Her husband had come back from the dead — didn't she have the right to be? She couldn't tell that to Clifton, so instead, she smiled and said in a falsely cheerful voice, "I'm doing just great." She noticed the flicker of doubt in his eyes.

But he was right to doubt, wasn't he? She had gone completely bonkers.

Jason soothed away her anguish, then, lifting her in his arms, carried her up to their room. If she had any doubt that he was a bizarre trick of the imagination or a strange waking dream, he demonstrated through lovemaking that he was not. He had not changed at all. As he laid her down on the bed, undoing the buttons of her blouse and kissing the spot above her navel, she closed her eyes, feeling an ease of familiarity with which he caressed her. Her body stiffened first with resistance, her mind still unable to absorb this new and strange reality. But when his tongue probed the inside of her mouth, and she tasted him, a sourness that was not at all distasteful, but comforting, she realized that this was not a dream, that it was happening. How could her imagination dream up something so physically complete?

Her hands flew to his tie and began unloosening it. She wanted to feel his skin next to hers, hungered for it with an abandonment that made her fingers fumble with the knot. Jason grabbed her wrists and gave her a stern and disapproving look.

"What's wrong?" she asked.

He shook his head and explained that he can never take off the suit.

"Why?" she said, startled, sitting up. "I don't understand."

"I can't ever take it off. Ever."

She wanted to know why not, but when he began kissing her neck, she had forgotten why it mattered. He was there and that was all she cared about.

Each morning, Vanessa woke up with Jason at her side. In the beginning, when she was getting used to having him back, she thought it strange that he was always wearing his suit, which grew increasingly rumpled. Making love to him while fully clothed was also strange, though she quickly grew used to that. She was willing to make any adjustments as long as he was with her.

While she showered and dressed for work, he was downstairs fixing breakfast and singing arias. He did all the chores. Breakfast and dinner were always on the table and the house was clean, the dishes washed, and the bedsheets changed. Well, at least, for the most part. He burned dinner, crusts of food clung stubbornly to the dishes, and the linen was carelessly folded or stained by bleaches, but Vanessa didn't complain.

When he was alive (but isn't he alive now? or is he dead or undead? She wasn't quite sure what to call his peculiar status), he left all the household duties to her. It annoyed her, how the burden of keeping house always fell on her shoulders, though she worked just as hard as he. Now, every evening she returned home to dishes that needed to be rewashed or ruined dinner that had to be thrown out, but she didn't say a word. Every day was like a moment or an hour of her life returned to her.

Her colleagues must have noticed the change that came over her. Before Jason's return, they frequently asked how she was doing. Her boss had even offered to let her take a brief sabbatical to mourn in peace, though what Vanessa took from the offer was that her boss and her colleagues were uncomfortable with the depth of her grief. Of course, she realized they wanted not to be reminded of death, theirs, and everyone else's. But now that Jason had returned to her, they no longer avoided her or watched her with pitiful and uncomfortable gazes. Clifton had even remarked that she seemed to be glowing.

"I am?" she said, touching her face.

He probed her eyes closely, then nodded. "In fact, you look like you're a lady in love." He smiled with the confidence of a man who believed he was the source of this newfound glow.

When she arrived home in the evening, rescuing a roast in the oven from being charred, she smiled sweetly at her husband and bought take-home Chinese. After dinner, she went over some work she brought home from the office while he sang an aria from *La Traviata*. She sighed as his voice embraced her with its tremulous warmth.

Vanessa embraced the strangeness of her new situation. Undisturbed by the outside world, her day was complete each evening she returned home. With practice, Jason became a better cook. One night she returned after a particularly jarring day to find the steak broiled exactly as she liked it, medium rare with grilled onions on top. He had a glass of Scotch waiting for her and encouraged her to tell him about her day. Sometimes he rubbed her feet.

As perfect as her life became, Vanessa could not look past the suit. With each passing day, it grew more rumpled and frayed. There were stains on the shirt from cooking and lovemaking. Threads unraveled along the cuffs and the pockets. It stank. One Saturday, after he made her blueberry pancakes, she insisted on washing it.

"Sorry. No deal."

"Jason, it's starting to smell rank."

"Don't question a good thing," he said quite seriously, then kissed her on the lips.

As the weeks passed, Vanessa divided her time between the real world and the life she was rebuilding with Jason. Work occupied most of her time. Once her colleagues encouraged her to go out to lunch with them. As they ate club sandwiches and drank sodas at a nearby deli, she laughed and enjoyed herself far more freely than she had in months. She had attributed this to the fact that Jason was back in her life, but when she returned home later that afternoon and found him there, cooking for her and singing his arias, she became unsettled.

Something was wrong, though she wasn't quite sure what. While he cooked, she stared at him closely. His face was changing. It was shiny and soft, malleable even, like putty. The pores were more visible, dark freckles stippling across his cheeks and forehead. When he noticed her staring at him and asked why, she replied: "No reason," and then frowned.

One day, Vanessa's mother called and invited her to brunch the next Saturday. She looked forward to spending time outside the house, though she felt bad that Jason could not join her. He looked disappointed when she told him about the date. His eyes drooped as if they were about to fall down the length of his cheeks. She promised she wouldn't be long.

It was a warm day and a breeze blew in off the ocean. She and her mother drank tea and ate Cobb salad at an outdoor cafe. Vanessa felt more relaxed than she had felt in days. Her mother took note of this and said she was glad that she was no longer grieving. It was time for her to move on, she said. Vanessa sipped her iced tea through a straw and noticed Clifton approaching their table. They both gasped with recognition and surprise.

"Funny running into you," he said, smiling warmly as he glanced at Vanessa and then at her mother. Vanessa introduced them. "Now I see where Vanessa gets her good looks."

Vanessa's mother raised an eyebrow and smiled. "For that, you deserve a seat at our table."

"Don't mind if I do," he said and pulled out a chair.

They talked about her mother and Clifton mostly, work, and Vanessa. It was obvious that Clifton was trying to win her mother's favor, a vain attempt to gain an ally. More amused than upset, Vanessa sipped her tea and occasionally joined in their conversation.

After a half hour passed, Clifton glanced at his watch and announced he had to leave; he was meeting a friend downtown. Rising, he said goodbye to Vanessa's mother, then, glancing at Vanessa, said it was nice running into her. "It's a nice departure, outside of work, I mean."

"Maybe the both of you should try it more often," said Vanessa's mother.

Vanessa glared at her, stunned by her forwardness, but Clifton laughed and said, "Maybe." He smiled confidently, then turned and left.

"What was that all about?" Vanessa said, her voice sputtering. "He's my colleague."

"He's attracted to you. That's obvious enough. Or have you forgotten what that even looks like? Vanessa, baby, you've been out of commission too long."

"It's only been a year," she said, stabbing a half-eaten boiled egg with her fork. "And besides, I don't want to give him any ideas."

"Why not? You can't go around with your 'merry widow' act forever, Vanessa."

Vanessa gasped, then glared down at the salad. Her wedding ring, which she had never removed, glinted softly in the sunlight. She realized that she hadn't thought of Jason that entire time.

Jason was changing. His face was softer, blurrier. He was shrinking, or perhaps it was the suit that was growing in size. One evening, over dinner, he even seemed transparent in the candlelight. She stared at him across the table, frowning and blinking as though she was emerging from a dream.

Jason told her she was changing. She dropped her mouth in surprise.

"I am?" she said. He nodded. She asked how.

"I don't know. Maybe you don't love me anymore."

"I've never stopped loving you," she said, leaning against the table.

Jason smiled. His mouth stretched across his face, bearing enormous, white teeth. He got up and took her hand and began kissing her fingers. His lips felt rubbery.

They went upstairs and made love. After he fell asleep, she stayed awake, listening to the wind harass the trees and bushes outside. A terrible feeling came over her, and she could not quite identify what it was. It wasn't gloom or depression or sadness, but an uncanny feeling.

During a meeting at work, she tried to stay focused, but her thoughts wandered. She glanced out of the large windows in the conference room. Sailboats crowded the bay and fog obscured the top of the Transamerican Pyramid. She wondered what Jason did all day when she was at work. She wondered if he even existed at all when she was not home.

She worked late for the next three days. When she returned home at night, it was to a house that had grown fuzzier around the edges. Every time she walked through the front door, she felt like she was stepping into a dream. Jason still greeted her with the Scotch and water and the fine meal, but he seemed less enthusiastic. He stared at her while she ate. She asked him not to do that. "And besides," she said, gazing into his elastic features, "You really should eat something. You're ..." she was about to say that he was wasting away, but that seemed too ironically true. He was wasting away.

He blinked his large, sad eyes at her, but said nothing.

The next morning, Vanessa woke to a shock. Jason had changed dramatically. He was literally melting. His skin dripped down the side of his face and fell in large clumps along the hem of his frayed shirt collar. Though he was still thin, his body was losing shape. It was wobbly like Jell-O. When she saw him in the kitchen cooking, she screamed and clamped her hands to her mouth.

"What's wrong?" he said. His voice sounded broken and slurred, like a tape recorder played at the wrong speed.

When he tried to kiss her, she recoiled. A shocked, hurt look flashed in his eyes. She excused herself by saying she was late for work. He tried to get her to eat. He had made eggs Florentine and it looked and smelled delicious. But she could barely look at Jason. She fled the house.

At the office, Vanessa plunged into her work to distract herself from her troubles at home. She had reports to read and write. She was already backed up. A stack of data was piled on one end of the desk. She told her secretary to hold all her calls and kept the door closed. She remained there long after office hours. Most of the office workers had left and only the night janitors were in the building. The muffled hum of a vacuum cleaner drifted through the door.

When she couldn't use work to avoid the obvious anymore, she grabbed her coat and purse, turned off the desk lamp, and left her office. As she walked down the corridor, she noticed light pouring out of Clifton's door. She knocked and entered. He glanced up at her at his desk and smiled.

"Working late?" she said.

He laughed. "Not the only one, I see."

She shrugged. He asked if she was leaving. When she affirmed that she was, he asked if she was headed home. She considered this question for a few seconds, then breathed deeply. Before she answered, he rose, pulled his jacket from the back of his chair, and approached her.

"Let's go for drinks. God knows, I could use one now."

She let him take her arm and lead her toward the elevators, grateful that he offered her a chance to avoid home.

The bar was a block from their office building. It was small, darkly lit, and loud. Clifton found a spot near the back and ordered drinks from the bar. When he returned, he gave her a drink and a napkin. She thanked him. They began talking, mostly about work at first, quarterly projections, and regional performances, but eventually eased onto more personal matters.

Clifton complained about the dating scene, and how hard it was to find the right woman, offering his suggestion that modern life made it difficult to find an "old-fashioned romance." He was ladling it on thick, and under any other circumstance, she would have cut him short. But that night, she relaxed under the steady flow of his voice, nodding and occasionally sipping her drink. She hadn't been in the dating scene for a long time, but she understood what he was going through.

"It'll happen, give it time. She'll come around and you won't even remember what life was like before you met her."

"Sort of like with you and Jason, I guess."

"Yes," she said, lowering her eyes, frowning. She had forgotten what her life had been like before Jason. She never imagined that she'd have to face life again without him, but at the very least, when she was single, she wasn't lost without the knowledge of having known him. She was struck by the irony that in some ways she missed those years before Jason when she was free not to miss what she didn't have. She thought of the altar she had arranged on her living room mantle and winced. It seemed like such a long time ago now.

"I'm sorry," he said. "Seems I brought up sad memories."

"No. It's all right. Listen," she began, setting down her glass, and was about to continue when something at the front of the bar caught her attention. A group of young people had sauntered in, their voices rising above the babel of ambient noise, and strolled over to the crowded bar. Behind them, something or someone flashed like lightning in front of the entrance. It happened quickly before her eyes could decipher what it was, but, like the clap of thunder right after a strike, she heard Jason's voice calling her name in her head. It was so clear and distinct that she glanced at the entrance again, expecting to see him there.

She started to rise and, in so doing, knocked over her glass. Clifton reached for the napkins to sop up the spilled drink. Vanessa grabbed her purse and started to leave. She had reached the entrance when Clifton grabbed her arm.

"Hey, what's up? Where're you going?"

"I have to go," she said, struggling out of his grip.

"Let me walk you ..."

"No. Please, I have to go."

She rushed out into the cool, fog-draped night, leaving the noisy bar behind her.

The house was dark when she returned home. Jason always had the lights on. She felt that, in some way, he was keeping the hearth burning. The warmth drew her in time and again. But now the shadows had returned, and she felt nothing but apprehension.

Her hand trembling, she unlocked the front door and stepped inside. She turned on the lights and gasped. The entire living room was in disarray. The books from the shelves were scattered on the floor and the broken shards of lamps and vases lay everywhere. A tremendous boom shook the air and rattled the walls like an earthquake, knocking down paintings and framed photographs. Her heart pounding, Vanessa ran to the kitchen where, just as she expected, Jason waited.

He had deteriorated significantly. His arms dangled at his sides like sticks of melted cheese, his hands dissolving on the floor. His face was globular now, one side sinking into his shirt collar. Vanessa cried out and clapped her hands to her mouth.

"You said you loved me," he said. There was another boom that rattled the kitchen so violently Vanessa nearly lost her balance. The oven door flew open and out burst a gush of hot air.

"You said you loved me," he repeated in that strange, mechanical voice. He started to walk toward her, attempting to lift his elongated arms, only to have them melt back toward the floor.

Vanessa screamed and ran out of the house.

She had been driving for a long time, sobbing and unaware of where she was going or what she was doing. When she reached San Bruno, she pulled of the highway and stopped at the first motel she saw. She checked in. As the clerk handed her the key, he gave her a strange, concerned look and asked if she was all right. She stared at him as if he were a strange thing that had dropped from the ceiling in front of her. Frowning, she went to her room. She stepped into the bathroom, and saw her image in the mirror. Was it any wonder the clerk looked at her that way? Her eyes were red and her face was caked and ashy with mascara and dried tears.

After washing her face, Vanessa went back to the other room and tried to rest, but she couldn't get any sleep. The lamp on the nightstand flicked on and off, the television turned on, its volume so loud that the occupant in the next room banged on the wall. She tried to turn off the set with the remote, but it was hopeless.

"Damn you, Jason!" she said, throwing the remote at the set. The screen went black. The lamp stopped blinking.

Dropping her face in her hands, Vanessa cried again. She wept as she hadn't wept since she heard that her husband was dead. She recalled with renewed fury the day her whole world collapsed. She was still at the office when two inspectors from the police department arrived and asked to speak with her alone. She was overcome with nausea even before she heard them say those impossible words, collapsing to her knees and letting out a howl that circled the entire office building, attracting the attention of her secretary and the office workers who crowded her door. For weeks afterward, she saw in their eyes what she imagined they saw that day: a woman in desperation.

She stretched out on the bed and cried well through the night.

When the sun rose, casting its pinkish glow through the motel windows, Vanessa had long dried her tears. She knew what she now had to do.

She checked out of the motel and drove back home. The squat Victorian looked fresh and new in the morning sunlight. It looked as if nothing unusual had taken place there. But the house inside told an entirely different story. It was just as she had left it the night before when she fled, everything torn and flung and rent asunder. There was a strange, musty odor in the air as if she had entered a long-enclosed tomb.

She called for Jason. He wasn't in the kitchen. She went upstairs to the bedroom and found him there. He sat on the edge of the bed, a glutinous mass of dark skin shaped only by the dark blue suit holding some semblance of physical form. His face had changed even more dramatically. One eye had fallen down his cheek. His lower lip draped the front of his stained shirt. The crown of his head had sunken in.

He tried to stand, but collapsed instead onto the mattress in a gelatinous clump of flesh. He grinned sheepishly. "I'm not myself today." His voice was even more distorted.

Vanessa shook her head as tears coursed down her face. "I'm sorry."

"About what?" she said cautiously.

"About last night. The mess I made. I was afraid I lost you."

She hugged her arms. "You haven't lost me."

He looked relieved, though his face collapsed into the blob. His eyes bulged like the lids of teapots.

"You don't belong here."

"Don't say that. I love you."

"I loved Jason," she said. "You're not Jason."

"Yes. I am." His voice slurred, becoming almost incomprehensible. His body roiled. Boils broke out all over it, popping with loud, gassy farts. He tried to rise again, his flaccid arms reaching toward her, but he lost his strength and fell back onto the bed.

"No," she said with more certainty. She reminded him of the Jason she knew. The man who taught her how to live, with arias and walks in the rain and lazy afternoons spent doing nothing but making love. "I have to let you go."

Jason looked at her. His face stretched obscenely into a grin. His grin and his gaze were sad, as though he knew what was about to happen and had resigned himself to it.

Vanessa leaned her head against the door frame. She was still for a very long time before she went to him.

"I'm sorry," she said.

"I know," he said.

"I love you," she said.

His lips moved, but all that came out were strange, gurgling sounds.

More tears fell as she undid the tie and removed the coat. There was an unmistakable odor of dirt and decay. Jason glanced up at her, her teardrops plunking into his fish eyes. She began unbuttoning the shirt and removed that, then unbuckled the belt, unbuttoned and unzipped the pants, and slid them down his flabby legs.

As she removed each item of clothing, he melted even more, so that he began folding in on himself into a jellied mass.

The mass slid off the side of the bed and oozed to the floor where it melted into the carpet and disappeared. All that remained was the tattered, dark blue suit. As Vanessa pressed it to her face, she detected the unmistakable, musky odor of her husband's old cologne.

BREATHE

JON HANSEN

I BREATHE IN THE NIGHT, its darkness running warm into my blood, then I breathe out the day. Its light is cold, biting my skin as it grows. There is no place to hide in it. Then, when the darkness is all gone, I sit back and rattle my chains. The silver links chime like bells, the sound echoing in my cell. The sound pleases me, but I'm always careful not to rattle them by accident.

If they came and found that the night still remained, they might not return.

Soon I can hear them approaching, feet shuffling in the hallway. The three great locks tumble open, one by one, and then my cell door opens to reveal the Mountain King. His eyes squint a little at the day I have made, before focusing on me.

"Your chains displease you?" he says. His tone is grave, polite, as if asking after my health.

"No more than usual," I answer.

He steps forward, lifting his feet so as not to disturb the day. "I would have them replaced with gold, if I could. You are worthy of it, but they would not hold you." Our talk is always the same. It was once a game we played, and now has become no more than a ritual, phrases asked and answered.

"The silver honors me sufficiently," I assure him, and he nods. Then in troop his men, the gatherers of the day. They carry bags woven from golden mesh and shovels with blades plated with gold. With swift precision they wield their tools, shoveling the day into the bags to be carried out into the kingdom under the mountain (or so I am told!) to provide the realm with light. As they work it grows darker in my cell. Their shovels move faster and faster, slicing through the thinning light. I can see nervousness start to pass among them, jumping from man to man. Still, they work on, unwilling to pass on the least morsel of the day.

They have reason to fear, of course. A moment, a flick of my hand, and I could seize an arm or a leg or a neck. Then I could see what darkness lurked in their meat.

But I do not. If they feared me too much, then the king might refuse to carry out the day. I would have to lie here among it, chained into place, unable to escape, forced to wallow in the cold light I had created until the end of all things.

For a moment I feel a tickling, as if I am watched by someone. I look up but see only the Mountain King watching me. His gaze is familiar to me as the stones in my cell; this was strange and unfamiliar, this regard. But the gatherers are tending to the corners, claiming the last sweepings of light. Perhaps I dreamed it.

As the last bag closes, the night has returned to my cell. The door opens and I hear them hurry out. The Mountain King's voice sounds different in the dark: "We thank you, as always."

How assured he sounded when first my cell opened! How afraid he now sounds! The texture of his fear ripples over me, its terror and uncertainty hot in my mouth. I smile unseen in the dark. The cell door closes and the three locks tumble shut, roaring like trumpets.

I sit back and breathe in the night once more.

•   •   •

Eventually I come to the end of the night. I rattle my chains and wait.

And wait.

And wait.

I wait so long that I am forced to rattle them again, my pleasure at doing so marred by my curiosity. What could keep them? I have resolved to rattle them once more when their footsteps start in the hall. But when the locks tumble open and the door swings wide, the Mountain King does not stand there. It is another. While I have never made a close study of their kind, I am certain I have not seen this one before. He is much younger, I think, less confident. He could be carved from fear.

He steps forward, all trembling uncertainty. "The king is ill," he says in a quaver.

At first, I say nothing. The king is my captor, not my friend. But I am anxious to have the day removed and he seems to expect something, so I nod. "How unfortunate," then nothing more.

It seems to be enough, for he gestures back into the hall. In a moment the gatherers of the day are at work. The uncertainty of the king's condition seems to affect them as well; their work is hasty, clumsy. One gatherer in particular, rather than starting near me when the day is strongest, instead begins at a distance. As the day is gathered from elsewhere in the cell, he is forced nearer and nearer to me to recover more and more of the light.

Now I can smell him in the growing darkness, his scent strong as it mingles with the twilight. It is intoxicating. As he works my thoughts stray: if I reached for him, would he see? As my fingers wrapped around him, would he scream? And most of all, what darkness flavors his flesh?

It is too much. I shift and the chiming of my chains fills the cell.

As one, the gatherers whirl towards me, fear in every face. Then, with great haste they seize their tools and flee. They are like shadows vanishing. A little of the day remains, collected in the cracks. As the substitute for their king begins to close the door, I can see the gatherer whose scent still fills my nostrils. He is staring back at me and is still there when the door slams shut.

I smell him still as I breathe.

• • •

Things go better for them next time. The king remains ill, but they are coming to grips with it. The fear running through them is bound, no more than an undercurrent flavoring the air. It does not interfere with their work. Only ...

Only the little gatherer, who tempted me so. I would have expected him to keep far away, clearing out a distant corner. But no. He is shoveling beside my chains again, and his scent is as strong as ever. It is like a strange flower blossoming in a cave, rich and ambrosial.

As the light disappears into the golden bags, I stare at him. He feels my gaze and looks up. A little smile tugs at my lips, but nothing more. To my surprise I think I see him smile back, but the warm darkness lies too thick to be certain.

I hear them scuttle out, and I find myself unable to look towards the door. My hope that he might be there watching is outweighed by the fear he might not.

This time the slam of the door shakes me as never before, each lock's turning a silver spike pinning me in place. All I can do is breathe, in and out, in and out.

• • •

Before the darkness is half gone, I hear footsteps in the hall. Not the tramp of many, but the quiet pace of one. The door swings wide and in steps a figure carrying a long torch; its flame flickers, as though caught by a strong breeze.

The figure stops before me but says nothing. Only stares at me in my chains. I cannot make out the face in the shadow of torchlight. But I breathe in, and the scent fills me. It is him: the gatherer from before, the one who smiled at me, the one whose nervousness had filled me with such elation.

My heart pounds in my chest as I look at him. "Who are you?" I ask.

He hesitates, and when he speaks, his voice is thin, youthful. "My name is Elan."

"Elan. Why have you come?"

"I wanted to see you again, alone. Without the others."

"Why? To gawk at the thing in chains?"

He shakes his head with vehemence. "No." The single word is almost a shout, rebounding in the cell as if it hoped to free itself. It dies away, finally, the silence holding us before he continues. "The king is dying." His words are softer now. "There has been talk about what to do with you among the court."

I blink. The king is the only one I have spoken to in so many, many years. For this I feel something for him, although it may be no more than familiarity. The other matter concerns me more. "And what have they decided?"

"Many of us," he includes himself with a gesture, "feel you should be released. The summoning that brought you here should be broken, to allow you to return home."

My home? I have been here for so long that I no longer remember it. I have only memories of being pulled from it. Cold green fire wrapped me, clawed my skin, before it cast me into the warm darkness. Strange faces stared down at me, silver chains locked around my wrists and ankles. I blink. Elan is still speaking.

"But the king's sons have decided that you will stay, locked in this cell and bound by chains." Elan hangs his head and when he raises it, silvery lines glitter on his cheeks. "The thought of it fills me with shame. That our people would do this to one as beautiful as you."

I shake my head. "I am not what you think me."

"No," Elan said. "You bring us the day. You are no monster."

He bends, setting the torch on the floor. "I searched long but could not find the key to your chains."

"There is no key," I say, but he does not hear me.

From beneath his cloak he pulls a short axe. "I will free you." The blade glitters in the torchlight as he raises it up, then down.

The first blow cuts the link with ease. As it snaps I gasp. A pressure from my mind lifts, one I had felt for so long I had half-forgotten it. My blood surges. "Again!" I say.

He swings again, and again, and again, then drops the axe. I rise up. Sensations flood me, a thousand memories forgotten, a thousand urges returned.

"Now you are free," says Elan, and I look down at him.

"Now I am free," I say, and stretch out my hand. My fingers caress his cheek, and although I can feel that he loves me, he fears me as well, this thing he has freed but does not truly understand. "You have my thanks," I say.

His voice squeaks even higher. "Will you depart?"

"Eventually," I say, and crush him to my chest.

Though his scent is the strongest I can remember, I do not taste his flesh. He is fragile, too fragile to endure such. And he has stirred other feelings inside me, long denied: desire and need. Those I cannot repress. He struggles, to no avail.

When I am spent, the torch has all but burned out. No matter. The day has grown stronger in the cell, although it is still only half finished. I cover Elan's trembling form with his cloak and stride out into the kingdom under the mountain, laughing as I go.

The people flee as I walk their paths, but some run slower than others. Each one I catch is filled with darkness, making them as a full wineskin, and I drink them down. With each one the daylight grows from me until I blaze like an inferno, light falling behind me in trails.

In the throne room I catch two of the old king's sons. The last, the new king, I trail deep beneath the kingdom to the quiet halls of dust where they lay their dead. He cowers behind his father's bier, and I devour him down to his anklebones. I do not partake of his father. His time has passed, and with it his flavor.

When I emerge, the kingdom lies deserted. Through the halls I search, seeking stragglers. I find none, only shadows.

For, to my surprise, the daylight is already beginning to fail. So soon? Did I tarry so long in the crypts? Confused, I follow the warm darkness, tracking it to its source, until I stand once more in my cell.

Elan still remains. At my appearance he flinches, pulling his cloak tighter in hopes of some protection. Something about him has changed. I gaze at him, curious, and then I see.

He, he is the source of the darkness. It spills from him with his every breath, filling the room. I laugh with delight. Had I done this to him? Or was it always within him, the cause of his strange pull to me? No matter. He is all that I need, all I desire, and the beauty it gives him draws me like a tide.

"You will stay with me," I say. "Always and forever. Always." The thought of it intoxicates me, and I shudder with pleasure.

Elan shivers. His left eye leaks a tear, a fragile diamond on his pale cheek. I reach out with a finger and capture it, bring it to my mouth. It is sweet beyond compare. "No," Elan whispers, shaking his beautiful head.

"Yes."

"No!" he screams. In a breath he is gone, footsteps fading in the hall. I follow.

Through the kingdom we race, him leading and I following, through galleries and passages and grottos. Twice I come across other strays, and twice I pause to taste before casting them aside. They do not satisfy.

I lose sight of Elan, but it matters not. His darkness cannot be denied, cannot be lost. Elan, Elan, Elan. He is all I can think of.

I track him into a great hall lined with towering statues, figures of grim majesty. His trail leads to a small door set in a corner. I enter and catch sight of him racing up a long tunnel. Darkness spills back down towards me, lapping at my feet in waves.

I follow to find him struggling with a latch. His face turns toward me at my approach. His terror is delicious. With desperate fury he throws himself against the door, trying to open it. I have almost reached him when it flies open and he disappears. I step through and catch my breath in wonder.

I am outside the kingdom, standing on what can only be the mountainside. Air rushes past me, clutching me. It is filled with scents unknown. I can see far, farther than I would have believed. I look down at a vast emptiness before me, set in shadowy twilight. At the bottom of it lies a great forest, ringed on one side by a great rolling darkness that can only be the sea. The air is cold but intoxicating. That I might not have ever have laid eyes upon this, had not Elan freed me.

The memory of his name electrifies me. I turn to see him running along the mountainside, burning like a silvery flame set in the night. He is crying, crying, crying.

I open my mouth to call to him but it is too late. He leaps out into the air. I race to him, afraid to watch him fall, but instead the darkness supports him. It spreads behind him like a cloud and I watch with longing and desire as he races away across the sky. Diamond tears fall from his eyes, each catching in the darkness to hang, marking a glittering path.

Breathe in the night, breathe out the day. I leap after him.

THE CLOCKWORK OCTOPUS AND A LETTER TO QUEEN VICTORIA

BRANDON CASE

I HUDDLED IN AN EMERGENCY TENT somewhere south of Balmoral Castle in the Scottish Highlands. Curled on my side amidst the frozen grass, I felt like a featureless egg in some forgotten nest left to the ravages of winter. My army-issued canvas blanket flapped above me, strung up on poles to block the blizzard's white wind. Nevertheless, gusts of snow burst through the flaps, stinging my exposed cheeks. Were the flakes still melting, or did the ice crystallize on my freezing skin? Until I checked, both realities would exist. I hated such indeterminate states, my too-many genitals making me one in society's view. Untucking a hand from my uniform, I reached up to my cheek. Still supple, the skin smooth minus wispy patches of stubble that'd never filled in: a beard that was not a beard, ever the source of mockery now I'd passed my thirtieth birthday.

I won't last in this blizzard. It was a hollow thought. Unfulfilled. An echo of me; this vacuum of potential. But what would happen to the letter I'd been dispatched to carry north to Balmoral? If I was doomed to die this night, I should write once more in my diary, so a future person could take up the duty from my frozen corpse.

With trembling hands, I dipped my freezing pen into its brass inkwell.

November 2nd, 1863

Storm impassible. Lost road south of Balmoral. Carry enclosed letter from Colonel Norcott to our Queen in greatest haste.

Lance Corporal Cecil Dryden

There. A record of my mission would pass into the future. I wouldn't ... which was fine — the future had always felt hostile to oddities like me.

Shoving my freezing hands into my red coat, I winced as they warmed. My makeshift tent shook and let in another burst of snow. I piled my backpack and gear over my torso, attempting to stave off the bitter wind. The light faded, leaving me in howling darkness. Winds like a pack of jubilant demons trying to get inside, to gawk at me, to pat my chest and groin in a vain attempt to classify my body. It was almost as bad as being in the city. My eyes closed, and I drifted into a black stupor.

But something changed.

Warmth bloomed in the air; the blizzard's shriek disappeared; brilliant light glowed through the gaps in my makeshift tent.

I jerked upright. My backpack and toolkit tumbled to the ground, and I called, "Hello?"

"Come out!" A man's voice, loud in the silence. "I want to chat."

"... God?"

"You're suffering hypothermia, not delusions. Come out of the tent!"

Woodenly, I crawled into the light. A sphere of perfect calm surrounded my tent, although snow raged in the darkness beyond. Stranger still, a wide hole pierced the air between two Scots Pines. Light and heat poured through the portal like ambrosia. My eyes adjusted, focusing. A man, leaning against a balcony. Behind him, glass buildings rose into a sky filled with elegant airships.

Weird! But beautiful and delightfully warm.

"My name's Ephraim," the man said. "Hurry, come closer. I'm not allowed to cross into your world, and we have little time." He was short, slim, and wore a long brown coat. His brass-colored cane seemed entirely nonfunctional, flexing whenever he put weight on it. The stitching and material of his outfit were poorly crafted, as though he'd fashioned them himself with little care. He ate cookies from a shiny bag. A cascade of crumbs dropped down his front.

The sweet smell made me salivate; I hadn't eaten in days.

Beside Ephraim was a brass octopus the size of a cat, wearing glass goggles and a top hat; the creature looked terribly frightened, scuttling nervously on its exquisitely crafted clockwork tentacles.

Amazing. I'd seen automatons, but nothing so lifelike. The two made an odd pair, with the octopus' sophisticated craftsmanship far outclassing the man. I said, "What do you want?"

"To save your life. We found your diary. You die tomorrow morning, unable to locate Balmoral and deliver your letter in the blizzard."

Creepy... but as plausible as a hole opening in the air, I supposed. Was I hallucinating?

The octopus anxiously twisted its tentacles and peered through the gateway — careful not to touch Ephraim. It noticed me watching, eyes going wide, the intricate brass irises expanding behind its goggles. It scurried out of view behind Ephraim, dragging one of its tentacles, which didn't curl properly.

"That's just Merriweather," Ephraim said, following my gaze. He kicked the octopus away. "Pay him no mind. Useless thing. We have important matters to discuss. I'm saving your life, remember?"

'Ephraim' seemed as much an affectation as his strange clothes. I decided to call him *Ephr*, the phonetics of which gave me a bitter chuckle. He claimed I'd die tomorrow morning ... "You're from the future?"

He laughed and popped another cookie into his mouth. "In the simplest sense. But you wouldn't recognize the planet I'm on. And the Hohmann timewell will close in less than a minute. I need to inject this syringe of Cry4 cryptochrome protein and nanites into your eyes."

Was he speaking English? And *inject what into my eyes?* I took a step back.

"None of that! The letter you carry is of utmost importance. You'll fail to deliver it without my aid, leaving an indelible mark on the future. War. Famine. Apocalypse."

Behind him, a young couple embraced on the deck of an airship. The scene didn't look very apocalyptic. However, I did believe the blizzard was only temporarily held at bay, and I'd likely die without aid. He was concealing something ... but I had very little to lose. I approached within reach of the portal.

Ephr lunged, grabbing my face. He slapped a device like brass opera glasses over my eyes. Two sharp pricks; the whirr of actuators; a strange, turbulent flow inside my eyeballs like they held schools of tiny fish. The metal device pulled away.

I couldn't see. Searing panic surged up my throat like bile. I shoved Ephr away and stumbled back. "What did you do?"

Another cookie crunched in front of me. The rapid *clink, clink, clack* of brass tentacles fluttered nearby. Ephraim said, "By tomorrow, you'll be able to see magnetic fields using quantum entanglement. Like a migrating bird. But it's time to close the portal; the rules of this game are very clear."

My vision slowly returned, revealing his outline against the bright skyline. "Can you give me some food? It'd help me fulfill the mission."

"Sorry, no can do. I'm not allowed to come through or leave behind any technology detectible by your civilization."

Neither of those applies to food, you ratbag.

"Oh!" Ephr called as the portal shrank. "Historical records are unclear whether you were a man or a woman. Now that I'm here ... well, which is it?"

I said nothing.

"Strong, silent type? A man! I was right, although the group will want concrete evidence to settle that side bet. Good luck tomorrow!" His portal winked out.

The blizzard slammed into me, more shockingly cold and dark for the brief reprieve. Scrambling into my makeshift tent, I heaped gear over myself, shivering violently.

Something cold and smooth squirmed against my legs.

I yelped and kicked.

The brass octopus, Merriweather, skittered into the corner, glowing faintly gold in the darkness. His wide eyes were enormously magnified by the goggles. He trembled, curling his clockwork tentacles around himself.

In a small voice, he said, "I'm sorry, but it's terribly cold. I stole you a cookie." He offered a perfectly round disk wafting the tantalizing aromas of cinnamon and sugar. "May I please lay with you?"

He speaks? There was no visible mouth ... the sound seemed to project through pores in his bell-shaped body. "Why are you here?"

"Ephraim isn't a nice man. I know it was against the rules, but ..." Merriweather twisted his tentacles, looking bizarrely guilty for a machine. "Please?"

He did look rather cuddly, with his top hat and cleverly articulated limbs. "You're metal. Why would you be so sensitive to cold?"

"Ephraim replaced my oil with a formula that seizes just a few degrees above human body temperature. It makes me more dependent. One of several alterations he forced upon me."

Forced alterations ... I shuddered and said, "He didn't create you?"

"Goodness, no! My clockwork would neither clock nor work. He installed clumsy limiters after buying me." Merriweather rotated to show his lame tentacle, snarled and useless. "Now I barely limp along."

I looked closer at the brass linkages. A small plate bulged out of place, incorrectly reinstalled. "And you'd prefer to be fixed?"

"Yes, wouldn't you?"

That's certainly what society dictates. Fixed, defined. No ... In my case, fixing involved alteration from my natural state. But I could respect his desire to return to his version of whole.

I accepted Merriweather's cookie — it was absolutely delicious — and grabbed my toolkit. Foremost, I was a tinkerer. I'd invented several devices, including a full-torso corset with mechanical linkages the wearer could operate themselves.

With a nod from Merriweather, I used a set of flat turnscrews to pry up the panel. Underneath lay a wonderfully intricate network of sprockets and rods. Truly beautiful workmanship. In their midst were the tines of a steel fork, crudely jammed into the cogs to stop their rotation.

Ephr, you flapdoodle. I removed the impediment and carefully reassembled the octopuses' brass plates.

"Oh my!" Merriweather flexed his tentacle, smoothly curling and rotating it. "Thank you ever so much!"

I nodded, shivering again, and tugged the backpack and gear over my legs.

Merriweather hopped from tentacle to tentacle. "May I please join you? The brass will be cold at first, but I produce some heat of my own ... just not enough. Beneath a blanket, I'll be like a toasty bed warmer."

Interesting. If he produced heat, it might help us both make it through the night. I unbuttoned my coat. The little octopus squeaked and scuttled over, nestling against my chest. There was just enough loose fabric to close the uniform around Merriweather. And he was right; after a few minutes, he warmed up wonderfully.

"Ephr referred to you by the pronoun '*he*'," I said. "Does that feel right to you?"

"I think I'm a he." Merriweather snuggled close. "In my head, that's what leaping sounds like. 'Heee!' Maybe for others leaping sounds like 'sheee!'"

I'd never been much of a leaper. Especially at the moment ... exhausted and holding an animated brass octopus. But I relaxed; with our combined heat it didn't feel like I was about to die. At least not tonight.

•   •   •

I woke to the sound of grinding gears, just audible beneath the blizzard's howl.

Merriweather trembled against my chest.

"Are you all right?" I asked. Unless I was much mistaken, his rasps were clockwork sniffles.

More grinding. "I'm fine. Just remembering Ephraim. He's a very lonely person. I think he changed my oil so I'd have to cuddle with him for warmth. You're much nicer ... but is it weird for me to miss him?"

"No." In my experience, such conflicted feelings were hardly strange.

I rose to check the weather conditions. Merriweather slid down to my leg, clutching it as I peered through the tent flap. Featureless white extended in every direction, the world hidden behind a veil of swirling snow. The Scots Pines loomed like formless ghosts, little more than outlines in the blank landscape. It was impossible to tell which direction was north. No wonder I'd died trying to reach Balmoral.

Merriweather shivered against my leg. "Can you see the planet's magnetic field yet? Concentrate on the sky, feel for the lines."

The ground and sky were indistinguishable, but I looked up at the vast, white expanse. Something *was* there. My mind slid around it, unable to focus.

"The stimulus is foreign," the octopus said, "and needs to be integrated with the parts of your brain modified by the nanites. Have you seen the aurora borealis? Try picturing that."

I'd seen the northern lights on plenty of occasions. They were abundantly colorful, but pinks and greens didn't feel right today.

From that blank expanse emerged lines of dull gold, the color of Merriweather's brass body, shimmering across the sky like ethereal pipes. They flowed ahead and to the right, northward, where I'd find the Queen to deliver the letter. And perhaps change my fate.

"Release my leg," I said, packing my gear. "I can't march through the snow like this."

"I'll die!" Merriweather said with a small squeak, casting horrified looks at the cold powder. "My oil will freeze, my parts will seize, and it's still too soon ..."

Too soon? To die in the general sense, or was he hinting at Ephraim's hidden plans?

Merriweather trembled and gazed up at me with enormous eyes. There was manipulation in that look, like a cat crying with the voice of a small child. It would reduce my risk to leave this creature who was still bound to Ephr. But he was undeniably alive; I couldn't let him freeze.

I needed my back free to carry the pack, and my limbs had to remain unencumbered to navigate through the brush. That left only one option.

With a sigh, I held Merriweather against my stomach. This would certainly complicate misconceptions about my sex. "Wrap your tentacles around my waist." I disassembled the tent and tied the blanket over my torso, covering the delicate octopus. My pack went on last, securing the canvas sheet. A large bump protruded from my front like a pregnant belly.

Spasmodic grinding rumbled beneath the blanket. In a halting voice, Merriweather said, "You're too good to me. There's so much I wish I could tell you. But a locked tentacle and adulterated oil aren't the only limiters Ephraim shackled me with." The grinding grew louder. "Don't ... Trust ... Bet ... Fake."

"Hush now," I said. Ephr's vazey plots were a secondary concern to dying in the storm. "We'll sort it out in front of Balmoral's hearths."

I plowed through knee-high powder, hunched against the white wind, following the brass lines arcing overhead. Ice crystals bit my face, turning the skin numb. The clockwork octopus warmed my core, and whenever I fell to my knees, certain I couldn't go on, he squeezed my middle, giving me the strength to rise.

A gap opened between the pines, and I stumbled onto a road. For a moment the swirling snow parted, revealing Balmoral's towers beneath the brass lines. I could've wept, but I was far too cold.

Guards met me at the castle's heavy door. They inspected my uniform and papers and passed me on to Mr. Brown.

"Good Lord, man," Mr. Brown exclaimed, leading me down a dark green hallway. "Your belly has gotten out of hand. You look nearly pregnant!"

I said nothing and entered a wonderfully warm study with a roaring hearth. The room was entirely decorated in plaid and smelled of pinewood. A round-faced woman with heavy cheeks sat in a chair, reading. She wore a voluminous black dress, despite being at home. Her shrewd eyes narrowed when she saw me. "You have a letter for me?"

"Yes, Your Majesty," I said. "From Colonel Norcott."

"You are late." She searched my face. "Give us a moment alone, John."

"I will be right outside." He bowed and left.

Why is the Queen giving me a private audience? I'd delivered letters to her before, but it was always a perfunctory experience.

"You are a queer creature," Victoria said, "like a man and woman entangled. But I had my suspicions when we first met. This confirms them. No man fattens at the rate you display. Tell me the truth of your situation, woman to woman."

Everyone claims my gender for their own. "It's nothing so intriguing as pregnancy, ma'am." I carefully dug in my breast pocket, trying to extract the letter without disturbing Merriweather's blanket.

"*TELL THE TRUTH!*" the Queen shouted.

Merriweather let out a squeak and lost his grip. The clockwork octopus slid down my legs, plainly in sight of the queen. Victoria gasped.

"I'm happy to explain," I said. "But please read this letter first, else disastrous consequences shall befall the future."

"N-No!" Merriweather clanged to the floor. His tentacles spasmed like he was having a fit. "Don't ... Letter ... Ephraim ... Fake."

On his underbelly, between the writhing tentacles, I spotted another misaligned brass plate. More evidence of Ephr's tampering. I darted a look at the Queen, who stared at Merriweather, apparently entranced by shock and fascination. Tossing aside the letter, I gathered my toolkit.

I opened the octopus. Inside his bell-shaped body lay a network of whirring cogs, gears, and spindles. At its center was a clear, gelatinous object the size of an egg. Gold vapor swirled inside, flickering with more sparks than there were stars in the night sky. Merriweather's brain. The handle of a steel fork jutted from the delicate structure. *Damn and blast that bloody man!* I gently removed the obstruction and replaced his brass plate.

Merriweather stopped twitching and heaved a sonorous sigh. "What a relief! Thank you ever so much. Ephraim shoved that fork in me, over and over, until he found the spot that broke my free will."

"That's awful," I said.

"What *are* you?" Victoria said.

The octopus scuttled to the fallen letter. "This is a fake. Ephraim forced me to destroy the original letter." He turned to the Queen. "Colonel Norcott advises you to wait out the storm at Balmoral Castle, given you refused to heed his advice and stayed dangerously late in the season."

"That sounds like him." Victoria sniffed. "As if I need to be told to stay out of a blizzard."

With a frown, I said, "The letter I died for was ... pointless?"

Merriweather gently squeezed my ankle with a brass tentacle. "Ephraim's society wagers on bending history in small ways. There are rules. He was only supposed to give you the quantum eyes. They knew the real letter was innocuous. But Ephraim wrote something dangerous in the fake. He commanded me to make the switch, see you to the castle, and bury myself in the snow."

"This clockwork creature is ... from the future," Victoria said. "And you fixed it with your little tools."

I said to Merriweather, "I'm glad you don't have to die in the snow."

"I'm glad you get to live, too!" The octopus hopped from tentacle to tentacle. "I don't know what Ephraim's letter says, but it doesn't have your best interest at heart. I suggest you destroy it unopened."

I'd always hated ambiguity, and it'd be uncomfortable to end my mission on an unknown. But Ephr's description of war and apocalypse replayed in my head. Along with his contempt. Maybe it was important to leave some mysteries intact ... *right* to allow their dualities, my duality, to remain unmolested, mixed, man and woman, neither and both. Warmth bloomed in my chest. "Your Majesty, may we have permission to burn this letter?"

Victoria waved dismissively. "With such mechanical skill, you are wasted as a messenger. Your strange friend has opened my eyes. You *must* work with my scientists to build more clockwork creations."

Merriweather let out a *'heee!'* and leaped into my arms. "That's no small change."

Such technological advancement might make Ephr's future unrecognizable. Or bring it to fruition. But my responsibility was to the present.

I settled Merriweather around my waist, tossed the fake letter into the hearth, and said, "Yes, ma'am," to the Queen.

For the first time, it felt like the future might hold a place for someone as odd as me.

Lena Ng loves to read short stories and one day decided to write them. Because she reads the strange and unusual, she writes about the strange and unusual. She shambles around Toronto, Canada, and is a zombie member of the Horror Writers Association. She has curiosities published in weighty tomes, including *Amazing Stories* and Flame Tree's *Asian Ghost Stories* and *Weird Horror Stories*. Her stories have been performed for podcasts such as *Gallery of Curiosities, Utopia Science Fiction, Love Letters to Poe*, and *Horrifying Tales of Wonder*. "Under an Autumn Moon" is her short story collection.

•   •   •

Of course, this story was inspired by Ray Bradbury's "Something Wicked This Way Comes", as well as his macabre stories in "The October Country". I love his creepy, yet darkly romantic, vision of the small town and the carnival that sweeps in, promising to fulfill dark dreams.

PROFESSOR PANDEMONIUM'S CARNIVAL OF CHAOS

LENA NG

FIRST CAME A DROP in temperature: the warm winds of summer gave way to chill autumn gusts, bringing with it a whiff of distant popcorn and cotton candy which drifted on the heels of shedding leaves.

Then it was the posters, awash in lurid colours of red and yellow: the Human Torso, a man consisting of a head and chest, placed on a cushion like a pearl; the Strong Man, with a long, sharp moustache and bulging biceps; the Webbed Creature from the Deep who carried a barely-clad woman. All kinds of Technicolor monsters leering out from their paper prisons. Posters which were stapled on telephone poles and hung in the windows of the laundromat, behind the bars of the convenience store, on the dingy walls of the vacuum repair shop. The whites of the images' eyes carried a yellow tinge and they seemed to stare at you as you walked past. "Professor Pandemonium's Carnival of Chaos" read the slogan beneath an image of a rabid wolf's outstretched, slavering jaws. "One night only."

Finally, we saw the resurrection of a tent on the outskirts of town: striped in red and white, bigger than a church. It seemed to cast a long shadow.

The carnival had come to town.

I was fifteen at the time, a boy big for my age, but my brain still had a ways to go. On the day of the carnival, I went with my grandfather, a grizzled old man of beard and sinew, and tattooed skin sleeves of skulls and roses. Since it was a gray day of mist and drizzle, no one else wanted to go and he said he'd come along to keep me company.

We gave our tickets to a gaunt man whose face was covered in white make-up. The make-up was so thick, his face looked like a macabre death mask with empty holes for eyes emerging from it. I couldn't help but stare.

Inside the gates, the calliope's music ran slowly, in a jerky manner, like that of a music box winding down. The carnival's games seemed odd and dark. The barkers called to us. "Come here, boy," one called, who was wearing a red-stained shirt, like that of a butcher. He balanced a glass bottle with murky water on his palm, containing a fist-sized, round piece of meat. "Don't you want to win a heart in a jar?"

Another held cages with cane toads that croaked. The man himself had a broad, frog-like face. "Cold-blooded pets," he called. "Step right up for a cold-blooded pet."

We moved past the hawkers selling scorpions on sticks and crickets leashed by a red string. An automaton, which looked like a ventriloquist's dummy wearing a swath of red cloth wrapped around its lacquered wooden head, was encased in glass. It had a sign overhead that said "Truth-teller. Ask your questions." I peered at it through the glass and shrank back as it swivelled on its base and clacked open its jaws.

Finally, I saw a game I was familiar with — target shooting with a BB gun. I fired off three shots, but the balloons, the size of tomatoes with a cartoon devil's face printed on them, remained unpopped.

Grandpa held out his gnarled hand for the gun. "Here, kid. Let me show you how it's done." He aimed the BB gun and shot the blue balloon in the top right corner. Then in quick succession, he shot the green balloon in the top left corner and red balloon dead centre. He handed the gun back to the game operator.

"Grew up on a farm. Learned to shoot an acorn from between a squirrel's paws." He let me pick out a prize. I chose a big, plastic sword with a blue glass jewel in its hilt, as though it were forged by barbarian. I tied it within its sheath to my back.

We made our way through the make-shift rows of the carnival stalls, passing tables of strange curiosities of many limbs and heads. We walked by a poster reading "Madame Le Fou, Palm Reader and Fortune-Teller."

Grandpa gave me a wink. "Let's see what she has to say about you," he said.

I pushed back the red velvet curtain, the fringed tassels dragging on the floor. Madame Le Fou sat at a table which was covered in black linen. She wore heavy make-up with kohl-rimmed eyes and violent, red-stained lips. "What is your name, boy?" she asked.

"Kane," I replied.

The corners of Madame Le Fou's lips turned up and she held out her hand. Grandpa reached into his back pocket and gave her a five-dollar bill. She tucked it into the waistband of her skirt before she gazed into her crystal ball, tracing her scarlet nails over its surface. She furrowed her brow. "Tonight, you will face the challenge of a life-time. You will either learn to meet this challenge ..." the crystal ball magnified further her widened eyes.

"Or what?" I asked in a hushed voice. I saw nothing in the crystal aside from her reflection.

Madame Le Fou looked up at me with a ghost-white face, the candle light illuminating her fear. "Or you will die."

Grandpa snorted. "Let's go," he said, pulling on my arm.

We wandered around the rest of the carnival until we reached the red-and-white striped tent at the center of the fairgrounds. A painting on a wooden easel stood beside the tent's entrance. Like the posters around town, it read "Professor Pandemonium's Carnival of Chaos." The professor's darkly-cast, hypnotic face was in the centre of the painting. He was surrounded by ugly, dog-like demons, jaws bared, with yellow eyes, wormy red veins escaping from their irises.

We took a seat upon the bleachers. People jostled around us to get a seat. I waved to one of our neighbours, Mr. Lawson, who used to work behind the meat counter at the grocery store before his old knee injury flared up and he went on disability. He now walked with a cane. I nodded at couple of kids from school, John and Aaron, nice kids, but we didn't run in the same circles. I didn't run in any circles. I kept to myself and didn't have any close friends.

The lights dimmed. A drum-roll sounded. There was a bang and a puff of smoke and spot-light turned to the centre of the ring where a man appeared from the ether. He was a compact man with a head of gleaming dark hair, his face adorned by a sharply trimmed moustache and goatee. He wore a red double-breasted jacket, black breeches with knee-high riding boots, and a matching black top hat. He looked like the debonair devil himself, holding a coiled leather whip.

The audience went silent. The ring leader opened his arms. "Welcome, everyone, to the Carnival of Chaos. I am your host, Professor Pandemonium." He gave a tight smile that didn't reach his eyes. "Tonight, I will show you the wicked wonders of the world. Tonight, on the autumn equinox, when the night grows longer than the day, when the boundaries of fantasy and reality blur and weaken and break, on this night, lives will lengthen and lives will be lost."

His voice held such command, but I didn't understand all that he had said. The giant belching organ in the right of the tent began to play by itself, no musician at its helm, a melody ominous and menacing.

The music abrupted halted. The Professor reached into his pocket and threw something upon the ground. When the smoke cleared, the Professor stood outside a blue-lit dome which seemed to be made from light and energy. A loud bang and a flash of light, and within the dome, a monster appeared. It must have been a man in a costume, but the costume looked real. It was the size of a rhino, with foot-long spikes down the spine and a heavy, dog-like head with weighty jaws and large, glowing eyes. It growled and pawed at the ground.

The organ began playing again. With each crash of a discordant chord, another explosion, another flash of light, and inside the dome, another monster appeared. A giant, slug-like mass nestled on a tangle of eight, spidery legs. A dragon's head on a snake's body; the flames from its breath licked the dome but remained contained within.

The audience gasped. The Professor held a hand towards these horrific creatures. "These are the monsters of my imagination. Tonight, the boundary into reality will break, and the fantasy will be made real." He said some strange words, a spell perhaps. "*Fantasy ad realitatem.* Arise, my children. *Ab ortu solis usque ad occasum, carpe noctem.*"

My grandfather muttered the translation. "Fantasy to reality. From sunset to sunrise, seize the night."

Above us, the tent flap to the sky was pulled open and the moonlight shone upon the dome. With an electric sizzle, the blue light of the dome sank to the ground, forming a circular outline of light on the floor. The monsters stood before us uncaged.

The dog demon was the first to attack. Bounding into the bleachers, the audience scattered, screaming. Mr. Lawson, cane in hand, arose from the metal bench and stumbled. The dog demon was upon him, jaws clamped around his shoulder, tearing his arm from his body, blood dripping from its massive jaws. It crunched Mr. Lawson's head as though it were an egg before dragging the remains through the portal of blue light in the centre of the floor. Grampa grabbed me and we started running as the flames of the dragon scorched overhead, setting the striped tent on fire.

My chest ached as we sprinted down the aisles which had, in the dark, turned into a maze. The wooden truth-teller turned and clacked its jaws as we raced past. Its turban was the same colour as the flames. A look came over Grandpa's face and he turned to face the automaton. "Why is this happening?"

The automaton's eyes lit up. It said in a melodious, mechanical voice, "The Professor has sold his soul to live forever. But he must pay a price. One year for one life. The monsters drag the souls to hell, and for each, the professor gets another year on earth." The eyes went dark.

Grandpa banged on the glass. "Well, how can we defeat them?"

The automaton's eyes lit up and it clacked his jaws. "By turning fantasy into reality."

"What? How?" screamed my grandfather, but a flame shot out and the glass case holding the automaton exploded. The truth-teller was set on fire.

We ran through the carnival stalls, each one along our path going up in flames as the dragon monster pursued us. Screams seemed to surround us as we dashed past the target shooting game. Grandpa yanked me to a stop.

"Hold on a minute," he said. "The night when fantasy will be made real." He grabbed a BB gun. "Let's try it out." He concentrated for a moment, trying to remember the words *"Fantasy ad realitatem."* The gun seemed to grow heavier in his hands, and the BBs that he had held clenched in his fist, when he opened his hand, had turned into bullets.

I pulled out the plastic sword from its sheath, still carried on my back. Grandpa repeated the words, *"Fantasy ad realitatem."* The plastic blade gleamed into sharpened steel. It grew heavy in my hands and I awkwardly tried to hold it in a way where it would cut my opponent instead of myself.

A flash of flame as the dragon monster slithered closer. Grandpa turned and shot off two bullets in quick succession. Two small glints of light as the bullets ricocheted off the armoured scales. I held the blade and hacked at the dragon's

242

tail. Grandpa grabbed me by the neck of my t-shirt as the flame shot towards me. He dragged me under a table. I held the sword close to my chest.

As the dragon monster screeched, Grandpa put a hand on my shoulder. *"Fantasy ad realitatem,"* he said. My veins felt like they were set on fire. We got out from under the table and I held out the sword, the blue from the jewel's hilt glowing in the night air. The awkward weight of the sword turned familiar, as though it were a steely extension of my arm. Amazed, I spun the sword first with my right hand, then with my left, the edge of the blade reflecting the moonlight.

I held the sword in front of me as the flame bore down. The dragon's fire split into two, deflecting it away from me. It attacked, baring its teeth with outstretched jaws. I lunged, and with both hands around the hilt, plunged the sword upward through the top of the dragon's open mouth. With a last, blistering groan, the dragon fell heavily upon its side.

The rays of the distant dawn released tendrils of light throughout the carnival. The dragon's body started sizzling when touched by the light. It disappeared into cinders. We raced back to the remains of the striped tent.

Again, I held out the sword. I felt the white-hot hatred of Professor Pandemonium's glare as he leapt through blue portal in the floor. His two remaining monsters followed, squeezing through the shrinking portal, each dragging with it a twisted and broken body. The portal disappeared as the sunlight grew stronger. The sword grew lighter in my hands as it turned back into a toy.

Thirteen souls were lost that night. Thirteen years on earth gained, stretching longer that life that was based on blood, on innocent souls. Now, thirteen years have gusted by, and the autumn winds are gathering again. I can smell the carnival in the distance. The powers of the blade, they lasted for only that one night. But since then I've trained with the best fencers and swordsmen and sharp shooters in the country. When the lurid posters go back up and carnival comes back to town ...

I know the words.
I'll be armed.
I'll be ready.
This time, he won't escape.

A WALK IN THE GARDEN

ALEXANDER HAY

T HE AIR STANK OF OZONE and overripe fruit as the fireball consumed its target. Grunting in pain, the wizard — Ashford — grit his teeth and hunched his shoulders as another seething mass of energy gathered in his hands. Yet more corrupted dryads and Garden spirits tore their way through the trees and once neatly trimmed thickets.

With a snarl, the wizard threw the energy from his hands into the midst of the mob. This time, it exploded, tearing through their number in a blinding flash of mauve rage. The wizard, through the pain and the fatigue, couldn't help but feel a small jolt of pride at this point. Knowing when to raise or lower the power of the blast took no small amount of skill. He even smiled a little. Yes, he was good at this …

The blast cut down many of the creatures, but a number managed to avoid it or somehow stumble onwards despite terrible wounds.

"Oh, if you must ..." Ashford sneered, sarcasm dripping from his voice. He drew the gnarled wooden blade from his belt and charged forward to meet them, blotting out the pain within his stomach.

The things screamed as they fell upon him. The wizard roared back as he sliced one foe in half with his wood blade. Others tore at him frenziedly with their claws, some slashing through his robes or scratching his flesh. But the wizard was used to the pain and hacked and slashed his way through the mob, the faint power of his blade and its caustic sap lending him a strength a man of such slight frame would otherwise not be able to muster.

Finally, the melee came to an end. Splattered with mulched ichor and tainted blood, the wizard gasped for air, dropping down to one knee.

"Stay", he said to himself. "Stay a little longer." But the cancer spreading through his body seemed to resist, the pain peaking.

"Stay", he hissed, and wobbled to his feet. His eyes narrowed and the pain was blotted out once more. He limped to a brackish pool of water. In its reflection, he saw a tall, slender man, beard well-trimmed, his receding hairline exposed, the cap he used to cover it having long since been lost. His robes were ornate, but crudely patched up and reinforced for the long journey he had taken. It was weathered, and soiled, torn and stained with the blood of these things, and not a little of his own.

He was thirsty. He looked long and hard at the water. Tainted, like everything else here. The wizard swallowed hard.

"Sod it", he sighed. "Let's carry on."

•　　•　　•

The tower was as wide as it was vast, stretching high into the clouds and above. No building method of the time could achieve this, of course. But mages knew a thing or two about bending the laws of physics and ensuring the Tower of the Stars truly lived up to its name.

The wizard rose to his level via the great white disc which carried its passengers up and down the many levels of the ornate super-structure, where and as requested. Ashford had heard of some fellow mages who rode the air currents or who rose up to their level through sheer force of will, but he had no time for that sort of toil. He found it to not be in line with the proper dignity and composure of his Learned Society. More to the point, he liked the grace of it all, and since his illness took hold, he felt the need not to exert himself, except when he needed to.

He walked down a vast hallway, the gabled ceiling stretching half a mile above him. He walked past crowds of other mages, scribes, flunkies, apprentices, and menials. In some way, the tower was a small city unto itself in terms of activity and the sheer number of those who dwelt and labored there. Proceeding to a large set of double doors to the side of a side corridor, he knocked twice.

A pause.

"Enter?" As ever with Bronzefinch, the command always sounded like a question.

"It's me", the wizard sighed, as he entered.

Before him was a cavernous, sumptuously decorated study and surgery. It was lined with huge bay windows, through which one could see the dusk light and clouds below. A small, tidy, and almost simple-looking desk was at its center. There sat Bronzefinch, a creased, greying bespectacled man, consulting his notes.

"Oh, hello there, Ashford", he said to the wizard. "How are you?"

"Ill", Ashford replied. He walked up to the desk but declined the offer of the chair in front of it.

"Thanks, but I prefer to stand ..." For a brief moment, Ashford gazed out at the vastness of the sky beyond the glass. Then he focused again.

"In any case", Bronzefinch declared, laying his notes down. "I guess you're here to hear the prognosis."

"Go ahead ..." Ashford sighed. He knew where this was going, but still entertained vague notions of a happy ending.

"Well, I have combined my science and craft", Bronzefinch began, "and studied both the droplets of blood you provided and the patterns of your aetheric aura. I'm afraid ..."

"I'm done for, aren't I?" Ashford sighed.

Bronzefinch nodded.

"The ... corruption, or tumor, is spreading through you. Soon it will be choking your every life function like an overly ravenous parasite ..."

"Where would I be without your lurid metaphors?" Ashford said, trying to grin, but it mostly came out as a grimace.

"Erm ... Yes," Bronzefinch said and Ashford saw regret on his face.

"It's alright — I took no offence," Ashford hastened to say. But he felt tired now, and finally took a seat. Then Ashford asked the last question left to answer. The one he dreaded.

"I assume you can't cure it magically?"

"Alas no," Bronzefinch murmured. "You see the tumor is a part of your body which has been warped with magic. Because it is a product of your own power and feeds upon it, healing magic wouldn't be able to tell the difference. As far as the spells are concerned, you're perfectly healthy."

"What about cutting it out?"

"It's spread so far through your body ... I ..."

"You did what you could, Bronzefinch. What more could I ask for?"

Bronzefinch nodded sadly.

"What caused it?" Ashford then asked. He realized how futile the question was. After all, it would make no difference either way. But he was curious nonetheless, and the scholar within him was still alive and kicking.

"Magic courses through us all", Bronzefinch explained. "Mostly we can channel it through our bodies and minds, but sometimes the body reacts the wrong way."

"And it combines with dross and magical residue to create a cancer."

"Indeed." Bronzefinch coughed. Ashford knew he was being polite, but still had to ask a difficult question. "What do you wish to do now?"

Ashford had heard of mages interned with their books and left to die and mummify, or others who attempted the 7 Trials of the Divine and simply turned to dust in the process. Others headed off to far lands in search of a cure, no matter how tenuous. Others simply fell into their armchairs, drank port and waited to die.

None of these were Ashford's style, of course. He wanted to keep himself busy.

"I heard about The Garden", he said.

Bronzefinch's eyes widened in response.

"You know how dangerous that job is?"

"Someone needs to give it a try", Ashford sighed. "It's not like I have any other pressing engagements now."

For a moment, the two mages sat quiet, not sure of what to say next. Again, Ashford looked out of the great bay windows at the clouds outside and the amber sky above them. He mused on the fact that there he sat, a man capable of impossible things in an impossible, vast tower, and yet even he couldn't stop his body failing and death coming far too soon.

• • •

As fast as his tired legs could carry him, Ashford jogged through the grove. Already he could hear the Garden come to life, aware of the intruder that had entered its midst. There was the crunching and snapping of vines, thorns, branches, and sentient fungi coming to life clearly audible in the distance. Meanwhile the primal magical power being awakened pounded at Ashford's temples and rippled through his body.

How had the Garden been cursed, however? Ashford found time to ponder this, even as he ran. Created by the First People, when humans were still pondering stone tools, it had sat, quite pleasantly, all the millennia since. Self-contained and serene, the Garden and its strange plants, beasts, insects, and nature spirits, ran with a smoothness that would have shamed even the most pedantic of mages. Why had it become bloated, monstrous, malign?

Suddenly the ground before him exploded and a thing made of bulging, half rotten roots punched up from beneath the soil. It was at least twice Ashford's height, and its many tendrils writhed and jerked like snakes about to strike.

Ashford just managed to stop before the thing fully emerged, but its arrival still knocked him off his feet. Gritting his teeth, Ashford got up, pulled out his wooden blade and charged at the root-creature.

It slapped the blade out of his hand and nearly took off his head with another tendril. Ashford managed to dodge the second blow, but scores of other roots surged towards him, spinning themselves around his arms, legs, torso, and face.

Ashford felt the roots tighten. Realizing he was going to be crushed, he managed to get his left hand free. Biting through the tendrils which gagged him, his teeth crunching painfully as he did so, Ashford managed to spit out an incantation.

Red fire surged out of his hand and surged into the creature. Screaming, it erupted into flames, the rot that had taken it over making enough of its usually moist roots dry like tinder.

Ashford realized in horror that the flames had now engulfed the root-creature, and they were now quickly spreading along the roots that held him. He managed to pull himself free and pick up his sword, hurling himself away from the inferno. He could only hear the thing screech as it burned.

Ashford staggered onto his feet. Blocking out the pain, he ran around the still burning corpse and headed on his way. He tried to ignore the fact that the root-creature was once benign, a servant of the Garden. And it had just died screaming, as the fire ate it alive.

•   •   •

While the Garden was, for the most part, bound by its limits — the great walls which the First People built around it — the soil nearby was still permeated with its life-giving energy. This meant bumper crops even during famines, and so humans had long since settled the surrounding area. Just not too close. Not even the greediest farmer was silly enough to get near a place with that sort of magic coursing through it.

But now the Garden had been corrupted, and horrors had begun to climb over, tunnel under or simply gnaw through the walls, which were no longer able to magically repair themselves. There already had been deaths and missing people. This would only get worse as the blight continued to spread.

Angry mobs of farmers with billhooks and calivers had begun patrolling the night. They had no hope in hell against the things coming out of the Garden. But they were a threat to anyone they saw as "weird", and that included any mage, even those from The Tower. This aside, Ashford could already see rings of crude palisades put up with haste in the distance. They would not be able to hold those horrors back, not when the Garden's own walls would finally give way. A great darkness would be unleashed on the land, with the people in this region first to be snuffed out.

It was late afternoon when Ashford arrived in the town. It was a mix of stone and wooden buildings, with a rough cobbled road and a stream, long since fouled with manure and human waste, running through it crosswise. It was owned by several hard-nosed, money-grubbing farming families who either rented the buildings out or outright owned the businesses within. They'd be a new caste of gentry in the land, Ashford mused, if they'd thought of anything beyond money and feuds.

"So, Sunflower," Ashford said to his horse, "we'll be at the inn soon. Shall I set you up some hay and water?"

The horse blew through its lips with no small measure of annoyance.

"Yes, I guess you don't speak," Ashford agreed. Uplifting beasts with magic was a controversial topic amongst even the more radical mages, mainly because — Ashford suspected — they were scared of what their dogs, steeds, and familiars might say about them.

"Still, I'll make sure you get a good night's sleep!" Ashford said, again to the horse's bemusement.

They trotted into the courtyard where the Innkeep and his family were waiting to greet Ashford, almost like he was a minor noble. In a sense, he was, of course. The local mages had made sure his room and board had been booked in advance, and the town knew he would be coming. They also knew why.

Ashford climbed down. "This time tomorrow we'll be back for dinner!" he whispered into Sunflower's ear.

The horse gave Ashford the *You stupid bloody human* look that only a horse can give. Ashford nodded sadly in agreement. Horses were sensible, as a rule. Wizards, most assuredly, were not. The odds of him coming back were slim.

Instead, Ashford busied himself greeting his reception committee. This was made up of the Innkeep, a barrel-shaped burgher who'd built up his meaty frame in the fields before ordering his younger brother to do the dirty work while he ran the inn.

Then there was his dour wife who was like a scowl with arms and legs ... There was a gaggle of cute, but nervous looking small children ... And a rather short, plain, nondescript older daughter, who lowered her eyes, and looked like she was sorry for even being there.

"A pleasure to meet you!" Ashford said, offering his hand. The Innkeep'sthick, heavy mitt grasped it a little too tightly for Ashford's liking.

"A pleasure to have you here, Master Ashford," the Innkeep rumbled. He was trying a smile, but it had withered on his face with a frown. "We're honored by your presence."

Ashford was used to pain, thanks to what was slowly killing him, so managed to ignore the attempt to crush his hand. He put on a brave face — something else he had a lot of practice with.

"I will do all in my power to lift this curse that has fallen upon your area," Ashford said. "Rest assured, the matter will be resolved, and I'm sure my stay here will be fruitful for all concerned."

The Innkeep almost guffawed but managed to hold it back. "We don't have trouble growing fruit around here."

Well, the fruit's now trying to eat you, Ashford nearly said, but he feigned a laugh instead.

Annoyed, the Innkeep turned to his family with a grimace.

"Wife, show our guest his room. And you layabouts!" he addressed his children. "Take his belongings and make sure they are all carried in WITHOUT BREAKING THEM!"

After they all collectively flinched, the children and the older daughter all quickly and efficiently moved to take Ashford's bags and luggage off his horse he was riding. None of them dared say a word. Out of the shadows, a stick-thin, petrified stable boy emerged to take Sunflower to his lodgings for the night.

"Will you be joining us for dinner tonight?" the Innkeep asked as he followed Ashford and his wife into the dark, smoky inn. It didn't sound all that exciting.

"No, I must apologize. I will be going to bed early tonight. I'll be up at dawn, and heading off to ... Well, you get the idea."

Ashford couldn't help but detect a look of relief on the old brute's face.

"Yes, very good. Master Ashford. I'll have your dinner brought up for you."

"That's very kind," Ashford said, now feeling just a bit nervous.

He could feel the odd mix of deference and chippy sulk the big man greeted him with. His stay brought prestige, but also envy. It was always the worst snobs who looked down on some and scowled at others.

Ashford glanced over his shoulder. *That went well*, the horse seemed to snort sarcastically as the stable boy lead him away. Ashford couldn't help but agree with him. Was this how he was to spend his last days?

Life was, indeed, a series of punchlines, none of which were all that funny to those they befell. Ashford could feel the cancer again. It was gnawing at him, and the pain was getting a little too much to endure.

•　　•　　•

Hacking his way through the honeysuckle that was trying to glue him in place, Ashford realized he'd just walked into a trap. He could hear strange ululating cries and shrieks all around him. And then ... Silence. What had happened? A stillness had befallen the Garden. Ashford strained to listen. He could almost hear the Garden growing and spreading like a wet, vile series of bubbles boiling and popping, and the strange croaks, belches and chirping of corrupted toads, insects, and birds.

Suddenly, they were upon him. Once elegant deer, of a kind refined by the magic of the First People, they were now emaciated, ulcerous things, spitting burning bile and shrieking as they rushed to crush Ashford underfoot.

Ashford replied with a cone of purple, blue, and red fire, cutting the head off the nearest deer-mutant, before whipping another into its peers with a telekinetic shove. Amidst the chaos, burning, smoke and screams, a great stag, sickened to the point of rotting, and yet bulging with perverse life and power, bounded towards Ashford. With a cry, Ashford set his sword and counter charged.

•　　•　　•

After the Innkeep's wife had given him a joyless tour of the building, Ashford was free to go. With some relief, he then retired to his room, took out a carefully wrapped bundle from his travelling chest, and laid it out on the plain, old oak bed. It was a mixture of tools, tinctures, bottled herbs, and vials full of swirling, writhing and even oozing strangeness. It also had a small silver-plated dish into which he gently tipped small, measured amounts of each substance. Placing it on its stand above a candle on the simple, wooden table nearby, he carefully heated the mix with a stirrer made of black glass, reciting incantations, and bending probability to his will.

The philter cooled, but still glowed and throbbed with hot air and strange energies. It was now a bizarre, simmering liquid rainbow of color. With no small measure of reluctance, he lifted the bowl to his lips and drank. It tasted of fire, shocked his tongue, and felt like molten wax going down his throat. Ashford grimaced for a minute while it went down.

The potion worked, insofar as it held the cancer off, and held back the pain. But soon it wouldn't work at all, and Ashford knew the time to do whatever the hell he was meant to be doing was now.

With a sigh, he took off his robes and donned a loose smock and hakama. Pushing aside the bed and much of the room's furniture, he made himself enough room to begin his sword forms with the same old long, heavy training stick he'd used to train all these years. It kept him sharp and was still as good a form of exercise and meditation as it was when he first took up fencing all those years ago. Most of the old school taught learning to fight and — heaven forfend! — even light physical activity was a distraction from magic. But Ashford didn't really care. It worked for him.

He then proceeded from one sword form to another, with enough speed and force to wear him out, though nowhere as much as when he was still well. This annoyed Ashford no end.

Finished at last, and soaked with sweat, he mused on how much of his health had already been lost. He'd managed two hours on good days. Now it was less than one. Looking up in a daze, Ashford then realized he was not alone.

It was the Innkeep's daughter. *Short, plain, nondescript.* She was young, but dressed up like she was a grandmother in tones of brown and plain linen designed, it seemed, to help her blend in with the inn's dark oak gloom. She stood squat, or perhaps, weighed down by everything. She looked tired, her small eyes blinking in the spluttering light of the room.

"Errm, Sir? I brought your dinner ..." she said, apologetically.

Without prompting, she walked to the table and laid down a simple wooden tray. On it was a large bowl of rustic stew, some rough brown bread, and a small jug of beer. Simple fare for someone on a budget, but not *too much* of a budget. After all, Ashford wasn't here for a good time, but he was hardly going to starve either.

The girl half nodded, half bowed and then scurried away. But then she stopped. Even with her back turned, Ashford could tell she was rubbing her hands, anxiously. She looked back at him, nervously.

"Y-you're a wizard, aren't you?" she asked.

So much for travelling incognito, Ashford sighed. The inn must have had a steady stream of wizards — be they of the Tower, amateurs, or half-mad hedge witches — passing through all the time. It's easy to learn how to spot one. You learn to pick up the signs — the theatricality, the faint crackle in the air. And, sometimes, the odd, strange event. Accidental cantrips. Cats and furniture that start talking. Hauntings. Strange wisps in the outhouse. Ashford could still find it in him to cringe at the less discreet mages out there.

But then Ashford grasped what was going on. *This girl watches*, he noted. *She asks questions.* He sighed, realizing she was looking for honest answers, and obliged her.

"Yes, Miss. I am a high sorcerer of The Tower", he said, in a matter-of-fact way. For all the wonders he had seen and taken part in, it all seemed a bit embarrassing now. Almost day to day.

The girl blinked at him, surprised. The Tower of Stars had a reputation that preceded it. But she probably never imagined that one of its mages would end up before her, looking like a half-drowned ferret in baggy clothes, and waving a wooden stick about.

"Erm, I—I've never seen one of you before. I guess —"

"You expected a little more ..." Ashford pondered the right word. "Gravitas."

"I'm not quite sure what that word means, but I guess", the girl frowned.

A silence. Ashford gingerly laid his glorified stick on top of the dresser, next to his dinner.

But then the girl lit up for a moment. "What's it like?" she asked. "Being one of you."

Ashford was caught off guard. Being a mage was so natural to him that putting this into words had never crossed his mind. What he found himself saying surprised Ashford as much as it had shocked the girl.

"I'm dying," he breathed. "The magic … It caused a great illness we can't cure. Not even us, with our knowledge. I don't have long. You could say being a sorcerer has killed me."

An awkward pause. The girl looked to the ground, nodded, and began to turn away.

"I guess it was too good to be true." She looked up suddenly. "I mean — sorry — I do get all sorts of silly notions in my head, that's what mother and father say. I shouldn't pry. No."

But then Ashford realized something, at the same time as he said it. "I have no regrets."

The girl's small eyes become like saucers for a moment, her eyebrows arching up in surprise.

"But, if you don't mind me saying, it is killing you."

"Yes, you have a point there," Ashford mused. "But it's also let me see and do amazing things. Help people. Bend the elements to my will. I —" Ashford blinked. "… Don't regret it."

"Do all sorcerers die like you will? I — oh bother. I've said something stupid again."

"No," Ashford said, shaking his head. "Not all of us. Most die of something else. I'm just, well, *unlucky*, I guess."

"But doesn't it come at such a cost? I mean, well, is it really worth dying for?"

"Everything comes at a cost," Ashford sighed gently, as much to himself as to the girl. "The only question is whether that cost is worth it."

"And is it?" the girl asked. "I mean, are you sure?"

•   •   •

Ashford left early the next morning, taking only his horse and saddle. Slipping out of the stables and setting forth at a near gallop, Ashford went forth on his mission, determined and mournful.

The road gave way to a track, then a trail, and then, finally, open fields and grasslands. Ashford couldn't help but notice how the corruption in the Garden had begun to warp the grass and patches of trees and shrubs. He saw twisted and sickly plants, with strange and unearthly colors.

The vast, high walls of the Garden finally loomed in the distance. He slowed Sunflower down, dismounted and patted the side of the horse. The rest of his journey would have to be by foot.

"Hang around if you want", he murmured. "But you don't have to stay. Whatever you do, don't eat the grass."

Within the hour, Ashford was upon his objective. Burning his way through the diseased vegetation that blocked one of the cracks in the wall, Ashford finally entered the Garden.

It was now overgrown and made into a nightmare of vile mutation and grotesque verdancy. Already, he could feel the place come alive as if ready to destroy this invader. Long-haired things, once the nemoral apes that helped tend the Garden, now red-eyed, tumorous savages, swung down the branches towards him.

Ashford sneered and pulled out a small twig from his pocket. It was somehow still weeping sap, and budding leaves. The last uncorrupted part of the Garden. Focusing his magic through the cutting, it began to grow and take form as a wickedly sharp, long saber, made of living wood and pulsing with green energy.

Several of the ape things hurled themselves at Ashford. He blasted them apart with magic from one hand and slaughtered the rest with his sword. He considered their corpses, noting how their insides were riddled with growths like his own. Casually, he walked deeper into the overgrown and diseased avenues, terraces and bosquets of the tainted Garden.

•　　•　　•

For a brief moment, Ashford pondered the girl's question. "Yes." he said, nodding now. "I've lived a good life. Perhaps one that you'd have to be mad to choose. But sometimes it's right to be mad. I'm just sad it's coming to an end. Do I sound arrogant for saying that?"

"Well, you are being honest, I suppose" the girl said. "How old were you, when you started?"

"Ooh, a good question ..." Ashford said. "I was young. Ten or so, I think. My parents thought it would be a good idea — it stopped me blowing their house up with my experiments."

"Ten?" the girl said. "You were so young. Not like me. I'm an old maid. I turned 15 last week."

Fifteen! Ashford remembered looking up to his older sister when she was 15. She seemed so tall and mature, like their parents. *A grown up.* Now, in his prime, 15 looked like a fetus. Had he gotten that old? He had outlived his sister twice over. She never got to be a grown-up, just a memory.

"Fifteen is not *that* old", Ashford said to the girl/fetus. He'd never had the chance to be a parent, but he'd taught enough 'fetuses' at the tower to realize how wizened he was getting.

The fetus almost gasped at the scandal. "My mother was thirteen when she married my father", she said. "I mean, I was going to end up a spinster until my father arranged for me to marry Perkin, the blacksmith's boy. He's a good enough groom, I guess."

Ashford imagined something half-way between a loping sweaty oaf and a slab of rock.

"Did your father even ask you first?" he asked, taken aback. Deep down, his sphincter clenched at the impertinence of his question. But still, he had to know.

"Oh, Father doesn't need to do that," the girl said. "It helps the family, you see. He gets a lot of land for the dowry. And some extra sheep!"

The Innkeep, Ashford realized, was the sort of person that liked putting fences up, and kicking anything that didn't get behind those fences. Did he even see his daughter as anything more than cattle? Ashford knew the most powerful magic wasn't being able to raise the dead, or cast fire and lightning, or travel across the land with a thought. It was being able to forget that other people had minds and souls too. Or not even care in the first place.

"I hope it works out well for you", Ashford said, as politely as he could.

The fetus blinked. "I think I can hear Father calling. He must be wondering where I've gotten to."

"Thank you for dinner", Ashford murmured, as the girl slipped away to meet the loud, ugly voice downstairs, wondering where the hell she had gotten to.

She closed the door behind her, gently. Ashford took a deep, cleansing breath. He closed his eyes, raised his head and lifted his arms up to his side. Green and blue and white-purple fire began to orbit his hands and forearms. It felt good, even as he could faintly feel the cancer begin to burn inside him again. He was ready. It was time.

Then he opened his eyes and shook his head at the wretchedness of being young and at the mercy of others.

•　　•　　•

As Ashford drew nearer to the Garden's heart, the Grand Arboretum, the plant life became ever more impenetrable, misshapen, and actively hostile. The constant flow of magic energy through his body and sword were taking their toll. He felt dizzy, hungry, parched — all the signs that his magic was now wicking away his own life force.

Worse, this was making his cancer burn even more than ever. He could almost feel it spreading now. Ashford had hoped that the mission would not worsen his illness. Now he knew the strain meant he had days, not months, to live if he even had the good luck to survive at all. Ashford guessed he should have torn at his breast and lamented. Instead, he just swore a lot.

Suddenly, a vast black shape flew out of the tree line and swooped down towards him. It was an insect, like a stag beetle, but far too bizarre and huge to be truly called as such. Seconds before it clasped him in its pincers, Ashford could see the thing was a strange mix of lucanid and mutated plant life. He saw ferns, fungi, and grubby small trees with sharp branches growing out of its carapace, and faint hints of leering, ugly faces in the bark.

Then he was in the air, the great creature carrying him who-knows-where, its pincers crushing his already sickened insides. Ashford snarled as he thrust his sword into the brute's one good eye.

He scrambled out of its loosened grasp and hauled himself up its back, even as the beast writhed and lost control of its flight. Casting a fire spell, he ignited the plant parts of the beast. His nose stung with the smell of burning, rotting wood and chitin. The beast reared up in pain, hurling Ashford in the air, before it crashed into the ground below, wrapped in flames.

"This doesn't look good," Ashford thought as he felt himself falling. With a supreme act of will, he managed to slow his descent with his magic, but still slammed into the ground with a hard thud. This alone would have hurt, but now he could feel his cancer blazing inside of him.

In pain, Ashford slowly rose to his feet. He found himself in a vast, empty clearing ... 'Empty' — who was he kidding? Sure enough, strange mists surged into the clearing, and began to take form. He grit his teeth when he realized what had finally come to confront him.

Once, the Twelve Custodians of the Garden were beautiful amalgams of plant, spirit and automaton, each hand crafted by the First People to oversee their Garden. Now they had become hideous parodies of themselves, more dead than alive, yet growing, always growing ...

Now fully formed, they stood before Ashford, glaring at him with utter malice. Clutching his side, Ashford readied to fight, knowing he would not be able to prevail against these beings alone. But then he smiled.

Before the Custodians could attack, he called forth his trump card, a mighty rubric which summoned a hoard of blazing knights from the Realm of Plasma itself. No single mage could have done this. Ashford knew other mages had been waiting for his signal and were now channeling their magic from afar. With a thought, he reached out to one of them — *thank you once more, Bronzefinch, my dear friend.* He felt a deep sadness then, before rage took over, and he led the charge.

The melee was a sight to behold — burning knight and corrupted Custodian alike torn apart and destroyed in the battle. Half blind with pain, Ashford himself fought savagely, hurling jets of flame and hacking furiously with his sword, which seemed beside itself with rage at what its kindred had become. For a moment, it seemed the Custodians had won, having cut down the last Fire Knight. But they were much weaker now. With casual ease, Ashford blasted them to ash, or slew them with his sword.

Suddenly, it became too much. Ashford fell to his knees, barely holding himself up with his arms. He was now coughing up blood. How long could he last? Weakness swept his body, as he fought to remain aware. But with a sneer, he got to his feet and, somehow, began to jog towards the Arboretum that he could now see in the distance. Sensing the end was near, ever more fouled dryads and flocks of mutated birds attacked. He hacked through and incinerated them all with barely a thought.

•　　•　　•

The next morning, the Innkeep's daughter woke early. There was something in the air, she sensed, but her parents were hardly the kind to pick up on it. She was always too fanciful, her head in the clouds. That's what they told her, in any case.

Still, curiosity made her creep out of the inn and into the courtyard where Ashford had first arrived just days ago. As her eyes got used to the dawn gloom, she found the wizard's horse standing there in that casual way of its kind, almost as if it had been waiting for her.

The horse looked up at the girl, half forlorn and half sanguine. If a horse could sigh like a stoic, the girl thought, this horse would have done precisely that.

The stupid bastard finally did it, Sunflower's face seemed to say. *You wouldn't happen to be looking for a horse?*

Despite everything, the girl found herself saying yes.

•　　•　　•

Much to his own surprise, Ashford finally made it to the Grand Arboretum, soaked in sweat, blood and butchery. The Arboretum's last line of defense was a now filthy, green scum-laden moat broiling with Who-Knows-What swimming in its depths. The only way in was via a bridge of living thorns that had, if anything, become even sharp, barbed, and vicious since the corruption had taken hold.

With a faltering but dogged voice, Ashford commanded the bridge to let him through. The bridge fought back, spawning ever more barbs and thorns. With a snarl, the wizard muttered a spell composed by the First People themselves, and bent the bridge to his will, its thorns yielding. Blood trickled out of his mouth as he crossed into the main structure. His vision became ever more blurred. Was it blindness, or tears?

The Arboretum was the heart of the Garden, an ornate frame of wood that had been grown into a grand structure, its 'glass' in fact membranes of transparent, magical chlorophyll. These had become slimy and misted over by the malaise, the structure itself a distorted parody of its former delicacy and grandeur. Here, the corruption was at its strongest, and the once mighty insectoid and arachnid defenders of the Arboretum had become too bloated and weakened to pose much of a threat.

Even on the brink of death, Ashford could tear them apart with casual ease. *How anticlimactic,* he tutted to himself, through the pain, as he cast them aside with contempt, powerful telekinetic spells doing their work, even as they made his heart strain and his veins hemorrhage.

Finally, he reached the center of the Grand Arboretum, and saw the cause of the horror. It dwarfed him.

"What to do with you?" Ashford mused.

Once, the epicenter of the Garden was a great, beautiful ebony tree, barely possible in this reality in its proportions and intensity, and crowned by a vastness of emerald leaves. But now it oozed and fruited before him, some sick amalgam of weed, tumor, fungus, and malignant spirit. A Hobgoblin Presence! No wonder even the magic of the First People could not resist it.

Knowing it was under attack, the Goblin Tree hissed as it spat poison spores of rage and contempt, hurling spines and spells in equal measure.

Blood erupted from Ashford's mouth as he repelled some attacks with his own spells, deflected others with the force of his mind, and blocked the rest with his sword. But he knew the Corruption had over-extended itself. He could defeat it. He would.

"How do you like them apples, you rancid git!" Ashford coughed, as he drew upon every last ebb of strength, every ounce of hatred and fury, and even the toxic magic of the cancer itself, hurling it all at the Goblin Tree through his sword, which blazed with green light as it erupted with the full force of its power. Slowly, horribly, Ashford tore the blight apart with brute force, his bones snapping and his organs failing under the strain.

As the thing began to wither and die, it revealed the fragile, stunted remnants of a stripling tree underneath its receding filth. Here remained the last vestiges of the True Garden.

With a horrible shriek, the Goblin-Tree finally dissolved into nothingness, waves of destruction sweeping throughout the Garden, devastating it, but also purging every last trace of corruption. The chlorophyll panes of the arboretum exploded as it did so, and even the rot that had spread beyond the walls withered and died.

Ashford swayed, all but delirious amidst the total havoc, as the Arboretum partially collapsed around him. He fell to the ground, but somehow crawled to the stripling, finally pulling himself toward it by seizing its trunk with his hand and dragging himself as close as he could, managing to stand one last time.

"Still life in you ..." he rasped, pressing his sword against the stripling, melding the two and giving it just enough energy to not only live but, slowly, gradually, grow again.

He'd done it. Ashford laughed, as he fell to the ground once more. The Garden had been saved, and perhaps the world itself. *Not bad for a retirement do,* he mused to himself.

But now a great tiredness fell upon him. He closed his eyes and drifted off to sleep.

•　　•　　•

Everything comes at a price.

The girl found herself pondering what this really meant as Sunflower cantered along the road away from the town she'd spent her entire life in. She'd miss her siblings.

Still, at least she wouldn't have to marry Perkin, she sighed. That was always a plus.

But then the girl gasped when she saw where the horse was taking her. The Garden!

Almost as shocking was the land surrounding it. She'd heard rumors that the grasslands, copses, and hedgerows there had become "wrong", and she dared not find out any more. But now they all looked like they'd been harrowed by fire, blackened and burnt.

Then Sunflower carried her through the shattered gates and fallen walls of the Garden and into its interior.

The girl was stunned as she witnessed the utter desolation within. What had not been burned to ash had been left scorched and stripped of life. Even now, a pall hung in the air, and ash still softly fell from the sky.

Yet here and there, the girl could see tiny flecks of green as life slowly returned to the Garden, and even hints of weak sprouting and seedlings somehow poking through the ash.

The girl knew enough about farming to know plants didn't grow this fast normally, even in the fertile soils her family and their like had farmed for years beyond count. No, magic was at play here, but it would surely take decades, even centuries for even the Garden to heal.

As the horse continued its tour through the desolation, the girl could, out the corner of her eye, see tiny movements, and even forlorn figures flitting between the scorched trees in the distance.

A tiny number of the Garden's native magical creatures had survived, purged of their blight, alongside its wildlife. In time, creatures from outside would join them, and the Garden would host a new forest, perhaps wilder and more chaotic than the First People had intended, but a rebirth for all that.

Even the shattered shell of the Arboretum showed signs of recovery as Sunflower trotted over the now-harmless thorn bridge and into its heart. The vast frame still looked like a blackened ruin, but hints of clear chlorophyll had begun to regrow in its grills. In the coming years, the branches of the arboretum would slowly come back to life and reshape themselves, if a little less perfectly than they were before. Nature had its own symmetry.

Sunflower reached the shattered center of the Arboretum. Ash and wreckage were all around. Then the girl covered her mouth and all but cried out. *The Wizard!*

Before her, a strange stripling stood before her — weak and frail, yet already showing signs of shoots and budding growth. Part of it looked strange, almost like it was a sword or similar thing that had melded with the rest of the young tree, but the girl knew that it was sometimes easy to see shapes where none existed. Right?

Yet what shocked her was the skeleton lying face down in front of the tree, the side of its skull turned towards the girl and what was now her horse, as if it had expected her. She knew that, ordinarily, it would take weeks for a body to decay to this point. But there was nothing ordinary here.

All traces of flesh had gone, and even the robes the wizard had once worn had been reduced to only a few tattered remnants. The girl was only barely able to recognize the patterns she'd seen on Ashford's clothes a few days before. The Garden had already made good use of his body. Soon, his bones would break down and in turn be absorbed by the healing soil. In every sense, he had helped the Garden not only break its curse but live again.

Sunflower hung his head, perhaps sensing that his own worst fears had come true. The girl wept but still patted the side of his mane. "It's all right," she said, gently. "He's free now."

Wiping her eyes, she took a deep breath. She understood now what price was worth paying.

Time we left, Sunflower seemed to say as he turned to leave. The girl agreed.

Slowly, the horse trotted out of the Garden's ruins, and back onto the road. Gently, the girl tapped his sides with her heels. And so, they began their journey towards The Tower of Stars, and whatever the future held for them there.

Xauri'EL Zwaan is a mendicant artist in search of meaning, fame and fortune, or pie (where available); a Genderqueer Bisexual, a Socialist Solarpunk, and a Satanist Goth. Zie has published short fiction in, among other places, *Galaxy's Edge*, *Polar Borealis*, *Transform the World*, and *We're Here: The Best Queer Speculative Fiction of 2022*. Zie lives and writes in a little hobbit hole in Saskatoon, Canada on Treaty 6 territory with zir life partner and two very lazy cats.

· · ·

"Opportunity Knocks" was my first ever published piece; it was originally printed in 2011 in Spectra Magazine, one of the earliest experiments in an online-only format for short speculative fiction. It sadly soon fell victim to the exigencies of fast-changing digital marketplaces, but it was a harbinger of the future. I was in a bad place when I wrote this; I try to be a bit more upbeat these days, but I think the raw hopelessness and anger of it is still valuable.

OPPORTUNITY KNOCKS

XAURIEL ZWAAN

S EEN FROM FAR ENOUGH AWAY, our Sun has rings now. They're quite beautiful, in their own cold way; they're broad and bright and when the light catches them just right they sparkle like crushed diamonds. They follow the orbits of the planets we inhabit and they are composed of our discarded tools, our broken machines, our frozen shit and piss and corpses. They are the debris of humanity, floating gently in space.

•   •   •

Sebban Texis Cale was 15 Mars-years old, and he had hit rock bottom. He had lost most of his value cycles in the big virtual-economies crash, and the slow bleed of everyday expenses took the rest. He'd had to sell off his rotothopter, his collection of antique Nintendo cartridges, and as many augments as he could be without and survive. His sharemates left him; he lost his job at the greenwashing plant after one too many hard nights soaked in the haze of cannabis liquor and had to kill his pet squid and eat it one day when the pantry was bare and the cold wind was blowing over the Utopia Plains. He traded his quonset for an efficiency tank, then traded that for a free room in the share-alike commune. The share-alikes tried hard to help him, as was their way; but by then he was spending too much time hazed out and couldn't do the work they required of him, so they apologetically handed him a few hundred value cycles and a week's worth of nutrition packs and showed him the door.

Mars is not kind to the homeless. Being poor there is practically a crime, and justice swift and sure. When there's nowhere left to go on Mars, you better get off.

Within the day he was on the state-sponsored shuttle bus to Phobos. Mars wanted him gone as much as he wanted to leave.

●　　●　　●

On the planet-side of Mars, there are billions on billions of people, feeding and breeding like rats in a warren. All the corpocrats really want is to be rid of them, one way or another; if the companies can't extract enough value from them, they're worthless. The share-alikes and the gift-givers and the government ground-breaking plantations do their best to save who they can, but there are limits to what a few scattered charters can manage. In the end, the vast bulk of them are left to quietly starve, and the barren soil of Mars is made ever more fertile with their ground-up, composted remains.

Out in the orbs, there's precious little room to be had, and even less food, water, or air. Nevertheless, a place is generally found for those that need it. There's always work to be done in the orbs, even for those so hazed out or blissed in or amped up or broken down that they can barely tell left from right. Out there in the orbs, the logic of Malthus gives way to that of Bentham; it's *always* share-and-share-alike out in the orbs, but not in the way of the twee little planet-side communes with their charters and councils and behavioral norms. Nobody really *wants* to live in the orbs; but they are necessary, and they draw people to them who are willing to do what's necessary. They are not lawless, but their laws are simple and harsh. Thieves, rapists, murderers, saboteurs, and false witnesses face the cold justice of the void. Everyone else gets by.

Cale worked his way from one orb to the next, doing whatever jobs came to hand. Drugs were hard to come by and held dear in the orbs, and without a steady supply he managed to regain a little equilibrium. He left each station with a little more to his name than he'd come with. Eventually, he managed to make it all the way to Earth Orbital; he traded the enjoyment of his body for a one-way trip frozen in the cargo hold of a rust-bucket ore hauler, following a half-brained notion of touching down on Venus eventually.

Venus was a paradise, they said; anyone could start a new life there — stead a farm, build a factory, hell, found your own charter colony where you made the rules and said who came and who did what. Food was so cheap as to be practically free, they said, and the vast terraformed fields would grow all the hops and cannabis a man could ever need.

If he'd only headed the other way, he sometimes thought to himself later, out to the belt or to Jupiter and Saturn, he could have really made something of himself. He could have struck it rich on titanium or deuterium, become captain of a million-ton water barge; maybe got out to the freezing freeholds of Neptune where *anything* goes. When he got to Earth Orbital, he found that his information was out of date and badly distorted. Venus, it seemed, had decided it didn't want to end up like Mars — or, heavens forbid, like Earth. It was now limiting immigration to those with special skills or unique augmentations.

•   •   •

Sebban Texis Cale was running out of options.

Venus was right out. You couldn't even step foot in their orbital stations now without a migration pass. Mercury, where real fortunes were being made on the Array these days, wasn't even an option; he couldn't possibly afford the advanced augments it took to be able to survive the heat of the swollen sun. Luna was a hive of corpocratic drones; his references were most certainly not up to snuff for a position in Marketing or Accounts Receivable. The captain of that tramp hauler had offered him passage back to Phobos, leering and licking her space-bitten lips; but to what point?

The orbs were living purgatory; he could hardly expect better there than to slowly fall apart from lack of senescence treatment, packed into a sardine can with all the other dead-enders and petty criminals and assorted trash that Mars cast off, eating their own shit and drinking their own piss for whatever time their telomeres had left in them.

As for the Belt and beyond, his successively clearer mind knew it was a fantasy. All the good asteroids were locked up by the big mining unions, and the chance of finding anything of real value in the leftover dross was negligible. Jupiter space was dominated by the Ganymede Borganization, and Cale was rather fond of his identity, pathetic as it might be. The water mines and barges were a family business, run by exactingly bred hereditary eugenic clans.

The next generation ship bound for Centauri wasn't due to depart for another decade or so. And Jah love alone knew what they got up to on the anarchist freeholds out in the cold, black ass-end of the solar system, or what he would have to do to survive there.

And he really couldn't stay on the Earth Orbital, playground of the richest of the rich. He was surrounded by luxury here, mountains of wealth he couldn't touch; and already he was starting to hear the siren song of warm, green liquor again. He could almost taste the rich smoky haze that would blot all his troubles away for an hour or three or five. It was available practically everywhere here, one of the very few things on Earth Orbital that came cheap. He was starting to feel almost desperate enough to try and find a way down to the planet, where the Naturists would be happy to at least give him a clean death.

Then he found his salvation.

It was on sale in a used shuttle bay run by a jacked-up third-sex podling in one of the seedier parts of the back-end roll; where the servant class came for their groceries and other contraband, and the playboys and playgirls and playhijras came to play with fire. It was buried in the back, as if ashamed of itself, behind battered luxury yachts and refurbished mail boats and obsolescent government moonjumpers sold for a song; but Cale was drawn to it, as if by a magnet, as if by fate. The instant he saw it he *knew* that this was the last chance he'd been looking for; he knew it in his bones.

It was about as rudimentary as a spaceship could get; a one-man plastanium canister, barely more than a gussied-up escape pod. It was rigged with a basic life-cycle system, a quad of tiny but adequate chem thrusters, an anachronistically powerful sensor system, and a slapped-on toroid cargo hold of almost ten times its own tonnage. The shuttle dealer, its stochastics intuiting a potential sale, was more than happy to tell Cale all about it.

It was an almost abandoned ship class known as a ring picker. The idea, said the dealer, its four arms twitching as it manipulated the torrent of commercial data streaming past its contacs, was to take it out on trips around the debris ring that generations of human habitation in space had left in the planet's wake, sorting whatever might be salvageable out of the tons upon tons of floating garbage. Not a glamorous life, no, nor even a particularly dignified one, the dealer said, its emotional modeling algorithms perfectly attuned to its mark's desperate yearning. But for a man who knew how to take advantage of arbitrage, yes, who knew how to sift the gold from the dross ... with no man your master, just you and the stars and the treasures in other men's trash ...

The name painted inexpertly across the canister's battered hull was *Opportunity Knocks*.

Cale gave the hijra every last value cycle he had as a down payment and took his new home out into the ring within the hour.

•   •   •

At first, Cale saw his ring picker as a steppingstone to bigger, better things. He could build up a little nest egg, he thought, and invest it in something stable like wellstone futures or prediction mutuals; then maybe think about training as a terrafarmer or getting some second-hand Mercurial extreme-temp augments. A few trips around the ring quickly showed him otherwise.

There was a reason the pickers had gone out of style and were now washing up in such questionable surroundings as Honest Asbel's Carnival of Orbital Transit. A dozen generations of human waste had been well and truly picked over; and there wasn't much of value left. The best and biggest hauls, the museum-quality pieces and still-working technology, had all been found, picked, hauled in, and sold. He'd come along far too late to make his fortune in the ring. What little salvage he was able to bring in each trip was barely enough to cover the cost of refueling, topping up the water and yeast tanks, and servicing his debt.

By then, however, he no longer cared. Sebban Texis Cale had found paradise. The ring was enormous, its total mass rivaling Luna, and almost anything imaginable could be found there provided that nobody really wanted it. There was always just a little more junk out there to be picked; some bit of burned-out booster rocket or plasma casing or circuit block that could be reused, repurposed, melted down for scrap.

He cut down on supplies by sucking in ancient, frozen biosolids best left undescribed and dumping them into the tanks whenever his life cycle meters started to redline. The profits were just enough for him to start buying a bottle or two of cannabis liquor whenever he was in port. Neither steerage, maintenance, nor retrieval generally required his active attention. He was free to spend the majority of his time drifting through the ring, hazed out just enough to blot the memories away.

He got to know the rest of the few pickers still operating, a society of lost and broken loners with nowhere lower to fall. They had a community, of sorts; a social code based mainly on having mutual respect enough never to pick the same vein at the same time. They were a taciturn lot, but once they got to know his transponder frequency they opened up and made him one of their own. They would swap stories on the far side of Earth's orbit, long meandering broadcasts on ancient radionics arrays; hard luck stories a lot like his own, lies and tall tales about their exploits back in the real world, legends of ancient Earth and of the first folks to colonize the solar system. He once assisted another picker in distress, shaking off the cannabis haze just long enough to lock holds and drain half his water. After that the pickers even started treating him with a little respect.

It couldn't last; of course, he knew it couldn't, though he tried long and hard not to let himself admit it. Every trip around the ring, the pickings got slimmer and slimmer. The rest of the ring pickers started departing one by one, dead or sold out or just disappeared off into the endless night somewhere. The ones who were left fell to fighting and grew jealous and wary; one particularly grizzled hand had been murdered, so it was whispered through the ether, over a megagram of crumbling heat shields — his pod ripped open by plastanium claws and left to decompress while the killer went his merry way.

Every trip, Sebban Texis Cale swore to himself, would be the last. He would sell *Opportunity Knocks* to the scrap yard along with the trash in its hold, and ... do something with the money. Something. And again and again he ended up going back out to pick the ring over one last time.

The end, when it came, was sudden and sharp. He hadn't been listening to the radio chatter, lost in the warm soft haze; hadn't heard the rumors jumping from one picker to another, or had just dismissed them as another attempt to warn him off the shrinking veins and thought no more about it. But this time, not a single other picker was left out there to greet him as he drifted gently along the strands of mostly ice and the things encased within, scanning desperately for some chunk of metal or crystal or ceramic or something, anything, that would serve to pay the bills. He'd made it just about halfway around the ring and had barely filled a tenth of his cavernous hold, when his radar pinged off the new ship.

It was massive, big enough to swallow *Opportunity Knocks* and a hundred like her. At the front was a massive ramscoop, a field of magnetic force radiating out for miles on miles, gently shepherding each and every bit of debris in front of it down into a vast sucking maw. Its name was *Last Chance*, and it was registered to Omnicor Hypercorp, the leader in waste reclamation.

Had he been lucid enough to keep up with the newsfeeds, Cale might have spotted the minor item announcing its commissioning and explaining its purpose: to scrape up the last remains of the trash rings colonial humanity had left behind, magnanimously cleaning up this menace to orbital navigation, before heading out into the Oort cloud to establish a competitor to the Saturn water run.

In a panic, he fired up the radio and desperately harangued the pilot of the *Last Chance*. This is my livelihood, he begged them. This is all I have. By what right do you come out here and scoop it all up and take it away, you who have never known cold or hunger or loss? You puppets of the corpocrats who sit like kings at the top of this dunghill of an existence, why could you not just leave well enough alone? You have ruined everything!

After long seconds, the reply came: Your trajectory is interfering with our salvage operation. Alter your flight path or it will *be* altered — for your own safety.

He refused; fired his boosters directly toward the ramship's squalid orifice, in the faint hope that his body and ship might jam up the sorting mechanisms within.

Of course, he had no such luck; the designers, in their offices in the Lunar warrens far away, had planned for every contingency. A beam of magnetic force caught his picker and flung him carelessly out of the way. The *Last Chance* continued on its course, sucking up the last dregs of the ring as it went, and left Sebban Texis Cale floating gently through clean, empty space as his life cycle meters fell slowly into the red.

SANDSTORM IN THE HOURGLASS

RICHARD ZWICKER

C HRISTIAN TOWNE LURCHED up the stairs to Niles Castle's third-floor apartment. He could have taken the elevator, but he didn't feel like waiting for it. Ever since he'd turned 19 and left his 20s behind, he'd felt his slimming body bursting with energy. There was something to be said for living in a dimension that went backward, which he'd been stuck in for nearly a quarter century. Every day he got younger, yet he was spared the question marks of youth because he'd already lived through them.

Also, his follically-challenged scalp had bloomed a full head of curly black hair in the past four years. These advantages were trumped by several inescapable facts: this wasn't *his* dimension, time wasn't supposed to go backward, and if he waited too long, he would be unable to operate his time and dimension-spanning Sideways Machine, which was his only means of escape. Niles's door was ajar. Towne burst in. Niles looked up from his bowl of cereal and cup of No-caf, a coffee substitute.

"Niles, I'm going to leave this dimension."

"Not *that* again." Niles scratched his goatee, the mustache of which had recently thinned. Towne noticed he'd also grown a zit on the left side of his face.

"This time I mean it. I put in my notice at school."

"How could you? Your students need you." Though a temporal expert and inventor in his own dimension, Towne taught high school art in this one.

"No, they don't. If there's one thing I've learned working two decades in education, it's that everyone — teachers, administrators, students — is replaceable. Plus, my resignation has probably added three years to the superintendent's life. That's my only regret."

"OK, but why now?"

Towne sat. "Because every time I sit down to do something, I waste twenty minutes playing an insipid video game. Because I've started thinking cat videos are funny. Because at some point, I'll become so juvenile I'll lose the ability to operate my Sideways Machine."

"Which is a good thing," said Niles. "From what you've told me, the Sideways Machine is like hard drugs. It takes you somewhere else, but you can't be sure of where or whether you can get back. Why can't you just relax?"

Towne winced. "And smell the No-Caf?"

"No. You'd need the nose of a beagle to do that. But, you've got your entire childhood ahead of you. You're going to get cuter than ever. You'll be free to make really obnoxious comments. You've earned the right to enjoy yourself."

Towne shook his head. "I'm not meant to be here. Time is not supposed to go backward."

"So you've always said. It's forward to me."

"So *you've* always said. Look, I know I'm unlikely to get back to my dimension strand, but for my own sanity, I've got to find one that goes forward, in my definition of the word." He hesitated. "And I just want to say goodbye and thank you for your friendship."

Niles was touched, as Towne was not the type of person to wear his heart on his sleeve. "I still think you should share your knowledge of time and trans-dimension travel with the world. Millions of heads are better than one."

"Maybe someday, but I don't think any dimension is ready for it yet."

"Is there nothing I can say that will change your mind?"

"Well, if you suddenly recited *The Epic of Gilgamesh* in the original Akkadian, it would give me pause, but no, I have to go. Farewell, my friend." With that, he embraced Niles and left.

There was another reason Towne had to leave this dimension. His hormones were driving him nuts. He'd get an erection just thinking about the Empire State Building. He'd never married, but hardly any marriage in this dimension could survive couples entering their adolescence. That wasn't surprising when most people first married in the equivalent of their 70s. At that age you had different needs from a middle-aged person or a youngster.

Somehow, Niles's marriage had survived until he was the equivalent of 27. He'd subsequently had affairs, but none lasted. When you got younger, you played the field, because no one person could satisfy another. The play-acting, the quest for self-definition, the inability to resist bawdy jokes — Towne just couldn't go through that again.

He entered his garage, where for years he'd parked the Sideways Machine, a tarp hiding its odd appearance, which looked more like a giant spider than a vehicle. All he'd packed were some clothes. His computer files were safely downloaded on his phone. Tossing the tarp, he got inside the SM and drove to a deserted field on the outskirts of the city, where for each of his eight trips, he'd always taken off and landed. The last six times, however, he'd ended up somewhere else. With each jump into the no-man's land between dimensions, he encountered fierce dimensional storms. Despite securing himself to his seat and donning a helmet, he'd been knocked unconscious on several occasions. Just the thought of it caused a headache.

"Here goes ... I don't know what," he said, as he started the SM and began driving across the field. Once he'd reached the speed of 140 kilometers per hour, his craft left the ground. After flying three kilometers, he floored the speed pedal. Within sixty seconds the sky exploded, and he found himself swept into the dark zone between dimensions. Winds buffeted and shook the SM, as if to insist that no one was supposed to be here.

He momentarily eased up on the pedal. The faster his speed, the more forceful the winds became, but speed was necessary for the SM would jump into another dimension. He remembered some classmates in school who loved to speed in cars and how he'd always thought drag racing was one of the dumbest sports in the history of humankind.

He accelerated.

The SM shook so badly, everything lost its shape, and yet, at 400, 500, 600 kilometers per hour, he was still stuck between dimensions. He reached 700, 800, 900. Without warning, another flying vehicle appeared, heading straight for him! Never before had he encountered traffic between dimensions, and he had no way to communicate with the on-coming vehicle. At the last moment, he swerved right, but the other vehicle did the same, grazing Towne's SM, which spun out of control. Fearing he might lose consciousness, he programmed the SM to switch to autopilot once it reached another dimension. There was another explosion, then nothing.

• • •

Towne woke up in the familiar field off Route 131. Had he returned to the backward dimension, or somewhere else? At least he was in one piece. He turned on the SM. The engine sounded like a damaged hairdryer. He pushed it into the woods then walked four kilometers to the nearest bus stop.

As he rode to his downtown apartment, the houses, stores, and vegetation all looked as he remembered them. If only he had reached a dimension he could live comfortably in.

Entering the lobby of his apartment building, he glared at the ugly purple carpet, the light smell of mold, and the lack of a name for apartment 3A. For 5B the name "TOWNE" had been handwritten on a piece of tape, slightly peeling off. For the first time, was he about to meet a copy of himself? There was only one way to find out.

He pressed the button.

"Yes," said a voice, a bit high pitched. He couldn't tell if it was male or female.

"I'm here to see Christian Towne," Towne said.

"Who are you?" the voice asked gruffly.

"My name is Christian Towne."

After a short silence, the voice sputtered. "What did you come back for?"

"Come back? I've never been here."

The voice swore, then the buzzer rang, unlocking the door. Towne entered the elevator and pressed button 5. When the doors opened to the fifth floor, a middle-aged balding man with an untamed beard stood waiting for him. He looked identical to the man Towne had been the first time he left his dimension.

"You've never met me?" asked the older Towne.

"I would have remembered."

The older Towne pulled on his beard. "If anyone ever criticizes me for implausibility, I'll kick them in the ass. Follow me." He led the younger Towne to his apartment. The walls were plastered with posters, like a college student's dorm room. It was an idiosyncratic collection, however, of relative unknowns from the worlds of sports, politics, Hollywood, and literature. In pride of place was one Ken Poulsen, a utility infielder who postponed his wedding to compile a major league career of one hit in five at bats with the 1967 Red Sox.

Towne had always wondered if his marriage had survived. Another poster showed the grade Z character actor Mel Welles selling a flower in the original *Little Shop of*

Horrors. On top of a bookcase stuffed with double rows of books sat a bust of Benjamin Harrison, the 23rd president of the United States, which Towne hadn't seen since he'd accidently knocked it over and smashed it while dusting. From that he'd coined the phrase, "from dusting to dust."

The older Towne noticed his interest. "Do these things mean anything to you?"

"Yes! I didn't think I'd ever see them again. They say material objects aren't important, but I've come to love how they are the only things that don't change."

"Someone who looked exactly like you said the same thing to me two days ago. I helped him repair his SM. This morning he supposedly returned to the dimension from which he came, which he said went backward."

The younger Towne's face got red. "Why did he do that?"

"He didn't want to live in a dimension where there was two of us. I told him just by our different ages, we were not the same, and that he was better off not messing around with inter-dimensional travel. He wouldn't listen."

"That sounds like me."

"And me. So, are you coming from a dimension where time goes backwards?"

"Yes! Does it go forward here, younger to older?"

"It does."

"Thank God!"

"You might want to wait on that," said the older Towne. "There is one difference between you and the guy who left this morning. Your voice is lower."

"Now that you mention it, yours is a bit high, and you talk fast."

"Did anything odd happen on your way to this dimension?"

The younger Towne's eyes widened. "I grazed another vehicle just before I left the backward dimension."

"Could you see the driver?"

"I was more concerned with his vehicle."

"He had to be the other you, leaving this dimension. I wonder if the accident put you out of sync, somehow. Nothing surprises me now."

"But why would there be another me? Before I went there, there was none in the backward dimension, and the Towne of this dimension is you. So this other Towne is from yet another dimension."

"How many dimensions are there?" asked the older Towne.

"In theory, an infinite amount, but that makes it all the more unlikely that someone would stumble into the ones I've been in." He thought for a moment. "Unless ... there's always been a lot of turbulence in the buffer zone. I wonder if by crossing dimensions, I've somehow fused the strands of both of them, so that when someone later goes into the buffer zone, he or she is more likely to end up going where I went."

"Is that possible?"

"There's no guarantee that any of the rules of science apply between dimensions. The thing is, this is the first time I've used the Sideways Machine in twenty-five years. It seems unlikely that a version of me in another dimension would be out in the Sideways Machine at the same time."

"Not if there's an infinite amount of chances. The strands might get more fused each time someone travels on them. What if that means more Townes doing the same thing, creating a loop?"

"That's a ghastly thought," said Towne.

•   •   •

The older Towne, who said to call him OT, set up a bed in a spare room while Towne took a shower. Nothing stimulated the sweat glands like inter-dimensional travel. Speaking of stimulation, he noticed a pair of panties hanging over the shower nozzle. After his shower he asked if OT was into wearing clean women's underwear.

"No, but my wife is. She's a gender studies professor at Boston University. It's a three-hour commute, so she sleeps on a friend's pullout three days a week. She'll be back tomorrow."

"I've never been able to marry. You'll have to tell me your secret."

OT's shrugged. "Limited energy."

Towne nodded. "Speaking of which, if you'll please excuse me, I need to replenish mine. Even nineteen-year-olds don't have an unlimited supply." He collapsed onto the spare bed. Was *he* the first Towne or merely a copy? Would more be coming? What were the implications of OT's voice being higher? As he lay there woolgathering, his last thought of the night was he couldn't have counted sheep if his life depended on it.

Towne woke up the next morning unsure of the day, time, or dimension. His watch said 4:17 a.m., which was odd, as behind a pulled shade, the sun appeared to be shining. Lifting the shade confirmed that it was mid-morning. Towne checked his other watches — he always wore three due to a joke on *The Three Stooges*, where Curly revealed it was how he told the time. Towne later tried to break the habit but felt naked without them. His other two watches confirmed the 4:17 time.

Outside the window, lines of cars zoomed down the main street. Somehow this dimension had solved traffic congestion. Outside the room he heard OT talking to a woman, though he couldn't make out the words. He got dressed, ran his hand through his long, bushy hair, and opened the door. He saw OT sitting at a table next to a middle-aged woman with reddish, shoulder-length hair and brown eyes that flashed with irony.

"You've risen from the dead," OT said, but something was indeed wrong with his voice, which raced as if he were on amphetamines. "Christian Towne, this is my wife, Vanessa," he spewed.

"It really is happening again," said Vanessa, quickly extending her hand as if she were trying to catch a sinking line drive. Towne took it warily.

"Pleased to meet you." It was the most common of pleasantries, but it made both OT and Vanessa recoil.

288

"I was afraid of that," said OT. "You're moving and speaking slower than yesterday. You're out of sync with this dimension, and it's getting worse. There's no time to waste. We must repair the Sideways Machine while you can still help. And since I'm an IT director and not an inventor, I'm going to need your help."

They drove to the field then towed the SM to the side of the road by OT's apartment building.

The damage turned out to be superficial. The left wing had a meter-long crack and a belt had snapped. Otherwise, the mechanics appeared undamaged, but there was another problem: because the Sideways Machine was from another dimension, it, like Towne, was out of sync, and slowing down. As constructed, it was unable to attain the necessary speed to do an inter-dimensional jump. Towne and OT worked through the night, increasing power, but to a dangerous level.

"How will I be able to drive this thing?" said Towne, his words drooling out of his mouth. "I'll have the reflexes of a bog person."

"I will drive to the field," said OT, speaking deliberately slow, though to Towne the words streamed together in a torrent. "For the rest, we'll have to depend on the autopilot."

By the time they returned to OT's apartment, verbal communication between Towne and the couple was nearly impossible. OT's and Vanessa's words flowed together like a laser beam. OT and Vanessa found it difficult to concentrate when Towne's words oozed out like molasses. In the kitchen they communicated by notes.

"Have you decided where you're going to go?" said the note OT handed to Towne.

Towne wrote his answer. "I will return to the backward dimension, if I can. That's probably where the fused strands want me to go anyway. There's a chance the version of me that returned two days ago will be there. Alone, I've been unable to return home. Perhaps if multiple inventors of the SM — no offense — put their heads together, it could finally happen."

"None taken, but wouldn't he be just as out of sync *there* as you are *here*? And if so, wouldn't he have to leave, just as you do?"

"That's occurred to me. I will set the Sideways Machine to arrive the day before I left. If the other me does make it back, that would not only ensure I avoid the collision, but it would also give me time to meet him. Then, if necessary, I could bring him back out between dimensions and return with him. If it solves my sync problem, it would solve his."

"The Sideways Machine time travels, too?" asked OT.

"That was supposed to be its original function. The dimension travel was an accident that kept compounding."

"Life tends to do that."

• • •

Laying in bed, doubts assailed Towne. He'd devoted much of his life to temporal and dimensional travel, in part because he felt there had to be a better time or dimension than the one he was living in. But with each trip he took in the Sideways Machine, he ended up somewhere worse. It was like not being satisfied with a facelift, but each one made you look more like a Martian.

Having lived extensively in his own dimension as well as in a backward one, he'd extended his life beyond the 90 or so years allotted to most people. Was his being out of sync now so different from what happened to the elderly of his dimension? Old people needed more time to process and felt as if life was careening out of control, leaving them behind. Only a few days ago he was in the backward dimension, slowly making his way to childhood. It had happened so fast, but didn't everyone think that?

He woke up to grasping hands carrying him out of his bed. After he finished his morning ablutions and ate breakfast, OT and Vanessa strapped him into the Sideways Machine. It was as if someone had pressed the fast-forward button. He had no chance to react. As OT drove the SM to the departure field, he felt like he was in a barrel going down Niagara Falls. He had become a passive figure, something he'd never been before.

Before Towne realized what was happening, OT stood outside the SM. He might have waved, but it happened too fast for Towne to be sure. The SM began moving forward at an accelerating speed. Towne thought, if for some reason I have to override the automatic pilot, I won't be able to drive this thing. OT has sent me to my death! He noticed the SM was gaining altitude, flying over houses and trees. Could this work? He noticed a note taped to the dashboard. It was from OT.

"I wish I could have got to know you better, because in doing so, I would have learned more about myself. I'll have to be content with the takeaway lesson: *Never invent a Sideways Machine!* Godspeed, whatever that may be!"

The SM made the jump to the buffer area connecting dimensions. The dimension storms were less severe than earlier crossings, and within minutes he achieved the jump point to the backward dimension. Suddenly, he saw another SM approaching. How was that possible, when he was arriving the day before he'd left? Sensing he was no longer out of sync, he switched to manual control. He veered right, but seconds later, the other SM adjusted its direction, right for him. It made no sense, but the more one used the SM, the less anything did.

Towne veered left, and the approaching vehicle adjusted, as if it were a mirror. He watched it get larger and larger in his view screen. *The pilot has got to be me,* he thought, *and there's a reason he's targeting me. He couldn't have known I was returning two days early ... unless he saw me arrive then went back in time to meet me.* Once more Towne veered to the right, and the oncoming vehicle matched it. Perhaps it was time to start trusting himself. He braced for a direct hit.

●　　　●　　　●

Niles and Towne stood in the field, as the two SMs exploded overhead.

"Do you think it worked?" asked Niles.

"It will take a couple of days to be sure," said Towne, visibly shaken. "There's probably a strand where there are still 27 Townes running around, but in this one, there's a good chance I'm the last one left. That's enough."

"Do you feel like a murderer?" Niles asked.

He shook his head. "I feel like someone who, at the last moment, cancelled their ticket on the Titanic."

•   •   •

When Towne had returned to the backward dimension and met the 27 other Townes, finishing his sentences, jockeying for position, diminishing his worth, he realized the only solution was to go back in time. Once there, Towne confronted his two-day earlier self before he left the backwards dimension and convinced him to stay. That would eliminate the other Townes, with the exception of he himself, the man OT and his wife packaged into the Sideways Machine, who had caused all this disruption. He insisted he pilot the fatal collision of the two SMs. That eliminated all but one of the Sideways Machines, which was parked a hundred feet from the two men.

"Niles, you always told me to destroy the Sideways Machine, but I never listened until now. Thanks for ... existing."

"What are friends for?" Niles asked.

"That's something we're going to continue to find out."

There was only one more thing to do. Towne overloaded the engine of the SM and backed away. In less than 60 seconds, it exploded like an intense regret.

Towne turned to Niles, whose car was parked on the side of the road. It was back to a life that hadn't turned out the way he planned, that he would slowly lose control of. But he was finally going to accept it as his.

"Let's go home," said Towne. "We're not getting any older."

Evangeline Giaconia is a queer writer, artist, and world traveler. Her writing is driven by her love for queerness, myth, and social transformation. She currently resides in Gainesville, Florida, where she works in a library and is often found knitting and reading interesting books turned in by patrons.

ARISTOMACHE

EVANGELINE GIACONIA

I

T HE BOAT BOBBED UP and down on choppy waves, young fear suffusing the sea air. It was a sour, familiar smell. Aristomache stood on the pier and watched the futures of seven girls and seven boys slowly drowning. An equally sour, familiar voice interrupted her contemplation.

"Aristomache?"

The man of the hour, disguised for the moment as a youth, poorly. She turned to face him and could not help the curl of her lip, echoing the curl of disgust in her gut the sight of Theseus evoked. He thought he could pass as a boy like *that*? With his man's leer and his man's swagger. She fought to conceal how angry his presence made her. The reformer, they were calling him. Already the myth outstripped the man.

He was golden and glowing as he reached her, even under the dirt he had smeared on his face. "What in Hades are you doing in Athens?" he demanded. "I thought we'd been rid of you four years ago."

"So good to see you too, brother."

Theseus scoffed, baring his teeth. "You're no sister of mine."

Aristomache looked back out at the turbulent sea, boat rocking on waves of terror. "I'm not staying long."

Theseus followed her train of thought — it was the same as his, after all. "You're going to slay the minotaur?" It gratified her that he didn't scoff at *that* thought. No matter how he despised her, he could not deny the truth of her prowess.

She merely shrugged. "I will slay whichever beast presents itself to my blade." She flicked a dismissive gaze over him, just to see him steam. "One for whom my blade has long been thirsty presents himself now."

Theseus put a hand to his hip, but he was unarmed, as was she. "Go to the crows, Eupraxia. You are a joke."

Eupraxia. *Good conduct.* The syllables of her old name, cast off in the sea long ago, grated on her ears. "I am neither of those things. Not anymore. And the girls on this ship have no need of your ... help ... brother. Go back to Pirithous and pant over some other women."

He sneered so hard it distorted his entire face. "I've heard tell of *your* women, bitch. You shouldn't be allowed aboard. They're supposed to be delivering maidens, after all."

Aristomache tried to push her rage back, but her heart was rocking like the ship in the waves. In one fluid move she stepped past him, kicking her heel behind his. The sound of his breath punching from his lungs as he hit the ground was infinitely satisfying. He looked up at her from the dock, furious but unwilling to engage further. Unwilling to lose.

Aristomache smoothed her chiton. "There is one woman whose favor is always with me, and it is Aphrodite Anadyomene. Don't think to blaspheme her again."

Theseus scrambled up and turned his back on her, shooting one more poisonous barb over his shoulder like a tantruming child. "How far Eupraxia has fallen, from her father's obedient daughter."

She folded her arms, chin tilted up in a manner calculated to drive his irritation skyward. "And how far Aristomache has risen. Begone, O great reformer, and reflect on the irony."

He skulked away like a kicked dog, leaving Aristomache to approach the ship. She would be glad to leave Athens again, no matter the danger she would be sailing into. She called up to the sailors. "Send the youngest girl down. I will take her place."

II

All shores reminded Aristomache of her rebirth. Whether she was departing the Athenian beach, shore packed with ugly memories, or arriving on the Cretan dock, surrounded by petrified youths, the sound of waves upon sand would always center her. It reminded her who she was, and who she was no longer. She relived the day she had gone into the ocean as mourning Eupraxia, and emerged shorn and salt-soaked Aristomache, with the blessing of a goddess.

It was bittersweet, that memory. Rebirth only follows desolation.

By the time they were led off the boat, Aristomache was thoroughly ill with the youths' panic. She had done what she could to comfort them on the voyage: gave the girls a shoulder to cry on, as well as those boys who finally surrendered to terror. Arriving in Crete, however, all fraying tethers to sanity seemed finally to snap.

Had Aristomache truly been in their place, she would likely have snapped too. Knossos sickened her. They were paraded down the street to the palace like returning heroes, citizens cheering and throwing flowers at their feet, while their hands were chained and they were led on a rope like cattle.

In the palace they were greeted with a night of revelry. King Minos himself made a speech to greet them, his entire family arrayed around him like decorations. He praised Athens for their tribute, a twisted gleam in his eye, and thanked the youths for their bravery. The crowd of assembled nobility laughed and tittered as the king proclaimed his indebtedness to King Aegus and the Athenian citizens.

A feast ensued after Minos finished his sarcastic oration. Wine was plentiful, with figs and honey cakes and a dozen other delicacies. The Athenian youths stuffed themselves, overwrought and clumsy with despair. They drank like they hoped they'd still be drunk in the morning when they were set into the maze. A few enticed party-goers into last minute, frantic trysts, trying desperately to live before they died.

Minos watched over the twisted bacchanalia with cool speculation, a malicious smirk on his face, eyes gleaming. Aristomache's blood sang for his heart as she watched him over her cup, brimming with wine she would not partake of. Her fingers itched to curl into fists. She kept them still, and observed his wife.

Queen Pasiphaë sat dull-eyed and listless beside Minos. Aristomache had seen that look before. Her own kingly father had plowed through four women in search of a son-bearing womb. Her mother had been the first to be discarded, and when he had finally sired a son, even he had been unsatisfactory. Aegus swapped out heirs like hats. Her father's legacy was a trail of trash he dropped behind him, once useful and now worthless.

The look in Pasiphaë's eyes was depletion, and Aristomache knew it well.

She saw it in his children too, seven of them. They skirted the edges of the perverse festivities like skittish animals, eyes haunted, shoulders hunched.

Only one was not so timid. She caught Aristomache's eye by the color of her hair, rich red-touched gold, and held it with her strong jaw, clenched at the revelry that surrounded her.

She was also watching Aristomache, a carafe of wine in fine-boned fingers, her eyes dark and angry.

Aristomache tipped her wine cup to call her over, though it was still full. The princess' walk was stiff but graceful, and Aristomache admired the rage in the set of her elegant shoulders. Such obvious defiance was a welcome relief from the youths' despair and the unholy glee of the other partygoers. It mirrored Aristomache's own heart.

"You aren't like the others," the woman said softly, glancing from Aristomache's face to her brimming cup.

"No," Aristomache agreed. "I volunteered for this sacrifice, Princess Ariadne."

The woman's mouth tightened. "You know me."

"I've heard tell of your beauty." Aristomache smiled and was gratified to see the princess raise her hand to stifle a laugh. "I am the elder sister of Prince Theseus of Athens. Aristomache, daughter of Meta."

Ariadne frowned. "I do not know of you."

"Few do. I used to go by another name."

Ariadne's eyes skipped over Aristomache's muscled arms. "You are no youth. You say you volunteered for this madness?"

"I will *end* this madness," Aristomache swore. "In the name of Aphrodite Anadyomene, whose blessing I carry. Though my suspicions are deepening that ending it does not necessarily mean slaying the beast. This madness runs deep."

She let her gaze flick around at the revelry, knowing her disgust showed on her face. She also caught Ariadne's subtle frown at her phrasing. "You take exception to the word 'beast'? You feel sympathy for the monster who slaughters the youth of my homeland?"

"I feel sympathy for my *brother*." Ariadne's strong jaw was clenched, and Aristomache was sure it was anger, not fear, making her hands tremble minutely around the wine.

"I would hear more of your tale," Aristomache said.

The carafe shook so forcefully the wine nearly spilled. Aristomache extended her cup, and Ariadne took a deep, settling breath before pouring the barest amount into the full vessel. "Do not sleep tonight. When the moon is high, meet me in the garden below your room."

"I will be there, Princess."

III

"How could I have never heard your name?" Ariadne asked.

They stood among a riot of moon washed crocus blooms. The garden was a floral paradise, the air perfumed, the infinite silk sky dotted by the myriad souls of bygone heroes.

Aristomache brushed her fingers over a crocus petal, then plucked it. With care, she tucked it behind Ariadne's ear, savoring the soft brush of her sunshine hair and the high blush that bloomed across her face.

"Why would my father announce the birth of a daughter? Aegus hungered only for sons, but even his son by his fourth wife Medea proved insufficient. Medus was my cherished brother, yet when Theseus came, even he was cast off."

Aristomache had to look away from Ariadne's face then, unwilling to let her see the force of her old rage. "Medea was my teacher, beloved by myself and my mother. She advised the king against replacing Medus as heir. For this, Aegus exiled them both."

Memories swept her away for a suspended moment, superseding the stars. The boat carrying her beloved mentor away from her. The slap of Aegus' hand against dear Medus' face. Her mothers' desolation at her lover's exile. And over it all, Theseus: intruder, usurper, ruiner.

"What did you do?" Ariadne's musical voice brought her back to the present, like the lyre of Orpheus.

"I left," Aristomache said. "I reinvented myself, gave myself new purpose: to hunt down injustice and slay it, as I could not do in my own home." She let out a great breath, heavy with regret.

Ariadne traced her hand down Aristomache's cheek, a melancholy smile on her face. "You live my wildest dream."

Aristomache caught her hand and dared to press a brief kiss to it. "Tell me of your brother."

The sadness in Ariadne's eyes deepened, and she dropped her eyes to the crocuses flowering beneath their feet. "These are his favorite flower." Tugging Aristomache with her, she sank to the ground and nestled into the blooms, turning her gaze to the night sky.

"My brother was born of the wrath of a god." She traced Aristomache's knuckles as she spoke. "I will not speak his name. Minos slighted him, and for my father's crime he induced insanity into my mother and made her fall into perverse lust for a white bull." She spoke the horror dispassionately. "My eldest brother was the result. Asterion."

Her lip trembled and she sighed, looking from the stars to the ground. With her free hand, Aristomache stroked her hair slowly.

"They call him *monstrous*," Ariadne spat. "But he is wise, and gentle, and a gifted poet. He studied statecraft — he was the only son for a time, horrid as Minos thought him. I always thought … perhaps it was delusion, but I saw a good king in him. We used to play games imagining how different it would be when he ruled. And then my other brothers came."

Her face had tightened, holding back tears, but now they came tremoring down her cheeks. She jerked her hands up to dash them away violently, but Aristomache caught her face and ran her thumbs gently under her eyes.

"My father no longer had need for a beast of a son," Ariadne continued bitterly. "Asterion was first confined to his room, then sent to the country, and finally locked in this wicked maze for the last three years. All the while my mother deteriorates, my siblings are but sheep, and Minos terrorizes his subjects."

Aristomache pulled her close, and Ariadne leaned her head on her shoulder, tears subsiding. "You say you are here to end this madness. Then save my brother. Even if that means killing him, for I am sure he is dying from this life. We all are."

"I will do all I can," Aristomache swore, stroking her hands down Ariadne's lovely back. "All Aphrodite guides me to do. But no one has yet escaped from the maze."

Ariadne turned her starry face up to Aristomache, her lips parted and gleaming. "I will help you."

When Aristomache kissed her, she felt Ariadne's soft lips turn up in a smile. When she pulled her down into the crocuses, Ariadne pressed gentle kisses to her breasts. When she buried her mouth between her silken legs, Ariadne called her name softly in the darkness, a blessing as holy as any goddess'.

During the night, Ariadne left Aristomache dozing in the crocuses and returned in the early hours. She carried a gleaming ball of thread the color of her rosy lips. "Come back to me," she demanded.

"Yes, Princess," said Aristomache.

Ariadne smiled, kissed her cheek, and tucked a crocus behind her ear.

IV

The labyrinth gaped dark and damp in front of her.

The youths, frenzied, desolate, and still slightly drunk, lit out into the maze the moment their ropes were loosened. They screamed and fled from shadows of imagined beasts, tripping into walls and over themselves. Aristomache stood in the cavern entrance and let them pass.

She had only the flower behind her ear and the ball of thread, which Ariadne had unspooled and wound many times around her waist under her chiton. Now Aristomache unwound it again and fastened the end to a boulder just inside the cavern entrance, tugging to ensure it held.

In addition to the thread and flower, Ariadne had given her one more precious thing: directions. Go only forward and down, turning neither left nor right.

Aristomache steeled her nerves, gave the line one more tug, and entered the labyrinth.

She lost track of time almost immediately. Shadows encroached further and further until there was nothing but darkness and the ghostly sensation of the walls around her, rising up to the heavens. Panic began to build up as she stumbled through the artificial night. How was she supposed to turn neither left nor right if she could not even see the path?

All she had was the thread in her hands and the flower behind her ear. She could only recall the taste of Ariadne's lips and hope the memory would suffice to ward away the terror.

But something happened as she remembered the puff of Ariadne's breath and the sunrise touch of her fingertips: the thread clutched in her fingers began to glow a faint rosy light. It stretched behind her, a heartstring, illuminating her path.

The labyrinth coiled on and on, and Aristomache ventured unerringly forward into the belly of the snake. After an unknowable period of time, she stumbled upon a sight that made her leap backwards in disgust: human bones. Barely visible by the light of her thread, they lay in a curl of eternal despair. She stepped respectfully around them and plunged on, but the tableau grew more and more frequent the closer she prowled to the center of the maze. To her dismay, it also became easier to ignore them.

Quite suddenly, after a long not-time of groping along the endless cold walls, between one curve and the next she came to the center.

The middle of the maze was a tiny space framed by eight archways and lit by a single torch on the wall that cast eerie blue shadows across the dirt floor. The sudden light forced her to blink away sunspots before she could see the monster.

It was an indistinct heap of fur and skin in the middle of the octagon. Its back rose and fell in slumber. The light barely reached it.

She gripped Ariadne's glowing thread close, apprehensive in spite of the princess' assurances, and sent a short entreaty to Aphrodite before calling out: "Asterion?"

The being erupted out of sleep with a snarl, scrambling to

all fours, tail lashing. It took everything in her not to flinch backwards. She could see now that it was a man with the head of a bull, filthy with grime. His hands, caked in dirt and blood, dug into the ground. He wore only a loincloth and metal collar, from which a chain bolted him to the floor, forcing his crouch.

"Asterion," she repeated. "Do you yet comprehend speech? I am Aristomache. Your sister sent me."

The minotaur shook his head like an animal, then sat back on his heels and wiped his hands across his eyes like an exhausted man. When he looked at her anew, his deep black eyes were pools of starlight.

"Of course, I understand you," he spat. "Living like an animal cannot make me one, no matter how much Minos wishes. Which sister do you speak of? For one would have me dead in this cave, while the others I would beg you for word of."

Aristomache took the crocus from her hair and tossed it to him. Asterion caught and held it like it was the most fragile of birds, pressing his wide black nose to the petals. His starry eyes went soft.

"Ariadne," he whispered.

"It was she who told me how to find you, who gave me this thread to guide us both out."

"I have long worried over her treatment at the hands of our father, without my presence to absorb his ire."

"Your other siblings may be cowed, but she stands apart. She approached me, saw I was no sacrificial youth, and gave me the tools to free you."

Asterion smiled. "And my mother?"

Aristomache remembered Pasiphaë, dim-eyed next to her husband. It must have shown on her face, because Asterion gave a low bellow of grief.

"I did not speak with her," Aristomache said, "but she looked … unwell.

Asterion's face twisted in animal anger. "I will kill Minos. I should have done it long ago."

"First we must free you," Aristomache said. She walked to him and examined the collar around his neck, wincing at the sight of metal fused to fur by dried blood.

"There is no keyhole," Asterion said. "I befriended one of the youths once, convinced her to examine the collar. She tried for two days to open it before she died of thirst."

Aristomache had no way to pry off a band of solid metal. There was only one thing to be done. "Give me the flower."

Asterion passed her the crocus with a puzzled expression, and she took it to the small torch on the wall. Gently, she held it out for the fire to lick, and held it in her cupped hands as it burned.

"Aphrodite Anadyomene, goddess borne from the sea, accept my offering: a true token of a woman's love. Help your sea-borne champion, Aristomache."

She gritted her teeth as the crocus burned to ash in her palms, breathing slowly through the pain. When Asterion gasped, she turned, letting the cinders fall.

Every time she witnessed a miracle of Aphrodite, she was as awestruck as the first. Asterion's chain had fallen to the ground, and his collar had blossomed, transforming into a necklace of crocuses.

Asterion rose from his crouch for the first time in three years with an agonized moan. He staggered back and forth with dizziness, and she stepped forward and caught his bulk with her shoulder, grimacing at the touch of blood-matted fur.

When he had finally steadied, he pulled away from her and knelt back down to the floor, head bent. "May the gods bless you. Had I any agency in this kingdom, I would grant you any boon you asked."

"Stand," Aristomache said. "I already have a goddess's blessing, and I do not act for payment."

"Then why?"

Aristomache took his hand and pulled him from the floor. "For the innocent youth of Athens. For my past impotence. For the freedom of a wronged man, and the death of a monster."

Asterion's ears flicked back. "The death of a monster. But you have freed me, not killed me."

Aristomache grinned. "You are not the monster in this country. Tell me: would your people follow a bull?"

Asterion stared at her, starry eyes bright. "You mean to put me on the throne."

"Your sister told me you studied statecraft, that you would have made a gentle ruler. Couldn't Crete use such a king?"

Asterion paced the circle of his confinement, thick hands smoothing the fur on his face, pressing his ears down. She felt his agitation growing and also his excitement.

"There was a time I thought I would rule," he murmured. "When I was Pasiphaë's only son. It was a child's delusion, but I thought of myself as a future king. Before my brothers were born." A bull couldn't smile, but his nostrils flared and his eyes shone.

"You don't hate them?"

Asterion shook his head. "When Minos barred me from lessons, they would sneak to my room and teach me what they remembered. The people barely know me ... and yet, I am the eldest son. With the support of my brothers ..."

"Will they give it?"

"Glaucus, the youngest, would give it in a heartbeat. He is too sweet for bloody rule. Catreus, the second, will oppose me. Deucalion, now the eldest after Androgeus' death, has always hated his lot as heir, but he does not easily give up power. Thus, it falls to my sisters."

"How?" Aristomache asked, marveling at the tapestry of family politics. Hers had always been black and white. Or black and red.

"Ultimately, it will be Xenodice's deciding voice, as the eldest daughter. Deucalion values her opinion over all. If Ariadne and Phaedra, the youngest, can sway her to my favor, then he will bow to my dubious authority as eldest. That leaves only Catreus and Acacallis in opposition, and me with the majority." His night-sky eyes grew cloudy. "It was my third sister Acacallis who encouraged my imprisonment. The prospect of facing her brings me no joy."

It took a significant effort of will to follow the convoluted alliances. "Ariadne is with you, of course. But Phaedra?"

Asterion's eyes softened. "Phaedra was the child of my heart. She attempted to fight Minos when I was condemned to this fate."

Aristomache's heart clenched with longing for Medus, her own beloved prince, whom her father had turned on. "Then we leave this place and go at night to Ariadne and Phaedra," she said, pushing back memories of heartbreak.

Asterion turned wild eyes on her, his arms outstretched as if he could encompass the world. "From birth, my life was something to be hidden and reviled. For the last three years, I thought it forfeit. Now, I see hope."

"Then let's make haste while it lasts. For we must still gather up thirteen intoxicated youths from this maze."

V

They crept through the palace gardens, a woman- and bull- shaped shadow. They had deposited the now hung-over youths inside a sea cave. To get them out of the maze they'd had to tie them to Ariadne's string, navigating to the exit as a weaving lunatic caterpillar.

"There is her window." Asterion pointed three stories up.

Aristomache picked up a small stone and threw it through the drifting curtain. It took several tosses before the curtain was pulled back. Ariadne's heart-shaped face peered out, the sight making Aristomache's own heart flutter. When Ariadne saw them, her hands flew to her mouth. She disappeared from sight, returning a moment later to roll a ladder down from the window.

Her dress swayed in the night breeze as she descended, and she leapt the last few rungs directly into her brother's arms with a joyful whisper of his name.

He staggered under her weight, and they fell to the ground, she pressing kisses all across his white muzzle — he had washed the filth off in the ocean.

"Be careful with me, sister," he groaned, though he was laughing all the same. "I am much weakened from my time in the maze."

"I will never let you go again," Ariadne swore. She looked up at Aristomache, face shining. "Excepting this once." And she leapt upon Aristomache and kissed her across her face as well, whispering adoring thanks.

"What now?" Ariadne asked, taking both their hands. "Flight?"

"No," rumbled Asterion. "Aristomache has a better idea. Where are Phaedra and Xenodice?"

"Abed, if they can stomach it after watching the sacrifice. I've told them nothing of my plans."

"Your lady plots to put me on the throne."

Ariadne looked at Aristomache, one fine eyebrow raised and a high blush on her cheeks. "I see. And so it all comes down to our eldest sister." Aristomache marveled at how quickly her mind had worked it out.

"Do you think it possible?" Asterion asked.

"It would not be," Ariadne said, "had Xenodice not recently taken a lover Minos would never approve."

Asterion's ears flicked forward, intrigued. "And who is this lover?"

Ariadne laughed softly. "Truly, it is Icarus. She sneaks into his workshop once a fortnight and thinks no one notices. As if her strange mechanical trinkets could be coming from anywhere else."

"Then I have won," Asterion said in satisfaction. "All that remains is to see it through."

"Not yet," Ariadne said. "For there is still myself."

Asterion and Aristomache looked at her in surprise. "Yourself?" Asterion asked slowly. "Sister, was it not you who conspired my release?"

Ariadne met his eyes, chin up, jaw set. "I will no longer be used as a pawn in a game of war. I will no longer accept the suits of men, and I shall live without fear in my own household. And if I should choose to leave, I will not be forestalled. I love you, brother, but I must know that rule will not turn you into my father."

Asterion, holding her gaze, slowly knelt at her feet. "Ariadne. Beloved sister. For the times you read me poetry in the dark, I promise. For the times you brought Minos' wrath upon yourself to spare me, I promise. For our evenings finding new constellations in the stars, for our days climbing trees, I promise you. But also for the sake of my future rule, I promise: I shall be no Minos. Not to you, not to anyone."

The sharpness of Ariadne's smile cut straight through Aristomache's heart.

VI

The ease with which the coup was staged was testament to how reviled Minos was.

Asterion strode through the halls, flanked by his siblings — though a few of them looked grudging — and a foreign warrior woman, and soldiers lay down their arms. Minos' personal guard knelt to Asterion in front of the king's chamber doors.

Only Aristomache entered Minos' rooms with Asterion. And only Minos was inside, reading by a lamp. When they closed the door, he set the papers down carefully on his desk. The very sight of him turned Aristomache's stomach.

"You," Minos said to Asterion. "Monster that haunts my nightmares, returned in the flesh. And with what?" He looked at Aristomache in outraged confusion. "Some woman? Even I never expected you to find a girl with such tastes as your mother."

Asterion snorted in anger, and Aristomache raised the sword she had taken from a soldier. "I am Aristomache, eldest child of Queen Meta of Athens. In the name of Aphrodite

Anadyomene, I come seeking justice for our twenty-eight youths whose lives fell victim to your sick pleasure. My blade has long sung for your blood."

"And you come with this creature," Minos said in disgust. "So it is a coup? As if Crete will follow the minotaur at the heart of a maze of nightmares. They know you are a devourer of children."

"I am no such thing!" Asterion bellowed. "In that hell-maze you made your architect design, I killed only in defense of my life, and no piece of flesh ever passed my lips! I would have died before becoming so depraved!"

"Liar," Minos snarled. "How could you still live?"

"The will of the gods," Asterion declared. "Which will not save you tonight." He turned to Aristomache. "Lend me your sword?"

Minos stood, hands clenched around the edge of his desk. "You would not dare."

"I would do it," Aristomache offered. "If you have truly never killed, then let me, for I have killed many."

Asterion shook his head. "Even wielding you as my blade, I would still be the killer. If I am to strike him down, I shall do it with honor." He glanced at Minos, whose fury was mutating to a dawning horror.

Impressed, Aristomache handed him the sword. Asterion took it, steadying his breathing, hands firm around the hilt.

"Minos of Crete," Asterion said, advancing. Minos was unarmed, and now he was panicked, scrambling back from his desk towards the window. "Accept your end with honor, if you can. Certainly, you could not muster up any by which to live."

And indeed it turned out Minos could not, for he flung himself out the window before Asterion could come a step closer. It was a choice so unexpected that Aristomache's heart jolted with sick adrenaline as she ran and peered out the window with Asterion. Minos' body lay broken and still on the path three stories below.

Asterion blew out a huge snorting bull's breath and stared at the sword in his hand. "No matter what anyone says,

I know in my heart I still killed him this night." He proffered the hilt to her. "Thank you, Aristomache. You are welcome in my kingdom for as long as my sister wishes. And if you would remain beyond that, I would even hide you from her wrath."

Aristomache laughed and clapped Asterion on his soft, furry shoulder. "I gladly accept your offer, King."

"King," Asterion said in wonderment. He looked out the window, not at the broken body of Minos, but to the sky, stars reflected in his eyes. "But where is the queen?"

Upon their return to the hallway, siblings and guard alike knelt to Asterion. Aristomache joined them immediately.

"You four," Asterion said to the soldiers. "What are your names?" They told him. "Pledge yourselves to me by Aphrodite Anadyomene."

If they found the command strange, they did not show it. The moment the goddess' name passed their lips, a crocus sprouted from the flagstones at Asterion's feet, blooming radiant purple. Everyone assembled, Asterion included, gasped and prostrated themselves before it, murmuring prayers. Stunned, Aristomache offered a prayer of her own: *Sister Aphrodite, thank you for blessing this king. May he earn what has been given.*

Asterion rose, dragging the attention back to him. "I gladly accept your service and thank you for it. This night I charge you to defend my siblings with your lives." They nodded, looking from the flower to Asterion in equal parts wonder and terror. "Rise. And please — someone tell me where mother is."

Ariadne stood and took Aristomache's hand, face grim. "She often sleeps on the roof. I think to be closer to her father. I'll go with you."

Asterion nodded, and turned to his eldest siblings. "Deucalion, Xenodice: Make a list of things which need my attention. I imagine first among them is the freedom of Daedalus and his son." Xenodice brought a hand to her mouth, and Asterion did not comment. "All of you, stay together. I do not trust any of my siblings to be truly safe this night."

VII

Ariadne led them to the fourth floor of the palace, where she pulled a trap door from the ceiling. Aristomache ascended first in case of danger, but the roof was empty save the senseless queen. She sat cross-legged, face upturned to the jewel-studded cloth of the sky. She hadn't noticed before, but now Aristomache saw that Pasiphaë shone slightly in the dark, as if sunshine was trapped beneath her skin.

Aristomache extended a hand for Ariadne, who released it immediately to go to her mother. Pasiphaë hardly moved when her daughter knelt next to her, and Aristomache was struck with cold fear that she would not even recognize Asterion.

The new king settled on Pasiphaë's other side, observing the queen's vacant skyward stare. "Mother." He took her hands gently. "Mother, do you see me? Or do your eyes search only for Helios?"

At his touch, her gaze slipped from the sky to his eyes, and for long moments she still appeared entranced. Then, to Aristomache's relief, something in the queen's face shifted. She raised trembling hands to smooth the fur around Asterion's eyes, pet his snout, and at last began to cry.

"Mother. My queen." Asterion's starry eyes glimmered. He stroked a broad hand down her pale hair. "I killed your husband. Minos lives no longer, so fear him no longer. And know that whatever you wish will be yours."

"My son."

At her mother's voice, Ariadne stifled a sob. Aristomache stopped resisting the pull in her stomach and went to her, arms wide. Ariadne fell into her embrace and hid her wet face in Aristomache's neck, shoulders shaking.

"My beautiful Asterion," Pasiphaë said. The queen smiled, and though cold moonlight shone down on them, they were suddenly as warm as if they stood in a summer sunbeam.

VIII

Crocus perfume drifted in through the window, ushered by a gentle sea breeze. Ariadne, gazing at her across their pillow, tucked a lock of Aristomache's hair behind her ear and kissed a whispered question across it. "Stay?"

Aristomache pulled her close and traced the curve of her back. "For a time. But Princess, I am called out into the world same as I was called here."

"Then," Ariadne kissed solar bursts up her neck, "come back to me?"

Aristomache tilted her chin up and kissed her long and slow, then pulled achingly away, breathing out into the space between their mouths: "Yes."

David A. Hewitt was born in Germany, grew up near Chicago, and lived for eight years in Japan, where he studied classical Japanese martial arts and grew up some more. A graduate of the University of Southern Maine's Stonecoast MFA program in Popular Fiction, he currently teaches community-college English, but has in the past worked as a translator of Japanese, an instructor of martial arts, a cabinetmaker's assistant, a pizza/subs/beer delivery guy, and a pet shop boy. His fiction has appeared in *Underland Arcana, Amazing Stories.com*, and *Metastellar*. His translation credits include the anime series *Gilgamesh, Area 88, Kingdom, Welcome to the NHK*, and *Kochoki: Young Nobunaga*.

•　　•　　•

"The Adventures of Zeedae and Them Gol-durned Genset-D Boys" is a parody of a popular TV show of yore which, after one viewing, my father forbade me from ever watching because — and he was right about this — it was deeply, deeply stupid. Obviously, I proceeded to watch it with clockwork regularity at friends' houses, but the subtle, yet permanent damage it did to my brain eventually mutated and metamorphosed into this deeply, deeply silly story. I would like to dedicate it to my most excellent writing group, the Phoenixes, who will read anything I write, no matter how bizarre and uncalled for.

THE ADVENTURES OF ZEEDAE AND THEM GOL-DURNED GENSET-D BOYS

DAVID A. HEWITT

S O YOU MUST'A HEARD how once upon a time, Zeedae
Genset-D done got herself into a heap'a trouble and landed
in a Perilous Eventuality Subsector detainment hexa-cube.

You *ain't* heard? Huh. Maybe you ain't from around these
parts?

Here's the thing: them Genset-D boys and their DNA-
affiliate kinsperson Zeedae was always gettin' on the wrong
side of the Subsector Enforcement Authority, and especially
of its leader, Boss Hrrrgh. Ol' Boss Hrrrgh done had it in fer
them boys since they left the recombinator birthin' unit, on
account of they'd been adopted by Mentorbot JSE Genset-D,
against whom Boss had a deep and longstandin' grudge.

Now ol' JSE, he was a fine mentorbot, dispensin' affection
in such a way as to evoke the neuro-emotional development
that leads to sound and balanced adults. But somewhars

along the way, Mentorbot JSE's self-conception A.I. went a little haywire, and he took to distillin' off-market Navjuice.

Now everyone knows ain't nobody permitted to man'facture and distribute Navjuice but with a license, and you can bet your bottom Galactic Exchange Unit that ol' JSE Genset-D warn't gonna have no truck with them Subsector Authorities, corrupt as they were. He done struck out on his own and I'll be goldurned if his Navjuice warn't just as good or better than the Authority-licensed stuff, with a tangier flavor, and leavin' the navigator feelin' high as a super-orbital omnisatellite to boot. It was on very rare occasions known to cause blindness, but that was easily reversible with space-age opti-medical treatments.

And how did Zeedae get herself tangled up in all that mess with the Authority? Well, if you ever heard anythin' about the Genset-D boys, you know they've a great fondness for hotroddin', runnin' the less-trafficked interplanetary and interstellar routes at speeds that ain't, strictly speakin', legal. Well what's true of them boys is also true of their DNA-affiliate Zeedae. She's pretty as a moon risin' acrosst the Butterfly Nebula, but she also has a taste for speed, and the odd dose of Mentorbot JSE's off-market, off-kilter Navjuice don't help that none.

Why, three shots of that Navjuice and she can make Q-space calculations an' burn quantum-improbable routes just as well as them boys or even better. And hoo-ee, Zeedae had near as many run-ins as them Genset-D boys theirselves with Briscoe T. Ponetrain, the Subsector Magistrate — the *Sub'strate*, they call him for short. Many's the time that ol' Sub'strate Ponetrain and his dep'ty-bots thought they done catched a live one, only to be left in Zeedae's spacedust or tricked out of issuing an Enforcement Citation Chit by her allurin' charms.

This time was diff'rent, though. Zeedae had been spotted but evaded capture three times in one Lunar Circuit, and Sub'strate Ponetrain had lost patience. Story is that it was a setup: Zeedae's Spinrunner started leakin' fusion protoplasma as she was makin' a hotroddin' run, and seein' as no one seemed to be tailin' her, she done stopped for a refuel at a service module. But the Sub'strate and his dep'ty-bots were lurkin' right there at the refuel station, right on cue — awful suspicious, almost as though they know'd just where she'd have to stop when she run low — and they done popped her into a field-capture magnetipod on the spot, afore she could bring her considerable feminine wiles into play.

What's more, when they opened the hold of her Spinrunner, they done pulled out a quantity of ol' JSE's Navjuice, enough to warrant proceedings for smugglin' and off-market traffickin'. Now Zeedae and them Genset-D boys wouldn't never transport JSE's Navjuice in any quantity across jurisdictional lines for just this reason, so one could speculate that plantin' those quantities in Zeedae's storage hold was part of the setup.

Whatever the case may be, Zeedae done wound up locked into the detainment hexa-cube back at Enforcement Authority headquarters, and the Sub'strate himself saw fit to sit in as part of the security detail to make sure she stayed there until proceedings could be held.

At this point they done had Zeedae dead to rights, them E.A. types, and it was startin' to look like an open fight might be the only way to free her, though that hadn't never been the Genset-D boys' style. No, they always preferred subterfuge or sh'nanigans when it come to stickin' it to the Enforcement Authority, or else pure vehicular speed and finesse.

So there's Zeedae, despondent, waitin' in the cube, with the legal game rigged against her as it always was for that Genset-D family. And to top all, ol' Boss Hrrrgh shows up. He come in, and he's physically nothin' but a big space-slug with a vaguely human-lookin' face; in he slinks, mainly for the purpose of gloatin' over finally incarceratin' a member of the Genset-D kin.

There he were, with the hexa-cube door open, in order to better gloat at Zeedae from close quarters, and Sub'strate Ponetrain's right there beside him in case she should try to make a run fer it. Now you'd think that with the Sub'strate standin' shotgun while ol' Boss runs his mouth, a gal with that amount of charges and evidence stacked up against her, she'd have no choice but to play up to them in hopes of gettin' fair treatment and proceedings. One might think — but that would be one who don't know Zeedae.

"Well, well," says Boss Hrrrgh, "if we ain't got Zeedae Genset-D right here in our own little detainment hexa-cube. By rights it ought to be the entire Genset-D gang in here, the whole criminal lot, but this surely is a start. JSE Genset-D's smugglin' operation has been a thorn in my side for too, too long, and here we have ourselves some evidence to start bringin' it down." Now he done leaned in at Zeedae in revolting giant space-slug fashion, and went on.

"I think we all know, my dear, sweet girl, that you're not to blame here. No, it's obvious that your old Mentorbot, old JSE, must've talked you into carrying his contraband cargo in that Spinrunner of yours. Now sure, the way you've got it souped up for speed is technically unlawful, but that — why, we can chalk that up to youthful indiscretion. It's the bootleg Navjuice that's the real concern. Now that: surely an innocent young sweetheart like you was carryin' it all unawares, or was manipulated into doing so by that conniving ol' Mentorbot JSE?"

It's a known fact that space-slugs can't wink, but if they could, Boss Hrrrgh surely would've, at this juncture. He'd offered Zeedae a way out, plausible deniability, and all she would've had to have done was to return the figurative wink, and reach out and take the bait. It was partly true anyway: the Navjuice they'd planted in the vehicle *was* in fact a sampling of Mentorbot JSE's bootleg product, which they'd confiscated elsewhere. And Mentorbot JSE was indeed the brains, the heart 'n soul of the bootleg Navjuice operation. Zeedae and her kinspersons the Genset-D boys only got involved in rare emergency circumstances; JSE Genset-D done his best to keep his young wards out of all that, to keep their noses clean.

All Zeedae had to do was admit to two things that were in fact true: Yes, the substance they'd pulled from her storage hold was Uncle JSE's legendary off-brand Navjuice, with its distinctive odor and taste; no, she hadn't put it there herself nor had any awareness of such a thing bein' there. That would've been enough for Boss Hrrrgh to have Sub'strate Ponetrain send his dep'ty-bots on over to arrest Mentorbot JSE for conspiracy to transport unlicensed Navjuice across interplanetary lines.

But even if she only had to tell the truth, Zeedae weren't no snitch, nor was she one to ever, ever betray her own kin. And Boss Hrrrgh and ol' Sub'strate Ponetrain, why, that stuff about "innocent young sweetheart" might'a been mostly hyperbole and persuasion, but my oh my had they underestimated this particular sweetheart.

"Boss and Sub'strate, sirs, I will most surely consider your offer," said Zeedae, batting her gen-mod long eyelashes at them both. "But I'm hoping that, right now, the two of you could help a poor girl out."

She turned to the bunkside table in the hexa-cube and bent over to pick up a tablet and light-stylus she'd been writin' with before they came in. She held the tablet up to show them, the sweetest and most ingenuous of looks on her face. She'd been calculatin' Fibonacci probabilistic travel branchings, as all jump-navigators must, and when she asked it to graph her equations, hoo boy — the *curves* she shown 'em on that screen! Boss Hrrrgh's eyes, already large as saucers, went wide as a starship egress-hatch, and ol' Sub'strate Ponetrain puffed up his cheeks and blew out a hypercharged breath. Hain't neither of them seen curvature like that before, and from a woman to boot; the Sub'strate blushed bright red, and Boss Hrrrgh's slug-cheeks turned a puce-like shade of magenta as Zeedae passed the tablet with them scandalous curves into their hands.

Did I mention they had misunderestimated Zeedae? Now, in their moment of distraction, she done slipped by them, kicked Sub'strate Ponetrain in the rump with her stylish magneto-heel to knock him fully into the 'cube with ol' Boss Hrrrgh, then slammed the phase portal shut, activatin' the Parabola of Silence as she did. Both of them, realizin' they'd been duped, hollered for all they was worth, but the sonic dampers done drowned out their voices entirely.

Still, Zeedae couldn't dilly-dally. There were two dep'ty-bots patrollin' around somewheres, and it was only a matter of time till they glided in. She held up the Sub'strate's T-com — she'd pilfered it right from his pocket as she slipped by — and whispered a pirate override code into it.

"Aries Two, Aries Two, you got your aural transmission implants on? This here's Wayward Ewe, puttin' out my thumb for a little pick-me-up. You read me, Aries Two?"

A voice come back, crackling with Q-space interference, and as it spoke the Sub'strate and ol' Boss Hrrrgh done pressed and bumped their heads against the phase portal, hollerin' and carryin' on like nobody's business, though with the Parabola of Silence ain't a peep could be heard from 'em.

"Well, now, Wayward Ewe, ain't your voice just music to the ears. We just happen to be in the neighborhood, about 17,000 kilometers straight up, fixin' to skim right past your current location. You wanna skitch a ride along with us?"

"Roger that, Aries Two. Zap me your Q-space paratrajectory; reckon I can find a way to hop on board."

Once she'd secured the paratrajectory fix on the Sub'strate's T-com, Zeedae poked her head out into the hallway. One of the dep'ty-bots was there, but was turned around facin' the other direction. She made a dash for it. But the sensory scanners on them 'bots had been recently upgraded, so it done detected her, and immediately registered the escape and begun firing its plasma-blaster. So there's Zeedae, a-dodgin' and a-skippin' like gangbusters, down that hallway, and I'll be goldurned if one 'a them plasma bolts ain't scorched her shoulder somethin' painful afore she dived 'round the corner to where the dissolution transporter, what you and I'd call the D-jumper, was located.

She's still clutchin' the Sub'strate's T-com, with that paratrajectory loaded into it, and just as the D-jumper is firin' up, the dep'ty-bot comes glidin' around, plasma-blaster to the ready — not one but *two* dep'ty-bots now. They done paused to stare down Zeedae just as she's steppin' onto the D-jumper pad, and she could'a been fried into plasma-broiled fricassee by them guns — if not for the brand new snap-judgment ethics-ometer that had newly been installed in the dep'ty-bots along with their sensory upgrades. That ethical-judgment algorithm done took a fraction of a second to make the call, so that at the very moment the plasma-blasters spat out their phase-shifted hot death, they hit only the empty space where Zeedae had been standin' a millisecond before.

•   •   •

Aboard the ol' Gen'ral Grant, Lau and Buuk Genset-D and Zeedae were now a-huggin' and a-kissin' cheeks, but their rejoicin' didn't last long.

"Buuk!!" Lau had noticed the proximity monitor flashin', which couldn't mean nothin' good.

Buuk squinted at the display. "Enforcement Authority orbital drones, right on cue."

Zeedae looked to one, then the other of her kinspersons with them puppy-dog eyes. "Boys y'all know how much I love the way the Gen'ral Grant handles. Can I drive?"

"Why, all respect for your aptitude, Zeedae, but it was your drivin' that got you into this fix in the first place!" said Lau with a guffaw.

"Fasten them spacebelts," said Buuk. "Things's about to get bumpy!"

Buuk threw hisself into the pilot's seat as the others strapped in, and his fingertips tapped all over the equation screen quick as a Grebtak rodent fleein' a seven-legged Snarlepticus. Them orbital drones, flashin' red on the monitor, loomed closer and closer, and a plasma-beam shot past the bow — a near miss.

"It's now or never, Buuk!" hollered Zeedae.

"All right, Gen'ral G," Buuk whooped, "do your thing!!" He swiped an open palm across the equation board and the familiar rosewater-and-phosphorus smell of Q-space entry suffused the cabin.

"Buuk," said Lau, "Why's the Gen'ral all a-shakin' and a-shimmyin' like this?"

And indeed it was. Molecular stability in Q-space travel is by no means a sure thing, so this was a disturbin' sign.

Buuk shot the others a mischievous grin. "Well, I plotted a slingshot Q-space jump around and out of the planet's gravity well, rather than a standard-curvature paratrajectory, to give them drones a little surprise."

Now the cabin was a-rattlin', a-vibratin', and a-rumblin' something awful. The three exchanged a look and all held their breath: their attractive young faces bent and warped as the probability stabilizers strained to keep 'em all in one piece. Then all the distortion halted abruptly as the good ol' Gen'ral Grant rounded the planet and made the jump clear of its gravity well, into the smooth sailing of less-bent interplanetary space.

Zeedae unstrapped and leapt over to the monitor just in time to see them drones fail to make the jump. They skimmed down into the planet's atmosphere and crash-landed right into an ocean, from which it was gonna cost Boss Hrrrgh a pretty Galactic Exchange Unit to have 'em extricated.

•　　•　　•

Buuk had busted out a vial of ol' JSE's Navjuice and poured 'em each a generous thimbleful when the transmission monitor done begun beepin' like all get out — on two channels at once, no less.

Lau tapped the first channel, and up come a holo of ol' Mentorbot JSE, large as life in 3.5-D full-rez.

"You boys manage to bust out Zeedae?" he asked.

"They sure did, Uncle JSE," says Zeedae, but Buuk couldn't never let that stand.

"Naw, JSE, Zeedae done busted her own self out; all we did is skip by and give her a lift up out'a there."

David A. Hewitt

"That's my girl," said JSE. "Them Enforcement Authority types oughta know that messin' with one of the Genset-D kin is sendin' the hounds up against the *wrong* pack'a repli-possums. Reckon I'll see all y'all back at the ranch in just a few blinks of a Gardozian Blizbop's eye."

"Roger an' out," said Lau, then tapped open the second beepin' channel.

And durned if it weren't Boss Hrrrgh and Sub'strate Ponetrain, in holo form, right there in the cockety-pit of the Gen'ral Grant.

"Why Boss," said Zeedae, "whatever could you be callin' up little ol' us for?"

The Sub'strate craned his neck and leaned forward, as though not aware that his image was bein' recorded globo-holistically from all sides and broadcast in 3.5-D.

"I'm gonna git you Genset-D boys, and you, Zeedae, and that Mentorbot of yours, the ringleader of the whole unlawful crew."

"Now, Sub'strate, Boss," interjected Buuk. "Y'all know we love you two. We Genset-D boys never did mean ya no harm. It ain't our fault we been in trouble with the Enforcement Authority since the day we was spawned. Ain't ya never gonna cut us a break?"

"I'll show you a break," sputtered Boss Hrrrgh. That space-slug in all his 3.5-D glory was a sight to behold, or more like a sight you ain't never want to behold twice, if you done seen it once. "We'll break up that smugglin' ring of yours, and when we do, you are all going to fry!"

"Aww," says Zeedae. "Generous of you to invite us over for a cookout. I do love me some deep-fried Q-transit Protein Supplement, but I believe we'll have to decline, with regards. Maybe another time, Boss."

"Or maybe never," threw in Lau, and flicked the screen to obliviate the unpleasantly lifelike holos of their unpleasantly lifelike nemeses.

"Well, we all know," said Zeedae, "that we ain't heard the last of the Sub'strate and ol' Boss Hrrrgh. For one thing, I'll be goldurned if I let them keep my poor Spinrunner in impound one Galactic Standard second longer'n I have to."

The three, Lau, Buuk, and Zeedae, each raised another vial of Navjuice, swigged it down, and off they went, exceedin' the Q-probability strictures for metaspace travel, the ol' Gen'ral Grant kickin' up a large fishtail of quantum spacedust in its wake.

N.V. Haskell returned to writing in 2019, luckily just a few months before the world shut down. Since then, she's had numerous short fiction publications and won the Writers of the Future contest, published in volume 38. She lives somewhere between suburbia and haunted creeks with her long-suffering spouse, rescue dog, and too many squirrels that she can't help but feed. After a long career in healthcare, she remains stubbornly optimistic. The first book in her series, *The Broken Bonds of Magic*, will be published in 2025 with Cursed Dragon Ship publishing.

•   •   •

I wrote "The Sky Keepers Daughter" over a twenty-four hour period during the Writers of the Future week-long intensive workshop, when each writer was given an item to use as inspiration. The item I received was a bullet casing which, of course, has absolutely nothing to do with this story. When I turned the casing on its end, I envisioned a pedestal where goddesses might stand and survey the world.

THE SKY KEEPER'S DAUGHTER

N.V. HASKELL

OUR MOTHERS AND GRANDMOTHERS have always held the universe together. They are the sun and the moon, the land, air, and life. But when a meteor burst through the gauzy fabric of Mother's sky, the world shook and screamed.

From my perch in the clouds, I saw the fiery ball hurtle towards the open sea with unprecedented violence. Gigantic waves crashed on vulnerable, unsuspecting shores. The meteor's impact devastated four islands, their populations drowned in an instant before Mahasa, the keeper of the oceans, could calm it.

Fear gripped me as I hastened towards the shrine. Five stony figures stood fixed atop their marble stands. Ten glassy eyes settled upon me as I entered. Their faces were similarly shaped, though varied in composition. From sparkling granite to milky opal, shimmering citrine to steady agate.

The sixth pedestal stood vacant, like a missing tooth in a gaping smile. Mother's statue was gone and without her protection, the world would burn.

The eldest and most ill-tempered of the guardians, Surya glared down with a scowl. Her sharp citrine edges melted everything at the slightest touch. Cool Chandra stood beside her bearing an opalescent placidity and a near-sympathetic expression. Beside her, in a descending line that was only altered through necessity, stood the rest of my matriarchal ancestors. Their subtle expressions ranged from concern to chagrin.

Grandmother Mahasa, composed of shades of deepest sapphire, remained perfectly still beside the empty pedestal. Her cheeks were newly etched, as if tears carved slivers of her stone away. She had seen her daughter taken and been unable to stop it.

These guardians, these women, had been set in stone for so long that they couldn't have moved to stop the abduction if they'd tried. Their job, after all, was to safekeep the world above and below. When one of them was compromised or ready to rise to the stars, the others had to work harder to maintain equilibrium. But in all the world's history, no guardian had ever gone missing before.

Mother's empty pedestal had been violently gouged and splintered. Shards of blue agate lay strewn about from where she'd been dragged away. My heart sank when I found a slender finger, now bloody and greying, behind the base of her stand. It looked the same as before she had transitioned into her role as sky keeper. The dismemberment explained why the meteor had struck the southern oceans — where a piece of the sky was surely missing.

The other guardians showed signs of strain as Mahasa struggled to control the tidal waves that now threatened continents. Worry strained the edges of her face.

"Who?" My whisper rebounded off their hard surfaces and swirled about the circular room. But they did not need to answer. There was only one amongst our kin that would have braved this act, and, with a heavy heart, I went in search of my troublesome sister.

Like the sun, moon, and world, the sky must rise above the needs of her few children. Compared to her, the four of us were just the weather. In order for the guardians to remain diligent in their prospective roles, distractions had to be done away with. Emotions tempered and cut off so that they may act with impartiality. The guardians had to see all creatures as their children, not just the ones they'd made or raised.

When Mother had ascended to the pedestal and transitioned into the blue agate that her sister had set, I had understood that she still loved my siblings and I. Metreyu, my sister, was less understanding. Resentment is perhaps too meager a term to describe her emotions, but it is the closest thing to equate it to. The last eon had seen her clutching tight to her grievances and avoiding the responsibilities that I and our other siblings were obliged to fulfill.

Metreyu would have hidden Mother well and the remaining guardians could not help me. Although they could see everything beneath the sun and the moon, they couldn't see into caves or beneath the wide branched canopies of forest trees. While the guardian of the earth could feel every step upon it, she could not always discern one step from another. A tribe of people dragging gigantic blocks across the sand might feel the same as a stone guardian being towed behind a reticent and stubborn daughter. The air guardian could not attend to any task for longer than a few minutes. Her thoughts flew away in long streams that never led to an end, only to a new beginning. And Metreyu would not be foolish enough to venture near grandmother's waters.

No. It fell to me to find my sister and mother before the other guardians weakened at the imbalance.

I began my search in the land of our father, though he had risen to the stars long ago. Tall intricate marble likings of him stared down in judgement, carved by worshippers who falsely credited him with casting lightning bolts and children across the world. With my eyes closed, I questioned the people who still worshipped him, but they knew nothing of my mother or sister.

When a few of the elder priests postured and hurled offensive words, I couldn't help my gaze turning hot. Their flesh morphed to granite and shale. The other people then cowered or fled, and I moved on.

Venturing to my younger brother's vibrant temples in the high, snowy mountains, I impatiently watched as Sivu's devotees offered up their neighbor's children for sacrifice in exchange for the safety of their own. While sandalwood incense wafted in yellow ribbons through the thin air, my brother sat upon his throne and sneered at his worshippers with disregard. Sivu had always been cruel and I'm not ashamed to admit some satisfaction when his eyes finally found me, and he flinched. The hems of his concubines' red saris fluttered as they trembled and scurried behind his throne when he warned them not to look upon me.

"Metreyu has stolen Mother. Have you seen them?" I asked.

Sivu sniffed as he sat a little taller. His eyes shifted subtly away before he answered. "Not in years."

There was bitterness in him, and I reminded myself that he had handled abandonment in his own way.

"If she isn't returned soon, her form will begin to fail, and the sky will fall again." I warned.

His tongue nervously worked the inside of his cheek as he leveled black eyes upon me. "That won't affect me or mine here in the mountains." His tone held false authority, as if repeating lies that had become his own truths.

"The entire world will suffer without her. How much can sea and earth endure before they grow weary?" I asked. "You must remember when the guardians grew ill, and chaos took hold. Everything fell still. The mountains crumbled then. Yours will fare no better."

Sivu's black eyes shifted toward the white-capped peaks that cut across the horizon. His fingers trailed down his jaw to tug at the length of black beard upon his chin while his lips pursed in contemplation.

"Do you remember when mother lifted the sky back up so that air and sea could move again? Imagine what will happen to the other guardians if she does not return."

Sivu's silence was heavy. One of the women behind his throne cried softly.

"You could replace her," he said. "It's almost your time, isn't it?"

Annoyance dusted my breath. "You know that is not my role. They made us in pairs. One is the setter, and one is to be set when the time comes."

Beneath my gaze, his body stiffened and shimmered subtly, until I blinked and looked away. I could have set him then if I'd wished it. But, according to my grandmothers, the men never lasted as long when they were made keepers.

He cleared his throat before shifting nervously in his seat. "Ask Yoshen. He always understood Metreyu better than the rest of us," he said. "That is where I would go."

I nodded politely. "Come visit us, brother. It would do your grandmothers well to see you."

He clasped his hands together attempting to still the tremble that worked its way through them and refused to meet my eyes. Sivu gave a curt, dismissive nod.

A woman with high cheekbones and wide eyes peeked curiously from behind Sivu's seat, unintentionally drawing my gaze. Someone hidden beside her cried out as she morphed into rose and gray dappled granite. Her last breath was a soft, dusty sigh that hovered in the air as I left.

Yoshen lived in a northern wooded glen, nestled amongst tall pines and thick-coated beasts that slumbered through the winter months. He didn't seek the company of others, though would provide aid if someone fell ill under his watch. The locals revered him as a monk or a myth. In time, he might become both.

He sat cross-legged upon an old stump with his face turned toward the distant warmth of Surya's sun. He'd always been her favorite grandchild, and no one bore him any resentment for it. Yoshen's kindly nature made him everyone's favorite, in one way or another. He watched me approach with eyes dark and warm as fresh turned dirt in spring.

"You've lost her," he said. There was no accusation in his tone, though part of me wanted to take offense.

"Metreyu has taken her."

"Did you think she'd come to hide here with me?" Yoshen asked. He smiled gently until I looked away, fearing the damage I might do.

"Sivu thought you might know."

He scratched his shaved head. "Where would you go if you wanted to be alone with mother?"

"I was never alone with her, you know that." I shrugged as if it never mattered, though knew he understood the sting of that truth. "Being the setter fell to me when Auntie rose to the stars. And Metreyu knows her duty."

He uncrossed his legs and patted the space beside him. "You were too young to become the guardian's setter and keeper. It was too much for you then."

I settled next to him, enjoying the warmth of his shoulder against mine as the sun smiled upon us. Yoshen offered a quiet companionship that calmed every creature in the vicinity, including myself.

"It had to be me," I said finally. "Metreyu doesn't have the steadiness of a setter."

He placed a gentle arm around my shoulder and, though physical gestures were a rare thing amongst any of us, I leaned toward him.

"How long can you be away from the others?"

"I have a little longer until they soften," I said.

"I suppose our sister will have to be set now, too." His words flitted away with the wind, though their weight made me slump.

"Yes, I suppose so."

Squeezing my shoulder, he nodded slowly. His voice was heavy. "Have you tried the forgotten caves?"

"The one with the glyphs that we drew as children?"

"If I wanted to speak of childish hurts and longings without the audience of my siblings or ancestors, I would take her there."

I looked too long upon his profile until his skin shimmered with a jadeite iridescence before I closed my eyes. He squeezed my shoulder once more before releasing me.

"I will visit when all is settled," Yoshen called. I departed without looking back.

It was a long trek to that musty cave a continent away. Each step left a trail of shale and sandstone formations that jutted from the ground behind me but, as I tired, those changed to slate and schist.

Metreyu had rolled large boulders before the cave entrance to keep it hidden from the sun, moon, and air. They had all warned Mother of Metreyu's nature from the moment we were made. I was the strong one, they said. The steady and reliable one. They labeled my sister demanding and stubborn. Selfish and unruly. They never hid their opinions from our ears. But they didn't know my sister. Truly, she was none of those things.

Metreyu needed more than I did — more attention, more comfort, more consoling — and she was wounded for never having those needs met. We were not the same, but I had tried to understand her.

Until this.

Beneath the willing touch of my fingers, the boulders crumbled, blowing away in silt-fine particles that drifted away in the wind. I descended into the dark cave, following the narrow tunnel for a long while until a flicker of light warmed the limestone walls. I did not try to quiet my approach. It would make no difference.

Mother's blue striated body sparkled in the fluttering light. The agate still held strong. At the broken edge of her right little finger, a stark contrast of red and white juxtaposed against the blue outer shell - a reminder of what used to be flesh. Metreyu sat on the ground, rubbing her thumb over mother's absent digit as she mumbled and wept.

"I didn't mean to hurt her," she said. She glanced at me over her shoulder, black hair flowing like a curtain that folded around her face. "I never got the chance to explain everything. You understand, don't you?"

Mother's eyes tracked me as I moved slowly toward them. "I understand that you have not gotten the resolution you'd hoped for." I tempered my words with a gentleness inspired by Yoshen.

"I just wanted to talk," she whispered again. Her cheeks were wet and raw. "It's difficult to speak freely up there. You know how the others judge my every word."

"I'm sure that you didn't mean to hurt her." I was only a few feet from her. "But you shouldn't have brought her here without permission. Family does not equate to property. And her finger ..."

"It was an accident! I forgot how heavy she is now." She sobbed again, wiping the back of her hand across her nose in a long sweeping motion.

"There was a meteor ..." I left the sentence hanging. It was unlikely that she would care about the thousands of lives lost, and it would only cause mother grief. I lay a hand on Metreyu's shoulder, letting the weight of it instill a certain amount of gravitas. A shudder wriggled up her back, lulling her sobs into a thick silence. "We must return her before the others begin to falter without her."

Her shoulders rolled back, posture stiffening as she settled in for a fight. She glanced at me briefly before gazing at mother's stony face. "I struggled without her. So did Sivu. So did Yoshen. I know that you did too, though you never complained."

My hand drifted from her shoulder. "Did complaining about it help you? It never changed anything, only made you more comfortable with your misery."

Metreyu struggled to stand on stiffening limbs, grasping mother's hand to haul herself up as I continued. "I never had the luxury of wallowing in self-pity, sister. Someone had to keep the guardians set. There was never any time to indulge myself. I have always had work to do."

Her eyes widened as ripples of green malachite shone through beneath patches of her skin. "What are you ...?" She gripped Mother's arm with sudden understanding. "No, please. I still need to ..."

In a moment of panic, she swung a heavy arm toward me. The new weight of the limb threw her off balance. She stumbled while trying to remain upright and knocked Mother sideways.

I abandoned Metreyu's setting and leapt to catch the sky keeper. But I was not fast enough.

Metreyu screamed as Mother shattered upon the floor. Blocks of blue striated agate tumbled and broke into smaller pieces as the inside of her split open like a geode, revealing ruby and white quartz innards. She had broken into small, unrecognizable bits that shimmered and glowed.

A blinding light rose from her remains and disappeared through the dirt ceiling. Mother was rising to the stars, there'd be no bringing her back now. Knowing that she would rest beside her stone-setter sister didn't ease the pain of losing her.

The surrounding ground shook and groaned in sharp, sudden blasts. The sky was falling. Neither Surya nor Chandra could stop it. Our grandmothers, aunts, and all the lives they sought to protect would soon suffer. The world would be shaken clean unless ...

Metreyu stared transfixed at the rocks scattered around us. We watched stoically as the blue agate transformed into bits of decaying flesh and congealing blood. When another wave of shakes threatened us, understanding dawned in her eyes. My sister wrapped her arms around me and wept.

•　　•　　•

I gently wipe the dusty particles from crystal and stone limbs while the women's eyes look beyond me. The guardians are busy tending to their duties and, though it has taken the breadth of eternity, they have finally accepted Metreyu as one of their own.

My sister stands upon the sixth pedestal, her figure cut in sharply angled aquamarine as her unyielding arms reach upward to brace the sky. I linger over her, speaking my love, though she cannot return it.

Yoshen comes frequently with bright-colored flowers, but never stays for long. He prefers the woods and glens to this austere space. Sivu visited us with his twin-made daughters in tow. One is quiet and steady, the other is rash and loud. Soon they will stay here and call me auntie until my time is done.

There is peace in the quiet company I am caretaker of. For as long as the sun burns and the moon encircles us, I shall keep them all together. Until it is my time to rise to starlight.

Hugh McCormack is a writer of short stories, based in London, UK. By day, he's a nonfiction writer/editor.

●　　　●　　　●

"The Tome of the Watermelon Harvest" is about navigating the treadmill of life when you're led by a half-blind philosopher. It was inspired by life and half-blind philosophers, not so much by treadmills. It was also shaped by the landscape, mythology and watermelons of Greece.

THE TOME OF THE WATERMELON HARVEST

HUGH MCCORMACK

A S THE SUN'S RAYS first peeked over the courtyard walls, the archivists brought out my burden. Four of them carried it on their shoulders, one under each corner of its wooden case. My hooves shuffled as the archivists held the tome above my paniers, and shuffled some more as its solemn weightiness came down upon my back.

When the tome had been secured, the one they called Theodore tugged me forward by a rope. Like the others, he wore long blue robes, but his beard was a little longer and curlier, his hat a little wider, and his odor a little stronger. Yet for me, it was the keenness of his tongue and the eagerness of his whip that set him apart.

We left the hard stone of the courtyard by the high arch of the Archive's main gate and descended the broad path past the olive grove. Pale dust puffed up and hung serenely in the light dry air, and cicada song reverberated from the wizened trees, as though to wish us farewell.

At the crossroads we took a faint stony path unfamiliar to me. It was only on this path that the tread of hoof on ground took on an easy rhythm, and the trudge was established. Ahead, the scrubland stretched out as far as I could see, silently awaiting the inevitability of the day.

•   •   •

Like any archivist on any trudge, Theodore was difficult to ignore. His flapping robes never left the panoramic scope of my eyes, his smell never made peace with my nose, and his clumsy footfalls never found the rhythm of the trudge. If that wasn't enough, I also had to endure the patter of his voice.

"Well, Buridan, here we are on the road together."

I thought he must be speaking to someone else, since I'd never been called 'Buridan' before.

"As we go, I'll pass on to you some of the great wisdom of the Archive."

Then it dawned on me that I had a new name, since no other human or beast was in sight, and it seemed unlikely he was addressing one of the stoical shrubs that stood within earshot.

"I only wish you could understand me. It would change your life if you did."

I snorted. For all their great wisdom, it was strange how the archivists always assumed you couldn't understand if you didn't speak.

"So, you must be wondering where we're heading."

I was not. Instead, my attention had been cornered by a fly that had somehow tracked me down in the open scrubland.

"Well, the Grand Archivist has chosen me to go to Krestena to perform the rituals of the watermelon harvest, one of the traditions he wants to revive."

It was one of those small flies that prized speed over subtlety and that always seemed reluctant to actually land.

This, in simple terms, meant its irritation would be drawn out but mild, more in the ear than under the skin.

"This is why our undertaking is so important, by far the most important of your life."

The fly had started circling about my ears, a tactic that was particularly irritating. I lowered my head slightly, held it for a moment, then threw it back, simultaneously flicking both ears. The buzzing vanished, and I thought I must have hit my target. Yet, a moment later, it was back.

"Are you listening to me, Buridan?"

Fearing a whip might be near at hand, I resolved to ignore the buzz and focus on the patter.

"As it's over twenty years since the people of Krestena last saw the Tome, they must have forgotten much."

Twenty years? This was barely comprehensible to me. It was the time needed to create twenty donkeys, and I hadn't met twenty donkeys in my entire life.

"Which is why I'm taking it there."

Despite my best efforts, I couldn't stifle another snort. It was clear that Theodore was not taking the tome anywhere, but rather it was my legs and back that bore it.

"I hope you're not ill." He peered at me suspiciously. "We've a long way to go, and if you can't maintain the pace, we won't arrive by dusk, when the harvest ceremony begins."

Even though I always wanted to know when I would be liberated from my burden, discovering I would first have to toil a full day under the summer sun was never going to make my tail dance. But now, coming on top of the fly's endless goading, it sparked a primal urge.

I stopped in my tracks, raised my head, and my bray burst out. For many heartbeats it declared itself, its forthright passion echoing across the empty scrubland. But then came the sharp snap of a whip, instantly cutting it short.

•   •   •

When I first saw the small copse of trees, the sun was burning my haunches, and my shadow was scampering under my hooves. At first, I presumed the copse was a mirage. Mirages were common on a summer trudge, manifesting when you were distant and vanishing as you neared, just like cicada song.

"The hermitage marks the half-way point of our journey, and we'll rest there awhile."

Through the morning, Theodore's monologue had guided me through countless pages of the most revered tomes, but it had faded away a while ago, leaving just the rhythm of the trudge. So used had I become to this, that his voice now seemed like an intrusion. But at least I'd learned that the copse was no mirage.

"Those trees are tamarisks. I would know this even if I'd never seen them before."

As we approached, the snigger-snicker rhythm of cicada song started up from the branches, but it was the fresh fragrance of water that had captured my attention.

"You see, tamarisks have a whole page in the Tome of Botany, and the trees you see achieve the form, if not the beauty, of its illustrations."

I barely heard his words. As soon as we entered the shade, I spotted the stone trough next to the well. Forgetting the risk of the whip and defying the burden of the tome, I rushed forward, pulling the rope out of Theodore's hands.

"Have patience, Buridan!"

My ears flicked his words away as if they were a clumsy fly. Nothing could distract me from the promise of the trough water, not even the dark specks floating in it.

"Buridan? Strange name to give a donkey."

This new voice came from a man who sat on the shady doorstep of a ramshackle one-room shelter, just a few paces away. Like Theodore, he wore blue robes and a long beard, although his robes were sun-faded and his hair was grey.

"Georgius?" Theodore peered into the shade. "Is that you?"

"Who else did you expect? Welcome to my hermitage! You must sit down and rest. You've already come a long way."

Theodore slumped down on the doorstep next to the hermit. After removing his hat, he accepted the ceramic flask offered to him.

"So why have you renamed him Buridan?" Georgius asked, when Theodore returned the flask.

My ears twitched.

"I've named him after Jean Buridan, the philosopher. Or rather, after his ass."

"Of course. But why choose Buridan, and why a philosopher at all?"

Theodore laughed. "Well, a few months ago I conducted an experiment on him. I wanted to see if Buridan was right about donkeys. Specifically, if a donkey is offered two desired things that are the same distance away but in opposite directions, would it really be thrown into an insoluble dilemma and be unable to take either."

My hooves began to shuffle. While most of my days seeped silently from my memory like water from a leaky trough, the day of my ordeal held on like a famished leech.

"So I led him to a spot exactly equidistant from food on his left and an open gate on his right, and then removed his rope. I even stood well back, so I wouldn't distract him, yet still he didn't move. He couldn't choose between satiation and freedom."

It goes without saying that I knew perfectly well which temptation I wanted more, since one would last only a few hours and the other a lifetime. But I am a serious, contemplative creature who had never tasted freedom, and whatever lay through that open gate was unknown to me. I couldn't seize my freedom because ...

"He was too stubborn."

... I was too wary.

Theodore was laughing now, just as he had on the day of my ordeal. Beside him on the doorstep, Georgius was stroking

343

his beard and shaking his head. As I'd now drunk my fill of water, I moved on to a bundle of hay next to the trough.

"You've a lot to learn about donkeys," Georgius said. "They're not really stubborn – they just choose not to move when they're not sure what to do."

I paused my eating, to be sure I would catch every word of archivist wisdom, but I couldn't stop the shuffling of my hooves.

"Then he's just too stupid to know what to do," Theodore said. "In any case, I whipped him, so that next time he'll know better."

"I'd wager that next time he'll do exactly what he did last time. You should have more respect for what he is."

"I don't know why you say that. He's my favourite donkey, full of personality. He does funny things and makes me laugh. But however much I like him, he has a lot to learn, and the whip is the only teacher he understands."

I resumed eating the hay. Wisdom was clearly subjective.

•   •   •

Theodore's monologue resumed soon after we left the hermitage. The joyousness of his tone jarred against the serious rhythm of the trudge.

"People often wonder at the magnificence of the Tome of the Watermelon Harvest. Did you know that, Buridan?"

I knew that I wondered how the tome managed to compact the weight of so many watermelons into its pages.

"But it's not the most magnificent tome in the Archive. That is indisputably the Tome of Equinology."

Theodore turned his head to stare directly into my left eye with both of his, and a strange grin emerged.

"You've heard of the Tome of Equinology, haven't you?"

I had not. Moreover, given that the tomes travelled courtesy of my paniers without any concern for my well-being, the opportunity to learn about yet another tome was not likely to make my tail dance.

"It must be well-known, even in the stables?"

I wondered if Theodore ever opened his eyes when he went to the stables. The only things well-known there were whips and sticks and flies. Even the rats skulked about in the shadows and made no effort to socialise.

"It's a bestiary, all about you. You donkeys. Everything there is to know."

Despite myself, my ears twitched. Theodore stared at them, smiling broadly.

"Not just donkeys, but also horses and hinnies, mules and zonkeys, onagers and unicorns."

It seemed a congested tome. But not too congested for me, as the continued twitching of my ears confirmed.

"And you should see the pages on donkeys. The calligraphy exemplifies the classic imperial style, and the swirling patterns and variegated flowers of the illustrations are considered the finest work of Basil the Younger. Only the pages on unicorns can compare, and only then because unicorns are the noblest of all beasts. You know perhaps that they are the lords of Elysion?"

He stopped, and the rope tightened, turning my head and breaking the trudge. He was standing there, beaming, directly into my left eye.

"You know about Elysion, don't you?"

In the Archive and on my trudges, I'd heard many exotic placenames, from Argos to Arcadia, Corinth to Constantinople, but never Elysion.

"Not far from here, just over the horizon, lies a wondrous land. Its vast fertile fields are carpeted by the greenest grass, crossed by the freshest streams, and cooled by the serenest shade. Donkeys and other equines laze and graze to their hearts' content, roaming wherever and whenever they choose. There are no archivists to obey, and no work to be done."

Even as Theodore started laughing, I was already in Elysion, already consuming and consumed by bliss. In contrast to my ordeal, when I'd had to choose between sustenance and freedom, it seemed that in Elysion both were simultaneously plentiful.

"Maybe one day you'll find your way over the horizon and experience its magnificence yourself."

My breath slowed to hear more, and my heart pounded to learn when he would take me there. Instead, his laughter resumed with greater vigour, and clattered on and on for no apparent reason, like the pulsing rhythms of a cicada choir.

•   •   •

The sun had descended almost to the horizon ahead and fatigue was gnawing, when at last we crossed Krestena's old stone bridge and entered the town square. A sea of people was there, filling the dusty ground from the riverbank behind us to the two-storey stone buildings ahead. On seeing us, the people fell silent and stared, and parted to let us through. Even though their numbers made me nervous, and their collective odour made me curse the sensibilities of my nose, I couldn't stop my ears twitching or my tail dancing, as the liberation was so near.

We stopped in the centre of the square where a large empty table was draped in scarlet fabric. A man dressed head-to-foot in purple robes stood beside it, and he stepped forward to greet Theodore. As they talked, the crowds gathered round, and my hooves began to shuffle.

The man in purple then gestured with his arm, and several pairs of hands started pulling at my paniers. As the great weight of the Tome of the Watermelon Harvest finally lifted from my back, my excitement overcame me. I started braying and kicking out at the air, scattering the crowd behind me. The liberation, the passing of the burden from donkey legs to human legs to table legs, was always the highpoint of any day.

•   •   •

By dusk, I was tethered up to a post at the edge of the square. Groups of people wandered by as the light waned. I'd emptied the trough beside the post, and with my stomach satiated and my burden gone, I seemed to be floating like a cloud. I even had company: a small speckled gecko, a statuesque extension of the trough's stone and an ally in the unending fight against airborne tormentors. Maybe in the fields of Elysion I could feel like this every moment of every day, as I roamed without tether and communed with my donkey friends.

I was roused from my reverie by a fragrance. My hooves shuffled and my breath stopped as my senses scoured the drifting crowds. Yet there was nothing but faceless people.

When at last she came into sight, I could see only her ears. Then she emerged in all her beauty: from the smooth curve of her spine to the regal rhythm of her stride, the vibrant whiteness of her nose to the soft mottle of her hide.

When she spied me, she flicked her ears in that nonchalant playful way that only debonaire jennies can truly master. And of course, I had no choice but to bray as loudly as I could. When she replied, her voice was as clear as the purest water. Again and again, I tugged on my tether, trying to go and greet her properly, but the post was firmly planted, and the rope securely tied, and my weary limbs strained in vain. So, I resumed braying and was unable to stop, even though this meant I couldn't hear her replies.

She was led to a dusty space by a man in black wearing a hat even broader than Theodore's. The man raised his arms, then his voice.

"Townspeople and farmers of Krestena, gather now to see this amazing sight!"

He repeated these words several times, and the passing people started looking round. Some of them slowed to look longer.

"Marvel at the dance of life, performed by the unique and astonishing Zoë the donkey!"

The gathering crowd began to obstruct my line of sight, so I moved first left, then right, until I found a clearer vista.

"In the dance of life, Zoë becomes a unicorn, the greatest of all equines, and dances to the rhythm of the tambourine."

After tying a long wooden horn to her forehead, the man held a circular object above his head and started tapping it with a stick. To my astonishment, Zoë began to prance to the beat, flicking her ears and tail as she went. Her hooves, head and tail were all synchronised, as if she were a marionette tied to the stick. Round and round she went, my eyes following her every step and gesture, my ears and tail doing their best to mimic hers. The people started clapping and whooping, as though they too wanted to dance with her. Finally the man in black stopped the beat and raised up his arms.

"Zoë, the dancing unicorn!"

The cheers and applause were loud and only stopped when the man in black cracked a whip in the air. The sound startled me, and I backed away, but Zoë's reaction was more refined. She reared up on her hind legs, and for many tail flicks held herself upright, as lofty as a human. She started braying and snorting, her song of triumph echoing across the square. I tingled with excitement as the purity and passion of her voice poured through me. I had never been so proud to be a donkey.

"Zoë, the greatest of all equines!"

The crowd cheered and started clapping above their heads and continued long after Zoë had returned to four-legged pragmatism. I lost sight of her as the people flocked about. For a moment I caught a glimpse of the man in black in among the laughing, smiling human faces, his huge coin-consuming hat held out boldly before him, but Zoë just seemed to have disappeared, swallowed up in the smelly human sea.

I pulled from side to side, trying to catch another glimpse of her, but without success. It was only when the crowd had finally dispersed that I accepted she had gone. Her scent lingered a little longer, but soon I was left in the calm cool of the failing evening light, alone except for a silent gecko and a troupe of inspirations that whirled around my head.

•   •   •

Next morning's trudge back from Krestena was like no other of my life. I barely saw the path or the dust or the stones, barely heard the clump of hoof or the buzz of fly, and barely smelled Theodore's hat or robes. Even the dead weight of the tome seemed somehow elsewhere, as though I shared its burden with another. Instead, I spent the morning alongside Zoë in Elysian bliss, dancing the dance of life. Together we pranced, sang and stood up on our hind legs.

Before Zoë, every donkey I'd met had been a beast of burden, compelled to carry and to pull, and bore its yoke with perseverance, patience and pride. But Zoë's dancing hooves had opened my mind to a different world, a place where we could graduate from the trudge, express ourselves with character and creativity, and be appreciated for our individual traits and talents.

I realised then that I too could follow Zoë's hoofprints. I didn't have to wait to be led to Elysion by an archivist but could venture there on my own. I just needed to be liberated from burden and rope, to be offered again the choice of my ordeal. And once in Elysion, I would be free of burden and rope forever.

"Are you following me, Buridan?" Theodore was looking at me in that way he did sometimes, his two eyes peering into my left. "Everything's changed. You see that, don't you?"

All morning, to my surprise, he'd been walking in time with the trudge and staring down at the ground in silence. Even his hat, for all its impressive size, seemed to flop lethargically. Yet now his voice had returned, shattering my reverie.

"Ever since I was taken to the Archive as a boy, I've always believed that if I studied all the tomes, I would learn everything worth knowing. That's why I go to the great library every day and pass my hours poring over their pages. But yesterday everything changed. The harvest rituals proceeded as they were supposed to, and everything was well. But afterwards, when I started talking with the farmers and townspeople, I realized there were ... gaps."

The forlornness with which he pronounced 'gaps' caused my back to stiffen. It was one of the great injustices of my world that an archivist's frustration would loosen his whip hand.

"Some things have been discovered recently, such as the invention of a metal tool that cuts watermelon stalks far faster than a knife. But other things seem to have always been known yet were not included when the tome was scribed. They say even the children of Krestena know that a beehive aids pollination, but the tome says nothing of this. Nor does it mention the pests to guard against, such as fruit flies."

It was one of those moments you hope will never come, but as soon as he uttered the word 'pests', a particular drone came to my ears, a drone for which they were on perpetual alert.

"Are you listening to me, Buridan? You understand the gravity of the situation, don't you?"

I certainly did. The tone of the drone was unmistakably that of a horsefly.

"For all its wondrous calligraphy and venerable illustrations, the Tome of the Watermelon Harvest is neither complete nor authoritative."

In the past, the arrival of a horsefly had driven me to bray hysterically or flee in panic, and once even to dive into a flooding river.

"And there are probably also gaps in the tomes on olives and grapes and other crops."

Yet this time, everything was different, as instead of a flood of fear I felt the call of a challenge.

"We might have to rewrite them all!"

The horsefly couldn't know how I'd been transformed, of course, as for all its biting power, it lacked any kind of sophistication.

"I don't know how we can manage it."

It didn't notice how easily my hooves kept to the rhythm of the trudge.

"We might take many years to gather the new information ..."

It didn't realize that I was calmly, patiently tracking its drone ...

"... and many more to scribe and illustrate the new pages."

... left and right, nearer and farther ...

"But the worst thing is …"
… and when it swooped back towards my rear quarters …
"… we'll have to acknowledge that …"
… it failed to foresee …
"… the farmers are contributing …"
… the force with which my tail would flail …
"… more to the harvest than just their labour."
… and end its drone forever.

• • •

"Georgius, come and help me. There's something I have to show you."

The hermit sat in the doorway of the hermitage's shelter, dozing in the shade of the tamarisks, exactly where we had left him the day before. At Theodore's voice, he stirred himself.

"Is anything wrong?"

As Georgius ambled over to the trough, my attention switched to the gleaming trough water and bale of hay beside it. I struggled to free myself, but Theodore held me tightly by the rope.

"Help me with the tome," Theodore said. "We can put it on the well."

I presumed I had misheard, as the liberation normally occurred only when we had reached our final destination, but Georgius went round to my other side, and with Theodore began to lift the tome.

As the great weight left my back, the euphoria of liberation started coursing through me. Even as Theodore and Georgius staggered towards the closed wooden hatch of the well, I was kicking the air and braying.

After only a few kicks, it dawned on me: I was unrestrained. Theodore hadn't tethered me to the trough and had let go the rope by which he led me. So, right now, it was like the day of my ordeal: I was free to choose between the path to freedom before me and the water and hay beside me.

Yet this time my decision was different. This time, I knew what I wanted, and was ready to seize it.

With a burst of speed, I left my world behind.

Like a messenger's horse, I flew out of the shade of the tamarisks and sped across the sunny scrubland, possessed by an all-consuming power and purpose. With my hooves drumming the ground, my empty paniers bouncing on my back like the lightest of riders, shrubs raced towards me, rushed past.

Behind me, through the dust of my passage, I could make out the diminishing figures of Theodore and Georgius waving and shouting from the edge of the trees. But they soon faded from ear and eye, dropping out of significance, until they were no more than horseflies swatted on the path.

•   •   •

By the time tiredness slowed me to a walk, I was all alone in the still, silent scrubland. The ground undulated away in all directions to the hills on the horizon, with just a scattering of shrubs and rocky outcrops to punctuate its emptiness.

Yet everything felt different. The blanched summer colours looked lighter and more variegated, the web of scents that patterned the ground seemed purer and more distinct, the muted soundscapes appeared to resonate in soft echoes, and the warm caress of the air felt gentler and more reassuring. The old familiarity of the landscape had been embellished with a mystique of newness, as though it was a place I'd never been before, yet also a place I should have come to long ago, a place designed for me.

Despite the midday sun, I started to forage. The morning's trudge had left me hungry and thirsty, so I nibbled at leaves and sought out the clumps of grass that tried to hide in the odd patch of shade.

Although I found little food and no water, somehow it didn't seem to matter. My hunger and thirst were subsumed by warm tinglings that originated around my heart then fizzed out to my legs, neck and head, freeing feelings that normally only came with a liberation. As I drifted from shrub to shrub, time seemed to stop, to become irrelevant.

So this was freedom. For the first time in my life, there was no archivist to control me, no walls to confine me, no tether to restrain me, no whip to coerce me, no path to lead me. I was free to wander wherever I wanted, tarrying or moving on as I chose, surveying the sights and sounds and scents of the scrub, measuring the lie of the land. I was no longer merely a carrier of archivist burdens or a servant to archivist whims, and I was no longer defined by some fanciful name hung round my neck. Whatever I had known before had gone; this day marked the beginning of the life I was supposed to lead. Now I only had to find Elysion, and everything would be perfect.

By the time I stopped my foraging, the sun was sinking behind the hills. Standing in the open, soothed by the drifting cool air, I was away from the shadows yet somehow still close to everything around me. As the sky darkened, the speckle of stars brightened, then inched across the blackness.

I started to bray into the night. Anyone — donkey or otherwise — that heard me would know I was free. Just as Zoë had had the freedom to express herself in dance, so I had the freedom to express myself in voice, without risking the whip. I hoped that somehow Zoë would hear me and come to join me and add her voice to mine. After all, it had been her dance of life that had inspired me to take my freedom, and it would be fitting if she were to live it with me.

By the time I stopped braying, my voice was hoarse.

•   •   •

The next morning drifted by like the gentlest breeze. I knew from Theodore that Elysion was close, so it seemed that I only needed to keep on foraging and sooner or later I would arrive.

During the hottest part of the day, I rested in the shade of an evergreen oak. I still hadn't found any water, and while food was easier to find, it was all dust-dry: the pale-yellow grass was wood-tough, the rugged bark crumbled as I pulled it from the shrub, and the brown-edged leaves flaked in my mouth. I knew that once in Elysion, I'd be able drink as and when I desired, but I was also aware that thirst never waited for any donkey. The conclusion was clear: I had to find Elysion as soon as possible.

When I left the shade, I pointed my nose towards the dome of the nearest hill and, even though I was now free to roam as leisurely as I chose, I took up the rhythm of the trudge. As I went, my mood rose and fell with the land, rising with hope as I climbed to a ridge, falling again when I reached the summit and saw no sign of Elysion on the other side. Yet I knew my fortunes could change in a whipcrack.

•　　•　　•

That evening, I imposed my defiance on the darkness, reminding the world of my voice and that in the morning my search would continue unabated.

Despite not being a mountain creature, I would climb the hill.

•　　•　　•

It was only with the coming of the light that I realised the enormity of my task. The dome-shaped hill towered over me; I'd never been so close to anything so huge. For a donkey weakened by thirst, it seemed too high to climb.

Then I recalled the verve and panache of Zoë's dance of life, and resolve refilled me. Even though I had neither the power of a horse nor the agility of a goat, I still had four sturdy legs. I scanned the slopes for the easiest way up and traced a route to a spur protruding out from the hillside. Although it was barely halfway up the hill, I realized that from this spur I'd still have the vantage point of an eagle, and would surely be able to see Elysion, wherever it lay.

When I finally reached the spur, I inched towards the edge until —

There it was, the whole world laid out before me, a vast panorama stretching from one horizon to the other, glowing hazily under the midday sun. I had never been so high before, never seen so far.

For a long time, I scanned the land for the fertile fields of Elysion. Yet I could see no verdure in the mottle of burnt yellows and sun-bleached browns, no bright colour in the gleaming smear. Even now, standing on top of the world, Elysion remained beyond the horizon.

After what seemed like the duration of a trudge, something wrenched me out of my despair: a dark blotch. Far closer than I thought it possible.

It wasn't Elysion, and Zoë wouldn't be there, but in that blotch I could imagine water, and wholesome food, and company. After two days of freedom, I was ready to ignore the other things that might also be waiting there, like the tails of a whip, the weight of a burden, or the drudgery of a trudge.

It wasn't Elysion, but right now it seemed like paradise.

●　　●　　●

When I entered the shade of the tamarisks, a fanfare of cicada song was resonating from the branches. Theodore was sitting with Georgius on the doorstep of the shelter, holding his hat in one hand and drinking from a ceramic flask in the other. I rushed for the trough.

I was already drinking when they noticed me. As they hurried over, I edged away along the trough without removing my mouth from the cool water. I was determined to exploit every last moment before Theodore's whip cracked out its punishment.

As they came up to me, I directed my gaze down, as subserviently as I could, towards the quivering surface of dark water, towards the hard wall of trough stone. I was determined: I would take it like the noblest equine.

The cicada song stopped.

I closed my eyes.

I braced my back.

"Buridan! You've come back to me!" At the touch of Theodore's first pat, my neck quivered. He started hugging me, and when I opened my eyes, his smile was there, right in my face. "I knew you would. You show up as soon as I return to the hermitage. Were you waiting for me?"

As much as this welcome flooded me with relief, my nose was swamped in disgust: the last two days had done nothing to subdue his stench.

"You should whip him." Georgius was right beside us now, a whip offered in his outstretched hand, its tails hanging down between his bony fingers like steel snakes. "Hard and right away."

Even though my hooves started shuffling, I continued to drink as fast as I could.

"Whip him? Certainly not." Theodore finally released my neck, turned to face the hermit. "All he did was make his bid for freedom, and that's natural for any creature with self-respect."

"Still, you need to remind him of his place, and emphasise that his escapade hasn't changed it. Whipping him is the best way to do that."

"I don't think you understand him at all. He's just demonstrated he's no longer a stupid, stubborn donkey, and he shouldn't be whipped for that. He's nothing like Buridan's ass anymore."

"Well, maybe you should be calling him Sisyphus, like the rest of us."

My ears twitched. It seemed a lifetime ago that I'd last heard my old name. Theodore was laughing, but — yet again — I didn't understand why.

"Sisyphus is the perfect name for him," Georgius continued. "He carries a tome all the way to Krestena, and then he carries it all the way back. For him the tome is meaningless ballast, so his task is as pointless and arduous as Sisyphus' task of rolling a rock up a hill."

Still laughing, Theodore came over to me. I was hoping he would give me another new name. I'd never liked 'Sisyphus', as I couldn't stand its sound; to my sensibilities, its smooth sibilance was sticky and slimy, like stream mud that sought to switch residence. In any case, now it seemed out of date, like a throwback to last year's harvest.

"Don't listen to him," Theodore laugh-whispered into my ear. "I know you're much more than a four-legged Sisyphus, and I've no doubt that one day you'll show me all you can do and earn the name you deserve. In fact, I'll take you with me, back to Krestena, this very afternoon."

My ears started twitching. One thing the last two days had taught me was that Krestena was a far more desirable destination than Elysion.

"You can carry the pens and parchments I need to gather new information about the harvest practices. How does that sound ...?"

He finished with a strange word I didn't catch. Maybe that word was my new name, a pointer to my future, or maybe it was as inconsequential as the buzz of a fly. But I wasn't paying attention, as I was already back in Krestena, at the edge of the crowded square, waiting for Zoë to emerge from the smelly human sea.

John M. Campbell grew up reading science fiction and loved imagining a future extrapolated from what is now known. Inspiration for his stories often comes from the strange realities of quantum physics and cosmology. Stories of his appear in *Writers of the Future* (Volume 37), *Compelling Science Fiction* (Issue 12), and in the *Dragon Gems Fall 2023* anthology (Water Dragon Publishing). John lives and writes in Denver, Colorado.

• • •

Enceladus is a moon of Saturn with an icy crust hiding a liquid ocean beneath that is likely conducive to life. We will someday send a probe there, most likely a tiny ice-drilling vehicle piloted by an Artificial Intelligence called NEMO, the Nuclear Enceladus Mission Operator. Jules Verne would have been delighted.

AN EXPEDITION TO ENCELADUS

JOHN M. CAMPBELL

F OR AS LONG as I can remember, I have always wanted to be an explorer. And a pilot. (Probably because I was designed and trained to be an explorer and pilot.) I am NEMO, the Nuclear Enceladus Mission Operator, the artificial intelligence who controls the *Nautilus* as we explore the depths of the ocean beneath the frozen crust of Enceladus.

Enceladus is the sixth largest of the more than eighty moons orbiting Saturn. Enceladus zips around the huge planet in thirty-three hours tracing an orbit that extends twice as far from the planet as the main rings. That is still close enough for Saturn's gravity to flex the icy moon as it passes by. The resulting friction heats its interior, which creates a liquid ocean under its frozen surface. The gravity also cracks open the crust, allowing the warm waters below to erupt as geysers. Those cracks are the route we will take to reach the ocean and search for life.

We begin our adventure hanging from a crane that the Enceladus mission lander extends over the vent of an active cryogeyser. The escaping water vapor and ice crystals buffet the *Nautilus* since our ship measures only five centimeters long and one centimeter in diameter.

"Vapor exit speed fifty meters per second with heavy turbulence," I transmit to the lander, where it is relayed back to Earth along with video and telemetry. The lander has a powerful transmitter and sensitive receiver operating at a frequency designed to penetrate the ice up to forty kilometers.

"Extending control surfaces." These stubby wings allow me to counteract the buffeting. "Turbulence compensation: eighty-four percent."

"Opening collection ports. Starting impeller rotation."

The vapor plume rushes through the ports in the nose of the *Nautilus* as our micro-fusion reactor injects steam into the turbine that rotates the impeller. The turbine also generates power for the electronic systems, including me.

"Impeller speed increasing." The rising impeller rotation generates thrust as it expels vapor out the back and creates a vacuum that pulls in more vapor from the front. The *Nautilus* strains forward against the vapor gale, pulling the cable taut.

"Releasing cable."

I feather the impeller blades to increase thrust. The *Nautilus* creeps forward into the crevasse below. Forward-facing radar displays an image of the shape of the opening ahead.

I selected this particular geyser for the descent based on it having a large volume of discharge at a relatively low ejection speed. Both of these values indicate a comparatively large pipe connecting to the ocean below. We begin our descent at perigee, the point of Enceladus's closest approach to Saturn, when the gravitational forces are squeezing the cracks in the ice together and pressing the vapor channels closed. As the moon slingshots around Saturn, the orbital speed will drop, Saturn's gravitational pull will lessen, and the crevasses will open wider. In seventeen hours, when the moon reaches apogee, the channels will be open widest.

To achieve a depth of thirty kilometers, the *Nautilus* must travel at least twice that distance in negotiating the twists and turns in the cracks through the ice. If the ship averages one meter per second, we will make it to the ocean in the seventeen hours before Enceladus reaches apogee. Anything less, and we risk getting stuck deep in the ice.

I concentrate on the radar returns, steering the *Nautilus* down through the main shaft. Whenever the path splits, I take the wider gap in the ice, as long as the Doppler radar indicates sufficient flow volume. That strategy seems sound until the ship starts shaking.

"Experiencing turbulence. Radar shows multiple branches ahead, none of them large enough for the *Nautilus* to pass."

With no room to turn around, I must back out. I reduce the impeller speed, and the current begins to push the *Nautilus* back from where we came. I switch to the rear radar and steer to keep the ship centered in the channel. I make continuous adjustments to the thrust to control the boat's rate of ascent. When we reach the earlier intersection, I restore full thrust and turn into the other channel. The detour has cost half an hour of mission time.

"Backout completed," I transmit. "Resuming descent."

Like a race car driver, I increase thrust and speed when the channel straightens out, reducing speed as I approach a bend in the route. At one such bend, the Doppler registers a disturbance on the channel wall. An instant later, the radar image shows approaching clutter.

"Experiencing debris in the flow." I cut impeller thrust and steer close to the wall of the shaft where the radar shows an opening. Small chunks of ice ping off the hull. A cluster of objects appears ahead, returning glints of radar energy as they tumble toward the ship. Chips of ice act like kites in a gale as they sail and swoop, crashing into the walls and splitting into more pieces that the airstream catches and sends spinning forward again.

One chunk of ice hits the *Nautilus* broadside, causing the hull to ring and knocking the ship into the wall of the channel.

The ship bounces off the wall into the middle of the melee. I compensate and drive the ship to the wall again. Seconds later the hailstorm ends. Sensors register no damage to the hull, and all *Nautilus* systems show green status.

I issue an incident report, concluding with the words, "Give the *Nautilus* design engineers a pat on the back for me. Continuing descent."

After the debris storm, the flow rate diminishes by thirty percent. Around the bend and a few meters farther, a mosaic appears on the radar screen.

"Obstruction ahead." Shards and flakes of ice have stacked up in a pile across most of the shaft. Pieces move and shift in the current. Occasionally, a piece splits off and flies past us.

"Attempting a forced passage." I ease the *Nautilus* forward toward the largest opening. Although too small to pass through, the gap is large enough for the *Nautilus* to poke its nose into. As it makes contact, I apply extra thrust to push through the blockage. Some of the pieces shift, but the force of the current keeps them in place. I cut off thrust to allow the current to push the ship back, intending to make another run at shifting the debris aside. The ship doesn't move. It's wedged between the debris pile and the side of the tunnel.

Time for Plan B. The nose of the *Nautilus* is built like a drill bit for just such a situation. I retract the wings and extend diamond-coated cutting surfaces from the nose of the titanium hull. The blades trace a partial spiral that curls back from the tip.

"Initiating burrowing maneuver." I shift the drill into gear, and the motor begins to rotate the nose. The blades cut into the chunks of ice, clearing a path ahead. The current begins to send the *Nautilus* backward. I engage the impeller and push the *Nautilus* ahead. In a few seconds, the nose chops its way through the obstruction and reaches the open passage beyond.

"Maneuver complete. Continuing descent." I disengage the drill, stow the blades, deploy the wings, and proceed ahead.

"Mission time is four hours, forty minutes. Depth is nine kilometers." I check the biochemical sensors that sample the water flowing through to the impeller. "Sensors read methane, ammonia, and amines." I'm excited. The presence of these organic compounds makes the discovery of life more probable in the ocean below.

The next seven hours consist of steady progress with the *Nautilus* encountering few blockages and requiring minimal backtracking. At a certain point, I expect the channels to widen as we close in on the underground source of heat. However, the deeper we travel, the narrower the passages become and the more numerous the small tributaries. At each intersection, the choice presented involves smaller-diameter channels. Finally, further progress requires use of the drill.

By itself, the drill is capable of cutting through the rock-hard ice, but to assist the process, I route superheated steam through pipes embedded in the hull. The heated skin of the nose melts the ice, and the liquid water creates a frictionless layer between the ship and the tunnel wall. As the blades shave away ice in the wall and the nose melts it, intake ports draw in the resulting water and pipe it through to the impeller to provide a small amount of thrust forward. Progress downward continues, but at a fraction of the previous pace.

"Mission time is eleven hours twenty-nine minutes. Depth is twenty-three kilometers." The *Nautilus* has slowed to four hundred meters per hour. I fear we will not make the ocean depth before apogee, but we continue to press ahead.

•   •   •

Fifteen hours later the *Nautilus* breaks through. The radar shows a cavern eighty meters across empty of water. I open covers and switch on the six headlights arranged in a circle at the bridge of the nose.

"Breakthrough achieved at mission time twenty-six hours forty-seven minutes." Our video camera records shimmers of color reflecting off the ice walls, which are carved into waves and grottos by a past intrusion of heated water from below. The view inside is clear and still. I extend the control surfaces and feather the impeller blades to use what meager gasses exist for thrust. I move to one wall, point the headlights at it, and disengage the impeller. Now in freefall inside Enceladus, the camera records the blue folds of ice parading past the lens. At one-hundredth the force of Earth's gravity, the fall is languid. After ten seconds, the *Nautilus* falls at a meter per second and has travelled ten meters along the wall.

I point the nose down and locate the deepest part of the cavern. Radar displays a deeper hole on one side. I angle the *Nautilus* over that hole. By this time, the velocity has quadrupled, and the *Nautilus* plummets toward the bottom of the cavern. I turn the ship to a stern-down position and accelerate the impeller to high speed in an attempt to slow the ship's fall. With little for the blades to bite into, the pit at the bottom approaches quickly. The rear radar image shows the pit to be a meter wide and narrowing with depth, but how deep is uncertain. I keep the impeller running at high speed as the ship leaves the cavern and drops into the abyss.

The headlights illuminate the walls of the pit running away, and the nose camera shows its smooth, wavy features gradually closing around the ship. As the ship continues to fall, the radar begins to resolve spikes rising from the bottom.

At the last second, I steer the *Nautilus* on a path between spikes. The stern collides with the side of a spike, jerking the ship sideways before it strikes the bottom at high speed.

Instead of a crash, the collision is more of a plop. The *Nautilus* submerges into a slushy pool of ice and water at the bottom of the pit.

"I guess we're on our own now, Jules."

The presence of water blocks the radio link, so I feel comfortable speaking aloud to my alter ego. Jules offers a friendly ear and good advice.

The intakes begin pulling in a slurry the impeller blades can use to push forward. I manipulate the wing controls until

I have the nose pointing downward again. The radar picture is jumbled and only effective for a few tens of meters ahead. I aim the ship for the darker-colored spaces which indicate areas of more liquid water and less ice.

An hour later, the *Nautilus* hits open water.

"Mission time twenty-eight hours four minutes," I recite for the record, "the *Nautilus* has entered the Enceladus Ocean." Internal recordings will be the sole data repository for the future. "Outside temperature is 273 degrees Kelvin." That temperature is roughly the freezing point of water, but the presence of ammonia keeps it liquid.

Under thirty kilometers of ice, the water pressure outside is thirty atmospheres, equal to a depth of three hundred meters on Earth, the deepest SCUBA dive ever achieved. The bottom of this ocean is another ten kilometers deeper, equivalent to the Mariana Trench on Earth, but the water pressure on Enceladus is one-hundredth of the pressure on Earth at the same depth. The titanium structure of the *Nautilus* is more than sufficient to withstand the forty atmospheres required of it.

"Okay, Jules, let's see what we've got."

With the headlights for illumination, the video camera mounted in the nose shows clear water with no hint of color. Chemical analysis still shows organic compounds in the water, but at lower concentrations than before. The boat's path has deviated from the heat source that caused the eruption, so I began a spiral search. I monitor water temperature and organics concentration as I venture outward. After three rotations, I obtain a heading. I steer to that heading and search for a peak in temperature. As the temperature ticks upward, I notice an increasingly strong upwelling as well. The temperature peaks at 290 degrees Kelvin.

"Looks like we're over a hot spot." I aim the *Nautilus* straight down and accelerate to maximum speed into the current. At this descent rate, I should reach the ocean floor in an hour.

I keep the headlights on and the video recording our descent, but nothing appears within its range. After half an hour, the headlights begin to pick out tiny bubbles sliding by. Chemical analysis shows molecular hydrogen, which is a food source for methanogens that congregate around volcanic vents in the seabed on Earth. In another ten minutes, small clumps of matter begin floating by. Analysis shows bits of amino acids. With each passing minute, the clumps become more numerous, some in wavy filaments, others in fluttering membranes. I collect samples for later analysis.

"Better slow down before we hit the bottom," I tell Jules. The particles in the water now limit visibility to a hundred meters. The headlight beams probe forward as one of the six finds a clear path downward, then another. Random sideways movements appear among the constant upward drift.

"What could that be, Jules?" I check a playback of the video, slowing it down to see small points of light appearing out of the dark and moving through the rising clumps to take pieces before disappearing into the dark again.

The *Nautilus* continues forward into clear water, and the lights reach out to their maximum. A minute later, the bottom appears.

"Mission time twenty-nine hours fifty-two minutes. The *Nautilus* has reached the seabed." Here and there dark rocks peek through a carpet of fine, light-colored sediment. I inject air into the ballast tanks and use the control surfaces to level out the ship. We explore the area at a crawl, vectoring toward higher-temperature water. Then, a hundred meters away, I see it.

"White smoker ahead." A knobby chimney rises from the seabed, and a plume of white mineral "smoke" billows out the top.

Surrounding the chimney for several meters, clusters of material cover the ground. "Possible organic matter."

As the *Nautilus* glides closer, the material resolves into an ecosystem of tiny individual structures. Some of the structures form miniature castles with red flags or tentacles waving from their turrets.

"Looks like life to me, Jules." We have found what we came here for. Anchored to the seabed or to the side of the castles, delicate fabrics flutter in the turbulence produced by the smoker. As we approach, I see white worms squirming in the spaces between the castle walls. Tiny, gnat-like creatures flit around the waters over the castles. Filaments rise from anchors on the ground at numerous points around the chimney and disappear above the area illuminated by the headlights.

Maintaining the *Nautilus* a few meters away from the biomass, we circle the smoker, recording what the headlights reveal. At the edge of the cone of light another smoker appears.

"Look at the size of that plume." We move toward it. As we approach, the plume separates at the surface into three chimneys that merge into a single plume a meter or two above their openings. The biomass proves appreciably more diverse here. Even tiny jellyfish organisms float over the castles. Filaments also rise from the bottom here, some twisting into twine as they disappear into the darkness.

Beyond this smoker the seabed buckles up into a seam that leads to another colony clustered around another smoker. "I'm seeing what appears to be a fault line with smokers along it." A crack in the underlying rock has been sheared apart by Saturn's gravity and heated by friction as the contrary pulls of nearby moons Dione and Tethys move it back and forth. These fractures could account for the corresponding fissures in the ice at the south pole, called the "Tiger Stripes."

I decide to investigate the filaments that rise beside the white plumes. "Let's see where these strings go."

Keeping the headlights on the plume, I introduce air into the ballast tanks. The *Nautilus* begins to rise. After a few meters, the twine starts to unravel, and the filaments branch and intertwine. The intertwining becomes denser and spreads out into a loosely interconnected fabric that undulates in the water currents. Higher still, the delicate fabric encloses portions of the nutrient-rich smoke. Farther on, the edge of the fabric dips down, and we trace it to another filament bundle anchored to the seabed. Continuing around the vent, several more filaments contribute to the fabric that surrounds the smoker plume.

Continuing to rise, I back us off to take in the object as a whole. A white fabric with areas of red and black surrounds the smoke and billows out like a parachute over the column of heated water. A hole in the middle of the fabric lets the main smoke column continue through, as smaller puffs of smoke escape through pores in the fabric.

"What's that movement? Is something climbing on the fabric, Jules? Maybe a symbiotic organism siphoning off smoke nutrients?" Or even the byproducts of whatever the fabric organism is ingesting itself. Looking closer, I detect no such organism. Yet the impression of movement persists. Is it a reflection from the headlights? To test that theory, I turn off the lights on one side.

Refracted light from the remaining three headlights still provides dim illumination on the darker side, but that light does not explain what I observe. In the darker areas, pulses of light flit over the fabric in many different directions. I switch off the other headlights and adjust the video to low-light conditions.

"Would you look at that," I say to Jules. The field of view fills with countless spots of light that move across the total darkness like fireflies on a moonless night. In some places, the moving pulses split, and two or more pulses branch out in different directions. In other locations, pulses arise and depart on their paths periodically, like a heartbeat. Some nodes seem only to serve as a destination, receiving pulses, but not producing them. Others seem to be relay points, receiving pulses and directing them along one or more other pathways.

I ease the *Nautilus* forward to study the phenomenon more closely. At closer range, the number of pulses multiply as dimmer pulses appear in the fabric. As we watch the complex network of pulses before us, patterns emerge.

"I'm seeing periodic pulses like a heartbeat, but many others, too, in different frequencies that harmonize with the heartbeat. I see single pulses firing that create a cascade of other pulses across the whole fabric. And what's that, Jules?"

He has noticed a "Grand Central Station" node where a lot of the activity is concentrated.

I move the ship to center the camera on that spot. The fabric billows out, so I must adjust the camera to bring the image into focus. The fabric contacts the diamond porthole in front of the camera lens.

"Oops, too close." I reverse the impeller to gently pull away from the organism, but it remains stuck on the porthole.

"Come on, now." I pull back a little farther, not wanting to injure the creature. It doesn't budge. Maybe the headlights will frighten it off. I turn them on. Light diffracting in the water now appears in the video, but the fabric doesn't even flinch.

"I don't want to use the blades on you." The nose screw would cut us free, but I want to avoid becoming the Slasher of Enceladus.

"What do you say, Jules? A bit of heat?" I flood the nose heater with steam.

At the first hint of high temperature, the fabric tears away in a reaction akin to a human's involuntary response to touching a flame. "I guess Hot means Danger, Jules, even on Enceladus."

The diamond window retains a trace of the substance the creature used to adhere itself to the *Nautilus* — some kind of alien superglue. I reverse to a safe distance and extinguish the lights. We record a new set of cascading pulses that continue for ten minutes before subsiding into the more typical patterns we first observed.

"I'm wondering, Jules. Was that predatory behavior? If so, what does the prey look like?"

A few minutes later, a ribbon-like flatworm swims by. The dark spots on the worm's side must contain photoreceptors that attracts it to Grand Central Station. The fabric billows out to envelop the flatworm. Question answered.

•   •   •

For the next sixty hours, we explore the area along this oceanic rift, cataloguing and sampling the environment and its life forms. Now it is time to return to the surface. Enceladus is rapidly approaching its bigger sister-moon, Dione, which it does every two orbits. Dione's gravity would tug Enceladus in the direction opposite from Saturn, stretching the moon's rocky core and adding another pulse of tidal heating. We are counting on it to loosen up the geyser pathways.

I select the area above the rift that exhibits the greatest flux of heated water. The hot water will have carved caverns into the ice, and the upper movement of water from below maintains a constant pressure. The caverns act as wedges to concentrate the pressure and force open the cracks in the ice that provide a pathway for the flood of water to the surface. We are timing our ascent to reach the caverns while the liquid water is flooding through the ice channels at the maximum rate.

"Time to say goodbye, Jules," I say. "We have amazing news to share with Earth."

I pump air into the ballast tanks to maximize the ship's rate of ascent. I spin up the impeller and steer the *Nautilus* into the rising water column. The updraft gives us a boost of acceleration before the boat settles into a constant speed. I keep the headlights on and the forward radar operating. The range of our sensors is only a few hundred meters in water, but I need at least a few seconds of warning as the ship approaches the ice at high speed. In the meantime, I monitor the water temperature and try to keep the *Nautilus* in the center of the plume.

When the ice appears, I'm ready. The radar sounds its warning, and I flood the ballast tanks to slow the ship's ascent. I steer away from the wall on the right to the higher opening on the left. An ice wall appears in the video on the right, with continuing darkness to the left. I keep the wall in sight to give myself a sense of our speed. If the *Nautilus* is in a cavern, the upper wall could appear quickly. If a channel leads out, I need time to react.

I need not have worried. A current seizes the *Nautilus* like it is a raft on a white-water river. I increase thrust to allow our wing controls to provide some maneuverability. The radar warns of an obstruction, and the video shows a wall encroaching from one side. The water bounding off the wall pushes the *Nautilus* away and up toward an oblong opening. An instant later the ship rushes into the channel and bangs off the sides.

"Whoa, now. We can't have this." I pull in the wings, leaving the minimal extent that allows some steering with thrust applied. As an extra measure of protection, I deploy the blades in the nose and activate the drill. It will fend off obstructions and provide some rotational stability like a spinning bullet.

I keep the forward radar pulsing at its maximum power and lowest frequency to create a beacon that propagates best through the ice. The lander is listening for it. The *Nautilus* has no chance of reaching the surface through the same vent we entered, but I am aiming for somewhere not too far along the same Tiger Stripe at least.

The channel twists and turns, sometimes widening and sometimes narrowing. The *Nautilus* bangs off the wall around each turn, but her hull is built for this. When the headlights show a passage branching off, I take the wider option. As the ship rises through the ice, the temperature outside drops, but so far, the ammonia content in the water is sufficient to prevent crystals forming.

Depending on the speed the boat maintains, I estimate it will take anywhere from ten to fifteen hours to reach the surface — maybe more if we run into trouble. I hope the need for more burrowing will be minimal.

•   •   •

With each passing hour, the *Nautilus* moves upward. The narrowing channels create a greater push from behind by the water speeding through. That extra speed is tempered by the times we use the drill to get past a blockage. However, the average speed keeps rising. By the eight-hour mark, I estimate the ship is ten kilometers below the surface.

"On the bright side, Jules, we seemed to have passed the narrowest channels. Maybe the worst is behind us."

Another branch approaches, and I steer toward the opening with the greater Doppler reading. Just as we enter the new channel, another branch appears, and the *Nautilus*'s sideways momentum sends us down a narrow channel before I can steer us to the faster side. The channel corkscrews, sending us sliding along the wall into an ever-narrowing opening at high speed.

I reverse the impeller to slow us down, but it's too late. The nose of the *Nautilus* takes a final turn, jams into a fissure, and the stern slams sideways into the wall leaving us wedged in the ice.

With no flow of material through the impeller, the ship has lost thrust. I halt the impeller and deactivate the nose blades, which are impaled in the surrounding ice. I route steam through the nose tubes to melt the ice. Soon, a trickle of water loosens the nose and allows some rotation. The intake ports receive some water, but most of the water seems to be collecting in the cracks in the channel wall and refreezing to lock the ship in tighter.

After an hour, I can reactivate the nose blades, and they begin to carve the ice ahead of the ship. A mixture of water and ice shavings enter through the forward ports, and I turn up the feed channel heaters to raise its temperature as it passes through. I activate the impeller to send hot water out the back while we continue to carve some room forward.

The situation is turning into a race against time. In the short term, we need to keep enlarging the free space around us faster than the water refreezes to keep us trapped. In the longer term, we need to find our way back to an open channel before Saturn's gravity pinches off our escape route — perhaps forever.

I reverse the nose screw to move us backward while I send more hot water out the rear to melt the ice behind us.

Then I thrust us forward to intake more ice and water while I engage the screw to carve more from the wall in front of us. I repeat this backward-then-forward maneuver countless times as the hours pass, until finally I feel the hull tilting around the curve of the channel behind us. After two dozen more repeats of this maneuver, the stern pops free and slides backward along the narrow channel.

With no current propelling us from behind, a combination of the nose screw and gravity allows me to inch the *Nautilus* rearward. We finally reach the main channel, and by keeping the nose screw in contact with the channel wall, I propel the stern against the current until the nose pops free.

I deploy the wings and accelerate the impeller to turn into the current. We are sucked into the main channel and continue our ascent. We have lost six hours, but we still have a chance to make the surface before gravity squeezes shut our escape route.

Not long after, the water begins to freeze, creating slush. We continue upward but at a slower pace. I adjust the impeller to ingest the slush and expel it out the rear to maintain the ship's speed. A few minutes later, the vacuum from the surface penetrates to our depth, causing the slush to sublimate. As the ice and liquid water boil off as water vapor, it creates a foamy mixture that the headlights and radar can no longer penetrate. I am flying blind.

"What the hell is this, Jules?" The foam carries the ship forward, but my controls are sluggish. I feather the impeller blades but fail to gain purchase on this new type of fluid. The ship becomes a rudderless projectile inside a kinked tube of ice.

The *Nautilus* slams fore and aft against the ice wall, but the ship holds together. The higher she goes, the more the ice and water turns to vapor, until the foam subsides, and the tunnel fills with wind-driven snow.

"Finally. Here is something I can work with." The *Nautilus* flutters in the wind. I extend the wings bit by bit to stabilize the ship and harness the flow. I tune the impeller blades and manage to gain a modicum of control. Soon after, most of the snow has sublimated, and in the relatively clear air, the headlights illuminate the path ahead. I can now negotiate the turns with minimal contact against the walls.

The ice tube widens as other passages join and add the force of their winds to the gale. The only way to maintain control is to keep on top of the storm.

"If the water vapor travels at one hundred meters per second, I have to go a hundred and one." I ignore the fact that hitting the granite-hard ice wall at such a high speed would crumple even a titanium hull.

The radar shows glints off the walls, but clear in between. Then a return off the ice paints a line directly ahead. I flick the wings to move laterally. Half a second later, I pass a wall that bifurcates the passage.

Five seconds later the walls begin to march away from the center of the radar and video images. Then the screens go black.

Emerging from the corner of the screen, the video camera catches the imposing form of Saturn peeking over the white surface of Enceladus.

I engage the retrorocket system, which reroutes the superheated steam from the reactor to nozzles in the wings. That thrust reduces the boat's speed from two hundred meters per second to zero within a few seconds. By then, the *Nautilus* has risen to an altitude slightly under a kilometer. From that altitude, the lazy drop to the surface will take ninety seconds.

"The *Nautilus* has returned," I radio to the lander and the world, "with life from Enceladus."

With the last spurts of steam, I turn the ship to point its camera at Saturn. I broadcast the picture so the lander can lock onto our position.

"Congratulations, Jules," I say. "We did it."

Beside me, Jules Verne smiles.

SINS OF THE SON

STETSON RAY

WILLIAM GRADY began hearing voices on a Friday evening in late September.

He was on his way home from work when he heard someone say, "Can you hear me?"

Grady ignored the voice. He figured it was coming from one of his fellow train car passengers. People say all kinds of crazy things on the tube.

"Hello? Can you hear me?" the voice asked again.

Grady eyed the people around him casually, barely turning his head, not wanting to make eye contact with whoever was talking.

"WILLIAM GRADY, CAN YOU HEAR ME?" the voice thundered.

Grady winced and covered his ears with his hands. He looked at the woman sitting next to him, expecting her to have her hands over her ears as well, but the woman was behaving as though she'd heard nothing.

The voice boomed again, louder than before.

Grady cried out and fell to the floor and was sure that his eardrums had ruptured. He checked his palms for blood; there was none.

"I can hear you just fine," Grady said. "Please stop shouting."

A mother and her child got up and moved seats. A plump bald man followed their lead. Grady had always wondered what it would be like to be the crazy person on the train — one of those people who don't have to worry about rent or mortgages and are fond of talking to themselves.

"IS THIS ANY BETTER?"

"Please stop shouting," Grady pleaded, holding his ears again. "My head is going to split open."

A second voice said, "Turn it down." It was quieter, farther away.

"I'm sorry," said the original voice. "How's this?"

"Much better."

Grady looked around, but as far as he could tell, the owner of the voice was invisible.

"Where are you?" he asked.

"Don't worry about that," the voice answered.

"I've had a stroke, haven't I?"

"No, Mr. Grady. You are in excellent health as far as we know."

"Then why am I hearing voices? And who is *we?*"

The last few people sitting near Grady changed seats upon hearing him say the word *voices*. He didn't blame them. He knew the drill: you encounter a crazy person on the tube, you do your best to keep your distance. Grady had seen all kinds of strange behavior while riding the tube over the years, but there was one strange person in particular he had never forgotten:

A disheveled woman talking to herself rapidly, as though she were an auctioneer. She stank. There was debris in her hair. Grady and the rest of the commuters had given her a wide berth, but he couldn't help but listen to her ramblings. The woman was saying something about a bumblebee that had the wings of a rooster — an insect with feathered wings. As the train pulled into the station the woman began growling like a dog. Grady and the rest of the commuters had left the woman behind. They left her and went to work and had meetings and drank coffee and ate their lunches without ever asking the woman if she was alright, if she needed help.

Grady had looked for her on the ride home.

He did not see her, that day or ever again.

The train-car lurched and slowed.

The voice in Grady's head said, "I'll explain what's going on later."

"Later?"

"Yes. Now when the train stops, proceed as usual."

Grady did not respond.

"Is that clear?"

Grady whispered, "Yes," as the feeling something was terribly wrong settled inside him.

The train stopped and the doors slid open. Grady stepped out onto the platform and headed for the stairs. The crowd swallowed him. He looked around to see if anyone was watching him. No one seemed to know he existed.

The voice said, "When you are streetside I need you to proceed directly to your ex-girlfriend Sheila's apartment."

"Sheila?"

"Yes. Her flat is only a few blocks from your current location, is that correct?"

"Yeah, it's pretty close."

People were looking again. The crowd around him thinned. He might as well have been talking about bumblebees and feathers.

"Why am I to go to Sheila's? Did she put you up to this?"

"Proceed to Sheila's flat," the voice said quietly, like it was farther away than before. "I will give you further instruction once you arrive."

Grady stepped out of the underground and ducked into an alley to get some privacy. "No," he said, "I'm not going one step further until you explain what's going on."

"Proceed to Sheila's apartment."

"I will not. I need some answers."

"This is your last warning. Proceed to the apartment."

"I won't, and I want to know —"

A low tone rang inside Grady's head; with the sound came a feeling; it washed down to his hands and feet like cold water. He had to lean against a dumpster to keep from falling. His bones burned. His muscles contracted. His thoughts raced, scattered and wild. He tried to yell for help and out came a noise a startled walrus might make. The tone grew louder, loud enough to drown out the sounds of the world around him. Grady could not hear. He could not breathe. He was drowning on his feet, submerged in a pool of liquid electricity.

Then the sound was gone.

Grady gasped for air.

The voice said, "Unless you want that to happen again, you'll do as we say."

Grady vomited. He looked down at his trousers to see if he had wet himself and was surprised to find he hadn't.

"What was that?" Grady panted. "What did you do to me?"

"That was a specific sound that makes every nerve ending in your body light up at the same time. I can do that again any time I want."

"Please don't."

"Start walking," the voice said quietly, barely audible.

Grady shambled out of the alley.

"What am I to do once I get to Sheila's?" He waited for an answer. "Hello? Are you there?" He listened, but the voices were gone.

Grady wanted to do what he did every Friday evening: pop into Dooley's — the little pub around the corner from his flat — and grab a few drinks. But he kept walking toward Sheila's. He feared the tone — feared its return.

•   •   •

Twenty minutes later, Grady was standing across the street from his ex's building. And there she was, Sheila walking on the sidewalk, their son Walter dawdling along beside her. They didn't see him. They disappeared inside the building.

"I'm here," Grady said. "What now?"

He waited.

He asked again.

And waited.

The insanity of his situation came crashing down. Grady never came to visit Walter unannounced, so Sheila would want an explanation. If he told her the truth about the voices ... Grady imagined himself locked inside a padded room, nothing to do but bounce from wall to wall and wonder where it all went wrong.

His body acted on its own: he hurried down the sidewalk and ducked into the first pub he came across. He'd never needed a drink so badly in his entire life.

•   •   •

Three pints later, Grady was convinced he had imagined the whole thing. He wondered if he was starting to go crazy and hearing voices was the first symptom. His mother had gone looney in her later years. They say that kind of thing runs in families, so perhaps it had caught up to him. His depression had been getting worse for months, so maybe he had crossed some kind of threshold.

He said to himself, "I'll head to the doctor on Monday and get everything sorted out."

He finished his pint, paid his tab, and went to the loo.

He was standing at a urinal when the voice said, "Mr. Grady, can you hear me?"

"Loud and clear."

"Have you arrived at Sheila's yet?"

"I have not."

"Are you on your way?"

"Nope."

"Why not?"

"Because I'm not going to listen to the voices inside my head — I'm not crazy. And even if I am crazy, they have medication for that nowadays, and I intend to get a prescription."

"You are not crazy, Mr. Grady. Where are you?"

"Please, if you're going to be addressing me regularly, lose the Mister. Everyone just calls me Grady, always have."

"Alright then, Grady, where are you?"

"At the pub."

He was speaking loudly. He was a little drunk, and he didn't care if people heard him talking to himself. He went to the sink and washed his hands.

"How many drinks have you had?"

"Two or three, whatta you care? Maybe I'll have a few more."

"You need to leave immediately. Proceed to —"

"Yeah, I get it, I know where you want me to go, but I'm not going, and that's that."

Grady walked out of the restroom with the intention of having one more before he left, just to show the voice who was boss. Then he was on the floor, writhing and making noises, riding an invisible electric chair again.

The tone was louder than it had been before.

It shook the deepest parts of him, rattled him to his core.

People appeared above him. They looked worried. Their mouths were moving. A lady with bleached blonde hair was holding a phone to her ear and staring down at him, her eyes bulging.

When the tone stopped, Grady found himself saying, "Okay," over and over again. He fought to get his feet under him. One of the pub patrons said he needed to lie back down. Another said the word, "Seizure." And apparently an ambulance was on the way.

Grady ignored the rabble of concerned drunks and stumbled outside. He turned his head and puked. He did not stop walking. The sun was setting. Many people were on the sidewalks, headed out for food and drinks; most gave Grady a wide berth.

"Please tell me what's going on."

"If you aren't at Sheila's in ten minutes, you will receive another correction."

Grady picked up his pace.

It didn't take him long to reach Sheila's

"I'm here. What now?"

"Go upstairs and talk to your son," the voice said.

The voice may as well have told him to jump the fence at Buckingham Palace and storm the Royal Chambers. He would have almost preferred it had.

"I can't do that," Grady said.

"Grady, it is very important you talk to your son."

"Please, just leave me alone. I don't care if you correct me again. I'm not doing anything else you tell me to do. For all I know, as soon as I'm inside Sheila's flat you'll ask me to stab them both to death with a steak knife."

The second voice whispered something.

"We would never do anything like that," the first voice said. "We are here to help you."

"Thanks a lot. I feel so much better now. I always wanted to hear voices — you know, just go completely mad."

"You're not going mad. We suspect you are suffering from severe depression, but you are not crazy."

"I'm not —" he started to say depressed, but that would've been a lie. "Respectfully, I disagree. I've lost my marbles and I need medication."

"Please, Grady. I don't want to give you another correction, but I will."

Crazy or not, the last thing Grady wanted was another correction.

"I'll do it, I'll talk to my son, but you have to tell me what's going on." He was standing on the street corner, his hands on his hips, staring into the sky. "You say I'm not crazy, so make me believe it."

There was muffled talking — voices at the end of a long hall.

The voice said, "We wanted to wait until after you had spoken to Walter, but since you insist, I'm going to tell you, but the explanation might be difficult for you to accept. Are you ready?"

"I'm listening."

The voice said, "I'm speaking to you from the year 2068. That makes you the first person in history to receive direct communication from another time. You'll be remembered with the likes of Columbus, Armstrong, and Magellan. Congratulations, William Grady, your name now belongs to the ages."

Grady stood there, the words echoing inside his head. Something about it struck him as silly. He began to laugh. Not chuckle or snicker, but *laugh*. He bent over and held his belly and bellowed, tears running down his face.

"Twenty sixty-eight!" he balked, choking on his laughter. "I've gone totally bonkers!"

"You haven't," said the voice, "and I can prove it if you'd like."

Grady laughed a little more. "Sure, go right ahead."

"If you go upstairs and ask your son what his favorite memory of you is, he will tell you about the time you took him to the fair."

Suddenly it wasn't funny anymore. It felt personal. Grady started to ask the voice how it knew about that day at the fair then remembered the voice was him, was his own deranged mind; it knew what he knew. Still, what the voice had said intrigued him.

"That day at the fair was a disaster," Grady said. "There's no way Walter has fond memories of it."

"Ask him yourself. You'll see."

Grady stood staring at Sheila's building, debating.

"Fine."

He sprang across the street and poked the buzzer.

Through the speaker, Sheila said, "Yes?"

"Sorry to just pop in, but I need to talk to Walter."

"Grady? What are you doing here?"

"I'm uh — I'd really like to spend a minute with Walter, if that's alright."

A long pause.

"You didn't even call. You could've at least called."

"I know. I'm sorry. But if I could just talk to Walter for a moment, I'd owe you."

Grady stood listening to static pour through the intercom. Sheila was up in her flat, silently deciding his fate.

"It's not a good time. We're about to have dinner. Maybe we can meet up tomorrow at the park."

Grady couldn't wait. He needed to know if the voice was right about the fair. Also, he wasn't looking forward to being violated by the electric tone again.

"Tomorrow's no good. It needs to be tonight. Right now."

"Are you drunk?"

Maybe back at the pub, but not after receiving a correctment, and not after puking.

"I'm stone sober, I swear. Please, just give me a minute with Walter. I'm begging you."

Sheila considered.

Grady waited for eons.

"Come on up but make it quick."

The door buzzed and Grady darted inside the building. On his way up the stairs, he thought about that day at the fair with Walter, his only son. The whole day had been a disaster. It had been hot out, the ground wet and soggy from recent rain. The smell coming from the livestock pens had been stunningly pungent. Even so, the place was packed.

Grady remembered thinking that half the city must've driven out to the country to visit the little fair. He and Walter had waited twenty minutes in the sun to ride the spinning teacups — in hindsight, probably not a good idea right after lunch. Walter had spewed chunks the moment he stepped off the ride. His shoes and shirt were soiled. The children waiting in line had laughed, and Grady and Walter had gone home prematurely, their father/son day ruined.

Sheila must have been waiting by the door; she opened it before Grady could knock.

"Make it quick," she said.

She stepped out of the doorway, and Grady went in. He stood writhing his hands and looking down the hallway toward Walter's bedroom.

"Have you forgotten where your own son's bedroom is?" Sheila asked.

"Course not," Grady answered, then headed down the hall.

He took a deep breath and knocked on the door before pushing it open. Walter was sitting at his desk, his eyes fixed on a computer screen. Grady stood motionless in the doorway. The feeling that he was unwanted and uninvited was overwhelming.

"Your dad's here, Walter," Sheila called from the kitchen.

Walter glanced at Grady, then went back to his game. He had grown since the last time Grady had seen him. How long had it been? Five months? Six? More?

"You bring me something?" Walter asked.

"Uhm, not this time." Grady faked a smile and ran his hands down the front of his shirt.

"What are you doing here?"

Oh, you know, just doing what the voices told me to do. Say Walter, did you know that some bumblebees have feathered wings? That's right, just like roosters.

"Just wanted to pop in and see how you're doing," Grady said.

Walter made a dismissive noise. Walter wanted to play his game. Walter didn't want anything to do with his sorry excuse for a father. Grady would never say it, but he didn't really want Walter either. Grady had been at the right place at the right time and Walter had been an accident. Ever since Sheila had informed Grady she was pregnant, he had felt like an intruder, a nuisance, a deranged elderly relative who refused to die.

Knowing how to be a father had never come to him. Parents are supposed to love their children unconditionally, but that wasn't the case with Grady. It had taken him a long time to learn to love his son. Did Walter know that? Probably. Wasn't it obvious? Anyone with eyes could see that Grady had zero fatherly instincts.

Walter paused the game and said, "You dyin' or somethin'?"

"No, of course not."

"Then what are you doing here?"

Walter was far more attuned to the world around him than Grady had been at ten years old. Sharp as a tack, as they say. One of the smartest in his class. A good egg. A good kid all around. He deserved a better father than Grady. Much better.

"I've got an odd question I'd like to ask you, Walter."

"Go on then."

"Have you got any fond memories when it comes to me and you?"

"Of course I do."

"Really?"

"Well, yeah."

"What's your favorite one?"

"My favorite memory of me and you?"

"Uh-huh."

Walter leaned back into his chair and thought about it. "Probably that time we went to the fair."

Of all the moments that Grady had shared with his son, of all the pathetic attempts at bonding over the years, he would have never guessed the fair to be a fond memory, not in a thousand years.

But the voices had known.

"*The fair?*" Grady asked, narrowing his eyes.

"Sure. What's the big deal about that?"

"It's just — I'm sorry, but I don't remember one thing going smoothly that entire day."

"Yeah, but I had a great time anyways."

"What was so great about it?"

Walter took a deep breath and let it out. "You remember when I puked?"

"Of course."

"It's just ..."

"Just what?"

"I thought you'd be mad at me, that maybe you'd think me a sissy for puking, but you seemed so unbothered. You were so ... cool about it. And we even stopped for ice cream on the way home. I felt like you really cared about me that day, like I was really your son, like I didn't need to impress you or anything."

Grady was speechless. He crossed the room and knelt down in front of his son.

"I know we don't have the best relationship, but I care about you plenty, Walter. I'm sorry I'm not a better dad. I'm sorry for … Well, I'm just sorry."

Walter stared, a blank expression on his face. For a moment Grady thought they might hug, but they didn't. Grady wasn't sure what to do next. He loved his son, but he didn't know how to love him.

"Guess I'll be going now," Grady said, standing up. "I'll let you get back to your game."

He turned and headed for the door.

"You think we can go to the fair again sometime?" Walter asked.

Grady wasn't sure if he had heard correctly.

"You say, *go to the fair?*"

"Uh-huh."

Grady nodded. "Sure, we can do that. See you later then."

He stepped backwards into the hall and pulled the door shut slowly, Walter still watching him. Sheila was waiting in the kitchen.

"Don't start thinking you can show up here whenever you get drunk," she said.

"I'm not drunk."

"Please, I can smell it." She crossed her arms. "What did you and Walter talk about?"

Bumblebees and roosters.

"You know, just father-son stuff."

"That's a load if I ever heard it. Walter needs a father, not some drunk showing up and making empty promises. I went through the same thing with my father and I won't let it happen to my boy. You will not lead him on. Half in half out is worse than all the way out, so you can just go back to being absent. We both know that's what you want anyways."

Not knowing what else to say, Grady said, "I'm sorry."

He went for the door and Sheila didn't stop him.

Back on the street, Grady said, "You were right." He waited for the voice. "Hello? Are you there?" Grady knocked on the side of his head as though it were a door. "This is Will Grady calling the year twenty sixty-eight."

"Am I coming through?" the voice asked.

"Yes, crystal clear."

"How'd it go with Walter?"

"Alright I suppose. You were right about the fair."

"Now do you believe what I told you?"

Grady answered before he could think. "Yeah, I guess I do."

"Good."

Grady began walking down the sidewalk. He barely noticed the strange looks he received from the people he passed.

"Can I ask you something?"

"Sure," the voice replied.

"Why me? I mean, why did you contact me, of all people? Am I important to the future? Or do I do something terrible? Will there be assassins sent to kill me?"

The voices laughed, one much louder than the other.

"Don't worry, there'll be no assassins," said the voice.

"That's good to know." Grady realized something. "So if you're just some bloke from the future, what's your name?"

There was a long silence.

"Nate," said the voice.

"That's it? No last name?"

"We think it best to avoid telling you too much, as we aren't fully aware of the repercussions this conversation could have on the future."

All the movies Grady had ever seen featuring time travel flashed through his mind. Sometimes changing the past changed the future, sometimes it didn't. In one film, a small change to the past could alter the future. In another, you couldn't change the timeline if you tried. He thought of the story by Bradbury where the man steps on a butterfly and changes the entire course of history. Grady didn't think such a thing could happen. Surely time wasn't that delicate.

"Has anything changed in the future since we started talking?" Grady asked. "Is your Prime Minister still your Prime Minister?"

"Nothing has changed so far, though it might be impossible to tell if it does. As I said, you are the first test subject, and we don't know how much our conversation will alter things, if at all."

"So, is there anything you can tell me about the future?"

"What do you think?"

"No, probably not I'd say." Grady rounded a corner and caught a whiff of food and his stomach rumbled. "Can't you tell me one small thing? One little fact that might surprise me? Promise I won't tell."

"If I told you that England still hasn't won another World Cup, would you believe me?"

Both of them laughed, then Grady asked, "Would it be alright if I grab a bite to eat? I'm starving."

"No problem."

Grady ducked into a nearby shop and ordered a ham and cheese bap and took his meal to a corner booth — as far away from the other customers as he could get.

"Are you still there?" he said, quietly.

Nothing for a moment.

"Can you hear me?" Nate asked, but his voice was muffled.

"Yes, but not very well."

There was a grainy static sound inside his head, like someone was searching for the right frequency on a radio.

"Is that better?" Nate asked, clearer.

"Yes, much better. Why does it take you a minute to come back every time?"

"Each time we communicate we are both at slightly different points in time. We have to re-tune in order to get on the same wavelength again. Not to mention the potential micro-effects our conversation may be having on the timeline."

Grady listened while he ate, trying to understand.

"How are we ... I mean, what is allowing us to talk? Some kind of machine? Or ..."

"Even if I could tell you, it wouldn't be easy to understand. The process that is allowing this conversation to take place utilizes a great many technologies that haven't been invented in your time yet."

"I see."

Grady ate. None of the other customers paid attention to him. What would happen if he told them? He imagined standing up and saying, "*Attention everyone, I am the first man in history to communicate with the future. See this shirt I'm wearing? They'll hang it in the British Museum one day.*" He chuckled quietly and took another bite.

"You never did say why you contacted me, or how you knew about Walter and the fair."

"I'm going to be honest with you, Grady. You were not selected at random. You were chosen for a reason."

"Which is?"

"According to the current version of history, you die in roughly four hours."

A knot appeared in Grady's throat. He struggled to swallow the food he'd been chewing.

He choked out a single word: "How?"

"Suicide," the voice answered.

The noise of the sandwich shop faded. Grady was seeing through a tunnel.

"How often do you think of suicide, Grady?"

"Pretty often. At least once a week. Sometimes more."

There was no use in lying.

"How long have you been having those thoughts?"

"Wait, don't I have a choice? Do I have to die?"

"Of course not. That's why we contacted you. Our goal is to change your outcome. We don't know what spurred it on, but according to what we know, you leave Dooley's Pub a half hour past midnight and you are never seen alive again. They find your body Monday evening. Single gunshot to the head. No note."

Sins of the Son

Grady pushed his plate away, no longer hungry.

His thoughts went to his grandad's old pistol, which was unregistered, loaded, and hidden in his apartment closet.

"So I'm not important to the future? I'm just a guinea pig for some kind of government health program that saves people from offing themselves? Is that it? Retroactive suicide prevention?"

Grady waited, listening intently.

"Very close, but it's a bit more complicated than that. Originally, yes, we received public funding for research and development with suicide prevention as one of our primary goals, but at the present we are a private venture."

"Aren't there a hundred other blokes you could save?

"A thousand. Hundreds of thousands."

"Then why me?"

"In the future, your son Walter is a very wealthy man."

"Walter? Really? Did he hit the lotto or something?"

Nate laughed then said, "No, not that kind of wealthy. Walter is the richest man on the planet."

"Walter? The richest?"

"Yes, filthy rich as they say."

"Exactly how rich?"

"I'll put it this way: Walter was worth more than the next five wealthiest people in the world combined by the time he was forty."

"Walter's a billionaire?"

"Try trillionaire."

The word rang out.

It started with a T.

"How'd he get so rich?" Grady muttered.

"You know I can't tell you that."

"Did he invent — is Walter the reason the future can talk to the past?"

"Yes, but that's not what made him rich. Truth be told, to build the machine that is making this conversation possible, your son exhausted most of his fortune, and by using it to contact you, he has broken federal law."

"Talking to the past is a crime?"

"As of four months ago, yes. The government wasn't worried until Walter actually built the machine, and when they learned what he meant to do with it, they passed laws. They fear it will change things for the worse in our time. Most of the world agrees. Everyone is worried that Walter will destroy our timeline by using his machine. There have been protests for months. As we speak, there are dozens of protesters outside the compound which houses the machine. The government cut our power off months ago, but Walter saw that coming; we make our own power, have for years. They'll probably send in the Army Reserve when they find out we've made contact, but we should have a while longer to talk, a few hours at least."

It was too much information for Grady to process. He was staring out into space, mouth hanging open. The shop owner had noticed Grady and was watching him.

Nate said, "I know how it sounds, but I assure you it's true. If you still don't believe me, I can tell you the final score of a football match that hasn't started yet. You just can't bet on it, of course."

"No, I believe you."

And Grady did. He could see it all in his mind: Walter, a successful inventor, the Bill Gates of the British Isles; a sprawling compound; crowds outside the gates holding up signs that said things like, "*HELP THEM=KILL US!*" and "*YOU CAN'T SAVE THEM ALL!*" and "*THE PAST ISN'T WORTH THE FUTURE!*"

Grady believed everything.

"We thought it might be too much for you to handle initially, but Walter is here and he wishes to speak with you, if you're ready."

Before Grady could respond, another voice said, "Dad, can you hear me?"

The voice was different than he expected, but Grady knew that it belonged to Walter at once. There was no mistaking it. A father always knows his son. It looked like Grady had more fatherly instincts than he thought.

"Sorry to put you through all that," Walter said.

"No worries," Grady breathed.

"And sorry about making you go to mom's flat. We wanted to find out if I would receive any new memories after you talked to the past version of me."

"Did you?"

"Not yet."

The future remained silent for a few seconds.

"I don't know where to start ..." Walter mused. "I've rehearsed this conversation in my head for decades now, but I can't seem to remember a word of what I planned to say." He chuckled nervously. "I've moved heaven and earth to have this conversation, so to say I've missed you — well, that wouldn't quite cover it. I forgot what your voice sounded like a long time ago, so just sitting here and listening to you talk has been wonderful." Grady's eyes burned. "Sorry about those corrections earlier. It was for your own good, you understand." Walter paused. "Dad? Are you there?"

"Yes, Walter," Grady choked. "I'm here."

The weight of it was unbearable. To think of all that Walter had done just to speak to his father again ... It was hard for Grady to believe that anyone would miss him so much if he were to die. Opting out was no longer an option. Suicide was off the table, now and forever.

"I'm sorry I ever thought about leaving you, Walter," Grady said, wiping his eyes. "I've got good news: it worked. I'm not going anywhere, I promise. All your work has paid off. I'm proud of you, Walter, so proud."

There was a hiss of static and a pop, like someone had unplugged an old tube TV while it was still on.

The shop owner appeared beside Grady and said, "Can't have you talking to yourself, mate. Out you go."

The shop owner pointed toward the door. Grady tried to stand but his legs wouldn't work.

"Come on then," said the shop owner.

He grabbed Grady under the arm and guided him toward the door. Grady tripped over the entryway and fell outside onto the sidewalk.

"Sorry about that, Walter. I just got tossed out of a restaurant for talking to myself." Grady laughed at the absurdity of the situation. "Are you there?" Walter said nothing. "Can you hear me?"

Grady stood up and spun in a circle and held his head at different angles in an attempt to get a better signal. He vaguely noticed that people were watching him.

"Walter, am I coming through?"

He marched around in odd patterns and twisted his head and yelled for Walter over and over again. Two policemen appeared on either side of him.

"What's the problem here?" one asked.

"No problem," Grady said. "I'm just trying to ..."

Trying to what?

Communicate with my son in the future?

Catch a feathered bumblebee?

"Nothing. I just got a little confused. I'm sorry."

The officers eyed him suspiciously.

"Had a bit too much to drink?" the second officer asked.

"Yeah, guess I did. Got a bit carried away I suppose."

"Can't have you out here making a scene."

"Of course not. I'll go straight home."

The officers watched him.

One said, "Well go on then," and Grady took off in a fast trot.

As soon as he was out of earshot he resumed talking and trying to get something to go through. He tried the whole way home. He tried after he got home. He tried all night. But the voices were gone. Walter was gone.

Sometime around sunrise, Grady passed out while lying on his couch, still mumbling to himself.

•   •   •

Grady was standing in a field. Walter was riding some kind of spinning contraption. There were people all around, some eating cotton candy, some carrying oversized stuffed animals.

Walter was laughing. He was getting older, but he still loved going to the fair.

Two years had passed since the voices stopped. It had taken Grady months to accept that things had changed, that he wouldn't be hearing from future-Walter again. Sometimes he considered telling present-Walter about that night but knew he never would; it was better to leave the future in the past. And it wouldn't be fair for Walter to learn of the price he'd paid to save Grady.

Trillions of pounds.

Billions of lives.

An entire future stripped of existence.

Walter was blissfully oblivious, but Grady wasn't; he could feel the debt hanging over him every moment of every day. But the guilt was beginning to fade and he couldn't help but be proud of his son for doing what he had done. Whether anyone knew it or not, Grady was the world's only trillion-dollar-father. It had become his life's purpose to make sure that Walter got his money's worth, but he often wondered how well he was doing ...

The ride ended and Walter staggered over to Grady and looked up at him, a dazed expression on his face.

"Had your fill?" Grady asked.

"Yeah. I don't think I can handle much more." Walter rubbed his stomach with one hand.

Grady put his arm around his son and guided him toward the parking lot.

"Was it a good day?" Grady asked.

"No, it was a great day."

Walter was getting bigger. Soon, he probably wouldn't want to hang out with his father in public.

"Can I ask you a serious question?" Grady asked.

"Sure."

"What would you trade for a day like this?"

"What's that supposed to mean?"

"Would you trade the whole world?"

Walter thought about it for a moment. "I don't know. Probably not. Might trade France, or maybe Ireland. But the whole world? Not for a trip to the fair with an old bloke like you."

Grady couldn't help but laugh as they climbed into his car.

As they drove away from the fair, he gazed into the rear-view mirror and watched all the laughing families and happy children grow smaller and smaller until each and every one of them finally disappeared.

AFTERWORD

IF YOU'RE LIKE ME, daily life doesn't always allow us the time we want for reading or writing. So many times, I've started an amazing book, only to be kept away from it for a week and then ... no longer feeling as invested in the story. (Or, frankly, having forgotten good chunks of what happened ...)

Shorter works of fiction perfectly fill this void. Whether they're novellas or short stories, they've become a prominent and much-needed feature in today's publishing world.

Short fiction works beautifully across genres, but especially speculative fiction. Some of the best horror I've ever read are short stories. When you look at fantasy and science fiction, these authors must fit world-building, character-building, and plot all into one cohesive and entertaining bite that can be digested in one or two sittings. On top of that, they must reel you in and make you care — about the characters, about the stakes. This is no easy task! It's like trying to swim laps in a hot tub.

As a reader, it's so satisfying, though — to be given an entire little world that you can lose yourself in for a few hours. To fall in love with an author's writing from this singular piece. It's led me to look up those authors to get more of their work, and that's how you know the story really did its job. I enjoy going into something knowing that it's a complete piece. I will not be left on a cliffhanger; I will not be puzzling over side-plots that aren't set to resolve themselves until books two or three or ten.

Seeing short stories become increasingly popular in the world of books delights me, and I hope that trend continues. Keep reading them, and the authors will keep writing them.

Kelley York
author of *Into the Glittering Dark*

ALSO IN THIS SERIES

DRAGON GEMS (WINTER 2023)

Tales to warm your imagination during the cold winter months

Featuring stories from Christina Ardizzone, Matt Bliss, Gustavo Bondoni, Micah Castle, Nestor Delfino, C. M. Fields, Andrew Giffin, Emma Kathryn, Michelle Ann King, Jason Lairamore, Eve Morton, Lena Ng, S. Park, Arlo Sharp, Mar Vincent, and Richard Zwicker.

DRAGON GEMS (SPRING 2023)

Let your imagination bloom with these mind-opening tales

Featuring stories from Veronica L. Asay, Warren Benedetto, Jason P. Burnham, Michael D. Burnside, Laura J. Campbell, Arasibo Campeche, Jay Caselberg, Philip Brian Hall, Tom Howard, Tim Kane, Benjamin C. Kinney, Stephen McQuiggan, Mike Morgan, Sam Muller, Jason Restrick, and Elyse Russell.

DRAGON GEMS (SUMMER 2023)

Pass the long days with these short tales

With stories from Raluca Balasa, Gustavo Bondoni, Sasha Brown, Mario Caric, Jordan Chase-Young, Chris Cornetto, Marc Λ. Criley, Megan M. Davies-Ostrom, Malina Douglas, Jen Downes, R.E. Dukalsky, Allan Dyen-Shapiro, Lu Evans, LL Garland, Kai Holmwood, Steve Loiaconi, George Nikolopoulos, Antony Paschos, Christopher Rowe, Lauren Stoker, Adam Strassberg, Edgar Strid, DJ Tyrer, and John Walters.

DRAGON GEMS (FALL 2023)

Shiver during the long nights with these dark tales

With stories from Brett Thomas Abrahamsen, Mike Adamson, Christopher Bond, John M. Campbell, Arasibo Campeche, Brandon Case, Elizabeth Cobbe, Ryan Cole, Sarina Dorie, Monica Joyce Evans, P.G. Galalis, Kara L. Hartz, Brian Hugenbruch, Andrew Rucker Jones, Andrew Kozma, Steven P. Mathes, Jen Mierisch, Iseult Murphy, Ira Nayman, Tarver Nova, Frank J. Oreto, Anthony Regolino, and Lauren Reynolds.

Available from Water Dragon Publishing in hardcover, trade paperback, and digital editions
waterdragonpublishing.com

YOU MIGHT ALSO ENJOY

THE FUTURE'S SO BRIGHT

Out of the darkness of the present comes the light of the days ahead ...

With stories from Kevin David Anderson, Maureen Bowden, Steven D. Brewer, Nels Challinor, Regina Clarke, Stephen C. Curro, Jetse de Vries, Nestor Delfino, Gail Ann Gibbs, Henry Herz, Gwen C. Katz, Brandon Ketchum, Julia LaFond, R. Jean Mathieu, Cynthia McDonald, Christopher Muscato, Alfred Smith, A.M. Weald, and David Wright.

CORPORATE CATHARSIS
The Work From Home Edition

The boundaries between reality and fantasy have become as blurred as those between life and work.

With stories from Alicia Adams, Antaeus, Pauline Barmby, Steven D. Brewer, Dominick Cancilla, Adrienne Canino, Graham J. Darling, Derek Des Anges, Manny Frishberg, Alex Grehy, Jon Hansen, Alexa Kellow, Jack Nash, Helen Obermeier, Frank Sawielijew, William Shaw, Steve Soult, N.L. Sweeney, Kimberley Wall, and Richard Zaric.

Available from Water Dragon Publishing in
hardcover, trade paperback, and digital editions
waterdragonpublishing.com

Made in United States
Orlando, FL
14 December 2024

55571522R10245